Omo 312   C 140 c·52.

Jack Rann
OR
SIXTEEN-STRING JACK

LONDON: A. RITCHIE 6, RED LION COURT, FLEET ST. E.C.

NOS. 1 & 2, PRICE ONE PENNY.

SPLENDID COLOURED PLATE GRATIS.

THE LIFE and ADVENTURES of

Jack Rann

SIXTEEN-STRING JACK.

London. A. RITCHIE, 6, Red Lion-court, Fleet-street, E.C.

NOS. 1 & 2, PRICE ONE PENNY.
SPLENDID COLOURED PLATE GRATIS.

THE LIFE and ADVENTURES of
Jack Rann
SIXTEEN-STRING JACK.

London: A. RITCHIE, 6, Red Lion-court, Fleet-street, E.C.

man dashed on the heath from the Londn-road.

No. 1.

period, so great was his mo

Published by A. RITCHIE & CO.,

HANLY & Co., Lithographers, 152, Fetter Lane, London.

"JACK RANN'S LAST FAREWELL.

6, Red Lion Court, Fleet Street, London.

Published by A. RITCHIE & CO.,

HANLY & Co., Lithographers, 134 Fetter Lane, London.

JACK RANN'S LAST FAREWELL.

SIXTEEN - STRING JACK,

The Noble-hearted Highwayman.

THE BARGAIN ON HAMPSTEAD HEATH.

CHAPTER I.

THE MEETING ON THE HEATH.

THE night was dark and dismal, heavy clouds shrouded the heavens, and fitful gusts of wind swept on, with a spitefulness indicative of the coming storm.

It was towards the end of autumn, and the scene of our opening chapter was the famous Hampstead-heath—the report of many evil-disposed persons and the dread of every traveller journeying to or from the metropolis.

It was night, and, save the sound of the rising wind, nothing was heard in the neighbourhood of the heath.

The hour of midnight had chimed as a well-mounted horse-dashed on the heath from the Londa-road.

He rode some little distance, and then drew his steed away from the beaten track and listened attentively.

This horseman was a well-formed, well-dressed young fellow, who had perhaps seen some five-and-twenty summers; certainly no more.

His air was extremely jaunty, and a rather pleasant smile played over his features.

The most singular thing about him, however, was, that attached to each boot he wore *eight coloured strings*.

Had you seen him thus decorated and mentioned the fact in any part of Surrey or Middlesex, every nine in ten would have told you that you had encountered no other than SIXTEEN-STRING JACK, the most daring highwayman of the period, so great was his notoriety.

John Rann, or Sixteen-String Jack, was at the period of our tale one of the characters of the day. He was not alone notorious for his wondrous exploits on the road, but for the romantic and chivalrous traits in his character. Bad as he was, and bad as all must have been who followed his profession, there were many redeeming qualities about him which made him a special favourite with numbers of persons, and by the poor, to whom he was very charitable, he was quite idolised.

His life had been from his birth a most singular one, but it is not our intention to go into its details now, as we must confine ourselves for the present to the tale we have undertaken to write, and in which Rann will play a most prominent part.

The horseman, as we before stated, turned his black steed from the road, and drawing her to a standstill, listened attentively. as if in anticipation of the approach of some one.

He waited long and anxiously; becoming at last extremely restless and disturbed.

"Not yet, not yet!" he cried. "And if he does not come she will die in Newgate. Heaven and earth! If he should fail me! Mother hung, child starving—it is too horrible to think of!"

Muttering such sentences as these, he passed away another half-hour, and then, uttering an exclamation of horror, he continued,—

"If he should have come and gone! He would seize on the meanest excuse. If I missed him by a minute, he would fly, and I could have no hold on him. But no. The half-hour after midnight was the time appointed, and I know full well that I was before my time. Jack Rann never yet broke his word, or came a moment late in his life; did he pet, did he?"

This last sentence was addressed to his steed, and the splendid animal evidently knew full well that some kind appeal had been made to it; for, as Jack stooped forward and patted her shoulder, she turned her head and rubbed his hand in the most affectionate manner.

"No, mare; Jack never broke his word, and it is not likely he would begin at the moment when he is called upon to save the life of a fellow-creature and keep her child from starvation. Bah! he will come. The bait with which I have tempted him must bring him here; and, once here, as Heaven is my judge, he shall not leave the spot alive, unless he makes a written confession of his guilt and her innocence. They may tell me that I should not interfere with the concerns of other people; they may say it will serve me right if I get into trouble over this; but I care not for their idle word. Let them say, but let me do! I never yet forgot a kindness, and it is too late in life to break off old habits. No, Jack; do not think of hardening your heart now; let it rather become still more impressionable, for you do more than sufficient wrong to be easily balanced by a little good on an occasion."

The mare pricked up her ears, and twitched her near fore-leg nervously.

"What is it, old girl?" asked Jack.

The beautiful mare repeated her movement.

"Again? What can she mean? Let me listen!"

Jack lowered his head and listened in the most attentive manner.

"I hear nothing but the wind. A false alarm this time, old girl. Never mind; you are so often right that you can afford to be wrong once upon a time."

Again the mare moved about uneasily, and threw back her ears.

"Hilloa, pet! you do seem obstinate to-night. What is the matter with you?"

Once more the mare repeated her movement, but this time in a far more decided manner than she had previously done.

"Let me listen again. She may be right after all."

There was a sudden lull of the angry wind, and Rann sought to catch the sounds he expected.

This time he was more fortunate.

Distinctly on his ear fell the sounds of a horse's hoof, beating on the hard road.

"Hurrah!" shouted Jack. "he comes at last. Now for it."

In another minute a horseman rode rapidly up to the spot opposite which Rann sat on his mare.

Rann just touched his steed with his heel, and she sprang into the road, beside the other horse.

"Hilloa!" shouted Rann.

"Back," cried the horseman, "back! I am armed; and if you advance, it will be at the peril of your life."

"Psha!" cried Rann, "is that the way you treat gentlemen with whom you have appointments?"

"Who are you?"

"Jack Rann; or more familiarly speaking, Sixteen-String Jack, entirely at your service."

"You are he who wrote me to meet you here to receive certain documents you were to surrender up?"

"I am he."

"Then our business is soon over; let me have them and depart."

"Stop, stop; we cannot separate thus. Our business over! Forsooth, it has not yet begun."

"I have no time to waste."

"Mine is also precious; but you will have to listen to me."

"Not against my inclination."

"Yes, against your inclination."

"What! Ernest Malvers stay at the bidding of a cut-purse villain—a hunted felon?"

"Just so. You will have to do precisely what you say. And as to Ernest Malvers ruffling up his feathers at the bidding of Sixteen-String Jack, I can tell him he has stood to many a worse man. Besides, are we not equals?"

"Equals! how so?"

"How so? Did you not call me a hunted felon?"

"I did."

"Well; and perhaps you will have the goodness to inform me what you are?"

"A gentleman."

"Bah, Ernest Malvers, you too are a felon, although not a hunted one; and you know it. We stand here on equal terms. Now, what have you to say?"

"I say no man trifles with me."

"And I say the man is not born who ever trifled with me. You put your hand in your pocket! Mark me, if you draw it out, you are a dead man."

Jack drew a pistol and pointed it at the head of his adversary.

So quick was this done, that it took Malvers by surprise, and he involuntarily drew back a step or two.

"You have weapons in that pocket," said Rann, still keeping his pistol pointed. "Pull out your hand, but do not produce a weapon with it, or, by Heaven, sooner than you can raise your arm a couple of bullets will be crashing through your skull."

Malvers, rather chapfallen, did as he was ordered.

"And now," continued Rann, lowering his pistol, "we can resume our conversation. Where were we? Oh, I know; we were having some slight dispute about our relative positions; but we will dismiss the theme, and turn to another more interesting to both."

"Ay," said Malvers, "let us be quick, for this is painful to me."

"I am myself on thorns," said Jack; "but still there is much to be said and done, and we must go through with it steadily, step by step; and painful as it may be to either or both parties, we must miss nothing."

"I do not understand you."

"No, but you will presently."

"I only know that you profess to hold certain papers which are useful to me, and which you have promised to deliver up on receiving the sum of money you have demanded. If you mean to do this, do it at once, and take your reward, for I dare not stay here longer. And, moreover, beyond this, I cannot see what you have to do with me or I with you."

"Oh, all in good time, friend. Never hurry. Now, are you prepared to listen to me?"

"I have no alternative."

"True, you have not. Now, attention. Five years ago

you were travelling from Canterbury to London by post-chaise. On alighting you dropped some papers, which fell into the possession of the postilion."

" How know you that?"

" Oh, easily enough: I happened to be the postilion. You see I am still on the road, but no longer in the old line. But to resume. The papers you lost were of so much consequence to your liberty and good name that you dared not make inquiry about them, preferring to lose them rather than let the world know that you were a forger of wills and deeds of transfer. Oh! oh! you start, do you? Poor fellow! I have touched you so nearly, have I?"

" Go on."

" I will. It's rather interesting, is it not?"

" Go on," cried Malvers, impatiently.

" Well, sir, at first I thought I would burn the documents I became possessed of, but I changed my mind. Twelve months afterwards I heard of a death and of an extraordinary will case, in which your name was mixed up. I bethought me of my papers, and said to myself as I glanced over them, ' My friend Malvers has committed a forgery of a will, and the real one, stolen by him and then dropped in the post-chaise, is in my possession. I should be an important witness in the matter, but I shall not bother about it. Let them get over it as they best may. They are all rich, and there will not be much harm done in one member of the family having more than the others.' So, Mr. Malvers, I put my papers back into their resting-place, and allowed things to go on as they chanced, without my assistance."

" Well, well?"

" Well, sir, a few weeks ago the name of Malvers became again familiar to me through reading a singular charge of murder against a lady of that name."

" My wife!"

" Just so—it turned out to be your wife. But do not interrupt. The case was in everybody's mouth, and I could not help being struck by its peculiarity. A poor, harmless, inoffensive woman was accused of committing a most desperate and revolting crime. The evidence against her was circumstantial. Loud groans were heard issuing at midnight from a house in the neighbourhood of Fleet-street. The watch rushed in and found your wife stooping over the mangled body of a youth, who, being identified, proved to be her cousin. This youth, it is said, stood in the way of her becoming possessed of a considerable property, and to remove the obstacle she committed one of the most desperate crimes on record. On being found in the position I described, she was questioned by the officers, and gave so confused an account of the affair, that the suspicions against her rose to certainty. A jury found her ' Guilty,' and a judge sentenced her to death."

" It is so. I believe Augustus Darfield was the object of my wife's bitterest hatred, and I must concur in the justice of the sentence passed on her."

" Villain!" cried Rann, " oh, miserable villain! My soul revolts at holding converse with you; but I will strive to control my passion and finish my task in comparative coolness. Hark ye! In disguise I sought out your wife in the condemned hole of Newgate. I found her there, with her poor innocent babe slumbering in her lap. I saw her anguish, and at a glance I discovered her innocence. I made myself known to her, for she well remembered my parents, heaven rest them! I told her I was prepared to devote myself to her rescue, and drew from her the real facts of the case, which, in pity for you, she had long concealed. She told me that you had drawn Darfield to your house, that you had planned his murder, and that the crime was committed by Francis Austin, another cousin of the murdered man, and, after your wife, the next heir to the property which had long tempted him to crime. She further told me that she knew you were in league with this wretch to effect a division of the property after her death, which you sought to bring about by systematic ill-usage and diabolical cruelties; but that, in spite of all, she had determined to die, and thus save you and your brother murderer from the scaffold. I swore to her that she should be saved, but she made me promise not to compromise you. I am pre-

pared to treat with you now. Write a confession of the murder, regardless of the safety of your wife's cousin, and I will deliver to you the papers by which I tempted you here. Refuse, and I will make you a prisoner, and drag you to justice at the risk of my own neck."

" I will refuse."

" Tempt me not—I am a desperate man!"

" You are a villain, who would endeavour to frighten me into a confession of a crime which was committed by my wife."

" You lie, and you know I speak the truth!"

" I do not know it."

" Tempt me not, I say, or the scaffold shall be your doom."

" Die, dog!" said Ernest Malvers, drawing a pistol from his pocket, and presenting it at Rann's head; but fortunately the flint missed, and no harm done.

In a second Rann was at the throat of his opponent, and grasping him as in a vice of iron, he wrested his weapons from him and left him powerless.

" Fool that you are," cried Jack, " do you think to best me? You are as completely in my power as if every muscle in your body were unstrung. I am your master, and you must obey. I give you five minutes to decide. Will you write the confession, or will you go to Newgate? Mark me, I know where the murderer is to be found, and I will drag him after you. I have a clue which will complete the chain of evidence against you, and nothing can save you. I give you the chance of life at the request of your poor wife. If you do not accept it on the terms I propose you know what will follow."

" Listen, Rann. This woman can be nothing to you. Let me go hence, and keep your tongue quiet, and ten thousand pounds "——

" Cease!" cried Jack; " ten thousand empires would not tempt me. You are mistaking your man. Be certain, I have no inclination to play the villain. Your wife shall be saved—it is for you to say on what terms. You know my determination, so do not play with me beyond my powers of endurance. You have just two minutes more."

" Will nothing tempt you?"

" Have you decided?"

" Rann, spare me!"

" Yes—on the terms proposed."

" Rann, Rann, I will enrich you—I will place you in luxury for the rest of your life—only spare me!"

Rann drew forth a stout cord.

" You have one more minute," he said.

" Oh, Heaven! will nothing tempt you!"

" I am inexorable. Now, the time is up. How is it to be?"

" Must I confess?"

" You must; and you must also give a clue to the whereabouts of your accomplice, and some facts which will lead to an immediate acquittal of your wife."

" I cannot."

The rope was thrown about his body and tightened.

" Oh, Rann—Jack, Jack! Spare me."

" You have had my answer."

" Must I then die a felon's death?"

" You have an alternative."

" I will write."

" Very good; I thought you would."

Jack slackened the rope."

" But there are no writing materials. How can this be done?"

" Oh, I am not unprepared. Here are my tablets. Write."

The man saw that he was completely beaten, and accepting the tablets from Jack, he wrote, with a faltering hand, the following lines:—

" I, Ernest Malvers, do confess that my wife is innocent of the crime for which she is condemned to death. The real culprit, acting on my instigation, is Francis Austin, my wife's cousin, who will be found hiding at 'The Red Rose' beer-house, in the Minories. We tempted him to my house, and there Austin beat him to death. The clubs he used will be found under some rubbish in the cellarage; together with a part of Austin's coat, which was torn off by the murdered man. The motive which led to this crime was the possession of the property of the murdered man, to which Austin was, after my wife, next heir."

Rann carefully perused this document, and then said,—

"It will do, and here is the will I promised you. It was by that I drew you hither, and I give it you; although I do not know what use it will be to you, as you will have to quit England immediately. However, that is not my business. I made a promise, and I always keep my word. Adieu."

Rann handed Malvers a bundle of papers, and setting his horse in motion galloped away over the heath, leaving the brutal husband gazing after him in extreme bewilderment.

———

CHAPTER II.

THE CONDEMNED HOLE OF NEWGATE.

IN the famous condemned hole of Newgate Gaol, on the night of the opening of our tale, sat a young and, despite the awfully careworn features, very beautiful female. On her knee lay an infant, on which she gazed with extreme tenderness. It was her own darling boy.

"God bless and protect you, my poor, innocent babe," she said; "In a few hours you will be motherless, and cast on the mercy of a cold and friendless world. I commend you to your Heavenly Father's care, for he who gave you birth has cruelly deserted both you and your poor broken-hearted mother."

The poor creature burst into a flood of passionate tears, and drawing her child close to her, moaned and wept over him for more than an hour.

She was interrupted by the entrance of the chaplain of the prison, a fine, elderly gentleman, whose face bespoke the goodness and greatness of his heart.

He approached her gently, and laying his hand affectionately on her head, spoke to her in a calm and sweet voice, which at once arrested her tears and somewhat composed her perturbed feelings.

"Daughter," he said, "the hours pass quickly; it is after midnight, and the fatal hour approaches with a swiftness which will soon place thee over the gap which lies between thee and another world. It is time that we turn our thoughts heavenward, and cease to grieve over the affairs of this world. It is ordained that thou shalt suffer; it is meet that thou dost bow to His will without a murmur, for He in His infinite wisdom knoweth what is good for thee."

"'Tis well, sir," she murmured, "but I do not weep for myself; it is for my poor babe. Oh, I cannot leave him thus without a murmur! It is not in human nature for a mother to quite her child, her first and only one, without a murmur. It may be good for him, it may be good for me, Mr. Ashton; but, oh, it is hard, very hard, to teach the heart that lesson."

"It is, my poor child, it is; but thou shouldst try."

"I do try, sir, indeed I do; but it is all without avail. May I ask, sir, has any one inquired after me?"

"No, daughter; didst thou expect any one?"

"Yes, sir; I did expect—a friend."

"To take leave of you?"

The poor woman was silent.

"I see," continued the chaplain, "you yet hope for a reprieve. Oh! dismiss the thought. It is idle to hope; believe me, there is no earthly chance. I have done my best for thee. I have petitioned the minister. I have sent a most influential deputation to him, but he will not move in the matter. The answer is, that the law must take its course."

"Ah, they do not believe me innocent?"

"No, child, they do not."

"But you, Mr. Ashton, you cannot think me guilty?"

"It is impossible to be long with thee and entertain the faintest suspicion. No, my daughter, I would stake my life on your innocence; but it is very hard to make the world think as I think."

"And I shall die?"

"God has willed it so."

"Then Heaven have mercy on me!"

"Amen."

The poor creature, who, as the reader will easily imagine, was no other than Malver's ill-fated wife, bowed her head over her child, and gazing on it tenderly, again burst forth into a flood of tears.

"Who, who will give thee a crust of bread, though thou should starve, after I am gone?" she cried. "Oh, my poor, darling babe, who will succour thee?"

"I will," said the chaplain; "yes, my poor soul, I will. I have no child of my own, and I will adopt thy little one, and love it as if it were born to me. I am not rich, but I have enough for him and me."

"Oh, Heaven bless you for those words, sir; they are balm to my bruised heart. Heaven bless and reward you for your goodness."

"It will, it has. Charity brings with it its own reward; the pleasure of doing good is sufficient satisfaction to the Christian."

"Now," cried Mrs. Malvers, "now I feel that I can pray with you, sir; my heart is more at ease."

The poor soul placed her child on the hard couch, and fell on her knees beside it.

"Father," she said, "I am resigned to thy will: let it be done."

There was a noise behind her which attracted her attention. Turning, she beheld an old man with long white hair and beard; he was habited in a loose surtout which reached his ankles, and completely disguised his figure.

The gaoler accompanied him, and said to Mrs. Malvers——

"Here is an old man who says he knows you. He can remain with you half an hour. I will not wait. The presence of the chaplain will be sufficient."

The man withdrew, and turning the key in the lock, went away.

Mrs. Malvers gazed at the new comer for an instant, and then exclaimed——

"I do not know you, sir."

"Hush," said the old man, coming close to her, and whispering in her ear; "it is I, Jack Rann."

Mrs. Malvers started.

Collecting herself, she said,—

"You can speak; Mr. Ashton will not betray you."

"Who are you, sir?" cried Mr. Ashton, unable to understand this strange scene.

"Oh, sir," said Mrs. Malvers, "he is an old acquaintance, who seeks to save me. He is unfortunate, and is hunted by the authorities. He dares not reveal himself for fear of detection; you will not betray him."

"Heaven forbid, if he is in thy service," said Mr. Ashton.

"I would and will save her," said Rann. "Hark ye, sir, here are the proofs of her innocence. It is the confession of one of the real culprits, who has escaped from the power of the law. The other, as you will see, may be traced by the instructions therein given. Will you exert yourself for her?"

"I will," cried Mr. Ashton, rapidly glancing over the paper, "I will. Yes, yes; if there be but time to get to the office of the Secretary of State for the Home Department and see him. The work of death can be stopped, and the guilty brought to justice."

"My husband!" cried Mrs. Malvers. "Jack, Jack, you have betrayed him and deceived me!"

"Do not accuse me wrongfully," cried Rann "I have saved you, but he is free."

"He has escaped?"

"Yes; by this time he is far away. I do not think they will trace him."

"Heaven bless you for that!"

"Oh, don't thank me, Mrs. Malvers; I swore to save you at all risks. Your husband complied with requests which placed him beyond danger. Had he refused to obey me, I would, even at the risk of incurring your bitter hatred, have dragged him to the scaffold, and forced him, on the fatal drop, to rescue you from a death you did not deserve."

"You are a good and brave man," said the chaplain, tapping Rann approvingly on the shoulder, "and I admire you."

And then, remembering that he was addressing a criminal, and evidently a notorious one, he continued, "At least you are brave, if you are not good."

"Oh, sir," said Rann, "I am well enough, as men go. I might be better, and I might be worse; at all events, I am not the man to see the innocent suffer for the guilty."

"But," said Mr. Ashton, "this is a waste of time; we must away. How shall I get to the minister's house?"

"How!" cried Jack, "why, jump up behind me on my mare, and I will fly with you."

"It is a matter of life and death."

"It is; and I will whisper it to the mare, and you shall see how well she understands the importance of the mission."

"Adieu, my child," cried the chaplain. "If we do not return in time, commend thy soul to heaven."

"*If* we do not return in time! By Jove, chaplain, you don't know what sort of stuff my mare is made of."

CHAPTER III.

MALVERS PUTS THE MURDERER ON THE SCENT—JACK ON THE WATCH—A LIFE AND DEATH STRUGGLE.

MALVERS remained in the position we described at the end of the first chapter for some moments. His senses had almost deserted him, but making a gigantic struggle to rid himself of the oppression under which he laboured, he at length shook it off.

"It is like a dream," he cried; "it is like a hideous, incomprehensible dream. Would that I had been dreaming!"

He glanced on the papers he still held in his hand.

"Alas!" he continued, "alas for the sad reality! Who is this fiend, this Jack Rann, who has started up in my path and marred my plans? Oh, he shall suffer for this before I have done with him! But now I must take action. Another hour, and my confession will be in the hands of the authorities. My wife will live, Austin will die in her stead, and if I do not fly I shall share his doom. What can be done? Ah! a sudden thought. If I could but rescue Austin the authorities will imagine the paper to be a vile forgery, planned for the purpose of rescuing the condemned woman, and they will not revoke the sentence. It is a desperate hazard; but if successful, all would be well. The stake is worth playing for, and I will make the attempt. Yes, yes; to the Minories — to the Minories!"

The horseman goaded on his horse in the direction Rann had taken.

The beast, frantic with pain, appeared to fly over the heath like a winged creature.

The stones flew from under its hoofs, and still the lash was applied and the spurs used.

"On, on!" shouted Malvers, "hey, on! It is life or death! On, on!"

He shouted and screamed like a madman, and urged his steed along at a truly terrible pace. One false step, one stumble, would have ended his career; but he thought of nothing but the task in hand.

He saw only a halter before his eyes, and he determined to evade it at all risks.

Thus he argued with himself:—

"Rann will seek out some one to execute his commission for him. They will have to go to Newgate, thence to the authorities, thence for the officers, and thence slowly to the Minories. If I can but make this beast sustain its pace I shall be there a full hour before them—I can snatch Austin from their grasp, and my wife will pace the scaffold in a few hours."

Again he applied the whip, again he yelled to his horse, and urged it on at the top of its speed.

The poor creature became bathed in foam, but it was a remorseless horseman on its back. It was a crime-stained man driven to desperation who urged it forward.

The thought of an ignominious end was in his mind's eye, and he hesitated not to evade it at all risks and under all circumstances. He killed men, and could not, therefore, be expected to care for the death of a poor horse. The blood spurting from its side was naught to him. He had seen the crimson tide flow from wounds in the human body, and he shuddered not.

"To the Minories!"

That was his only thought.

How he got there was naught to him.

But there was an avenger on the track. There was a man as desperate and determined as himself working against him; and we have yet to see in whose favour the game of life and death terminated.

*　　*　　*　　*　　*　　*

Jack's mare flew over the ground, to the utter consternation of the good old chaplain, who, in all probability, was never before placed in a position so novel and perilous.

There he was, on a blood mare, his arms encircling the waist of a daring highwayman, positively flying through the streets of London in the dead of the night, bound on an errand of life and death. They were *en route* for the West-end of London, where the principals of the Home Department of the Government resided.

That there should be no hitch, no delay, the chaplain had concluded to trust to no one but himself; and deeming it advisable to at once place the facts in the possession of the First Minister of the department, he at once rode to his residence, determined that nothing should prevent him from obtaining an audience, late as the hour was.

The minister resided in St. James's-street, and thither Rann hurried his splendid mare. Down Ludgate-hill, up ill-paved and still worse lighted Fleet-street, with its oil-lamps swinging to and fro in the night-wind, and its croaking watchman drawling forth the hour of the night, and assuring the peaceful citizens who chanced to break their slumbers that "all was well;" through the Strand, by Charing-cross, into Pall-mall, filled with chairmen and lacqueys—for it was the height of the London season, and the West-end was in its full glory—and thence to St. James's-street, where were to be seen a still greater collection of chairmen, many blazing flambeaux, and throngs of bedizened servants; for the Minister of the Home Department was that night entertaining a large party of his friends and partizans at dinner, with cards and the inevitable *soirée*.

Through these things Jack had to pick his way as he best could; and for a man presenting his appearance (it must be remembered that he still wore the garb and beard in which he ventured within the precincts of Newgate,) he created a noise which surprised his hearers into admiration of his powerful lungs.

Several watchmen endeavoured to retard his progress, but the sight of the chaplain assured them that all was well, and that the errand of the noisy rider of the blood mare was not to be checked.

After a struggle our hero succeeded in gaining the door of the house he sought.

"Dismount," he said to the chaplain; "there is not a moment to be lost. Waste no more time than is necessary for her life hangs but on the merest thread."

"Trust me," said the chaplain. "I am alive to the vital importance of the errand."

He sprang to the ground, and hurried into the entrance-hall of the house.

Here he was accosted by a bevy of servants, who demanded his business.

"My business is with Lord Lismouth," said the chaplain.

"I fear you cannot see him to-night," said the servant, with respect in his tone, "for his lordship is much engaged."

"Of that I have no doubt," said the chaplain; "but my business is of the most imperative nature. I am chaplain of Newgate, and life and death depend upon my interview with his lordship. Pray tell him this, and you will oblige me."

"I will convey the message," said the servant, "but I fear his lordship will refuse to see you."

"I have no such fears," said the good old priest; and the servant departed on his mission.

During his absence, the chaplain engaged himself by gazing at the stream of light which filled the grand hall in which he stood, and in listening to the melody and laughter which reached him from the upper apartments.

"No wonder," he said, "that these great ones have so little thought for the poor wretches amongst whom my life is passed; for what is there in common between this scene and the one I have just quitted? Nothing, nothing! It is hard to bring the mind to believe that such a mighty contrast could be found within a circle so small."

The servant returned, and beckoning the chaplain to follow him, said—

"His lordship will grant you an interview, sir. Pray follow me."

The man led the way to a small retiring-room in the neighbourhood of the brilliant suite of apartments thrown open to his lordship's guests.

"Remain here, sir, and his lordship will be with you presently," said the man, immediately withdrawing.

In a few minutes the minister, a fine old gentleman with a truly noble cast of countenance and distinguished bearing, entered the room.

Without the slightest preliminary remark he commenced business.

"Now, sir," he said, "I understand you have important business with me. I need not say that this is not the place and time for business, because I am convinced that you are well acquainted with the fact, and that you would not intrude if you had not sufficient excuse for doing so."

"You are right, my lord," said the chaplain; "I should not have intruded on your privacy without sufficient excuse, and I will take care to be as brief as I possibly can, now that you have done me the favour of receiving me. There is in Newgate a poor woman under sentence of death, and whose execution is fixed for to-morrow."

"Ah, you refer to Mrs. Malvers; a very sad case, Mr. Chaplain, a very distressing case; but I trust, after the very decided manner in which I have already expressed my views on that matter, that your business is not to further importune me in her behalf?"

"I am here to ask a reprieve for her, my lord, but not on grounds of former applications."

"Then I may at once tell you, sir, that unless you have convincing proofs of her entire innocence of the crime with which she is charged you do wrong to come here, for my mind is made up on the point."

"I think I have proofs which will satisfy your lordship that I do not come here without sufficient reason. Will your lordship do me the favour of reading this paper?"

The chaplain drew forth the confession and placed it in the minister's hands.

Lord Lismouth gave a rapid glance over the scrawl.

"How was this obtained?" he asked, as he finished the perusal of the document.

The chaplain had no wish to reveal the source by which the confession came into his hands, and so endeavoured to evade the question.

"It was brought to Mrs. Malvers to-night by one who had just left her cruel husband."

"Where is this husband?"

"That we do not know."

"Really, sir, this is most suspicious," said the minister; "the document may be a clever forgery, produced by some friend of the unhappy woman who lies under sentence. I do not think I should regard it in any serious light."

"For the love of God," cried the clergyman, "do nothing hastily. On my veracity I believe that document to be valid. Of the innocence of the poor woman I am well convinced, and if she perishes, my lord, her blood will be upon your head alone."

"You speak warmly."

"Oh, yes; but pardon me, my lord, I feel deeply on the subject, and cannot tutor my tongue to set phrases. Oh, believe me, this unhappy woman is as innocent as your own wife of the crime with which she is charged and for which

she is condemned to suffer. That paper reveals all, and to treat it as a fabrication is to wilfully destroy a precious life. If I were not fully convinced of this, I should not be standing in your presence on this occasion."

"You see, sir," said Lord Lismouth, "my responsibility is a great one, and I have no wish to abuse the power I wield. I grant that you believe this woman innocent, but I have no real *facts* before me. There is your *belief* and a pencilled scrawl, which might have been written by the prisoner herself, for aught I know. There is no witness's signature. There is no one to vouch for its authenticity. Under these circumstances it only rests with me to grant a provisional reprieve."

"A provisional reprieve?"

"Yes. If you can produce either the husband or the cousin of this woman before the time of execution, the sentence shall be delayed."

"But if he should have escaped?"

"I can do no more."

"Think, my lord, oh think of the awful responsibility which rests upon you! Think that if, as we reach the scaffold with the real culprit, we see the fatal bolt drawn, and the innocent victim launched into eternity, you alone are to blame. Oh, think of this. Delay the execution for a day, in order that the innocent may have a chance of life."

"It is not in my power to do so," said the minister; "and I still think that you are imposed upon, and that this woman is the real culprit. Take this."

The minister had written something on a paper, which he now handed to the chaplain. It ran as follows:—

"*To the Governor of Newgate.*

"You are hereby empowered to delay the execution of the woman now lying in Newgate under sentence of death, for the murder of Augustus Darfield; provided that Francis Austin or Ernest Malvers, persons presumed to be implicated in the crime, be placed in your charge before the hour of execution.

(Signed)   "LISMOUTH."

As the chaplain glanced over this order his heart failed him.

"Heaven help her," he cried; "her doom seems sealed."

"There is no help for it," said Lord Lismouth. "It would, you may rest assured, be more pleasing to me to see this poor wretch live than die; but I have a duty to perform for those who have placed the authority of the office I hold in my hands. Society must be protected, and I trust I shall never fail in my duty."

"Amen," said the chaplain; "but, my lord, there may be such a thing as too much zeal. God grant that this case may not prove illustrative of the fact. I humbly take my leave."

The poor old chaplain withdrew.

"Umph!" said the minister, as he prepared to return to his guests, "umph! A stupid old man, that. I wonder who selected him for the office of chaplain of Newgate."

No matter who did so. Certain it was that no better representative of the office could have been found.

His lordship returned to his friends, and soon forgot that there was such a place as Newgate in the world.

The chaplain retraced his steps to the street, and there found Jack awaiting his return.

"You have been an intolerably long time," cried Jack; "but what cheer—what hope?"

"But little, I fear."

The chaplain then recounted the substance of his interview with Lord Lismouth.

"Little hope!" said Jack, as the narrative was brought to an end; "little hope!—bah; you know nothing of the matter. There's every hope."

The chaplain shook his head.

"You think not," said Jack; "but we shall see. I never failed a friend, and the mare never failed me. All you have to do is to hold on, and keep as close to me as possible. Now, then, for the Minories. On, mare! Ahoy,—ahoy, girl!"

The shout was sufficient. The bonny mare bounded forward, and was soon retracing her steps in the direction of the City. Quick as she had flown to the West-end, her pace had been nothing to that at which she now covered the ground.

It appeared to the chaplain that the houses flew past him in one continuous wild flight. All was confused and dim. The lights danced past him, and things lost their natural forms.

In his ears rang the clatter of the mare's hoof's as she dashed fire from the rough flint-stones in her mad gallop, and the excited voice of Rann, encouraging the steed onward.

"Hoy, mare—good mare—on, on—hey up—hey up—on on. Hiss-s-s! up, up—hey! on!"

At every fresh shout the mare tossed up her splendid head, as if in token of recognition of the orders she received.

Her nostrils were extended, and foam broke out all over her sleek body. Her eyes were filled with wild excitement, and despite the heavy burden she bore, there was no diminution of the speed, no relaxation of a muscle. On, on, she sprang, as lightly and gracefully as a fawn.

Onward, to the dark, dangerous, and terrible precincts of the Minories—the quarter of the very worst thieves and cut-throats of London.

Sure-footed as a racer on a well-kept course, she continued her way, extending her limbs to the utmost, and bounding on, nearer and nearer the goal.

The instinct of the animal taught it that extraordinary efforts were expected, and being used to the excitement of the flight and the chase, it seemed to thoroughly appreciate the position in which it was now placed, and strove with might and main to win the approval of its master.

Rann used neither whip nor spur; his shouts were sufficient to urge his mare onward. At the sound of his voice she would redouble her efforts, and at length dashed into Lagsman-street, in which place was situated the "Red Rose" public house, a den for thieves and rascals of the worst class.

"This is the place," said Jack, as he drew rein at the door of as repulsive a house of entertainment as one would wish to enter.

"What do you purpose doing?" asked the chaplain.

"You will see. Dismount."

Jack and Mr. Ashton sprang to the ground at the same moment.

"I will enter," said Jack. "If Dick Turpin or Tom King should chance to be within, they will lend me a hand; if not, I must do the task by myself."

"What task?"

"What task? Why, the seizing of Austin. I'd drag him out though he were in the centre of an army."

"You will not attempt to enter the house without the assistance of officers of justice?"

"Officers of justice! Show me one who would dare enter that house with hostile intentions."

"Is it, then, so dangerous?"

"It is death to anyone who is not branded with the stamp of crime. Hush!"

"What do you hear?"

"I hear nothing."

"But I do. It is the tramp of a horse—an unusual sound in this neighbourhood. Let us draw on one side and see what is in the wind. Silent, mare!"

Jack, the chaplain, and the mare, the latter making but the faintest sounds as she moved over the stones, stole away into the shadow of the houses, at some slight distance from the inn.

In a few moments they beheld a horseman, hot with haste, dash up to the door of the inn, and, dismounting, demand admittance.

"Hilloa!" said Jack, in a whisper, to his companion, "hilloa! there's a nice game a' foot here."

"Who is it?"

"Who is it? Why, Malvers, come to put Austin on the scent."

"Unfortunate."

"Not at all. Quite the reverse."

"What do you mean?"

"Simply that to drag Austin from the house would have been a task of the greatest magnitude, but to seize him as he comes out will be comparatively easy work."

"But are you assured he will come out?"

"From what other purpose but to bring him from danger is Malvers here?"

"True—true."

"Hush! they have admitted him; now for work."

Jack touched his mare, and then stole back to the house, outside which the horse ridden by Malvers stood motionless. Jack applied his whip to the jaded brute, and it galloped off with all the haste it could make.

"So! we win the first move. His horse is gone, and now we shall see if we can't have him."

"Pray do no violence."

"Violence! How shall we deal with violent men if not by violent measures? However, the work is not for you. Stand back, and let me do the task alone."

Jack approached the door of the house and applied his ear to the keyhole.

"Hist!" he said, "they come. Now for it."

He drew his pistols, and stood prepared for what was to follow.

Withdrawing a pace, he watched the opening of the inn door. Malvers, accompanied by a young man, who proved to be Austin, sprang through the doorway and into the street.

It was the work of a moment, for the proprietor of the "Red Rose" did not allow unwelcome guests the chance of entering his premises without his sanction; but, quick as the movement of opening and shutting the door had been accomplished, the men who had effected egress had not time to move two paces before Jack had confronted them.

"Stand!" cried Rann, presenting his pistols.

"To whom?" shouted Austin, raising a pistol he bore in his hand.

"To Jack Rann, the avenger of Darfield."

"Back, fool," cried Malvers; "back, or we fire upon you."

"Fly, Ernest Malvers," shouted Rann, "I have nought to do with thee. Fly, it is with this villain I have business."

"I will never desert him," cried Malvers.

"Then you must share his fate, for he shall be in Newgate before another hour has passed over his head."

Malvers attempted to beat down Jack's weapons, and at the same moment Austin fired.

The bullet passed through Jack's left arm, but he moved not.

Discharging his pistols at the pair, but without effect, our hero clubbed one of the weapons and rushed at Austin. They struggled until they reached the road, close to the spot where Jack's mare stood.

At this point Malvers skulked behind the highwayman, and dealing him a tremendous blow on the head sent him to the earth, and he fell under the mare.

At this moment Malvers, seeing lights in the street, turned and fled. Austin now grasped his second pistol, and, cocking it, was taking deliberate aim at his prostrate foe, when Jack's mare seized him with her teeth by the shoulder and forced him to drop the weapon.

Austin howled with pain and endeavoured to drag himself from the hold of the mare, but the faithful creature clung to him with the tenacity of a bull-dog.

Meanwhile Jack shook off the effects of the blow he had received and sprang to his feet.

He at once grappled with Austin, and seizing him with his left hand held his throat until he was well nigh suffocated.

Meanwhile the lights kept approaching, and it became apparent that the whole force of the night watch was bearing down to the spot.

"Fly," said Jack, to the terrified chaplain, "fly, or it will be too late."

He sprang on the back of his mare as he spoke, and dragged the almost inanimate body of Austin after him.

In a moment the mare dashed away, and the stupefied chaplain was surrounded by a crowd of modern Dogberries.

CHAPTER IV.

FOLLOWS JACK AND HIS PRISONER.

AWAY flew the black mare, and Jack, without bestowing a second thought on the chaplain, dashed in the direction of Newgate.

THE MARE SAVES THE LIFE OF SIXTEEN-STRING JACK.

He had seized his prey, and that was all he cared for.

"Ah!" he cried, "I have you now, and she is saved."

"Whither are you taking me?" cried Austin, as soon as he recovered his reason.

"To the gallows, man, to the gallows."

"Oh, prithee, release me," cried the abject wretch, finding himself powerless, "prithee release me. I never did you harm."

"Maybe not, but you have committed murder, and you would allow one who is good and innocent to mount the gallows in your stead. That one, a poor helpless woman, I honour and love as dearly as though she were my own sister. I have registered an oath to snatch her from the gallows and place thee in her position. I have said, and I will do it."

"Listen, I am rich, I will"—

"Silence, lest I cheat the hangman of his due by strangling thee at once. Silence, and tempt me not, for it is useless."

Rann directed the course of his mare to Newgate, and there, after a gallop of a few minutes, he drew rein.

Without hesitation he sprang from his horse, still holding the murderer in his grasp, and applied himself to the knocker at the principal entrance.

It was now almost daylight, and the authorities of the prison being astir, the pair were admitted, the mare following Jack through the gates.

"What! Mr. Jack Rann voluntarily inside the gates o' Newgate?" said the turnkey, "Vel, this here is rum Why, what game is up?"

"A bad one. Here, I've turned honest, and taken to your own trade; see what a brute I've brought you as a commencement."

"Why, who is this gentleman?" asked the turnkey.

"Who? Why the murderer of Darfield."

"Vot, the cove as Mrs. Malvers is a going to swing for at eight?"

"The same, only this gentleman's presence saves Mrs. Malvers the trouble of going through the ceremony."

"Vel," said the turnkey, "you alvays vos a rum bird, and there vos never no getting at yer; but you had best come before the deputy-governor."

"All right," said Jack, pushing the now utterly speechless and dejected Austin before him, "but give an eye to the mare."

"Oh, she shall be all right. I say, Jack, it was rather soft of you to come here, after all. You won't require the mare again in a hurry."

"Oh, sha'nt I? We shall see."

"So we shall, Jack."

They now approached the office of the deputy-governor, and entered it without ceremony.

It was a curious place, was that office.

The walls were of coarse plaster, and the only adornments were a variety of instruments usually carried by those who uphold the majesty of the law.

Over the fireplace was an enormous blunderbuss, attached to which was a card, on which was printed the word "LOADED"

THE REPRIEVE.

as a warning to those who approached it to keep their hands off.

Near this instrument of death were a number of pistols of every possible size and shape.

The next conspicuous articles were the swords and hangers, which looked remarkably bright and dangerous as they glistened on the walls.

Then the eye fell on a variety of sticks, staves, and bludgeons; and above all on a score pair of handcuffs, or "darbies," many of which had doubtless graced the wrists of some of the most notorious criminals of the generation.

At a desk in this singular apartment, poring over the last number of the "Hue and Cry," was the deputy-governor of Newgate—a small, bustling little gentleman, dressed in a suit of shabby brown, and shoes all the worse for wear, and face and hands all the more repulsive for absence of soap and water.

Flitting about this important luminary, there were a number of smaller stars in the shape of gaolers, thieftakers, and watchmen, all of whom exhibited a repugnance to the keen morning air by drawing as near the fire as possible.

"Hillo," said the deputy-governor, "and who have we here, so early in the morning?"

"Why, no!" shouted several of the officers in a breath. "It is—it can't be—and yet it is—SIXTEEN-STRING JACK!"

"Yes, it is I," said Rann; "and what do you make of that?"

It was evident that the limbs of the law could make nothing of all of that, and so they contented themselves by staring from one to the other, and ejaculating—

"Why, no, it can't be! How queer!" and other interjections of a similar stupid nature.

"Why, what has brought you here, Jack Rann?" asked the deputy, glaring at Jack from over his spectacles.

"I have brought you a murderer," said Jack. "Behold the destroyer of the man Darfield!"

"Why, Jack, what do you mean? Mrs. Malvers killed Darfield."

"Nothing of the kind; this is the real murderer. Mr. Ashton will explain all."

"Mr. Ashton! what has he to do with it?"

"Everything; he has procured a reprieve for Mrs. Malvers, on condition that this brute be brought here; and here I have brought him."

"But where is the reprieve? where is Mr. Ashton?"

"Where?" echoed Jack. "Oh, good God! he should have been here by this."

"Where did you leave him?"

"In the Minories!"

"And you expect to see him here?"

"Fool that I am! What have I done now?"

"Well, you have not done much unless you can produce the reprieve or Mr. Ashton. We can't stop an execution on your word, Jack."

"True, true; but he will come."

"Are you sure he did not fall into the hands of the gang?" asked the deputy.

"More probably into the hands of the watch, for they were upon him when I fled."

"Just as bad. He will be taken to some remote watch-house, and before anything could be done eight o'clock will have tolled from St. Paul's, and the bolt will have fallen."

"No, no!" cried Jack in an agony of terror, "that must not be. You cannot sacrifice an innocent woman like that. I am sure you will delay the execution until the return of the chaplain."

"We will do nothing of the kind. The under-sheriff will be here at half-past seven, and at eight Mrs. Malvers will die, unless Lord Lismouth's reprieve, if there be such a thing, is in our hands."

"Oh, Heaven!" cried Jack, "what shall I do?"

"Well, I do not see that you can do much, Jack, for you see you are yourself a prisoner."

"No, no!" said Jack; "you would not be so cruel as to deprive the poor woman of one chance of life. You will let me go forth again to complete the work I have begun."

"I don't know about that. There is something strange about the case. How do we know but what Mr. Ashton has been purposely thrust out of the way, and this tale trumped up to gain time for projecting some plot or other? No, no, Jack, we can do little for you."

"But you will let me seek Mr. Ashton?"

"No."

"No! Oh, do not, do not say that."

"Why, Jack, you have forgotten one thing that will save the life of the woman."

"Have I? Have I? Name it."

"It is the confession of your prisoner. If he confesses the crime. there would be an end to the bother."

"True," said Jack, turning to Austin, "true; and now, man, if there is one spark of humanity left in you, confess your crime, and save the poor soul who lies below, suffering in mind and body for your infamous deed. Confess, confess!"

"I have nothing to confess," said Austin. "All I know is, that I was violently attacked by this man in the Minories, and dragged here, I know not wherefore. This is, as you suspect, some infamous attempt to save a guilty woman. I beg you will place this man under restraint and set me free."

"Not so fast," said the deputy; "all in good time, young man. If you are innocent, you will not mind being detained here a few hours."

"But I do mind. My business"—

"Your business cannot be very important, or you would not be found in the Minories at the hour at which you confess to have been there; so say nothing on that score. Look here, Jack. It appears to me that, after all, there is something in your tale. You are too old a bird to thrust yourself inside these gates without sufficient cause, and so I am inclined to give some credence to the assertions that you utter."

"Bless you for that," said Jack; "that is kind of you."

"Now," pursued the deputy, "they say that the chief peculiarity of Jack Rann is, that he never yet broke his word "—

"It is so, or I should not have been here now."

"Good. On the faith of that saying I am inclined to allow you to pass without the prison. Before you go you must swear to me that you will devote yourself only to the business you have in hand, and that as soon after eight o'clock as possible you will deliver yourself up to me, a prisoner, on the many charges I have here booked against you."

"This I cheerfully swear. I would desire nothing better," said Jack.

"Then you can go, and, if your errand be as good a one as I believe it to be, God speed you."

There was, after all, a heart beating under that dirty cuticle; one would not have thought it, on getting a first glimpse at the hard features and cold grey eyes: but there are singular contrarieties in human nature, and a observer may, perchance, make a mistake when glancing at some types of the human countenance.

"I shall be back before eight," said Jack, "either bringing with me the proofs of Mrs. Malvers' innocence, or ready to die with her on the scaffold."

"Not so bad as that, Jack," said the deputy; "we shall let you off this time, with something less than a halter."

"I trust so," said Jack.

As he passed into the prison-yard, the clock struck six.

"Two hours!" said Rann, "two hours! Heaven and earth, man! what have we not to do in that time!"

As soon as Jack was gone, the deputy ordered the gaolers to lock up the suspected man.

"Why am I to be used thus?" asked Austin. "Is the word of a common cut-throat and desperate highwayman to be taken before mine?"

"No matter," said the deputy, "no matter. There will be plenty of time for you to assert your innocence hereafter; and, before you go, a word of advice in your ear. If you would desire to make old officials believe in your innocence, don't conduct yourself as you are now doing—your actions being as unlike those of an innocent man as anything I ever beheld in my long experience."

"Indeed!"

"Yes, indeed!"

"You are a most impertinent old fool," said Austin, "and you will regret this conduct."

"Perhaps so. I have regretted many things in my time; it will be no novelty to me."

"I shall inform the Governor of——"

"Pooh! away with him! we want no such stuff here."

Mr. Austin found himself rather roughly handled, and thrust away into a cell, without further ceremony. Newgate is not, and never was, a place where etiquette was particularly well observed.

    *   *   *   *   *   *

Turn we now once more to that condemned hole wherein the poor woman and her child lay shivering in the cold.

It had struck six, and still no appearance of Rann—still no sign of Mr. Ashton.

"They have failed!" she cried, her poor swollen eyes again overflowing with tears; "they have failed, and dare not come to me. Oh God! what shall I do? In two hours—two short hours, I must leave thee, my poor lamb. I must quit thee, and seek a world where all is good and just; but I leave thee branded as the child of a murderess, to fight with a world which will have no sympathy with thee. God protect thee and watch over thee, for I must die."

Then she pressed her poor babe to her heart, and covered it with kisses. She deprived herself of much of her scant clothing to protect it from the chilly air, but as she did so her tears would break forth again, for the thought of who would do that for her infant when her eyes were closed in death came upon her, and the image of her darling—pale, emaciated, neglected, scorned—presented itself to her mind's eye.

Then came one ray of hope. She had heard of people being snatched from the very scaffold; she had read of persons rescued from the stony grasp of death.

Why should not this be her case?

But the gloom gathered again, and she saw no hope—not one little ray to gladden her.

Meanwhile, the moments stole away, and the fatal hour of eight was fast approaching.

And neither Jack nor Mr. Ashton came to her.

Without the gaol was assembling a vast throng of people to witness the execution.

Such a crowd as can only be seen at such places was gathering there. A wild, godless, fearless, cruel gang, who awaited the coming sight as a treat of the highest order.

As their yells rose and their number increased, so died out hope; and death—death was staring the innocent woman in the face.

CHAPTER V.

THE CHAPLAIN—THE REPRIEVE—THE MIRACULOUS ESCAPE FROM THE LOCK-UP.

"HILLO!" said one of the many watchmen who surrounded the chaplain; "hillo! what's the meaning of all this riot?"

" It's nothing; at least nothing that I can explain. I pray you let me pass. Do not detain me. A life hangs upon me."

" What a pity, to be sure!" said the watchman, with mock sympathy. " Who'd have thought it? Let you go! You must think us green."

" You certainly will not detain me."

" Oh, won't we?—we shall see about that. Bring him along."

" I implore, I entreat you, not to detain me. I have done nothing to warrant detention, and must implore you to release me."

" That's all very fine, my friend, but it will not do for us. You must come away to the lock-up."

" No, no; I cannot remain here another moment. Life and death hang upon my presence elsewhere."

" Dear me, that's very distressing; but, unfortunately, we are too old to be caught with such chaff; so come along."

" Whither will you drag me?"

" To the lock-up in Aldersgate-street."

" For the love of Heaven, do not serve me thus! Do you not see that I am a minister? Is not my cloth sufficient to protect me from such insult and degradation?"

" Not if we know it. The make-up is a very good one, but we are not to be taken in by it. You must come with us; and so no more talk about it."

" Come along," cried the watchmen, in a chorus; " we ain't going to stay here and chance being scragged by some o' your friends and mates. Come along!"

It was in vain that the chaplain protested; his captors would listen to nothing he had to say.

" The fellow who galloped off with the man across his saddle was a highwayman, and you was with him—that's enough for us."

Mr. Ashton wished to explain the circumstances of the case and relate the history of the unfortunate woman he had tried so hard to save. But he might as well have appealed to savages. All he could get for his pains was the brutal reply that they dared say it was all very fine and clever, but they were down to such trumpery dodges, and were not to be taken in so easily.

Through the streets they hurried their helpless prisoner, and at last brought him to the lock-up in Aldersgate-street.

It was a miserable cage, usually filled with the lowest and most dissolute brawlers.

The morning had now broken, and the inhabitants of the various cells had fallen into slumber. The stench which arose from their dens was overpowering, and it was with eloquent earnestness that Mr. Ashton begged that he should not be confined in one of them.

" No use, my man," said the principal watchman, " no use at all. We ain't going to give such a desperate bird the chance of flying away. In with yer, and no nonsense, or you'll get but rough usage, I'm thinking."

" Since you will detain me," cried Mr. Ashton, " will you send some one to me whom I can trust to take a packet to Newgate?"

" Oh, Newgate be blowed! shut up your noise and go to sleep."

The door of the cell into which the chaplain was thrust was slammed home, and he was left to his meditations.

Of what description they were the reader can readily imagine.

The life of a human being depended on him, and on him alone.

He had in his possession that which could snatch her from the hangman; and there he was, confined in a noisome dungeon, without the power of stirring hand or foot to snatch her from the inevitable doom which hung over her.

He knew that Jack had secured the real murderer; but that was useless without the production of the reprieve. He blamed himself for the weakness and confusion which led him to disregard Jack's urgent request that he should fly.

" Oh, if I had had the sense of a child," he cried, " I should have evaded these hardened men, and have flown to succour the innocent. Craven heart that I am, to have succumbed thus!"

Alternately upbraiding himself and beating at the door of his cell to attract the attention of those without, the first hour of his imprisonment passed over.

" Alas! alas!" he cried, as the broad daylight burst into his cell, " in another hour or two it will be too late, and she will have suffered. Oh, the child—the poor, innocent, defenceless child!"

The thought was maddening, and it was with renewed energy that the good chaplain applied himself to the task of attracting the attention of those without.

" Men, men!" he cried—" if men you be, pray release me. The sun rises high in the heavens, and ere another hour has passed it will be too late. Release me—release me! Gold, bright gold—all I possess in the world, shall be yours, if you will but open this door and allow me to fulfil my mission."

" Curse your mission!" cried the sleepy and sullen watchmen. Just go to sleep, wil yer, or we'll give yer something that'll make yer."

With this they closed their eyes again, and attempted to resume the slumber from which they had been aroused.

" I implore—I entreat"——

" Shut up, or we'll smash yer head in."

That was the threat which silenced the poor chaplain.

His repeated cries had, however, aroused the inmates of the adjoining cells, and they forthwith commenced a very animated conversation on the very subject which so agitated the chaplain.

It was evident that he was surrounded by a gang of miscreants of the worst order.

" Deuced unlucky to be shut up here, and such a treat going on at Newgate," said one.

" What treat?" asked another.

" What treat? Why the hanging of that woman for the murder of her cousin, to be sure."

" Oh, is that this morning?"

" Yes."

" I shouldn't mind seeing it."

" I'm sure I shouldn't; she deserves it."

" Awful affair, wasn't it?"

" Yes, for a woman to be mixed up in."

" What did she do to the fellow?"

" Oh, a mere trifle."

" What was it? It couldn't have been much of a trifle to kill him."

" Couldn't it? yes it could though; she only dashed out his brains."

" Ha! ha! ha! I wonder if it hurted him.'

" Hurted him—o' course not. It must be rather pleasant than otherwise."

" No doubt, but I'd rather him than me."

" So would I. But he's jolly enough now."

" Awfully jolly I should say. I wonder how he likes his companions."

" What companions?"

" Why, the worms, to be sure; they're fellows, only bedfellows in the grave."

" Ho! ho! ho!" roared the other, " that's a good joke."

The blood of the chaplain froze in his veins as he listened to these terrible jests.

They but increased his desire to fly from his bondage, but he was fast held in the noissome den, too fast to move; and still the minutes flitted away, and the terrible hour drew near.

" No hope!" he cried, " no hope!"

" Hillo!" shouted one of the two wretches to whose conversation he had listened, " is there anybody grieving next door?"

" Make no jest of my despair," cried the chaplain; " it is by far too serious a matter for laughter."

" Is it though? Poor old cripple! what are you in for?"

" Do not ask me, for I am too confused to speak."

" Not used to it?"

" No! Heaven in his mercy forbid."

" What a pity! Ah, you see, old sanctimonious, the morning's reflections don't come as pleasant as the night's jollity. I s'pose you got drunk and was caught sleeping in the gutter, or p'raps you were obstreperous and pitched into the watch—eh?"

" No, no; it is nothing of the kind, I assure you."

" Ah, your assurances won't go for much. How much d'ye think he'll get, Bill?"

" First offence?"

" Blest if it don't look like it."

" Then they'll let him off with a month."

" A month's imprisonment!" cried the horrified chaplain. " No, no; it is not so bad as that. But God knows I would willingly undergo that much incarceration, or even more, so that I could save her."

" Hillo! the old fogey is in love."

" Wno's the charmer?"

" Cease your badinage," cried the chaplain. " Lawless men, hold no further converse with me, for I am sick at heart, and cannot find words to answer thy brutal remarks."

" Come, I say," shouted one; " no cheek, or when we get out o' this I'll give you one for yourself as you'll remember. Blest if I don't, if I get an extra month for it."

The chairman offered no further reply, and the men left him unmolested.

Another hour passed, and the clock struck the hour of seven.

The deep tone of the bell seemed to clash through the brain of the poor chaplain and madden him.

In imagination he saw the unhappy woman led forth, her child torn from her, and her arms pinioned.

He could hear the shouts of the multitude, and picture the efforts of the executioner as he dragged the poor soul to the scaffold; and there he sat, powerless, helpless, with the reprieve in his pocket! He could have dashed himself to pieces against the rough walls of his cell.

The sound of the clock had barely died away when the clatter of a horse's hoofs fell distinctly on the ears of the minister.

" Heaven bless us;" he cried. " If it should be the highwayman!"

It was the highwayman. Long and tedious had been the search Jack had made for the chaplain, but falling across one of the several watchmen who had assisted in his capture, he was informed of his whereabouts.

The mare was unfailing; in spite of all the fatigue she had undergone throughout that long night she still answered the call of her master, and gallantly obeyed his touch.

In a few minutes after Jack had parted company with the watchman he darted up to the watch-house of Aldersgate-street.

The entrance to the lock-up was a wide one, and Jack hesitated not to ride in, mounted as he was, rather than to leave his mare in the street.

The floor of the little prison was of stone, and of course the mare traversed it easily.

On either side of the passage were the cells; at the extreme end were the rooms appropriated by the guardians of the night.

Jack hesitated not to ride into their very midst.

" Hilloa!" he cried, as the aroused watchmen tumbled off their benches; " hilloa here! You have a prisoner, the chaplain of Newgate; I must see him."

He sprang from the mare as he spoke.

Shaking themselves together, the watchmen rose and stared at the intruder.

It was in all probability the very first time a mounted horseman had dared enter the precincts of their dormitory in the abrupt style adopted by Jack; and the astonishment of the upholders of the law may be imagined.

" Hillo here!" shouted Jack, " are you all deaf? I say, you have a prisoner here, a clergyman."

" And I say we have two prisoners here—a clergyman and a highwayman. Now, what have you to say to that?"

" Nothing in particular, save that I am in no cue for argument or jesting. My business is of too serious a nature."

" Is it, though?"

" It is, man; it is. Will you answer me? Have you not the chaplain of Newgate under lock and key?"

" We have the chaplain of the Minories under lock and key, if that's what you mean."

" Do not mistake. The gentleman of whom you speak is really the chaplain of Newgate, who was in the Minories on a matter of life and deaf; you must release him instantly."

" Must we? how droll!"

" Fool, I tell you it is in his power to save the woman who is to be hung this morning at Newgate. He has the reprieve and her blood will be upon you if you detain him further."

" Come, none o' that gammon!" said one of the watch " we can't put up with it, yer know; and if yer think to get away again, you are precious mistaken. We know you."

" Oh, that we do," shouted the others. " Look at his boots —its Sixteen-String Jack! He's a nice one to be looking after the chaplain o' Newgate, he is!"

" I tell you, the words I speak are true. You will not detain me. You will let me see him,—you will let me bear to Newgate the reprieve, if you will not liberate him."

" Look here," said one to the other; " that chaplain cove has some swag about him that they want to get off, and this is the dodge they are down to; but it won't do, Jack; we are too old. Both you and your chaplain will go before the beak before you leave our clutches."

" I tell you I will not be detained."

" And we say, you shall. Come on, men."

They rushed upon Jack with the ferocity of wild beasts, and in a moment had him completely at their mercy.

" Now," said the one who had put so base an interpretation on Jack's motives in coming there, " now let him go in and talk over matters with his friend the parson, and much good may it do them."

Another minute and Jack was thrust into the cell in which the distracted chaplain sat rocking himself to and fro in unutterable anguish.

" You are come!" cried the chaplain—" thank God! you are come!"

" Yes, I am come; but I am useless. I, like yourself, am a prisoner. They would not listen to me, and all is lost."

" Oh, Heaven! Say not so."

" It is so. It is all over now. I have struggled in vain. Jack's word is broken at last."

The poor fellow buried his face in his hands, and gave vent to a flood of tears.

" All over!—all over!" he cried in anguish.

" Nay," said the chaplain, who forgot his own sorrow in that of the highwayman, " do not thus give way to tears. Let us think if something cannot be done."

" Too late! too late!"

" Nay, nay; Heaven will surely interpose for the innocent. Let us not yet despair."

" It is all over. It is ended."

" Since you have come, I feel there is hope yet. I am relieved of half my sorrow."

" Old man," said Jack with awful emphasis " I tell you to give birth to no false hopes. It is ended, I tell you. We are both prisoners. The mare is captured, and in a few minutes the poor woman will be on the scaffold."

" It is horrible!"

" Horrible;" cried Jack, " it is excruciating. Oh, God have mercy upon those fiends if I once get free again, for I will have none!"

" Be not rash."

" Is she not to die? Can I be calm, and she with her foot on the scaffold?"

Crash! Crash! Crash!

The door of the cell fell in, shattered into ten thousand atoms. In the passage Jack beheld his mare dashing out her heels right and left, and laying the band of watchmen to the earth.

The poor brute, with miraculous instinct, had beheld her master made prisoner, and on being led through the passage into the street had taken this mode of assisting him.

"There is hope!" shouted Jack, with a wildness approaching a burst of lunacy. "There is hope! Quick—the reprieve!"

The chaplain handed it to him, and he placed it between his teeth.

"Now," he cried, "I can save her, though a thousand fiends stood in my path!"

Dashing to the earth two men who attempted to stop him, he shouted to the mare to go on.

She obeyed, and actually fought her way to the door, covering the retreat of her master at the same time. In the street Jack sprang upon her back, and with a wild "hurrah!" dashed away.

At his heels, springing their rattles and yelling like madmen, came the whole troop of watchmen.

CHAPTER VI.

THE FATAL MOMENT.

THE clock had tolled the half-hour after seven.

The deputy-governor, accompanied by the gaolers, entered the condemned hole.

Mrs. Malvers was sleeping.

"Poor soul," said the dirty little deputy, as he wiped a tear from his eye, "poor soul! it's all over now. And to think that she was so near being saved!"

"Ah! it is sad. I s'pose there's no hope?"

"Hope! and she has but thirty minutes to live!"

Mrs. Malvers awoke with a scream.

Her cry alarmed her poor little infant, and it commenced a dismal wailing, which was only checked when the mother clasped it to her bosom, and by gentle words reassured it.

She then turned to the group of men who had entered her cell.

"Has he come?" she cried. "Is all well at last?"

The deputy hung his head and answered not.

The poor woman gazed upon him fixedly for a moment, and then her head dropped, and she murmured,—

"You need not speak. I read the answer in your countenance!"

"God bless you, my poor soul," said the old man; "it is my duty to tell you there is no hope."

"No hope!" she repeated, absently, "no hope!"

"It is past the half-hour after seven, and you must leave your cell."

The poor young creature shuddered, and held her babe more closely to her bosom.

"Shall I call in the woman?"

"What woman?"

"The woman who will take your child."

"Take my child?"

"Yes; it is time you parted with it. I should have hastened the separation; but I thought of the possible return of those you expect, and I determined to give you the last chance."

"The last chance!"

"It was the last; all is now over." He turned to the gaoler, and continued, "Call in your wife."

The man did as he was ordered, and a tall and rather ill-favoured woman entered the cell.

The young mother gazed anxiously at her, and turned her eyes away with a shudder.

And it was to such a being her tenderly-cared-for darling was to be handed!

"How shall I part with it?" cried the poor mother; "how can I hand it to another?"

"Painful as the ordeal may be," said the deputy, "it must be done, and speedily. In an adjoining room is the sheriff and the ——" he was about to say hangman, but he hesitated, and said, "officers, who await your coming."

"Yes, yes," she cried, "I know, I know. Give me but a few moments. Oh! you do not know the terrible ordeal a mother undergoes in parting with her only child."

"I do know," said the deputy, "for I have seen it more than once; and therefore I would urge you to be as brief as possible. By delay you will but augment your sorrow."

"You are right," cried Mrs. Malvers, "you are right. Let her—let her take—no, no, no, I cannot spare my babe! Let it be with me till the last. It is but a small request. You will grant it, will you not? and God will bless you."

"I would grant anything you would ask," said the deputy, "if I had but the power to do so; but in this instance I have none. The sheriff would strongly object. Besides, it is usual to pinion the condemned persons before they ascend the scaffold."

"But they will not tear my child from me. A last request —a request so poor and so easily granted—will surely not be refused. They will let my closing eyes rest on my babe. They will do so, will they not? Oh! tell me, tell me they will do so!"

"I dare not tell you that which would be false. They will not allow any such proceeding. Pray calm yourself, and hand the child to the woman. Heaven knows I would spare you, but if you do not hand over your poor babe I must tear it from you."

"Oh, God, that it should come to this!"

She laid her child on her knees, and buried her face in her hands.

The deputy observed the mother's grief, and motioned the woman to bear the child away.

She immediately obeyed, and advancing a step, hastily snatched the babe from its resting-place.

With a loud shriek Mrs. Malvers rose to her feet.

"One look!" she cried, "one last look—but one kiss, and then I will give it you freely. Indeed, indeed, I will!"

"It were best not to prolong the scene," said the deputy; "bear the babe away."

The woman hastened from the cell, and mother and child were separated.

It was a terrible sight, was that of the poor young mother wailing for the loss of the child so dear to her.

Horrible were the feelings which agitated her as she heard the child's cry dying away in the distance, as it was rudely hushed in the arms of the stranger.

The pang of death was nothing compared with the agony of that moment!

It was gone, and the last tie was broken.

After this she consented to be led forth from the cell without further hesitation. In the room where the pinioning was gone through she was met by the sheriff, the officers of the gaol, the second chaplain (in the absence of Mr. Ashton), and *the hangman.*

They all treated her with the utmost consideration, and strove to soothe the great sorrow that was upon her. Even the hangman, hardened by years of practice of his dreadful trade, softened at the sight of the condemned woman.

"It was many years ago," he said, "that I hanged one so young and handsome. It is a bad business, and I'd willingly get out of it, if I could. I don't like hanging women, especially those so like angels."

He spoke of angels! What did the thoughts of that man run on when they were not occupied in matters nearly connected with his daily life? Everything pointed to his thinking of death in its worst forms. It was natural to suppose that one whose trade was that of hangman should have thought of death, and death, too, in its worst phases. Old, bold, strong men struggling with it, with the fatal rope tightened round the muscular throat; of protruding tongues, of eyes starting from their sockets, of swollen faces, and thin blue lines about the throat, of icy hands, of blood, and of the dark grave within the prison walls! This, we say, it would be natural to suppose was the subject which would occupy the leisure moments of such a man; but here was one who, by his spoken words, gave the lie to such a supposition.

"I don't like hanging women, especially those who look so like angels!"

And he, perhaps, dreamt of angels! Fair faces, spotless forms, halos of glory about hair of gold, wings of silver, and robes of spotless white. He must have thought this, or he could not have spoken the words we have noted. And thank God for it! It is well that those whose offices lead them into the darker paths should have some bright spots to look out upon, or humanity would die away, and the brute nature reign paramount in the image of the Maker of mankind.

Well for that man, well for us all, if we could ever think of angels!

Mrs. Malvers gazed about her vaguely. Her head felt light and giddy, and a sickening at the heart and faintness came over her.

" Do your duty," said the sheriff to the executioner.

The man advanced, and went through the operation of pinioning the prisoner.

" You will say you forgive me before you die ? " he whispered. " I do not like people to die under my hand and not forgive me. I think of it sometimes, and it does not tend to make me happy."

" I forgive you," said Mrs. Malvers.

" Thank you—thank you! "

The chaplain commenced reading the prayers for the dead, and as the bell tolled the procession was formed, and a movement made for the scaffold.

The first note of the solemn messenger of death, the prison bell, hushed the vast crowd of spectators into silence.

As far as the eye could reach, in the open space before the prison, swarmed a dense mass of humanity, heaving and struggling to get a glimpse of the gallows.

The scene was an awful one. Men, women, and children were there. Beings of the lowest order of humanity—men who thought no more of death than of any of the incidents in the daily routine of the world—women soddened with gin, and deprived of all the more refined feelings of womanhood—and children reared in the lap of filth, educated in the school of crime, graduating for the gallows on which they looked.

The crowd was not wanting in other peculiarities. There were those present who, by their dress and manners, proved themselves to be above the common herd, and whose appearance at that place was perhaps more disgusting than that of the rabble, despite their retiring and unobtrusive behaviour.

It is not a little strange that such an exhibition should have the effect of assembling such an audience. The grave—the mysterious and terrible bourne from which no traveller returns—attracts multitudes to the foot of the scaffold to see a single individual start on the journey; and the subject is made food for wit, ribald jests, and irony. It is the means of affording thousands an excuse for a night's wild debauchery; it hardens the heart; it is a vehicle for the propagation of sin; and yet the institution is permitted to exist now as it did at the time of our story, when England was not the England of to-day, and the untutored minds of our ancestors could tolerate—nay, enjoy—bull and bear-baiting, cock-fighting, and pugilistic encounters between women.

If we cannot do without the hangman, why should he not ply his craft within the prison-walls, away from the gaze of such a crowd as that on which we are now supposed to be looking?

Why should death be made the vehicle for that mad enthusiast to yell forth his denunciations and frantic profanations of the sacred book he holds in his hand? Why should it be the means of drawing together that crowd of wild drunkards who have throughout the night glued their lips to the bottles they have brought with them, and fired their poor weak brains with the contents?

Why should it afford that crew of wild, weird women the chance of shrieking and screaming there, and rendering night hideous by their yells? and why, above all, should it admit of the assemblage of those children, who look on the scene as an excellent jest, and enjoy its horrors as if they were items in a banquet of childish sport?

Who shall answer these questions?

Turn we now to our history.

From midnight the crowd had grown and grown, until its size became alarming, and groans of suffocation and screams of pain went up on all sides.

The streets in the immediate neighbourhood were also full,

and as the hours passed the excitement became fearful to behold.

The crime of which Mrs. Malvers was supposed to be guilty had obtained a vast reputation, and people came from far and near to witness the execution of its projector.

Men wandered about the outskirts of the throng, vending what they termed the " life and confession of the culprit, with the true history of the crime "—a production which had served the turn of the vendors at least a dozen previous executions. These were eagerly bought, and their contents devoured with avidity.

It was a foretaste to whet the appetite for the banquet of horrors which was to follow.

These vendors drove a thriving trade, as did also the proprietors of the public-houses in the neighbourhood, which were crowded on an early hour the previous night.

Rooms commanding a view of the gallows were let at truly fabulous sums, and there the more respectable of the tribe of sensation seekers whiled away the night, relating their experiences of former executions witnessed by them.

Here is a group to whom we may listen.

The speaker is an old man, who " does " the executions for the newspapers.

" I remember the day Tony Harrison was hung; he who killed the four children at Richmond, and then attempted the life of his uncle; don't you remember ? "

" I've heard of him "

" Ah ! his was something like an execution."

" Was it ? "

" That it was. I shall never forget the scene."

" There was something extraordinary happened, wasn't there ? "

" I should rather think there was. My! that was a sight to come to see."

" What was it ? "

" Why, the rope broke."

" Did it, though ? "

" It did; and down came poor Tony with a crash. You should have heard the yell of the crowd."

" Awful, I s'pose ? "

" Frightful! "

" Well, was he killed ? "

" Not that time. He was horribly mutilated, and his neck was somewhat hurt, but he was far from dead."

" And they hung him up again ? "

" Yes, I should say they did; and we had to wait until a fresh rope could be found, which was no small bother, I can tell you."

" It must have been a thing to remember."

" It was. They had to carry him to the scaffold, and hold him under the drop while the hangman went through his performance for the second time."

" That was a sight! "

" It was; but I thought the mob would give way to the feelings which agitated it. Never was there such screaming and riot. They had to keep the hangman within the prison for many weeks. If he had been caught they would have torn him to pieces."

More of these fearful anecdotes followed, and were listened to with the greatest possible interest; and the old man became the hero of his circle.

At length the bell tolled eight, and the stillness we have before alluded to came over the crowd.

A few moments, and the procession mounted the scaffold.

" Hats off ! " was the angry roar of those behind who could not get a glimpse of the proceedings.

The surging of the human sea was stilled, and every eye was turned to the fatal spot.

Mrs. Malvers was led to the scaffold, and had to be supported as she stood there.

She was perfectly sensible of her position, but physically she was entirely prostrated.

Her appearance elicited a general murmur of sympathy.

" How young, how beautiful! She doesn't look like one who could commit such a murder."

The poor soul gave one glance at the sea of faces turned upon her.

The sight astounded her, and she turned her gaze heavenward.

The chaplain continued the dull mumbling of the prayers, and the preliminaries were hastily gone through.

"Have you anything to say?" asked the sheriff, advancing to the side of the poor woman.

"Nothing," she replied, "nothing, save that I am innocent, and that time—perhaps a few short hours—will reveal the whole truth of my oft-repeated assertion."

"It is bad," continued the sheriff, "to quit the world with a falsehood on the lips. If you are guilty, pray confess; remember, you have but a few moments to live."

"I am innocent."

The sheriff withdrew, and the hangman now advanced and drew the white cap over the poor woman's face.

There was a shudder amongst the crowd so visible that the poor woman could hear and feel it.

She prayed that God would deprive her of the sense of hearing and feeling.

The sensations she was experiencing were too much for her, and yet she was painfully alive to all that was taking place. She heard the words of the chaplain, she felt the terrible touch of the hangman, and at last she was moved under the fatal beam.

The rope encircled her throat, and all was prepared.

A hand clasped hers: it was that of the hangman.

"Good-by!" he said, "you are going to be an angel."

He hurried from the scaffold to draw the fatal bolt.

All was prepared!

Horrible moment of suspense! Agony ten thousand times concentrated.

The hangman's hand is on the bolt!

* * * * * *

"Hurrah! hurrah!" The shouting was in the distance.

"Stay your hand," cried the sheriff; "what means that cry?"

"Hurrah! hurrah! Sixteen-String Jack for ever! Harrah! hurrah!"

Nearer and nearer came the shouts.

"What is it?" cried the sheriff.

"It is Jack," cried the deputy governor, in a fever of excitement. "Call up the hangman; Jack has *a reprieve!*"

The hangman returned once more to the scaffold.

"Look to the woman; she faints."

"Hurrah! A reprieve—a reprieve!"

"Clear a way, clear a way for the bold Jack! A reprieve—a reprieve!"

The shout was taken up by ten thousand throats.

Stentorian lungs yelled out the words until the whole air was rent with them.

"Hurrah! way for Jack! A reprieve—a reprieve!"

On the outskirts of the crowd a horseman could be seen ploughing his way into the very midst of the throng.

It was indeed Jack, and in his hand he held above his head the sealed packet from the Secretary of State.

The gallant mare, imbued with the excitement of those about her, snorted proudly, and ploughed on through the crowd as if conscious of her own importance and that of her bold rider.

"Bold Jack, brave Jack!" cried the excited mob. "Jack's the man; room, room; fall back; let him reach the prison!"

"Hurrah for Jack! He has saved the woman."

"Make way there," cried the horseman, glancing up at the scaffold, "make way; it is death to delay me a second; I bear a reprieve!"

There was not much occasion for him to shout.

The crowd, a few moments ago thirsting for the scene of death, were now mad with frantic delight at the thought of the miraculous escape of the intended victim.

The men fell back as well as they were able, and made a lane for the horseman straight to the prison.

He was there in a few moments, and the ponderous gates opened for him.

He was within, and everyone hurried from the scaffold.

Mrs. Malvers was carried away dead faint.

The excitement had been too much for her, and she had succumbed.

In a few moments the sheriff had read the reprieve, and satisfying himself as to his validity, ordered that every care should be taken of the prisoner until the search of the house of Malvers had been completed.

"If it is as the accomplice reports the woman must at once be set at liberty. There can be no excuse for detaining her."

"Free!" said Jack, "free! and by my own contriving. Thank God, I have kept my oath."

"You are a brave fellow, Jack," said the deputy-governor, "a very brave fellow; and it is with regret that I am obliged to address you as my prisoner."

"Never mind," said Jack, "I have not broken my word, and that is everything. I suppose it will be my turn to mount your scaffold next. Well, it's a bad end, but it can't be helped now. Tell them, though, that I gave myself up to justice, and don't let them think worse of me than you can help; and above all, be kind to my poor mare. She will not trouble anyone for long when I'm gone, poor old girl! When she misses my hand she will pine away and die."

"Come, Jack, cheer up! You're not dead yet."

CHAPTER VII.

SHOWS WHY MR. PETER PATTYPAN MADE SOME CONFECTIONS.

ANY ONE in the habit of passing through Holborn at the date of this story, would not have failed to notice a very neat confectioner's shop not far from the brow of the hill.

The place was very clean, and the window dressed with all manner of tempting morsels, set out with an eye to effect.

True, at that time shop-windows did not admit of the display we note in the present epoch of history. Gigantic sheets of plate-glass were not as yet dreamt of, and interiors dazzling with marble, mirrors, and gold mouldings were only to be found in the mansions of the great, and there only rarely.

Nevertheless, the shop of Mr. Peter Pattypan was an extremely natty place, and, the small squares of glass and limited space excepted, really presented a very striking appearance.

Fine jellies and preserves were well exhibited; sweets were ranged in long bottles, with due regard for the laws of harmony of colours, and ices were represented by very tolerable imitations ranged in rows of glasses, and looked remarkably tempting in the summer, but in the winter were suggestive of anything but pleasurable sensations in the stomach.

In the window of Pattypan's shop was exhibited a large placard, on which was depicted in gold letters the following announcement:—

PETER PATTYPAN,
PASTRYCOOK AND CONFECTIONER.
Wedding Breakfasts provided. Balls, Routs, Pic-nics, &c., attended.

This card was the constant delight of Peter.

He used to view it from all points of observation. He would change its position half-a-dozen times a day in his endeavours to improve its effects on the passers-by; it was, in fact, Peter's hobby, and to him a never-failing source of gratification and amusement. Never was there such an enthusiastic pastrycook as Peter; he was really wedded to his business, and he certainly proved a very attentive and enthusiastic spouse.

His thoughts were confined to his shop, and his whole life was a long, uninterrupted dream of pastry and confections.

Peter was a little man of rather singular appearance. He bore about him the look of a confectioner. There was something in his face suggestive of cake and jelly. Jams appeared to be marked on his lips, and certainly nothing but sugar was in his voice, for a more even tempered, better disposed little man than Peter could not be found in a day's ramble. He was

JACK AND THE DEPUTY-GOVERNOR.

always nattily dressed in a light suit of clothes, over which he wore a white apron, sleeves, and cap, so bright and snowy that they gave one the idea of being kept in flour, washed in milk and glossed over with the whites of eggs rather than the iron of the laundres.

Such, then, was Peter's shop, and such was Peter.

It is only necessary to add that Peter was a bachelor, and that the best part of his well-furnished little house was let out as lodgings. His establishment was ruled over by a mild old lady, as harmless and pleasant as Peter himself, and who was assisted by a tall, raw-boned girl of about fifteen years, who was taken out of the workhouse by Peter, and whom he therefore named Charity; her surname was Dobbs. The peculiarity of this specimen of humanity was, as she expressed it, "that she was a orphin, and that she hadn't got no mem'ry; but she couldn't help that—cos why, warn't she brought up in a work'us?"

Charity Dobbs was allowed to have pretty much her own way in the establishment of Pattypan, but she had an awful enemy in Sam Snike's, Pattypan's apprentice and errand-boy, a juvenile with an overpowering propensity for leaping over street-posts, and keeping mice, rabbits, and guinea-pigs. He was, moreover, addicted to substituting the " v " for " w," and talking the most abominable Cockney English ever heard.

Sam was a legitimate street-boy of the period, and was never so happy as when sent on a long errand, so that he might enjoy himself by performing on the posts, worrying inoffensive dogs and cats, and playing at the games usually indulged in by boys of his class in the by-ways of large towns.

Sam, as we have said, was the sworn enemy of Charity Dobbs. He taunted her with her failings, accused her of having faults she never possessed, frightened her into fits with his small menagerie, and when not otherwise engaged, chevied her from the top of the house to the bottom, with an enthusiastic enjoyment of the sport worthy the keenest huntsman in the pursuit of his favourite pastime.

Now that we have done with Peter's house and household let us turn to his lodgers.

At the period of which we write Peter's best rooms were engaged by a lady and her infant son; in a word, it was Mrs. Malvers and her child.

Released from Newgate, she was brought to Peter by the excellent chaplain, and the kind-hearted little pastrycook received her and treated her as gently as if she had been his own child.

Peter exerted himself strenuously to add to the comforts and happiness of his guest, and her smiles repaid him for his care.

"And ample payment, too," he used to say; "it does one's heart good to get her to smile. Poor thing! she hasn't much cause for mirth."

The baby, too, was a source of great joy to him. He was never tired of extolling its merits to those with whom he came in contact. Sam he put down as a barbarian, because be created so much noise in his recreation of worrying Charity up and down stairs.

"Poor little boy!" Peter used to say, "I wonder he can ever get a wink of sleep with that scoundrel flying about the

DICK TURPIN, TOM KING, AND RANN BEAR OFF GRANTLEY.

house and making such a riot. I know the end of it will be that I shall break his neck and get hung for him, though he isn't worth hanging for—the wild, uncultivated brute !"

Every time the baby squalled a fresh onslaught was made on Sam. It did not matter in the least whether he was in fault or not ; he used to get all the credit of being the evil genius of the little one, and many were the boxes on the ear received by him for disturbing "the precious baby ;" when the true cause of its uneasiness might be traced to wind and teething, and other infantine ailments of a similar but indescribable character.

"Blest if I can stand it," Sam would say; "it don't matter a fig vere I am ; if that ere kid cries, it's put down to my account, and I gets served out for it ! If it varn't for Mrs. Malvers's kindness, I'd wish the little vun further ; but she's so good and gentle, a feller can put up with a few knocks on account of the baby for her sake."

And good and gentle Mrs. Malvers undoubtedly was.

She appeared to think herself one of the most annoying creatures in existence, and strove by every means in her power to avoid occasioning any trouble in the household of Peter, although every person with whom she came in contact positively idolised her, and would have flown to the other end of the world to have served her.

This, then, was the exact state of affairs in the Pattypan circle at the time we introduce it to our readers.

It was a bright day in the autumn, and precisely one month after the occurence of the event which has occupied our preceding chapters.

The Pattypan circle was full of wild excitement, for an order

had come in suddenly for the preparation of a great wedding-feast which was to be devoured on the following day.

Although everybody had been very busy during the seven preceding days, it appeared that everything had been put off to the last moment, and the amount of work to be got through was extraordinary.

Peter had called in the aid of numerous journeymen, and great were the exertions made.

Jellies lined every table in the house; ices of all tints blockaded the cool passage and courts; pastry found quarters in every hole and corner; and fruits, gallipots of jams, and confections lay about in wild profusion.

Charity's memory had gone entirely, and after breaking a variety of plates and dishes, and otherwise exhibiting her talents, she was confined to her chamber, with orders to stay there until such time as a clearance of the eatables admitted of her re-appearance.

Sam had, much against his inclination, to abandon his live stock and his pet amusement of worrying Charity, and confine himself to business.

Peter was quite overpowerd with excitement, and quite forgot the baby ; and Mrs. Packets, the housekeeper, declared she never saw such a bustle and shut herself up with Mrs. Malvers until the excitement was over. Throughout the live-long day more jellies, more tarts, more sweets, and more fruits continued to appear, until it became apparent that the house would hold no more, and it was quite a relief when the cart came to convey it to its destination.

And the occasion of all this bustle was the wedding of Mr.

Edward Grantley, a wealthy young merchant of the City of London, with Miss Rosalie Mellhurst, the daughter of a Hertfordshire gentleman of considerable property.

Pattyman had been honoured by Mr. Grantley, with the order for the wedding entertainment, and the heart of the pastrycook rejoiced; for, as he explained to Mrs. Malvers, he had known Mr. Grantley a number of years, and it was pleasant to think that old times were not forgotten.

"Ah! Mrs. Malvers," said Peter, "Mr. Grantley was not always the great man he is now. I remember when he used, as a little boy, to pass the shop and peep in at the sweets without a halfpenny to buy 'em; and now just see what he is—one of the first City merchants, and looked up to by high and low with respect and admiration."

"He was once poor and lonely, then?"

"That he was. I believe he was left an orphan when very young, and that he fell into the care of a very rich, but particularly disagreeable, old uncle, who treated him so cruelly that he preferred working hard for a crust of bread to enjoying the luxuries of his uncle's house. Following the bent of his inclination, he went as errand-boy to a City firm, and fought his way upwards. It was as the poor, struggling lad that I knew him most intimately; and, taking a fancy to him, I used to give him the little niceties he couldn't afford to buy; and yon see he doesn't forget me, and, when he is about to marry a great heiress, comes to Peter and gives him the order for this magnificent wedding entertainment. Oh! the dainties he will have! Such patties, such pastry, such fruits—ah, you must taste my black-currant jam, prepared from the original receipt. I'll go and send some to you immediately." And away went Peter to create further bustle among his assistants, and scoop up some jam for Mrs. Malvers.

The scene of excitement continued the entire night; and when the last cart had taken away the last morsel to the house of Mr. Grantley, at Hackney, Mr. Peter Pattypan lay down to snatch a few hours' rest before preparing to undergo the fatigues which promised to fall to his share on the morrow.

CHAPTER VIII.

JACK AND THE DEPUTY-GOVERNOR.

One month!

It was just thirty days ago we left Sixteen-String Jack within the gates of Newgate, submitting to his fate, terrible though it was, for the sake of keeping his word pledged to Mrs. Malvers.

A month had flown over his head, and he had been tried and condemned, and now awaited his approaching doom.

He bore up bravely, however, and frequently asserted that were it not for his mare, he should die without a care; but he could not quit the world and know that his poor, faithful beast remained behind him, with the chance of falling into the hands of those who would neglect and ill-use her.

She had been under the care of the deputy-governor since the day of the arrest of Jack, and the little old man had treated her as well as he possibly could, for the sake of Jack, for whom he had taken a strong liking. The poor animal seemed to pine for her missing master, and no amount of kindness could compensate her for the loss. She lost her high spirits, refused food, and was visibly declining; but this fact was not communicated to Jack, lest it should heighten his gloom, and make his few remaining days more wretched.

Poor fellow! he put the brightest possible face on the matter, and displayed his want of care by tracing his many ribbons about his irons, until he made them, as he said, "look quite handsome."

In the next cell to that occupied by our hero lay another condemned man, in the person of Francis Austin. He had been tried, and found guilty of the crime imputed to him, and was now condemned to die on the same scaffold as the man who had dragged him to its foot.

Jack had but three more days to live, and, as his time drew near, so his anxiety for his mare increased. He never, by word or deed, alluded to his own position and suffering. All his thoughts were centred in the animal that had so long borne

him, faithfully and patiently, through his many trying escapades.

When the deputy-governor entered the cell, on the third day preceding the one fixed for the execution, the question with which he was greeted, was—

"Well, sir, how is my poor mare?"

"All right, Jack," said the little old man; "all right. Don't look so fat as she used to, but still all right. Lor', how she does prick up her ears when the stable-door opens, just as if she expected her master to pop in, and spring upon her as of yore! And how miserable she does look when she finds it's only the ostler or myself that pays her a visit. Ah me! you were right, Jack, when you said she wouldn't live long after you. I never saw such a faithful beast in all my life."

"True, true!" said Jack, "she is a beauty, and I can't bear the thought of dying and leaving her to the care of the stranger. If she would only die before myself, I should be content; but to quit the world, and know that she is left to the tender mercies of a careless master, to be ridden or driven about without compunction, is too much for me, and I can't stand it. The thought preys upon me day and night, and makes me melancholy. Were it not for that, your gaolers and warders should not see a cloud on the brow of Sixteen-String Jack."

"Fine fellow, fine fellow!" said the deputy, with something like admiration in his voice, "fine fellow! It's a pity you should die, Jack."

"That's a queer speech for an official to use towards a desperate highwayman, Master Deputy," said Jack, with a smile.

"It may be, it may be," continued the little man; "but I can't help thinking of it, and it's with regret that I think you surrendered to me. I heartily wish you had never given me your word."

"Oh, psha!" said Jack, "it's as well to surrender to you as another. They would have had me some time or other, and I suppose it's as well first as last. It's not a pleasant thing to contemplate death on the scaffold, but still I have not many cares, and my only wish is that the matter will be speedily over."

"Speedily over! And have you no wish to live?"

"No wish to live? Heaven bless us, deputy; I should think I had; but what is the use of wishing to live when there's no hope? Surely you don't suppose that the Home Secretary will interfere in my behalf?"

"I'm not such a fool, Jack."

"Well, then, where's the use of thinking about living?"

"Jack, did it never strike you that there were other ways of saving your life besides the one that presents itself through the mediation of the Home Office?"

"Never."

"Hush! What do you think of escape?"

"Escape! What, from a condemned hole, and without a friend? Absurd!"

"Is it? Not quite so absurd as it looks, I'm thinking."

"What do you mean?"

"Hist! Do you want all the gaolers to hear what I mean?"

"Great Heaven! Deputy, do not raise any false hopes. I'm content to die. I've long ceased to think of life. Do not, therefore, bring back such thoughts unless you have some notion of saving my life."

"Jack, Jack, listen to me. It has been preying on my mind day and night that it was through me you got here. In the saving of a fellow-creature's life you risked your own. It was mean of me to take such an advantage, and I deeply regret it; you do not know how deeply. I would make some atonement. I would at least try to save you."

"You are a good man, Deputy, and I thank you sincerely for your kindness; but I fear even you cannot get me out of this mess."

"Be not too sure. I have my plans."

"What are they? Let me know them."

"Will you lower your tone? All the fellows within a hundred yards will hear you if you keep up that bawl."

" Well, I'm quiet now ; but do speak."

" Well, then. I'm going to bring a lot of your female acquaintances here to bid you farewell, by-and-by."

" Female acquaintances ! I haven't one in the world, except Mrs. Malvers."

" What of that ? I've manufactured a full dozen for you, and they are all so anxious to see you, that they will be here in a body this very day."

" I do not see your drift."

" No ? I thought you were smarter. Do you not comprehend that ladies wear a variety of cloaks and hoods, and that one or two would not be missed by the gaolers any more than an addition of one to the number of visitors who make their exit would be detected."

" I see. You would have me disguise myself and leave the prison with the females."

" Just so. Is it not an admirable plan ?"

" It is, indeed, if it can be carried out; but will they admit so many people as you propose should visit me ?"

" Why not ? "

" It is unusual."

" It is : but what of that ? "

" Only that I do not see why concessions should be made in my case any more than in that of other criminals."

" Do you know who admits the visitors ?"

" No."

" Then learn that it is myself. If I give an order for the admission of half a hundred, there is no one but the governor to gainsay it ; and as he is not in the way, I think we are pretty safe."

" You are a good friend to me."

" But a very bad deputy-governor—eh ?"

" I did not say so."

" No, but you thought so."

" I have no reason to entertain such a thought."

" Hang it, man, no one is answerable for his thoughts I say I'm a very bad deputy-governor ; but I'd rather have that character, than that they should say of me hereafter, I entrapped a man into a halter whilst he was in the act of snatching a fellow-creature out of one."

" You are all goodness."

" I wish I could say the same of you. But no matter ; in time you may mend your ways, and lead an honest life. If you don't it's no business of mine, and I shan't grieve ; and I tell you now, that if ever you get into my clutches again, I shall have no mercy."

" I shall try to avoid you."

" That's well ; but be assured, my friend Jack, the true way to avoid me is by the amendment of your mode of life. Be honest, and you need have no fears of me."

" Your advice is good, but I fear it comes too late."

" As you will. Whatever your fate, you cannot say I did not warn you against the gallows, which stares you in the face."

" I can only reiterate my thanks."

" Hist ! "

The deputy went to the door of the cell, and opening it slightly, looked out.

The turnkey was at the other end of the gallery.

He returned to the cell hastily.

" Here," he said, handing a small key to Jack, " here is the key of the irons ; conceal it."

No sooner said than done.

Jack hid the key in one of his pockets.

" It's all right," said our hero.

" Good. When you get out—if you ever do get out—go at once to the ' Black Swan ' tavern in Bishopsgate-street Within. You will there find your mare. I will leave orders that you are to have her on application. Once on her back I know you are safe. After that, you may do as you will, for I shall take no further heed of you."

" Never fear," said Jack, gleefully ; " once on the back of the mare, I am safe.

" Ah !" said the old man ; " you are safe ; but it's the sort of safety I should like to avoid. Oh, Jack, Jack, you rogue I and I wish I could make you amend your ways."

" All in good time, governor."

" In good time ! Hang it, man ; how much more rope do you want ? But it's no business of mine. Do as you will, but never say I did not do my best to make a better man of you."

" I never will, deputy ; and if ever you want a friend, and you may, depend upon it you will find him in the wild, lawless, ungovernable Sixteen-String Jack."

" I hope I shall have no occasion to look after you, Jack."

" I hope so too ; but there is no knowing what may befall a man in this life."

" That's true ; but Heaven keep off the day when I shall require the aid of a highwayman."

" So say I ; but it may yet come."

" Hang the fellow ! Be quiet ; you speak like an evil prophet, and make one feel as if he had a pistol presented at his head, and only two minutes given him to commend his soul to the care of Heaven. But good-by, Jack, and success attend you."

" Thanks, deputy, thanks. I dare say you think you do a silly act to-day ; but the time may come when you will bless your stars to think that you liberated Jack Rann."

" I see you are already thinking how you are to repay the debt you will owe me. Oh, Jack, you are a proud dog."

" I am a faithful one. Above all, deputy, remember I never yet broke my word."

" Oh, hang your word ! It gets you into more trouble than enough. A less scrupulous villain would go through the world much easier."

" I have no doubt of it ; but it's my pleasure and my boast that my word has never yet been broken."

" A pretty thing to boast of, truly, when that word has been pledged to robbery and bloodshed. But that's one of the contrarieties of human nature."

" It is, governor, it is ; but no matter."

" True, it is no matter ; and so good-by."

" Good-by, sir. God bless you ! "

The turnkey here put his head into the cell, and announced that there were about a dozen women, who professed to be relatives of Jack Rann, awaiting the deputy in his office, in order to obtain his consent to a parting interview.

" A dozen ! " said the deputy, with well-feigned astonishment : " why, Jack, have you a dozen female relatives ? "

" Cousins included," said Jack," " I have full that number."

" And they all take sufficient interest in you to visit you here ? "

" I suppose so. Women are generally to the fore when a man is in trouble."

" So they are, Jack ; but a dozen is rather too great a number to admit at once."

" It is a large number, sir ; but I trust you will allow them to come. It will be the last time they will see me."

" So it will, so it will ; I think they may come."

" Thank you, sir."

This conversation was carried on with great gravity before the turnkey, who listened to every word with strict attention.

" Humph ! " he said to himself, " the old owl makes a deal of fuss about letting a few poor women see their relative. I wish he was placed in Jack's position ; he'd know then how good it is to get a few words of comfort spoken to him ; more particularly as they're the last he'll hear in this world."

He was a kind-hearted turnkey, and the apparent reluctance of the deputy-governor to admit the females, trapped him into an act which he had no right to be guilty of—the quitting of the cell during the interview.

" There can be no harm come of it," he said ; " and I am sure I don't care about hearing the parting words."

If he had it would have been all the same, for the deputy had concocted a plan for calling him away from the scene.

" You may show the women this way," said the deputy to the turnkey. " I'll give them half an hour."

The turnkey walked away, and the little man whispered hastily to Jack :

" Mind, no bungling. It is the last chance."

" All right," said Jack ; " I'll not miss it."

" Good-by, then."

"Good-by, sir."

In another minute the cell of our hero was half-filled by women, who all pretended to be steeped in the deepest grief, to have a painful interest in the fate of the prisoner.

"Oh, Jack, Jack," cried one, "this is dreadful! To think that you must die!"

She clung to him with all the affection of a fond sister.

"It is sad, sad!" cried another. "Oh, that I should have lived to see you come to this!"

And she hung about him.

Another and another followed their example, until Jack was quite surrounded.

"Poor souls!" said the turnkey, "I'll get outside; this is the sort of scene I don't care about witnessing."

He walked out of the cell and seated himself within a few paces of the door. And from there he heard the crying and moaning continued with unabated fury.

"Oh, Jack, Jack! and will they hang you!" was the cry in a loud tone; and then in a softer one came the question, *"Where's the key?"*

"Don't cry; hanging isn't much; and I'll keep up a good heart." Here he handed the woman the key of the irons, and added, "Make no noise."

"Oh, it's sad, sad!"

Here there was a perfect hurricane of sobs, amidst which part of the irons were removed, without even a clink.

"Do you feel content, Jack?" asked one. "Are you prepared to die?"

"*Not quite,*" answered Jack.

"Ah, that is sad, very sad; you ought to be resigned."

"He ought, he ought," cried the others, in a chorus; and the other portion of the irons came off without attracting any more attention than had the first moiety.

"Do you feel happier now that you have seen us?" inquired another of the women.

"Much," said Jack, "much. *The interview is quite a relief to me.*"

The conversation went on, and at last Jack had slipped off his coat, and assumed the outer garments of a woman.

A long wig was placed upon his head, and his disguise was complete.

The coat, stuffed with a variety of articles of clothing to resemble the human form, was laid upon the bed as if its owner had thrown himself there in an agony of grief; and then the women began to think of going.

"Good-by," said Jack, muffling his mouth, as if his head was buried in the clothes of his couch, "Good-by. Don't say another word; it's more than I can bear."

The women, with Jack in their midst, began to quit the cell.

"Poor fellow!" said the gaoler, rising and casting a glance into the cell at *Jack's coat,* "poor fellow! it's very trying to him."

"Very trying," said one of the party; "the moment is more agonising to him than *you* can tell."

"Ah," said the turnkey, locking up the cell, "I know something of these matters. I've seen enough of them."

He led the way through the long passage, and into the deputy's office.

That little functionary was seated at his desk.

"You have not exceeded your time, ladies," he said.

"No, sir," one of them replied, "no, sir; we were not willing to take advantage of your goodness; besides, Jack was too overcome with grief to hear a long talk; so we have left him."

"Poor Jack! I pity him."

"Ah, sir, he is to be pitied—so good a heart—so true a friend."

"I believe so," said the deputy; "but you see the reward of an ill-spent life."

"We do, indeed."

"Well, good-by, good-by."

"You'll be kind to him during the few hours he has to live?"

"Oh, yes; he will be treated with the greatest consideration."

"Thank you, sir. That is a great comfort to us. Good day, sir."

The band of women now filed out of the office, and one of them, who appeared as if she wore a wig, turned and deliberately winked at the deputy.

"Curse the fellow!" mumbled the deputy, when the last one had quitted his office and stepped into the courtyard, "curse the fellow! he actually winked at me, and he had a broad grin on his face too—just as if he thoroughly enjoyed his awful position."

The deputy rose, and walked to the window of his office. He saw the party cross the courtyard. He beheld the wicket-gate swing on its hinges, and the next moment Sixteen-String Jack was out of Newgate, having made his escape under the very nose of the turnkey in the broad daylight.

"He's gone," said the deputy; "and a pretty go it would be for me if they ever found out that I had had a hand in it."

CHAPTER IX.

DICK TURPIN, TOM KING, AND SIXTEEN-STRING JACK JOIN A WEDDING-PARTY.

THE day of Jack's escape from Newgate was a jovial one in the village of Hackney, for it was the wedding-day of Mr. Grantley, the gentleman for whom we have already seen Peter Pattypan preparing so magnificent a feast.

Hackney was all alive, for Mr. Grantley was popular in the neighbourhood, and everyone was anxious to express, as they were best able, the joy they felt in the consummation of this happy event.

From an early hour the bells were kept in a state of agitation, and general excitement pervaded all with whom one came in contact.

Mr. Peter Pattypan was at Hackney at a very early hour, and commenced his arrangements forthwith. His sweets were set out to the best advantage, and had it not been for that rascal Sam, who was brought down for the purpose of assisting, everything would have gone on smoothly, and the joy of Pattypan would have been excessive; but Sam was a perfect marvel.

He first of all took a fancy to Mr. Grantley's pigeons, and forthwith devised sundry plans for catching a few, and transferring them to Holborn.

Caught in the fact, he underwent a severe boxing of the ears, and then a sound kicking, but that only damped his ardour for a few minutes.

A few jumps over the park railings set him right again, and then he commenced rabbit-hunting, for the purpose of adding to his collection at home.

Stopped at that, he prepared to make himself useful, which he straightway did by smashing all the crockery and bathing the cat in the iced water.

He next of all caught Mr. Grantley's pet terrier, and fed it on ice-creams and sherry, until the poor little dog was remarkably ill.

Receiving another cuffing for this, he applied himself to business for a period of ten minutes with extreme assiduity; but the sight of an unfortunate parrot upset his equanimity, and he straightway caught the unhappy cat he bathed in the ice, and shut her up with poll—a companionship productive of much quarrelling of a severe character.

Notwithstanding these drawbacks, however, Peter, in due time, had completed his arrangements to his own satisfaction, and was anxiously awaiting the arrival of those who were to do justice to his good things.

It was eleven o'clock, and the marriage procession was about to set out for the church, when two magnificently dressed horsemen dashed into the village, and, leaving their horses at the only inn of the place, inquired their way to the residence of Mr. Grantley.

It was pointed out to them, and they immediately walked in the direction indicated.

Arrived at the park gates, they paused and looked around.

"This is the place," said one to the other; "my life! but Tom King and Dick Turpin will be queer wedding-guests."

JACK ATTACKED BY THE THIEF-TAKERS.

It was Turpin who spoke.

"Ah!" replied the dashing Tom King, "queer enough, but still they may have worse within."

"Like enough. At all events, they haven't two smarter fellows, and I'm only sorry I can't introduce Black Bess amongst them; she would be an improvement to any party of aristocrats."

"So she would, Dick. If there's anything in this world more beautiful than another, it's Black Bess; and Heaven knows how much I envy you the possession of her."

"But this isn't business. Have you got your story well prepared?"

"Yes; I'm right enough. I tell you, though, this petti-fogging swindling isn't much in my line. I rather prefer a clear road, a dark night, and a fat carriage."

"And so do I. But what's to be done?"

"To be done? Why, the work, to be sure."

"And you won't fail?"

"Not if I can help it. It's all straightforward enough, and a tolerably honest piece of business; but it's a nasty time to bring trouble to a man's door, and I don't like it. Hark! Even now the joy-bells are ringing. Ugh! It's a black piece of business."

"So it is. What d'ye say—shall we give it up, burn the will, and let things take their course?"

"No, no; too much depends upon it. We cannot afford to pitch away thousands like that."

"True. Very well, then; to work."

They were about to push open the gate, when the clatter of horse's hoofs attracted their attention.

"Hillo!" cried King, as a horseman came pelting along the road, "that fellow is well mounted. Who the deuce is it?"

"Why, look at the strings on his boots—it's Sixteen-String Jack."

"Oh! nonsense. Jack's in the condemned hole of Newgate."

"That's Jack for a thousand pounds."

It was Jack; and in a few seconds he was beside his friends, Turpin and King.

"Hillo, Jack!" cried Turpin; "who would have thought of seeing you?"

"Not you, for one, Dick. I suppose you expected that by this time I was hard at it with the chaplain of Newgate?"

"That we did."

"Oh, I've given him the cut."

"Escaped!"

"Yes; as clever a thing as ever you saw."

Jack then related the manner of his escape, omitting, of course, all mention of the deputy's participation in the act.

"Capital!" cried Tom, as Jack finished; "capital! As clever a thing as ever I heard of. Why, Jack, you will be quite a hero in London before the day's out."

"Yes," said Jack, "too much of a hero; for I expect the inquiries after me will be more numerous than welcome."

"Just so. But you are right now. They won't get at you in a hurry."

"Not if I know it. They wouldn't have had me then had I not given myself up to them. But once bit, twice shy. Catch me at that game again."

"Ah, well, Jack! you did a brave thing, and deserved to escape."

" No more than I'd do again and again for the same person. But enough of that. What game are you after here ? "

" We have a small job on hand at this house," said King.

" What," cried Jack, " a robbery ? "

" No ; only an extortion of money. But since you are here you shall be in the swim. Listen. Some few weeks ago a will fell into my possession. On examining it I found it concerned Mr. Grantley, a young merchant, who is to be married to-day. I find that he is in unlawful possession of the property he holds, the whole of it being bequeathed to a charitable institution."

" Well ? "

" I propose getting a good thing out of him, and then handing over the will."

" That's it," said Turpin ; " will you join us ? "

" I see no harm," said Jack ; " there isn't much knavery about it ; only it strikes me the proper thing to do would be to give the poor devil the will, and let him be happy on his wedding-day."

" So it would, but we are hard up."

" So am I – penniless."

" Well, we have no choice. Are you with us ? "

" Yes," said Jack, " as long as all is square."

" Very well, then. Put up your mare at the inn, and come with us."

" But, I say, is she safe there ? "

" Safe ! " said Turpin, " my Bess is there. D'ye think I'd leave her there if all was not right ? "

" I suppose not, Dick. You think as much of Bess as I do of poor Meg. Dear old girl ! it's the first time she has seen me for a month."

Jack patted his mare affectionately, and the animal turned her head and acknowledged the greeting by rubbing her nose against her master's hand.

" Poor Meg ! " said Jack ; " there's not a finer bit of horse-flesh in the world."

" Barring Black Bess," said Turpin.

" Barring nothing," said Jack. " I know Bess is good enough ; but give me Meg."

" Every man to his taste," said King. " Now I've an idea that my White Wizard is the finest beast in the world, but I suppose I'm mistaken. However, there's no time to argue on the merits of horseflesh when such important business is on hand."

" True," said Turpin ; " let us hasten."

The mare was soon secured in the stables of the inn, and the three friends bent their steps towards Mr. Grantley's house.

At the hall door they encountered Mr. Peter Pattypan.

" Here's one who will put us in the way of finding Grantley," said King ; " he doesn't look particularly clever ; let us address him."

" Very good," said Turpin ; " pitch it strong into him."

" The top of the morning to you, sir," said King.

" And the bottom of it to you, sir," said Peter. And then he continued, " Let me see : apple tarts—pine-apple tarts—sweet apple tarts—sour apple tarts—then "——

" You seem to be very busy," said Rann.

" I am, sir," said Peter ; " very busy, indeed. I don't know you, sir ; perhaps you don't know me—here's my card ; and when you are pleased to favour me with an order, I shall feel much satisfaction in taking—hem—your money."

" So, so," said King, taking Peter's card, and glancing at it, " I suppose you provide the wedding dinner ? "

" You are right, sir, I do. Pine-apple tarts—plum tarts—and gooseberry fool."

" Pray who is the bride ? "

" Oh ! a young lady from Hertfordshire, with such lots of money, and all to be paid down after dinner."

" Indeed ! " said King, apart ; " that makes it all the better for us. Ready cash is better than promises. Indeed ! " he continued to Peter, " and she is very rich ? "

" Very rich. But I've no time to lose. Good morning, gentlemen."

" Stay," said King ; " where can we find Mr. Grantley ? "

" I do not think you can see him unless you are a guest. If so, he is in the breakfast room."

" Thanks," said King.

Turpin and Rann now advanced.

" My lord," said King to Jack, " this is a very celebrated personage, I assure you."

" Here's a lord," thought Peter ; " how I wish they would patronise my shop in Holborn."

" Yes, my lords," continued King.

" They are both lords," thought Peter.

" Yes, my lords, he is a very famous little man. I have the honour of introducing Mr. Peter Pattypan, the confectioner, of Holborn."

" Pattypan ? " said Jack, thoughtfully. " What, Pattypan, of Holborn ? "

" The same," said King.

" The very same," said Peter, quite delighted.

" Ah ! " said Jack, " the very cleverest confectioner of the day. I am proud to see you."

" His lordship knows me," said Peter to himself, boiling over with delight. " What excellent society I have dropped into ! " He had !

Jack's hand was in one of his pockets, and Turpin's in the other.

" Allow me to put my hand in my pocket," said Peter.

Jack held him tighter still, and said,—

" By no means, my dear Peter."

" Just to reach a card," said Peter.

" Do not trouble yourself—I have one."

He had more than one, for he had eased Peter of his pocket-book, which contained half a hundred.

" Since you will not permit me to trouble you with a card," continued Peter, quite unconscious of the fact that he had not one to " trouble " his friends with, " allow me to ask the favour of your patronage, and to express a hope that when you pass through Holborn you will favour me with a visit."

" We perhaps may," said King ; " you may depend upon it we never think it a condescension to visit good, prosperous tradesmen."

" Indeed," said Peter, " that is truly obliging on your parts."

" Not at all, not at all ! The obligation is all the other way, in general."

" If ever you should visit me," said Peter, " I hope you will make free with my pastry. I can recommend it."

" My dear friend Peter," said Jack, " we will not only be free with your tarts, but with everything else you possess. It's a maxim of ours to stand on no ceremony with the goods of our friends ; therefore, be assured that when we come to visit you we will spare nothing that come in our way."

" Do not, my lords," said Peter ; " it will do my heart good to see you walking into my pastry. I am sure the delight will be excessive."

" Will it ? " murmured Turpin. " I take leave to doubt that. However, no one can say that we came without an invite, or walked away with that to which we had not been made welcome."

" And now, my lords," continued Peter, " I must say adieu, for I have to fly back to Holborn for some more apricot preserve ; there's not enough for the guests. I'm your lordships' very dutiful servant."

With this little Peter stalked off, feeling several inches taller from his contact with the supposed notables.

" Poor little man," said Jack, as the confectioner went out of sight, " how surprised he would look if we were to pay him a professional visit and remind him of his hearty invitation. Ha ! ha ! I should like to remind him of this morning's interview."

" And so should I," said King ; " how blue the poor little fellow would look ! "

" Particularly with a pistol at his head, and our noble selves urgent for the production of his cash-box."

" That's all very well," said King ; " but it's time to think of business ; here we are at the hall door. Let us find some one to announce us."

A servant here bustled across the hall.

"Hi, you fellow!" said Jack, assuming the air of a dandy, "Hi! Where is Mr. Grantley?"

"He is at hand, gentlemen; are you guests?"

"Well, something of that kind. Will you lead us to your master?"

"Decidedly, gentlemen, if you are not on business."

"Oh, Mr. Grantley will be so in raptures to see us! Say three gentlemen, friends of his late uncle, would feel delighted to join the wedding party."

"Very good," said the man as he withdrew to perform his mission.

CHAPTER X.

DARK FORESHADOWINGS.

Mr. Grantley had just been making the tour of his house with his future wife. They had rambled together through the splendid apartments, and were now in an elegant little boudoir which the rich young merchant had furnished with exquisite taste for his beloved bride.

"Here," he said, as he seated the lovely girl on a luxurious couch, "here you will be as happy as the days are long, Rosalie. See, the window looks out on the London road, and from this spot you will be enabled to watch for me on my return from the City. Note to what a distance you can obtain an uninterrupted view of the road."

"Yes," said Rosalie, "I shall be very happy here; it is an exquisite place—far more beautiful than I thought you would be enabled to give me."

"Yes, Rosalie; fortune has certainly favoured us. A very few years ago I was but a poor stockbroker's clerk, striving hard to make both ends meet and eke out a bare subsistence for myself; and now I am rich and honoured, and enabled to offer you a home to which even your father can raise no objection."

"And that is saying much, for he is not readily satisfied."

"He is not, indeed."

"So jealous has been his care for me, that a fainter heart than yours would have given up the pursuit long ago."

"No, no, I do not think that. Against your encouraging smiles your father's frowns would have no weight. Many a time, as a boy, when I have seen you at your window, as I have passed along to my office drudgery, my heart sank within me, for the well known features of your father would present themselves before me and warn off hope; but I have looked up into your eyes, and doubts and fears have vanished, and I have felt that I had only to push forward in order to overcome all difficulties that lay in my path."

"Yes; but it would have been a long and tedious task for you, had not your uncle died intestate, and had you not inherited his vast wealth."

"It would. I dare not think how long and tedious the task would have been, and that makes me more thankful for my wondrous fortune."

"It is indeed wondrous—so wondrous—so like a dream—that I dread an awakening which shall dash the cup of happiness from our lips."

"Oh, nonsense, Rosalie; there should be no fears now. All difficulties are overcome, all sorrows ended. In a few short minutes you will be my wife. What can possibly happen now to interrupt our happiness?"

"I do not know; but within the last hour some vague, incomprehensible sense of danger has possessed me; a chill has come over me, and my heart has beaten wildly. I am not superstitious, but I cannot shake off the foreshadowings of evil which have presented themselves to me. Strange! While we were in the upper apartments, I looked out on the road, and my eye fell on two horsemen who, after gazing in this direction, turned away in the direction of the inn. I do not know why, but something whispered to me then, and the voice is strong within me now, that those men were, in some manner to play a part in this day's proceedings which will be antagonistic to our happiness. I never saw faces so expressive of evil."

"Rosalie, you are ill! Something ails you, or you would not speak thus. The excitement has been too much for you, and you are now suffering from the reaction."

"No, no, it is not so; but these may be mere idle fears and fancies, engendered in over-anxiety; they will pass off presently, perhaps."

"Just so. Let us now join our guests. It is time we were on our way to the church."

"Come, then," said Rosalie, rising and placing her arm within that of Grantly; "let us go."

They were about to leave the apartment, when the servant who had encountered the three highwaymen entered, and delivered his message.

"Three gentlemen, do you say?" asked Grantley.

"Yes, sir; three gentlemen—friends, as they say, of your late uncle."

"Indeed! That is strange. I always understood that my uncle made no friendships. What manner of men are they?"

"City gallants, if one may judge by their dress."

"Indeed!"

"Have not two of them scarlet coats, elaborately trimmed, and long glazed riding boots?" inquired Rosalie, anxiously.

"Yes, madam; all three are similarly attired."

Rosalie staggered, and would have fallen had not Grantley supported her.

"Tell the gentlemen I will see them immediately, and lead them to my library."

The servant withdrew.

"Look up, Rosalie—look up!" cried Grantly; "this is nothing. There is some slight business transaction to arrange—some trifle. Do not be so discouraged. A few minutes, and I will return."

She did look up, but there was no hope in the pale face.

"Alas!" she said, "I feel that the dark foreshadowings are about to be realised."

He pressed her hand and withdrew, feeling that the voice to which he had listened had a prophetic warning in it, to which it was in vain to shut his ear.

In another minute the young merchant was face to face with his mysterious visitors.

"Good morrow, Grantley!" said King, with extreme nonchalance.

"Sir," said Grantley, "you speak familiarly. Am I known to you?"

"Known to me! Of course you are!"

"And yet I do not remember to have seen your face before."

"Probably not."

"And now let me inquire what your business with me? This is not the time usually chosen for business matters, unless of extreme importance."

"Sir, this matter is of extreme importance—at least, to you!"

"Yes, to you!" echoed Turpin. "Of course, it's not much account with anyone else."

"Then I would have you come to the subject at once. Even now my absence from my post may be noted, and I have no time to lose."

"My dear Grantley," said Turpin, "your time is nothing to us. Our time must be yours."

"You are insolent," said Grantley, "and if I hear another such a speech from you, I shall thrust you from the house."

"You had best not."

"Now, no quarrelling," said Jack, "hang it, settle matters without having recourse to high words."

"With all my heart," said Dick; "I'm not the fellow to expend much gab over a job."

"Your business," said Grantley, turning impatiently to King, "your business"—

"Is soon told. You have become wealthy by the death of your late uncle. He left no will, and you, as heir-at-law, succeeded to all his estates and property."

"And pray what is all this to you?"

"More than you think for. Had your uncle left a will, you would have been very differently situated, for, if report

speak truth, he never had much affection for you, and you
wonld therefore be a very unlikely person to inherit his
wealth."

" Grant all this. What does it amount to ? "

" A great deal. Now comes the joke of the story. Your
uncle *did* leave a will, and 'tis in my possession."

Grantley was stricken speechless with amazement.

" I'll tell you how it came about," continued King.
" Your uncle died in the old house, where he had lived so
many years, in Gutter-lane. Now you disposed, shortly afterwards, of this dwelling and others adjacent to a builder, who
pulled them down for the sake of the materials."

" Yes, yes ! " cried Grantley, " all this is the truth."

" Well," said King, " from a concealed closet there tumbled
out an iron box ; it was unseen by the workmen, but I was
standing by, saw it, seized and concealed it, hoping to find that
it contained treasure, and in the presence of my friend yonder
broke it open."

" You did ; and how dare you, sir ? "

" Dare ! Oh, bless you, that's a trifle to what *we* dare do,
as you will find when you know us better. Well, we broke
open this iron box, and in it we found your uncle's seal ring
and his will. I've brought the ring just to convince you that
it's all right."

Here King withdrew his glove and exhibited his hand, on
the fore-finger of which glittered a massive ring.

" It is his ring," said Grantly, " I know it well. How
often have I searched among his hoards for that ring and without success. And the will, sir ? "

" I have broken the seals, and I find that the whole of the
property is left to the City of London Orphan Asylum."

" Is it possible ? "

" Oh, not only possible, but a positive fact."

" Have you this document with you ? "

" Oh no," said King, " we are rather too old for that.
What, bring such a treasure here ?—that would be too good."

" Well, man ; speak, speak, what is it you propose ? "

" Why, I propose to sell the will to you."

" Sell it to me ? "

" Yes ; you see we are anxious to serve you as we best can.
Now if we had taken the treasure to those who have the best
right to it, we should have been handsomely rewarded ; but, we
argued, here's a very good sort of young man who is about to
be married, and who deserves well ; why should he lose all
when happiness is in his grasp ? Why should the cup of joy
be dashed down when it is at his very lips ? By serving him
we serve ourselves. If he has a mind to reward us, he shall
have the will, and we will be dumb on the subject ; that's
what we said, and now I ask you what could we say fairer than
that ? "

" True, true ; but the dishonesty of the act ! Oh, I shudder
at it ! "

" Bah ! Who has most right to the money—you or a set
of ragged orphans ? why you, and you shall have it, only
agree to what we propose."

" Oh," cried Grantly, " were it not for her—were it not for
her, nothing could tempt me to this act of dishonesty ; but
how can I go to her and say ' I am a beggar, go hence with
your father, for I have no home for you ! ' "

" How, indeed," said Jack, " why, the act would be madness."

" It would be honourable."

" Psha ! " continued Jack, " honour is all very well sometimes, but when it steps in on such an occasion as this, the
best way is to pocket it, and keep it for some future occasion
when its promptings are less likely to lead to misery and utter
ruin."

It was a trying moment, and poor Grantley was not proof
against the temptation.

Few men would have been.

Years and years he had been struggling upward, striving
in vain to reach the longed-for haven. Then a chance had
thrown wealth and happiness in his grasp, and as he was about
to secure it, it proved to be a phantom, a mockery, and a
deceit.

What wonder then that the poor distracted man preferred
securing the aim of his life, to acting according to the dictates
of honour, and thus beggaring himself and bringing misery to
the door of her he loved.

Nine out of ten would have followed the course of Grantley
and accepted the advice of Jack, and have pocketed his honour
until a future occasion.

" You spoke of a reward," said Grantley ; " what is it you
require ? "

" Briefly, then," sad King, " we want five thousand
pounds."

" Five thousand pounds ! "

" Yes ; and the sum is not worth haggling about. You'll
receive your wife's dowry to-day in cash—and that's twenty
thousand, if report is to be credited."

" No matter—no matter. Where is the will ? "

" At our lodgings in *Knaves-acre*."

" Bring it hither, I will agree to your terms."

" Bring it hither ! " quoth Dick, " not if we are aware
of it."

" What would you then ? "

" You must put the sum named in your pocket, and as
soon as evening falls go with us to Knaves'-acre. There, and
there only I will give up the parchment"

" 'Tis a dreadful spot. Perhaps I am to be lured there to
be slain."

" Bah ! keep faith with us, and you are safe. Give the
money we demand with one hand, and with the other you shall
receive the will. There is such a thing as honour among
thieves, and I pledge myself and my comrades that unharmed
you shall return."

" Enough," said Grantley. " I must trust you. It is my
only chance. Oh, Rosalie, into what a miserable gulf of sin
am I about to plunge, to secure thy happiness ! "

" Nonsense, nonsense. It would be a sin to throw up this
chance."

" I cannot think so ; but no matter, I am resolved. Where
shall I meet you ? "

" Here. Why, my dear Grantley, you do not think we
could leave you ? No, no, we will join your guests and go
with you to church."

" You ? "

" Yes, all three of us."

" Do not dream that I would sanction such a thing."

" Oh, nonsense ; you have no choice."

" Let me implore "—

" Oh, absurd ! "

" But Rosalie—my father-in-law ! "

" Oh, we will make it all right with them. Three better-
behaved, and, if I may say so, better-looking fellows you have
not in the house, and we promise to be as amiable as you could
possibly desire. To be sure, we are all more or less acquainted
with the cells of Newgate, but in this bright plumage no one
will recognise the gaol-birds ; so come ! I'll take your arm,
it will give me an air of importance. Ha ! ha ! This is
fine fun."

" It is torture."

" Torture ? " said Jack, " I call it the height of jollity.
Lor, I never saw a man married—I wonder what it's
like ! "

" It's like having a tooth out," said Turpin, " at least to
the principals in the transaction, and when it's over, you look
as if you had stolen something and were afraid of being
detected in the fact."

" Why Dick," said King, " one would think you knew
all about it from experience."

" Heaven forbid," said Turpin ; " no, no, boys ; no wife for
me while I have Black Bess to love and be loved by."

The quartette now advanced to the principal *salon*, and the
three highwaymen were introduced to the company as military
gentlemen who had enjoyed the acquaintance of Grantley's
late uncle.

" He was a very worthy old gentleman," said Mr. Millhurst,
the father of Rosalie, " he must have been a man worth
knowing"

THE ESCAPE OF JACK AND MRS. GRANTLEY.

"Oh, he was," said Turpin, "a most extraordinary man. He bore a strong resemblance to *Guy Fawkes*."

"Complimentary!" said old Millhurst. "What rude fellows these military men are, to be sure."

The procession was now formed, and a movement made towards the village church.

Was Grantley happy?

Alas, no! He felt that he was dishonoured, and that for the first time he had done an act to merit the frowns of his fellow-men.

He was wretched, very wretched; but it was too late to retract.

He was at the altar, and a glance into the eyes of the poor trembling girl at his side was sufficient to make him attempt to palliate the offence of which he was about to be guilty.

CHAPTER XI.

NEWGATE ONCE MORE—THE CONDEMNED CELL—THE VISIT OF THE INJURED WOMAN—A STRANGE TALE OF A WILL—A SECRET REVEALED.

MR. PATTYPAN had not quitted his house over two hours on the morning of the marriage of Mr. Grantley, when one of the turnkeys of Newgate knocked at his door and demanded to see Mrs. Malvers.

Mrs. Packets was immensely alarmed at the appearance of such a visitor; and Charity, on hearing that the strange man was connected with Newgate, immediately took it into her head that she was "wanted" for some capital offence, and made up her mind that the scaffold was her doom.

This, as a matter of course, brought on strong fits, in the midst of which she capsized a table of crockery and smashed the lot.

The least disconcerted party was Mrs. Malvers herself, who bore the news of the advent of the Newgate official without exhibiting any sign of trepidation.

"Show the man to my room," she said to Mrs. Packets.

"Show him here! Lor' a mercy me, why you will never see him! Oh, suppose the people of the prison have changed their mind again, and want to hang you instead of your cousin! Oh, dear! oh, dear! get out on the roof, or up the chimney."

"Or down the coal-hole," suggested Charity; "there's a fine lock on the door, and barrin' rats, it's a capital place to hide; particularly if yer ain't afraid of the ghosts o' guinea-pigs; for that's were Sam hides all his."

"Nonsense, nonsense!" said Mrs. Malvers, "do run and show the man up. He will think it strange to be kept down-stairs all this time. There can be nothing for me to fear; it is some message from poor Jack Rann; rely upon it, it is nothing else. Come, my good friends, do show the man upstairs."

"Well," said good Mrs. Packets, "if you do insist, of course I will; but if he calls a hackney-coach and carries you away, don't say I didn't give you a warning, for I know something dreadful's going to happen"

"Nonsense," said Mrs. Malvers; "do as I wish."

Mrs. Packets, trembling in every limb, descended to do the bidding of Mrs. Malvers.

"You are to go upstairs," she said to the turnkey, "but don't hurt the poor thing."

"Hurt the poor thing! What does the woman mean?"

"I do *not* know; only don't do it, that's all."

"Touched in her head," muttered the man, as he walked upstairs; "poor old soul!"

In another moment he was in the presence of Mrs. Malvers.

"Good day, ma'am," said he, "I am the bearer of a letter for you."

"Indeed," said Mrs. Malvers; from Rann?"

"From Rann? Oh no, ma'am! Rann has escaped."

"Escaped?"

"Yes, ma'am, escaped, and in the cleverest manner ever heard of."

And the man here gave Mrs. Malvers an account of Jack's exploit.

"He is a clever one, he is," said the man; "in all my long experience I never remember such a go. But that ain't what brought me here; I'd almost forgotten the letter; here it is."

He handed a letter to Mrs. Malvers.

"You see who it's from," he said.

"Oh yes! It is from my unhappy cousin."

"Yes, ma'am. Ah! there's no hope for him, I fear."

Mrs. Malvers glanced over the note, which ran as follows :—

"Will you visit me at once? It is a favour I have no right to ask, but as my time draws nearer, I long more and more to hear you forgive the great wrong I have done you. I know that in your heart this is already done; but oh! to hear the words from your lips is what I long for. Do, do come; I have much to hear from you—much to say to you. I know you will come to me, and the thought makes me happier. At once—at once; I shall know no peace till I have seen you.

"Your unhappy cousin,
"FRANCIS AUSTIN."

"Well, ma'am," said the man, as Mrs. Malvers refolded the note, "what answer shall I take back?"

"There is no answer; but if you will wait, I will accompany you."

The lady hurriedly assumed her walking attire and prepared to quit the house with the official, to the no small consternation of Mrs. Packets and Charity, who made up their minds that she would never be permitted to return.

Laughing at their silly fears, Mrs. Malvers went forth and sped after her guide to the precincts of Newgate.

Arrived within the prison, she was, without delay, conducted to the cell of Austin, who was awaiting her arrival with agonised impatience.

"Thanks, thanks!" he cried, as he caught sight of her; "thanks; I felt that you would come."

"I have come, Austin; for ill as you used me, I could not let you die without the forgiveness you so much desire."

"That is good of you, very good - far more than I deserve, for I persecuted you sorely. I will not seek to palliate my offence; I will not tell you that my evil ways made me cling to life at any sacrifice; I will not seek to depict the fearful mental anguish endured at the thought of another world, for I have no right to weary you with such a tale. I will only say I have sinned and suffered, and now humbly beg your forgiveness."

"You have it, Austin. Heaven knows how truly I forgive and pity you."

"Oh! that is well. Such words give me hope for mercy hereafter."

"I am pleased to hear you say so."

"I could not say so until now, but since you have been here half my load of sin seems removed from me, and I am happier. Sit you down, I have much to say to you."

"You must be brief, then," said the turnkey; "for Jack's escape has made the authorities very particular, and a few minutes is all that can possibly be allowed you."

The man withdrew to the further end of the cell.

"Let me speak quickly," said the prisoner, "for I have a secret to reveal that must be told before I die. You know that I was an articled clerk to Mr. Lascelles, the solicitor, of Clifford's-Inn?"

"I have often heard that such was the fact."

"It was the fact. Would to heaven it had not been so, for to my associates in that place I owe my present position However, that is not to the point. One day, about eighteen months ago, an eccentric old gentleman of the City, a merchant, named Pardoe, came to the office and made a will, bequeathing all his property to the City of London Orphan Asylum. That will he took away with him. Eight months later he came again, saying that he wished to revoke his former will and make one in favour of his nephew, Mr. Grantley, a clerk in the house of the Messrs. Robcast and Haylow, of Milk-street. The second will was deposited with Mr. Lascelles. Two days after the document was signed and sealed Lascelles died suddenly, from an accident received in a fall from his horse. On the very same day Mr. Pardoe was found dead in his chair. Well-versed in trickery, acquainted with all the phases of fraud, and devoid of honour, I saw in these chances the way to make money. The first will, as I have said, was taken away, and I argued that it would, no doubt, be found by the nephew among the papers of the old man and destroyed, for to him would undoubtedly fall the lot to examine the papers. A young man who has been for years struggling upwards will be glad of the chance to acquire a fortune so rapidly, and will, I argued, have no delicacy about robbing an institution by the simple process of destroying the will of a half-mad old man. In the hope that this would be the case, I, the only living man who knew of the second will, stole it and concealed it."

"Oh! Austin, Austin, to what a depth of sin have you not fallen!"

"Alas, alas! it is so. But listen the moments are precious, and I have more to say. Trusting to be enabled to make money out of my villany, I kept the will secure, and awaited the opportunity of meeting this young Grantley, accuse him of destroying the first will, and demand a good round sum as the price of my silence."

"And you did so?"

"No. In the meantime your husband met me, and I was tempted into the crime for which I am now here."

"But the will! Is it to restore it to its owner, that you have called me hither?"

"Yes, yes; it must be given back to him."

"Where is it?"

"At the Red Rose in the Minories."

"Indeed!"

"Yes! whilst hiding there I secreted it in the attic in which I slept. It will be found at the back of the fire-place. Remove the bricks, and it will then be found in a cavity in the wall."

"But who is to fetch it? According to accounts, it is a fearful place, and one in which but few can venture."

"True. Can you not find some one whom you can trust to do the mission for you? I have been thinking of"—

"Sixteen-String Jack?"

"Yes."

"Oh, if I could but find him!"

"You may do so yet. Meanwhile keep your secret; it is one which must not be noised abroad, or the will is endangered."

"Yes yes: I understand that."

"And you will do all you can to restore this will?"

"I will, though I go alone to that fearful place to do so."

"Thanks. And when the will is in Grantley's hands, ask him to forgive me."

"I will."

"And now I have said my say. There is much more which I could tell you—much more which should be said; but they will not grant the time."

The turnkey now advanced.

"You see," continued Austin, "it is well I finished, for they are impatient for your departure."

"Now ma'am!" said the gaoler; and Mrs. Malvers rose from her seat to take her leave.

We will spare the reader the scene which followed—the agony and despair on the one hand, and the tears and true sorrow on the other. It was a pitiful sight, and made even the hardened turnkey weep bitter tears.

Mrs. Malvers at length tore herself away, and the poor, dejected criminal was once more alone.

CHAPTER XII.

THE DIAMOND NECKLACE—SUSPICIONS—THE JOURNEY AND THE PURSUIT.

"Now this is what I call remarkably jolly," said Tom King to Jack, as they strolled about the rooms, "remarkably jolly, to be sure. That fellow, Pattypan, is a king of confectioners, and his wares are delectable. I don't know when I enjoyed myself half so much."

"Nor I," said Jack. "Really the blaze of jewellery, the wine, and the breakfast, are the most tempting things in the world, particularly the diamonds, which have been making my mouth water all day long."

"And mine," said Turpin. "They certainly are very fine, and enough to make one forget that he is a guest, and turn thief on the spot."

"I know I shall forget myself before long," said Jack; "I've had my eye on the finest necklace I ever saw for more than an hour; I think it will be transferred to my pocket before we go."

"Let us separate, and if any business is to be done, let it be done without bungling."

"Trust me."

"I know I can do so. Remember, the day wanes, and in an hour we must be on the road with this pigeon."

They parted company.

The day was far advanced, and the three highwaymen had been making remarkably free with everything with which they came in contact.

Their behaviour had been, truth to tell, anything but gentlemanly; for as the wine mounted to their heads, the restraint they had hitherto put upon their tongues was withdrawn, and in spite of assumed airs of gentility the low-bred highwayman would out, and make itself apparent.

The guests, as a rule, began to keep away from the knights of the road, and they were thrown upon Mr. Grantley, who was agonised at their familiar insolence.

At length Rosalie became grievously alarmed at the conduct of those who claimed friendship with her husband. More than once she had seen her father's brow darken and his eyes flash, as the coarse jokes and rude laughter of these men rang through the chambers.

"Who are these terrible men?" she asked of Grantley. "From the moment I first saw them my soul revolted at them. Why do you not send them away?"

"I dare not, Rosalie."

"Wherefore?"

"I must not tell even you."

"They hold some unaccountable sway over you; I see you shudder at their approach. Tell me—tell me what it is, that something may be done."

"Rosalie, again I say, I dare not."

"Dare not?"

"No. They are here unbidden; but they were friends of my uncle, and so intimately connected with him and his affairs, that to offend them would be fatal to me. And now, Rosalie, I have something else to tell you. Do not tremble, do not be afraid—there is no danger threatening me; but I must quit this place to-night, and in the company of these men."

"What do I hear?"

"A terrible thing; but I assure you there is no danger in the matter. Business of the utmost import, which, to neglect, would be fatal to me, demands my presence with these men in London. I must go."

"Oh, do not go! I know these are bad men. I feel some horrible dread at their presence. Get them away, and abandon the idea of going with them."

"I cannot."

"Then I will follow you."

"You? Great Heaven! You do not know what you speak of."

"Why should I not go? If there is no danger for you, there can be none for me; therefore I will go."

"It is impossible; it cannot be. Will you not trust me, Rosalie?"

"I dare not do so. My dread of these men is too great."

"Do not fear them. They are friendly to me, or they would not be here now."

"I do not understand you. Pray speak more intelligibly."

"I can only tell you that a great danger—utter ruin—is hanging over me; but these men have it in their power to avert it. Shall I not, then, follow them?"

"If you trust them, I dare not doubt then. Go, and God protect you."

"Amen, dearest! In a few short hours I shall return to you."

"I trust so."

"I must now prepare for the journey. Excuse me as you best can."

"I will do so."

Grantley was about to move from his wife's side, when Mr. Millhurst approached him.

It was quite certain that he was in a raging passion.

"Mr. Grantley," he said, "I want an explanation from you."

"If I can give it you, I shall be most happy."

"Sir, you can and must. Briefly, then, who are the people you have introduced among your guests?"

"I cannot answer you."

"I thought so. Young man, since you will not tell me who they are, I will tell you. They are thieves and villains, and no fit society for my daughter and your guests."

"Sir, they are my guests, and I cannot allow even you to apply terms to them which cannot be substantiated."

"Cannot be substantiated! What do you mean, sir? I can substantiate all I say. Your precious guests have stolen a valuable diamond necklace. Now, if you say my description is unwarrantable, I tell you, sir, you are no better than they."

"Sir!"

"Sir! Oh, don't bluster, for I am not afraid of big words."

"You are my wife's father, and therefore at liberty to use language to me which I would not tolerate from any other individual; but beware how you go too far."

Rosalie here advanced, and laying her hand on her father's arm, said,—

"Cease—cease, father. Pray do not quarrel with my husband. These men have some business to transact with him which calls him away immediately; in a few minutes they will be gone, and no more notice will be taken of their inopportune advent."

"What's that? My son-in-law have business with thieves and robbers! Dear me! a nice state of things this!"

"Again, sir, I warn you not to apply such language to these men. Whoever they are, their being my guests must protect them while they remain here."

"Oh, bosh! your guests be hanged, and you too, sir. I tell you what it is, young fellow: if you don't explain, I shall think it my duty to remove my child from beneath your roof without delay."

"Dear father," cried Rosalie, "you speak in anger. You well know that I would not leave my husband."

"More fool you!"

"Rosalie," said Grantley, "you are a good, true girl. Bless you!"

At this point the three highwaymen joined the family group.

"Now then," cried Turpin, "come along—there's no time to lose."

"Time's up," said King.

"And," joined in Jack, "the sooner we are off the better."

"Mr. Grantley, are you going away in the company of these men?"

"I am. Oh, sir! do not speak to me now. To-morrow

I may be enabled to tell you all ; to-day nothing can pass my lips."

" Of course not," said King, " of course not. It's not reasonable to expect that you are going to bleat out your business to every calf that comes in your way. But no more of this. Hey for the road ! "

" Adieu, Rosalie—adieu ! " cried Grantley.

" Adieu ! " she said. " Heaven protect you."

" The gallows overtake you ! " roared old Millhurst, boiling over with passion.

Grantley was gone.

Rosalie withdrew with her father to a private apartment.

Sinking on a couch, she buried her face in her hands, and gave way to a violent flood of tears.

" Now," said Millhurst, " what means all this ? "

" I do not know," cried Rosalie ; " but I fear some ill will befall my husband."

" Hang him ! What abominable mystery is here about the fellow ? Nice work this, to quit his home and wife on his wedding-day ; and in company with a set of common thieves ! "

" Thieves ! Oh, are you assured of that ? "

" Assured of it ? of course I am. Lady Maskeville assured me that that fellow who was covered all over with ribbons stole her necklace ; and is a man like that fit company for your husband ? That's all I want to ask."

" Assuredly not. Nor would Grantley keep their company only that some awful danger threatens him. They have induced him to go forth with them to avert some danger. It may be some plan to rob and murder him. Oh, that I knew how to save him ! "

" Oh, nonsense ! He must be a bad man, and I think the best thing you can do is to quit his house without delay."

" Father, if he were, as you think him, a bad man—even a robber in league with robbers—he is at the same time my husband, and it is my duty to cling to him. But I *know* he is good and true as the sun, and I will not doubt him. He has assured me that threatening ruin alone tempted him forth in company with those men to-night, and I believe him."

" Well, well," said Millhurst, who was, after all, a very good sort of man when his temper did not get the better of his judgment ; " well, well—you may be right, after all. Women are further-seeing than men ; and if you trust to them, they generally bring you right in the end. But still I don't quite see what secret business any man can have with a gang of robbers."

" Perhaps not ; but be assured that Grantley has no business of which he would be ashamed. Hark ! I hear the tramp of horses."

They hastened to the window.

Some distance off, on the London road, they beheld Grantley, Turpin, King, and Rann, mounted, and speeding towards the metropolis.

" Heaven and earth ! " cried the wife, " I stand here prating when his life is in danger. How can I save him ? "

" What do you mean ? "

" Mean ! Is he not going perhaps to death, and are we not here motionless as statues ? "

" Well, the man has gone on his own account. He makes his choice, and must abide by it."

" He is my husband, and no harm must befall him."

" Certainly not, if you can tell me how to avoid it."

" Mount and follow him—that is the only way. Do not tarry a single moment."

" Psha ! What folly you women talk when excited ! How am I to follow him, not knowing a single inch of the road ? "

" Then some one must be found to show you."

" A nice thing this is to befall a man on his child's wedding-day ! Oh, dear ! I wish this union had never been dreamt of."

" No more words, but away at once."

Rosalie caught her father by the arm, and hurried him back into the breakfast-room.

The company had scattered over the house, and departed on their several ways, so that this apartment was almost deserted.

At the further end, however, were Peter Pattypan and his boy Sam. The former was engaged in packing away the plates and broken confectionery, and the latter diving into the depths of a bottle of Cliquot.

" Sam, you scoundrel, drop that bottle," said Peter.

" I vill ven it's quite finished," said Sam ; and then, smacking his lips, he added, " My eyes, but ain't it prime ! "

" Prime ! you villain, you are half-drunk now."

" Don't go for to tell stories on a chap," cried Sam, assuming the air of an injured innocent.

" All gone ! " cried Rosalie. " Oh, whom shall I get to aid you ? "

" I beg pardon," said Peter, turning round, " I'm sure I didn't see you ; but the butler told me I had best clear out this room, and get back to London with the broken victuals."

" To London ! " cried Rosalie ; " the very man ! *He* will accompany you."

" Here, my good sir," said Millhurst ; " so you know the road to town ? "

" Perfectly well. I may say I could find my way back blindfolded."

" Indeed ! Then you are my man. Can you ride ? "

" Provided I get a good hold of the pommel of the saddle—yes ! "

" That is well. I'll order the horses at once. You have no objection, I suppose, to hasten with me to London ? "

" Not the slightest."

" That is good of you," cried Rosalie ; " very good of you. Let your boy remain to do your work ; or, if you will, close up the room and return to-morrow."

" If it's all the same," said Peter, " I'd rather close it up and return to-morrow, for you don't know what a plague that boy is. Drop that bottle, you villain, and get out of it ! "

Sam here sprang nimbly over the table, and fled.

" As I'm to go back alone," said Sam to himself, " and quite empty-handed, I'll take good care to valk off some of the poultry, not to mention any rabbits I may come across."

" I make one provision before I start," said Peter ; " it's a duty I owe to those who depend upon me for a livelihood."

" What is it ? " asked Millhurst, hastily.

" It is that I get a horse that don't shy. If I had a restive animal I know what the result would be."

" Fear nothing."

" Well, I don't."

Peter was hastened round to the stables, and there two horses were hastily saddled for himself and Mr. Millhurst.

In a few minutes they were on the road.

" Now then," cried Millhurst, " make that brute move his legs."

" I don't know the way."

" Don't you ? Then I'll show you."

Millhurst turned, and grasping his whip tightly, lashed the horse ridden by Peter, until it moved much quicker than agreed with the nervous temperament of that amateur equestrian.

" Stop ! " cried Peter, " I know I shall be off."

" Oh, nonsense ! Hang on anyhow, and urge the horse forward. Life and death may depend upon your haste."

" If that's the case," said Peter, half-jolted to pieces, " I'll do my best ; but, really, this is an awful position."

Mr. Millhurst did not spare either steed, and as the little confectioner became used to the motion of the horse, and gained confidence in himself, he grew excited with the chase, and was as eager as his companion to keep pressing forward.

" I know a near cut," said Peter.

" Do you ? Where is it ? "

" Here."

They were at the gate of an extensive field

" Cross here, and we save a good half-mile."

" Good," said Millhurst, springing to the ground and opening the gate.

" But I say," said Peter, " it's trespassing, you know, and there's an awful ditch at the other end."

" No matter. On we go."

And on they did go !

JACK DEFENDS THE BOX SUPPOSED TO CONTAIN THE WILL.

As soon as the horses warmed to their work, they tore along like mad, and it was as much as Peter could do to keep his seat on the saddle.

"Look out," cried Millhurst, who espied the ditch. "Hey, over! Hold up your horse."

Peter did as he was ordered, in a kind of mechanical way ludicrous to behold.

"Hey, over!" he shouted, in imitation of his companion, and in a second he came down with a jolt on the other side.

"It nearly took my breath away," cried the poor little man, who, however, looked remarkably proud of his achievement. "Well," be continued, "who would have thought that I could have cleared a ditch in that style?"

"Who, indeed? Now which road do we take?"

"The one to the left."

"Come on then."

"All right. In a minute we shall be on the common."

"Then, as nearly as I can calculate, unless they have gone at the break-neck rate we have come, those we seek will soon be in sight. Now draw the rein; we must not be seen."

"Why not?"

"Because, if I am right, the men we seek are desperate fellows, who wouldn't mind using the pistol on us."

"The deuce!" cried Peter, turning pale, and pulling very hard at his rein; "if I had known that"——

"You would not have come? So I presume. But steady; here is the beginning of the common."

"Yes; here it is, sure enough."

They mounted a slight elevation, and then obtained a complete view of the road.

In the distance they beheld the group of horsemen that had preceded them.

"Hurrah!" shouted Millhurst; "there they are. Hang it, man, we are upon 'em now."

"Hillo!" cried Peter, recognising his acquaintances of the morning, "hillo! there's the three lords who were so civil to me to-day, but who, nevertheless, took care to ease me of my pocket-book and handkerchief."

"Indeed!" cried Millhurst; "then my worst suspicions are realised. Oh, Heaven! into what danger am I following that man."

"I say," said Peter; "if there's any danger, just say so, and I'll turn back."

"Do as you will. I am on the track now, and will not lose sight of my men. If you are not brave enough to help me through this night's work, get hence at once, for I would rather be alone than in the company of a coward."

"A coward! That am I not. I would not seek danger, but if you say that you require me for any good purpose, I'll stick to you to the death."

"Thanks, my good friend. Do you not recognise the fourth horseman?"

"Yes; it is Mr. Grantley. He in the society of those robbers! Then I'll not leave him till I see him well out of it."

CHAPTER XIII.

OLD MOSES GRIPER'S PLAN TO BETRAY JACK.

KNAVES'-ACRE, numbered among the things of the past now, but in its day the most notorious and most dreaded part of London, was a variety of small and dirty streets, deriving its name from the character of those who dwelt within its precincts.

Thieves and criminals of the blackest die harboured there, and it was a place in which but few could venture with any degree of safety.

The houses were mostly owned by a class of men called "fences," a term meaning receivers of stolen goods; but their business was not strictly confined to receiving purloined property.

They harboured thieves and highwaymen, and turned their houses into private taverns, where a nightly revelry held full sway, and scenes of violence were enacted with impunity.

Near Princess-street, in this wretched neighbourhood, resided an old Jew, named Moses Griper. He was reported as immensely rich, and through his mercenary habits and general contour, the report gained many believers; but none dared test the truth of the rumour, and whatever the Jew was possessed of remained as secure as if it had been placed in the Bank of England; for Moses was dreaded and feared by all the lawless wretches of the Acre, and no one attempted to molest him or his.

His power over the thieves was not a little singular, and formed a theme of wonder to many; but those who marked the traits of firmness and courage in the old fellow's character were not greatly surprised.

He would insinuate himself into the good graces of the thieves by every manner of artifice, and when, serpent-like, he had coiled himself completely about them, he would strike, and at once and for ever lay his victim prostrate at his feet.

In his power once, he would hold them there firmly as long it suited his purpose.

And yet this man was old, infirm, and afflicted with illness. Weak and physically powerless, he ruled over half a hundred strong men with a rod of iron.

This old Jew owned four of the wretched, old, tumble-down houses in Princess-street, Knave's-acre, and in one of these resided, when they were in London, Dick Turpin and Tom King; and a second was at times used there by no less a hero than Jack Rann. But Jack only came there in troublous times. When "not particularly wanted," he preferred a purer atmosphere, and was seldom seen in Knave's-acre.

It appeared, however, that Abraham Harding, the thief-taker, himself a Jew, well understood the habits of Jack; for no sooner did he hear of Jack's escape from Newgate, than, disguising himself, he bent his steps to the house of his friend, Moses Griper, with whom he was always in secret league.

"Ish Mishter Griper at home?" asked Harding, at the old Jew's door, a few hours after Jack had flown from London.

The thief-taker was admirably made up to represent a Jew pedlar, and the man who opened the door to him was so completely baffled by his acting of his assumed character that, although he had been several times in his power, he now failed to recognise him.

"I don't know," said the fellow, in reply to the inquiry; "better see for yourself. I suppose you are welcome here, or you wouldn't come."

"Not for the vorld, ma tear; I'm a great friend of Moses Griper, and he's alvays very glad to see me. Ve're quite like brothers, from doing so much business together."

"Well, you're the only two Jews in the world who have done business together and remain 'like brothers.' My opinion always was, that in a bargain between two Israelites the one always bested the other, and that the beaten one looked on the other ever after as the worst enemy he had in the world. Ha, ha! You're a rum set."

"Ah, ve are, ma tear—ve are! Not a bit like you good, kind, generous, brave Christians, eh?"

"Oh, none of your chaff. I don't want any of it. There,

you'll find old Griper in the kitchen, where, if my nose don't deceive me, he's frying pork-chops and onions."

The man closed and bolted the door, and the thief-taker walked away in the direction indicated by the man who had admitted him.

Sure enough, Moses Griper was frying pork-chops, and from all appearance he intended eating them at no distant period.

As soon as Harding entered the kitchen, he muttered a few words in Hebrew, revealing his real name and purpose, to which Moses replied that all was right.

He then looked up from his culinary employment, and said,—

"Ah, Mishter Bash, ish that you? Mr. Bash, vot d'ye vant to buy?"

"I vant a few good silver spoons, Moses, if you've got 'em to sell."

"Silver spoons! My! And Mishter Bash comes to poor old father Moses for spoons! My! Vy, I never see'd such things as silver spoons, much more have 'em for sale."

"Oh, deep, deep!" squealed the supposed Mr. Bash. "Deep! Yah, ha! Old Moses isn't to be done. Oh, deep, deep!"

"My! Hark at Mishter Bash! He to call poor, old, simple Moses deep! My!"

There were several men in the kitchen, and this conversation was held for the purpose of putting them off their guard, which was done most effectually.

"And to think that old Moses Griper, the good Hebrew, should eat pork!" said good Mr. Bash, assuming an air of intense disgust. "Faugh! the smell is poison—poison!"

"But the taste is lovely," said old Griper. "Ah, ah! vith the pepper, salt, and onions the chops is prime—prime. Von't you stop and taste 'em, Mishter Bash?"

Mr. Bash looked very like as if he would, whilst those by whom he was surrounded looked as if they would rather he didn't, for, as one of them murmured, "There ain't so many; and when them precious Jews do go into pork, they don't know when to leave off."

"Vell," said Mr. Bash, "I don't know but vot I vill, by-and-bye; but, you know, bishness first and pleasure afterwards. Vot about the spoons?"

"My! How he does go on about them spoons—as if an old man like me ever had any spoons vorth sellin'!"

"Now, don't be bashful," said the thief-taker; "but come along, and show me vot you've got to sell. I really vant the spoons, and I must have 'em; so don't delay."

"Vell, I don't mind saying that I have just a few old, vorn-out tea-spoons."

"Ah, I thought you had."

"But they're very thin, and not vorth taking avay."

"I don't doubt it."

"But, of course, if you must have 'em, you must"

"Of course, I must, and at once, too; so make haste."

"Here, Long Ned," said Moses, presenting his fork to a great, hulking fellow, who sat near the fire, "take that, and don't let the chops burn."

"All right," said Ned, seizing the fork, and jumping up to attend to the operation of frying; "I'll do 'em to a turn."

"You'd best," said the Jew, leading the thief-taker from the room.

He led the way up a flight of ricketty old stairs, and conducted his companion into a small closet, the door of which he immediately closed and locked.

"Now, Harding," he said, "vot is it brings you to the Acre?"

"Bishness of vast importance, my tear. Jack has escaped from the con'lemned hole."

"Vot! Sixteen String Jack!"

"Yes, the same."

"My! But that is a boy!"

"He is a boy; and it's a pity he's to go back to the prison; but there's no help for it; ve must have 'im."

"Vell, and vot's that to do with me?"

"Everything. You must deliver him up to me."

"Me deliver him up! Vy, vere am I to go and find him?"

"He'll come and find you fast enough to-night, and you know it. Vere vould he come, if not to old Griper's, ven things is so hot for him as they vill be to-day?"

"Ah, there's something in that."

"There s everything in that; and now vot do you say?"

"I say, *I'm afraid t* interfere with Jack."

"Moses Griper afraid!"

"Yes, old Moses ish afraid. That Jack's a perfect tiger; and if I should have anything to do vith this, he'll be the death of me for certain—to say nothing of vot those fellows, his pals, Turpin and King, vould do."

"Bah! Let them do. Think of the revard."

"You never said anything about the revard. Vot is it?"

"A hundred pounds."

"My! Vot, me attempt to deliver up Jack for a hundred pounds! I'd as leave think of cutting my own throat."

"It vill have to be done."

"But not by me. Scrag Jack for a hundred pounds! Vy, the lad's vorth a hundred a month to me."

"Vell now, do the thing neatly and well, and I'll try and make it two hundred. I vill, though I have to pay the money out of my own pocket."

Mr. Griper closed one eye, and looking straight at his friend with the other, seemed to say,—

"That's a proceeding I should certainly like to see you trying on."

"Vill that do?" continued Harding.

"No."

"Then vot vill do, you greedy old sinner?"

"Three hundred."

"Three hundred!"

"And not a penny less."

"Now, listen to reason,—"

"I don't vant to listen to anything; and I'd much rather have nothing to do vith the game. If you don't like my terms, get avay and leave me to my bishness, for I don't vant to be interrupted."

"Three hundred!"

"My! How the man stares! Vot's three hundred? You know the revard vill be all a thousand."

"A thousand!"

"Yes, a thousand. They give something for men who get out of the condemned hole of Newgate."

"Now, let us talk sense," said Harding, returning to the subject of his offer. "Let us say two hundred, and close the matter."

"I've said three, and if you haggle another minute, *I'll make it four.*"

This completely staggered the thief-taker, who, after a moment's hesitation, appeared to think it best to come to terms without delay.

"It's awful hard upon me," he said, "but I've no option, and so I must submit. Jack in our hands, and the three hundred is yours."

"Right. I'll do my best; but if there's any bungle, don't blame me, for I can't help it."

"Your vord is good enough for me, Moses; you can't afford to play me false, so I'll trust you. Now, vot d'ye propose?"

"I suppose he'll be here to-night."

"I've no doubt of it."

"It's rather unfortunate, for his friends Turpin and King are coming, and there's a chance of his being vith 'em."

"In that case it vould be desperate vork."

"So I say; better put it off for a day or two."

"No, no; he must be back to-night—it's a condition in the revard offered by the governor."

"Vell, then, to-night. Let me see vot can be done. There's no room for you to hide here; so you'll have to get into the next house. From vun of the vindows you can vatch the street, and if there's a chance of picking him up in that direction, just do it: and don't let us have a scene in here—it mayn't be pleasant."

"I understand. Then to-night, at dusk, I'll be here vith my men."

"Here's the key of the next house; by the attic vindows you can pass from vun to another; but mind, you promise me to take him in the street if you can."

"Yes, only you keep the coast clear."

"I'll do all I can."

"Very goot; and now I'll just take a few of them chops before I go. Yah, I like the smell of 'em, Moses."

"Now, you don't mean to say you'll touch 'em?" said Moses, quite alarmed at the prospect of being robbed of his savoury meal.

"I mean to say I'd touch anything, for I am as hungry as a greyhound."

"Then you'd best pay for some more chops, and I'll tell you vot I'll do, Harding—I'll find the nice onions and seasoning, and cook 'em for you for nothing. My! there now, isn't that true kindness?"

"Oh, you're dreadfully liberal," said Harding; "I vonder you don't ruin yourself."

"Ha, ha," laughed Moses, "ruin myself. That's very goot! Old Moses ruin himself! Ah, let fools and drunkards do that. I know better."

"I should think you did; and now let us get back to the kitchen."

"Yes; but I say, vot about the spoons?—you vant some nice silver spoons, you know."

"Vell, but you haven't any to sell, you know."

"Yes, but I have, real beauties; vil! you buy?"

"Not I."

"Real thumpers; all new."

"I don't vant any."

"Beautiful bargain."

"Oh, curse your bargain! Let us get back to the beautiful pork-chops."

CHAPTER XIV.

MRS. GRANTLEY HAS A DREAM, AND THE RESULT THEREOF.

Not long after dark the house of Mr. Grantley was completely deserted; the only stranger remaining being Sam, who, in consequence of the rain which began to fall, was invited by the servants to remain the night—an invitation which he was nothing loth to accept.

It was a dark, stormy night, and Mrs. Grantley, retiring to the room which her husband had set apart for her own use, ordered a fire to be lighted, and seating herself before it, attempted to read.

"Dear me," said Phyllis, her servant, "what a dreadful night!"

"Yes," replied Mrs. Grantley, "the storm is very violent; make a good fire; it grows very chill."

"It does indeed. Hark! Wasn't that thunder, my lady?"

"I think it was."

At this moment there was an awful peal of thunder, followed by lightning, and another, and another peal.

"There! there! there was an awful flash," said Phyllis, quite terrified. "I'll put the shutters to."

She rose and performed this office.

"There," she continued, "that's all right."

"Yes, it is better," said Rosalie, apparently quite dejected.

"Why, madam," said the servant, "how pale and ill you do look! and I'm sure I don't wonder at it—to think of Mr. Grantley running away like this! I'm sure, when I told them in the servants' hall, Mr. Briggs said,—"

"Hush, hush!" said Mrs. Grantley, "you know I cannot bear chattering."

"No, certainly, ma'am," continued the servant, "no more can I, ma'am; but when a man goes for to act in such a particular, rumbustious sort of a way, it's enough to make——"

"Leave me," said Mrs. Grantley, in a tone which left the girl no alternative but to obey.

"Yes, ma'am; but can I do nothing further for you?"

"Not at present. I shall remain here for some hours."

The servant withdrew, and Mrs. Grantley again attempted to

....d. She bent her eyes on her book, but she could read nothing.

She heard the wind shrieking through the trees, and listened to the angry peals of thunder which one after the other burst forth with deafening effect.

Her thoughts wandered to her husband, and as the blasts increased in vehemence, and the rain pattered against the windows, her heart sank within her, and she gave way to the feelings which crowded upon her.

Strong as had been her fortitude heretofore, she was now the poor, weak woman, whose resources were prayers and tears.

Long and fervently she prayed for the absent one, and at last sank into a light slumber.

Her sleep was disturbed by a dream.

She thought she beheld her husband seated at a table in a quaint old chamber; beside him were Turpin, King, and Rann. Distinctly as in reality, she beheld her husband produce a purse, which he appeared to offer to those by whom he was surrounded, on some conditions which he appeared to be expounding. Next she saw one of the men make a snatch at the purse, but failing in the attempt, grapple with her husband, and after a struggle, throw him to the earth. The whole of the three robbers were about to fall upon him with their knives, when a boy rushed from a closet in the room, and presented a pistol at the foremost of his adversaries. In the boy she recognised *herself*.

She awoke with a scream.

"It was a warning," she cried; "it was a warning for me to follow my husband! It is I alone who can save him. It is to me he must owe his succour. But how to follow him!—how to find him in London, and on such a night! Oh, Heaven! direct me!"

At this moment the door of the apartment opened, and the boy Sam entered.

"I beg your pardon, ma'am," said Sam; "but I'm 'fraid I've lost my vay."

"If he could only guide me," thought Mrs. Grantley; and then she continued aloud, "do you know the way to London?"

"I think as how I could find my vay," replied Sam."

"But at night?"

"Yes, as vell at night as any other time."

"Would you mind following me at once?"

"I don't mind it."

"Thanks; you shall be well rewarded. It is necessary that I should explain to you. Mr. Grantley is gone to London, I fear, on some dangerous mission. He left here with people whose honesty I doubt."

"And vell you might."

"What! Do you know them?"

"Don't split on a chap, and I'll tell yer."

"I promise secresy."

"Vell, then, them chaps vos Dick Turpin, Sixteen-String Jack, and Tom King, the highwaymen."

"Oh, horror!"

"I didn't dare say anythink, for if old Pattypan thought I knew such fellers, he'd be down upon me. Lor'! I knew 'em directly I saw 'em. I've met 'em often at Old Griper's place, in Knaves'-acre."

"Do you think you know where they are now gone?"

"I should say to that very identical place—Old Griper's, in Knaves'-acre."

"Stay here; I will return anon. Take no notice of the change in my costume. I have my reason in going forth disguised."

"I don't take any notice, ma'am."

Mrs. Grantley here left the room, taking with her a chamber candlestick.

"I must gain the servants' apartments," she said to herself, "and trust to chance to furnish me with a disguise. But anything will do, and there is not a moment to lose."

In a few minutes she returned, completely equipped in a suit of clothes belonging to one of the stable-boys.

Her long hair was hidden under her cap, and so complete was her disguise, that Sam did not know her until she spoke.

"Now," she said to Sam, "I am ready."

"Ready! Hillo! is that you; well, bless'd if I know'd you. My eyes, but that is a nobby get-up!"

"Not a word. Follow me."

"All right."

"Stay. I hear a footstep. It is my maid. Quick; blow out the candles, and remain quiet. They must not see me thus."

Sam did as he was ordered.

The next moment Mrs. Grantley's maid knocked at the door. Receiving no answer, she, after a slight pause, opened it and looked in.

"Poor thing!" she murmured, "tired of waiting and gone to bed, not wishing to disturb anyone."

The door was closed, and the servant was heard descending the stairs to the kitchen.

"Now," said Mrs. Grantley, catching Sam by the arm, "now to gain the door."

They stole through the passages, and in a few moments were in the road.

They had not proceeded many hundred yards before they were wet to the skin.

"It'll kill yer," said Sam; "I don't care about it, yer know; but it's awful for you. We had best get back."

"No, no," cried the woman, "we must proceed."

And they hurried on, and the storm continued to rage with unabated fury.

CHAPTER XV.

JACK AND THE OFFICERS—GRANTLEY IN GRIPER'S DEN—THE REALISATION OF THE DREAM.

It was scarcely dark when Harding and his myrmidons, three in number, took up their quarters in the house set apart for their use by Griper.

Well disguised, they passed in without notice, and straightway placed themselves at the windows commanding a view of the street, to await the coming of the anticipated Jack.

As the sun went down the storm arose, and as it increased in fury, so the hopes of the thief-taker died away.

"Wherever he may be, there he'll stay, on such a night. Hang it; never vos there such luck! Yah, yah! it is too bad to lose such a beautiful chance of making money."

"Oh, it's all right yet, governor," said one of the assistants; "it's quite right; this storm won't last for ever; and when it goes down, Jack will be here."

"But if the storm should last! Ah! the beautiful revard—a whole thousand pounds vill go, and I'm a lost man."

"Why, look out. Even now the clouds are breaking away, and the rain ceases."

"Yesh, yesh; that's very goot, but just heark to that wind. Oh dear, oh dear! I never heard such vind in all my days. I declare it's quite a judgment upon me for eating them nasty, beastly——"

"Hey? What?"

"Nothing at all. Vatch the vind and the rain, can't you, and never mind me."

"I thought you said you had been eating something beastly?"

"S'pose I do; is that anything to do vith you? Vatch the rain, vatch the rain."

"Well," said the man, looking out of the window, "this is the clearing shower; it'll break away now."

"Isn't it time," said the Jew, "isn't it time? Oh, dear, oh dear! hasn't it rained for the last hour as if it vas bent on ruining me. Just think that it should rain and keep away the beautiful boy ven he vas coming so nicely into my toils. Oh, it's enough to make a man mad, it is—it is!"

"Bah!" said the man, shrugging up his shoulders contemptuously, "you're always grieving without any cause. No wonder you're so thin and ugly."

"Don't you go for to insult me," said the Jew. "I tell you vot, my friend Boit; I'll get rid of you if ye- don't treat me with more r.

THE ESCAPE FROM THE STABLE.

"I would if I were you," said Bolt, who was a tall and powerful fellow, with a most determined cast of countenance; "do, and what will become of you? I should like to see you, for instance, attacking Sixteen-String Jack without me by your side to help you. Ha, ha! a pretty figure you'd cut; and for twopence I'd go off and leave you to do it without me. I don't much like the job."

"Oh, dear!" moaned the Jew, "vot a boy it is! Vy, Bolt, you vouldn't go off and leave the old man to his own resources, you know you vouldn't now. Oh dear, it vould be too bad—too bad—particularly as you know I didn't mean anything wrong. Only, old men vill be touchy, and young vuns should make every allowance."

"Oh bother your allowance! Don't go speaking to me like that again, or you'll see what I'll do."

The Jew was silenced, and for some time regarded the storm without uttering a word.

At length it became apparent that Bolt was right, for the black clouds broke away, and the moon was at times visible for a few seconds.

"There, I told you how it would be," said Bolt, with the air of a man who made a prophecy which had been realised.

"Yes," said Harding, "it's all right, there's a beautiful moon getting up, and it's not yet ten o'clock; there's every chance of their coming."

"Hillo!" cried Bolt, "look out there. Who's that coming up Princess-street?"

"Vy, it's four men, I declare," said the Jew. "Now vut of 'em should be Jack."

They waited in breathless anxiety for a few moments, and at last the quartette of individuals pointed out by Bolt came near the house.

As they advanced the moon shone out upon them, and revealed the three highwaymen and Mr. Grantley.

"That's our man," said Bolt, pointing to Jack. "What's to be done?"

"Keep quiet," said the Jew; "nothing can be done vhile he's in company vith such fearless devils as those. Vait—vait!"

They saw the street door of the next house open slightly, and the whole of the four men enter.

"Get you up into the attic," said the Jew to Bolt, "and then drop gently into the next house and vatch. I'll go down into the street and vait for any signal old Griper may hang out."

"Right," said Bolt, hastening from the room, "right. I'm fly to all the moves."

He sprang out of the room, and up the stairs to the attic, whilst Harding stole down into the street. He left the room open, so as to beat a speedy retreat on an emergency, and then drew close to the next house for the purpose of reconnoitring. He had not been there many moments before old Griper partly opened his door and looked out.

"Hist!" cried the fence.

"Hilloa!" whispered Harding. "Is all right?"

"Yes, as right as the sun. Vot's the game?"

"Vere's the men?"

"Close by, and all ready."

"Keep quiet a leetle time, and it vill be all right."

"I'm alive!"

"I've got Long Ned in the room. He hates Jack, and I do anything to cross him. Look here."

"Right—I'm listening."

"Bring the boys down into the passage, and keep the door quite ready. I've heard 'em say Jack is to go back to the stables and see the horses right while they look after the gentleman. Ven he comes out he vill give the signal—a long whistle; you'll then jump out and do your vork. D'ye understand?"

"All right."

The old Jew closed the door and then went back to his kitchen; and the thief-taker withdrew to bring his assistants into the passage, and get them ready for action.

He had no sooner withdrawn than Mr. Millhurst and Pattypan, drenched to the skin, came in sight.

They came swiftly, but quietly, to the house opposite that which the highwaymen had entered with Grantley.

"That's the house," said Pattypan, pointing to Griper's house. "Now, what is the next thing to do?"

"Keep you a strict watch here, and I'll run on and try and find the watch."

"All right."

Millhurst sped onward, leaving Pattypan on guard.

He was scarcely out of sight when the man spoken of as Long Ned came out of the house, and, mistaking Pattypan for the thief-taker, took him by the arm and led him into the shadow of the houses opposite.

"All right," he said, mysteriously.

"Is it?" said poor, simple Pattypan. "Well, I'm very glad to hear it."

"Jack's coming."

"Is he?"

"Yes. I heard them move, and so I came out. Where's your hands?"

"In my pocket," said Peter.

"Psha! I mean where's your pals—your mates?"

"I'm sure I don't know," said Peter, in a puzzled tone.

"What! ain't you Harding?"

"Not that I'm aware of. I'm Peter Pattypan."

"Oh, the deuce! I thought you were Harding, of Newgate."

"I shouldn't like to be."

"I suppose not. But I say, you're one of the right sort?"

"Well, I hope so."

"Are you in the fancy line?"

Peter thought his questioner referred to the confectionery line, and so without hesitation answered—"Yes."

"Ah! I thought so. You don't look like a rough-and-ready cracksman; but I haven't much time to talk to you, and if you don't want to get into a breeze, you'll be off."

"All right," said Peter, moving off, but at the first opportunity diving into a doorway near at hand.

In another moment the door of Griper's house opened, and Jack Rann came out.

No sooner did Long Ned set eyes on him than he uttered a loud, piercing whistle, and out of their hiding-place darted the thief-taker and his men.

Quick as they were, Jack was quicker, and jumping into the middle of the road, threw himself into an attitude of defence.

Upon him rushed the whole crew, and Bolt, the foremost of them, was sent to earth by a well-directed blow on the head.

The thief-taker immediately afterwards shared a similar fate, and Jack drew his pistol and fired at a third, receiving a shot in return.

In a few minutes he was master of the position, and had sufficiently collected himself to look around.

Brief as had been the struggle, Pattypan had had sufficient time to run across the road and enter the door left open by the thief-taker.

Finding he was not opposed, he closed the door and barred it.

Meanwhile Turpin and King, attracted to the window by the sounds coming from the street, saw what was passing, and instantly descending the stairs, ran to their friend's assistance.

"Hillo, Jack!" cried Turpin; "what is all this? You bleed; are you hurt?"

"Slightly," said Jack, who had received a wound in the shoulder, "slightly; but I think I have given them as good as they brought me. There's three of 'em down."

"And serve 'em right, too," cried King, greeting each of the prostrate men with a hearty kicking, "the dirty blackguards!"

"Ware Hawk," cried Turpin, catching sight of Long Ned, "in, or we may be nabbed."

They sprang to the door of the house they had just quitted, and burst in, taking care to close and barricade it after them.

"Hillo!" cried out old Moses, coming from his kitchen with a candle in his hand, and looking about for Jack; "Hillo, ma tears! vot has happened?"

"Happened!" cried Turpin; "Jack has been set upon by the hawks and half killed. That's all!"

"My!" cried the Jew, in well-feigned astonishment, "my! to think that they should have ventured into the Acre. My! my! the daring of the birds!"

"No matter," said Jack; "since they are in the Acre, all you have to do is to keep 'em out of this place. Mind, no tricks. One of the fellows was that abominable Jew, Harding. I saw him, and I half suspect who brought him here. If I was but convinced that I am right, I would never leave a hold on your throat till you fell a corpse at my feet. You know it. I *always keep my word!*"

"My!" screamed the old Jew; "the boy is clean mad. Vot, suspect old Moses of playing false, and bringing hawks into his nest of pretty, bright birds! It's too bad, too bad of you, Jack."

And the old hypocrite pretended to weep.

"Well, never mind," said Jack, somewhat softened at what he thought the old fellow's distress; "never mind. I didn't mean anything. Only it's hard to be set upon like this, and not know whence the attack comes. It's enough to make a man suspect his own brother."

"So it is, my child," said Moses; "so it is. But never mind; you're safe now. Oh! vot a blessed thing to think that you're safe. I'm quite as thankful as if it vos myself or my own flesh and blood. But your arm is hurt; let old Moses look to it."

"Not now," said Jack; "not now. It's only a flesh-wound, and the man above will be impatient for our return. Let us get back."

The old Jew lifted the candle above his head, and lighted the men up the stairs.

As soon as they had disappeared his whole aspect changed, and he went stamping back to his kitchen, moaning out—

"My! my! Three hundred pounds lost! The ass! the dolt! so nice as the fellow vos caught, too. A baby might have taken him!"

The highwaymen found Grantley pacing the little chamber in which he was confined, with quick and nervous steps.

"Come!" he cried; "why am I kept here? If this is not some plot, some vile chicanery, give me that for which I came, and let me go."

"Softly," cried King, "softly. Our friend Jack has been set upon by the thief-takers, and almost nabbed. Had it not been for that, we should have squared accounts, and you could have gone ere this."

"Well, now to business," said Turpin; "hand over the money."

* * * * * * *

By this time there were fresh arrivals in Knave's-acre, and we must for awhile leave Grantley and the others to look after the new comers.

Foot-sore, and almost dropping to the earth from exhaustion, Mrs. Grantley, accompanied by Sam, arrived at the door of old Griper's house.

"Here ve are," said Sam, who appeared to be quite in his element; "that's the house vere Turpin and King live, and the other belongs to the same landlord, but it's not so often used; been kept for chance custom. Now, then, vot's to do?"

"I do not know. Oh! if I could but be convinced that my husband was there!"

"Hillo!" cried Sam, glancing at the upper windows. "Look there! Vat d'ye see?

"Shadows on the blind, resembling those of the terrible men who were at our house to-day."

"Yes; there's no mistake about it. They're there."

"But how to get in?"

"That's the question. If there's any game up, old Moses von't admit us. But ve must have a shy at it. I'll knock; so you had best keep up your pluck and look as leary as you can."

"I'll do my best. Heaven help me!"

"Now for it," said Sam, approaching and knocking at the door thrice.

After a pause, the voice of the old Jew was heard within.

"Who's there?"

"It's me; the pastrycook's kinchen."

"Vell, my pretty little tear, you must go avay to-night; the house is full, and ve can't admit another vun."

"Nonsense, daddy; I must come in. I'm vet through, and it's too late to go home; so open the door."

"It's no use, my little boy. Go home, go home."

"It's no use, my old man. I von't go home, go home; so vot d'ye think of that?"

"You can't come in—that's flat."

"I say, Moses," said Sam, lowering his voice, "there's something wrong going on in there, or you'd let me in. Now if you don't submit like a lamb, I'll just alarm the neighbourhood, and get my pal to run for the vatch. They'll come fast enough if ve tell 'em your game's *murder*."

"Now, vot a boy it is," said old Moses, evidently alarmed at this threat; "vy don't he go home and go to bed quietly? Vot *does* he vant, knocking up respectable people at this hour of the night, and telling such awful stories about a poor old man?"

"He only vants a bed," said Sam; "and now you know if it's vorth your vhile to give him vun."

"Vell, vell; I'll tell you vot I'll do. The next house is empty. You can have the key of that if you like. If you only vant a bed you'll find a dozen there."

"Very good," said Sam; "that'll do."

"No, no," whispered Rosalie; "what would you do?"

"Hush!" said Sam; "I know vat I'm doing."

The Jew now opened the door, and, thrusting out his hand, gave Sam the key.

"There you are, you bad boy. Now go to bed and be quiet, and don't come knocking up the old man again."

"All right," said Sam; "you'll do now. That's all I vant."

The door closed, and Sam, catching Mrs. Grantley by the arm, drew her towards the next house.

"Why do we come here," she cried, "and he there?"

"Leave it to me." said Sam; "you can get from vun attic to t'other. I know the vay."

He applied the key to the door, and it opened.

"Step in," he continued; "I know the ropes, and vill put yer down to 'em."

Trembling with fear, the devoted woman followed her conductor.

Now, Mr. Pattypan heard the door open and close, and immediately rushed up to the top of the house and secreted himself under a bed.

"Dear me!" he said; "some of those villains are returning. What am I to do?"

Shaking like an aspen leaf, he lay under the bed, which formed his harbour of refuge.

The next moment the door of the attic opened, and Sam and Mrs Grantley groped their way in.

"Mind," said Sam; "it's very dark and dangerous. Step cautiously, or you may fall."

"It is a fearful place," said the lady.

"Ah, this is nothing," said Sam; "nothing. If this frightens ye, I don't know vot the other crib vill do. Now for the vinder."

Mounting on a chair, the boy unfastened the bolts of the little window, and threw it open.

"Mount the chair," he said, as he sprang up and crawled through the opening on to the leads.

Mrs. Grantley mechanically did as she was ordered.

"Now," said Sam, "I'll pull yer through."

Seizing the hand of the lady, he assisted her to clamber through the open window.

"That's all right," he said, as he stood with her on the narrow parapet; "and now for the other window."

He advanced a step.

"My eyes!" he said, stopping suddenly; "if the vinder's bolted on the other side, how are we to get in?"

"Oh, Heaven!" cried the lady; "do not hesitate. Let us effect an entrance at all risks."

"It vill be at all risks," said the boy, "for I shall have to smash a pane of glass to get at the bolts, and that's risk enough, I can tell yer."

"No matter."

"Very well, then; on we go."

They advanced, and to their delight found the window open. Bolt, in his passage from one house to the other, had forgotten to shut it.

"It's the first time as ever old Griper forgot to shut his vinders," said Sam.

Gently the boy lowered himself into the attic, and assisted his fair companion to follow him.

The astonishment of Pattypan at hearing and recognising voices so familiar to him, was something wonderful to behold.

The little man burst out into a cold perspiration, and almost fainted with fright.

Being entirely unacquainted with the propensities of his boy, he never dreamt of finding him in such a place and with such a companion.

"I must be dreaming," he thought. "Dear me, if I should have eaten too much of my own pastry, and drank too much of my own wine, and am now suffering from a horrible nightmare! Yes, that must be it. It's an awful fancy. I'll shake it off."

Forgetting that he was under a bed, he attempted to jump up suddenly, and, as a matter of course, received a blow which prostrated him.

Lying senseless for a few minutes, he at length recovered himself a little and began to collect his scattered senses.

Crawling from under the bed, he staggered about the room, holding his head tightly between his hands.

The moon now burst forth brilliantly, and he was at once able to see that all that had passed before him was no dream, no idle phantasy, but a strong and terrible reality.

"It was Sam," he said, dejectedly, "it was Sam, and he appeared to know the place well. There is the open window that he passed through. But his companion? ah, there is the mystery! How could Mrs. Grantley be in such a place, at such a time, and with him?"

He reflected.

But it was all in vain.

There was a dark and fearful mystery surrounding him which he could find no means to fathom.

He was involved in a tangled skein of thought, and he could not find the means to unravel the knot.

He would in all probability have remained pacing the attic for hours, had not the sound of voices arrested him.

"There are other people in the house," he said; "what am I to do? To be seen here is death."

The open window was before him.

"Yes," he said, "they passed through there, and I will follow them, though Heaven knows where it may lead me."

He clambered through the window and carefully closed it after him.

Following the footprints of Sam and Mrs. Grantley along the sliding parapet, he crawled into the attic-window of the next house.

He found it empty!

* * * * * * *

"You demand my money," said Grantley, to whom we now return; "the sum is a tremendous one, and before I give it you I must have the vill."

"No tricks," said Turpin. "Are you sure you have the money with you?"

"I have it, but I will part with my life rather than the money until I have the will."

"Oh nonsense!" said King; "we mean honourable dealing. Give the money with one hand, and with the other receive the will."

"But the will, the will," cried Grantley, with growing impatience. "I do not see it here. Produce it, and the money is at once yours."

He put his hand into his pocket and drew out a heavy purse.

"See," he continued, "here is the money. Now the will."

"It is in yonder cupboard," said King, pointing to a cupboard in a recess in the wall. "Take it out, Dick."

Dick went to the place indicated, and searched.

"Hillo!" he said, "I don't see it. *It is not here!*"

"Villains!" cried Grantley; "I now see through you. I am entrapped into this place to be robbed, perhaps murdered; but beware, for I will sell my life dearly."

"Now put down your hands," said Turpin; "such tactics will not serve your turn."

"I am lured here to be slain," cried Grantley. "Fool, fool that I was to trust myself with you. I see it all now, but I will fight for my life against any odds."

"Oh, rubbish," said King; "we brought you here on the square, and mean to act honourably by you; so no more talk of fighting."

"But the will?"

"I know not where it is," said King. "Believe me when I assure you I am in earnest."

"You appear to be speaking the truth, and yet"——

"Trust me, and I will prove my truth. This is very strange, but it will doubtless be explained."

"It beats my comprehension," said Turpin.

Jack now eyed his companion with distrust.

He did not understand and would not countenance double dealing, and the conduct of his companion began to look so much like it that he began to wish himself well out of the affair.

"I'm in with them," he said to himself, "and I can't well get out of it. But my word was pledged that no harm should befall this man, and I will see that he is properly protected here."

While yet Turpin and King were ruminating on the mysterious disappearance of the will, the door of the chamber was suddenly burst open and a man rushed in.

"Now then, Scarlet," cried Turpin, "what is the matter?"

"Matter enough! There's treachery here. There's a man below whom I found in one of the attics. At first I took him to be a comrade, but now find him to be a friend of that person"—pointing to Grantley—"who has followed him here to assist him."

"Ah!" cried the highwaymen in a breath, and all eyeing Grantley with looks of fury; "that is treachery indeed!"

"I knew not of it," said Grantley, earnestly.

"That I doubt," said King; "but who is he?" he continued, turning to Scarlet.

"His name is Peter Pattypan."

"The man whose pocket I picked this morning," said Jack.

"Well," said King, "keep him quiet."

"Oh, never fear! I've dosed him."

"Villain!" cried Grantley, "have you slain him?"

"Oh, look to yourself," said Turpin; "you'll find you've quite enough to do."

"Get back to the kitchen," said King, "and see that we are not disturbed."

"All right. I'm off."

Scarlet was leaving the room when King suddenly called him back.

"Who has been in this chamber to-day?" he asked.

"No one," replied Scarlet; "that is, no one but myself and old Moses. But why do you ask?"

"Because we've missed something from that cupboard."

"Hillo! Is that it? What is it?"

"A paper."

"Indeed! Then I think I can put you on the scent. I saw Moses open this cupboard and take out a paper, which he carried with him to the attic over this room."

"Ah! and did he leave it there?"

"Yes. No doubt you'll find it in the old trap in the floor."

"Do you hear that?" asked King of Grantley. "Now I should think you were ashamed of yourself for bringing your confectioner fellow to take care of you."

"I repeat I knew not of his coming."

"Ah! that's very well, but we don't believe it," said King. "Men of his sort don't interest themselves much for nothing, and this Peter is not the man who would have followed you here without pressing. However, there's no time to waste in idle words. For your double dealing you will have to pay doubly dear. Before the will falls into your hands you must hand us ten thousand pounds!"

"Ten thousand pounds! Ah, now I am well convinced there is no will, and that I am duped. Let me pass."

"You shall not quit the chamber."

"I say I will."

"And we say you shall not. But to convince you that we meant dealing honestly by you, we will give you a sight of the will. Dick—Jack, take this fellow to the kitchen, whilst I mount to the attic and endeavour to trace this missing document. If it be not there, woe to that old villain; for I'll have his heart's blood this night."

"All right," said Turpin. "Now then, Grantley—to the kitchen. You'll find it a jolly place if you can only stand old Griper's pork chops."

With this Jack opened the door, and the unhappy Grantley followed Turpin from the room, Jack following close at his heels.

Tom King now took the lamp, and mounted the stairs to the attic.

———

CHAPTER XVI.

PETER PATTYPAN DOES NOT CLEARLY SEE HIS WAY OUT OF DANGER.

IT is now necessary that we return to Peter, and see how he fell into the clutches of the ruffian Scarlet; but first we must briefly allude to those who preceded him into the den of robbers.

Sam, who appeared to know every turn of the Jew's house, led his companion into the front attic, and hiding her behind the curtain which hung before the window, he told her to remain quiet until his return.

"I shan't be long," he said; "but it's quite necessary that I should see vot's going on down below, for it's no good of our staying here if ve're not vanted."

"You are right," said Mrs. Grantley.

"Keep as quiet as a mouse," said Sam, "and I'll soon return."

With this he stole silently down the stairs, leaving his companion motionless behind the curtains.

Peter seated himself on one of the two beds in the back attic and endeavoured to collect his scattered senses, but the effort was vain. His thoughts were completely confounded, and he remained like one in a dream.

So completely oblivious was he to all outward feeling, that it was not until a hand was laid upon his shoulder that he began to remember his position.

On looking up and beholding a six-foot ruffian standing over him, he was, however, painfully reminded of his deplorable situation.

Trembling hand and foot, he awaited the result of the tall fellow's scrutiny.

"Now then, little one," said the man, "what are you doing on my bed?"

"Is this your bed?"

"Of course it is."

"Well, I wasn't aware of it, or I'm sure I would'nt have taken the liberty of sitting on it."

JACK IS CAUGHT IN A TRAP.

"I should think not. You'd be a bold one if you would willingly offend Will Scarlet."

"I wouldn't do such a thing for the world Mr. Scarlet."

"Very well, but what brought you here?"

"Well, I don't know, but I s'pose I got into the wrong room."

"I should think you had, and you'd best get out again."

"With great pleasure," said Peter.

"But stay," said Scarlet, "a mistake is a mistake, after all, and a man can't help making one occasionally; so there's no offence, mate."

"I'm glad of that," said Peter.

"Oh, not the slightest, and to convince you of it, we'll have a glass of brandy together. Have you got any money?"

"Oh yes—I've got—that is, I've got a few browns. I had a job to-day, and when I get a good job I generally dip pretty deep into people's pockets."

"Just as I expected," thought Scarlet; "a pickpocket! Well," he continued aloud, "let us go down to the kitchen, and old Moses will give us a drop of the right sort of stuff to drive away care."

"Will he, though?" said Peter, "that's very good of him; I'm sure I want something of that kind very badly."

"By the way," said Scarlet, "you'll find some people in your own line of business below."

"In my line of business?"

"Yes. Didn't you know? This is a house of call for them."

"Why, you don't mean that?"

"Indeed, I do."

"Well," thought Peter, "to think of my living all my life in London, and never to know that there was a house of call for pastrycooks in this place before to-night. How very odd!" he said aloud.

"What, odd that I should know what you are? Bless you, the moment I saw you I knew your business. Yes, the instant I set eyes upon you I said that man's a P. and C."

"A P. and C.!" said Peter.

"Yes, of course."

Scarlet meant a pickpocket and cracksman, but Peter readily enough thought that he must mean a pastrycook and confectioner. And so both parties still remained in ignorance of the real character of the other.

"And so," said Peter, as they descended the stairs, "you really knew who I was?"

"Oh, to be sure."

"Nice, genteel business, isn't it?"

"Oh yes; little warm work now and then, though."

"He means the baking," thought Peter. "Why, yes," he said, "that's true my friend; but then you see, we old hands—we leave the warm work to the young 'uns."

"Capital," cried Scarlet, in ecstacies with his new friend, "a man after my own heart. Ha! ha! ha!! I see you're up to everything."

They had now reached the kitchen.

"Well," said Scarlet to Peter, "what are you going to order? As it's your first appearance here you'll have to stand treat."

"Very well," said Peter; "order what you like."

"Here, Moses," cried Scarlet to the old Jew, who was seated by the fire with his back towards them, "here, Moses, come and take the new cove's order."

The Jew now rose and advanced towards his customers.

He looked very hard at Peter and did not speak.

"Now then, old 'un," said Scarlet, "a pint of brandy; and be quick."

"All right, ma tear," said the Jew, still keeping his eye upon Peter; "all right, Moses 'll get the brandy."

As he left the room he winked to Scarlet, and beckoned him to follow.

"Who's your friend?" he asked of Will, when they had quitted the kitchen.

"I don't know. Don't you know him?"

"Never see him in all my life before."

"Why, I found him up-stairs in the attic, sitting on my bed. He told me he had missed his room."

"*Ware-hawk!*"

"Well, but how could a stranger get up there?"

"I don't know, but the birds have been flying about to-night after Jack. P'r'aps vun of 'em got into the other house, and entered through the attic-vindow."

"Like enough; but I'm on my guard."

"Don't let him stop in the kitchen; bring him into the front room—ve can manage him better there."

"What's to be done?"

"Done; vy drug him, my tear, drug him. He must pay for coming into old Moses's house. Ha! ha!"

"All right," said Scarlet, "but be careful."

"I vill. Look you here, I'll get Swagger to manage it. He's so clever at that kind of thing."

"So he is; but be careful."

"I know my way," said the Jew, hobbling off as Scarlet returned to the kitchen.

"Now," said the burglar, returning to the kitchen, and addressing Peter, "now, my man, how are you getting on by this time?"

"Well, not very brilliantly," said Peter, who, on being left alone, soon gave way to thought, and became as puzzled as ever.

"Oh, I suppose you don't like this room; would rather be alone, eh?"

"Well, it's not a very enticing place."

"And abominably hot. Well, let us come into the front parlour and enjoy ourselves quietly together."

To this Peter saw no objection, and forthwith rose and followed his companion.

They now seated themselves in the front room, and awaited the advent of Moses with the brandy.

"I can't help thinking about this being a house of call for pastrycooks," said Peter, resuming the conversation he had held with the burglar whilst descending the stairs.

"For pastrycooks!" said Will in astonishment.

"Yes; didn't you say it was the house of call for men in my line?"

"Yes."

"Well, my line is the pastrycook line."

"Oh, ah, yes," said Will, quite puzzled. "Oh, I dare say. Just so,"

"And to think that Mr. Millhurst should have put the place down as a den of thieves, and run off to get the watch."

"The deuce he did!"

"Yes. You see we saw Mr. Grantley enter the house with some people of a doubtful character, and I found my way in through the attic window, whilst the old gentleman ran off to find the watch."

"Oh! a good arrangement."

"Yes, capital. But what is Mr. Grantley doing here? Can you tell me?"

"I'm sure I don't know."

"But who are the fellows he is with?"

"Oh, highly respectable gentlemen."

"Well, I thought so this morning; but, hang it, they picked my pockets."

"Quite a joke."

"Now I suppose it was."

"Oh, yes; only their fun."

"Ha! ha! yes their fun. What jolly dogs these noblemen are."

"Very."

"And to think that Mrs. Grantley and Mr. Millhurst should think them thieves, and trot us after them to protect her husband."

"Oh, ridiculous."

"Quite so."

"The murder's out," thought Scarlett; "I know who my friend is now."

At this point the man alluded to by the Jew as Swagger, entered the room with a bottle of brandy.

"Here you are, my boys," said he, the "real sort and no mistake."

Scarlett rose, and met his friend just behind Peter's chair.

"I'm off for a minute," he said, "but will not be longer."

"All right," said Swagger, "*I'll* fill *your* glass."

He said this with a significance which Scarlet perfectly understood, and he expressed his comprehension of his friend's meaning by a wink as he passed out at the door.

His errand was, as the reader is already aware, to the up-stairs room, for the purpose of putting the highwaymen on their guard.

Swagger filled a glass of brandy and placed the bottle on the table.

"Will you drink with me?" asked Peter, filling the empty glass placed before him, and handing it to the thief.

"Thank'ee, sir," said Swagger, "but there's a glass already poured out. I'll drink that with pleasure."

With this he took the glass he had filled for Scarlet, and tossed off its contents, immediately refilling it from the bottle.

At that moment the old Jew was heard calling from the kitchen,—

"Swagger, Swagger, vere are yer? There's a fellow says he von't pay for his gin. Come here!"

"Oh, I'm coming," said Swagger, leaving the room, which, however, he had not intended doing.

As soon as he was gone, Peter pushed his untasted glass towards the spot where the glass poured out for Scarlet stood, and drew that towards him.

"*He* drank out of that glass," said Peter, "so there can be no harm in it. I'm always particular in strange company."

He had but just made this exchange when Scarlet returned and with him entered Swagger.

A look was interchanged between the men, and Scarlet deeming all to be right, took up the glass placed for him by Peter, and swallowed its contents.

He was poisoned.

———

CHAPTER XVII.

MRS. GRANTLEY ENACTS THE HIGHWAYMAN.

THE wife of the unfortunate Grantley had not long been ensconced behind the curtains of the attic-window when Tom King entered the room.

He had been met on the stairs by Swagger, who took the lamp from him and volunteered to assist him in his search.

"The trap is hereabout," said King, as he stopped in the middle of the attic and desired his companion to lower his light.

"What ever could have possessed Moses to walk off this Grantley's will?" continued King, as he stooped to search for the trap.

The words were distinctly heard by Mrs. Grantley, who held her breath in suspense.

"Is it of value!" asked Swagger.

"Of value!" said King; "to Grantley it is of the greatest value. It's the will of his uncle, leaving all his property to the City of London Asylum for Orphans."

"Oh! then that accounts for the old 'un walking it off. He knows the value of good paper as well as most men."

" Then it's fortunate Scarlet saw him take it from the room downstairs."

" Are you going to hand it over to the gentleman?" asked Swagger.

" Well, I don't think we shall. He has served us shabbily, and we mean to pay him out for it. Moreover he has five thousand pounds about him, and if we can get that and still hold on to the will, so much the better for us. Hang the trap; where is it?"

The voice of the Jew was now heard calling again for Swagger.

" Come here, come here!" cried the Jew; " there's a dreadful mistake—a sad affair. My! vot shall I do! vot shall I do?"

" Hillo!" cried King; " what is that?"

" I don't know. The old 'un seems really in trouble this time. I'd better go down."

" By Jove! It may be our man cutting up rough. I'll go with you and return for the will directly."

The two men rose and quitted the room simultaneously, leaving the lamp behind them.

They had no sooner disappeared than Mrs. Grantley sprang from her retreat, and hunted for the trap.

" This then, brought him here," she said. " The will! the will! I must have it or all will be lost."

She searched eagerly, and at length found the trap in the floor.

Opening it, she thrust in her hand and drew forth a sealed packet.

King was now running up the stairs again, having found the alarm of the Jew was occasioned by the sudden disappearance of Peter Pattypan, and the stupor which had come over Scarlet.

He entered the chamber just as Mrs. Grantley had contrived to conceal the will in her bosom, and replace the trap-door.

" Hillo!" cried King, observing her, " how came you here?"

Rosalie at once recognised one of her guests of the morning, and collecting all her energy, replied, with an air of impudence,

" Ah, my friend, how d'ye do?"

" Why, I'm pretty well, my friend—whom I never saw before; how are you?"

" Oh! nothing to complain of. Have you been out to-night?"

" What! on the Heath?"

" Aye."

" Oh! you know me then?"

" I know you to belong to the Knights' of the Road, but forget your name."

" Sir, my name is King—Tom King, quite at your service."

" And I, sir, have the honour to be Dick Welldown, commonly known as Gunpowder Dick!"

" Gunpowder Dick! A most alarming name for so little a person."

" Sir, you need not cast aspersions on my size. I shall grow bigger."

" Just so. And do you belong to our profession?"

" I do; but as yet I have been only in an inferior grade of it. To-morrow night I commence upon the Heath."

" You do?"

" Yes, I do."

" Then, now I'll tell you what I'll do. I'll show you how to transact matters."

" Will you? Oh! thank you."

" Yes, I will," said King, entirely forgetting what had brought him here, and drawing two chairs to the centre of the room. " I've taken a fancy to you, because you are what all our profession should be—good-looking, bold, and well-spoken. Now, sit down and listen."

Rosalie was about to take her seat, when the will slipped from under her coat and fell upon the floor, but unobserved by both parties.

Just, however, as King was about to seat himself, his eyes fell upon the papers, and he stooped and picked them up.

" Hillo!" he said, " Grantley's will. The very thing I came for. How could it have come here? But no matter. Now listen, my lad,"

It may be readily supposed that the " lad " was in no humour for listening now. The only thought of the poor distracted woman was how she was to regain the papers.

" Now," continued King, " we'll suppose that you are mounted on a fine horse, scampering about the Heath, with a fine sky above you, but with the moon hidden at the moment you wish her to hide her face. Suddenly you hear the sound of wheels at a distance, you curb your steed, you draw your pistols thus, you wait till the carriage is level with you, and then you cry out, ' Stop!'"

Here Tom stood up and threw himself into a threatening attitude,

" Now," he continued, " your money or your life! Your watch! Thank you. Your rings! Thanks. Ah! I see a lady! There is no cause for alarm. I am Tom King, who never hurt a woman, nor ever will. But I must trouble you for your ear-rings and necklace."

" Good!" cried Mrs. Grantley, in well-feigned admiration. " That is, indeed, admirable."

" Yes," continued King; " it's brave fun. Now we'll suppose you get your rings. You then make another bow—low to the lady, slight to the gentleman; you touch your steed with your spurs, and away you go, cantering over the Heath, to your merry home, where you drain a goblet and drink ' Hurrah for the road!'"

" Excellent! Excellent!" said Mrs. Grantley. " Oh, if I could do it as well as that!"

" Live in hopes—live in hopes, my bantam! But now let's see what notion you have of robbing a carriage."

" Oh, I've no notion whatever."

" Psha! Then what's the use of going on the Heath to-morrow night?"

" To rob single travellers."

" My dear lad, it's a thousand times better to rob a carriage because you get three or four times as much by it. Come, suppose you rehearse it. I will enact both travellers. Imagine the lady sitting on the other chair. Now commence by stopping the carriage."

" If I could but disarm him!" thought Mrs. Grantley.

" Yes," she said aloud, " but how am I to stop you? I have no arms!"

" Ah, that's true," said King. " Here take my pistols; but mind how you handle them, for they are loaded to the very muzzles."

He handed his weapons unsuspectingly to Mrs. Grantley.

" Now," he continued, " you hear the smacking of a whip, you curb your horse, draw him into the shade, then suddenly dart forward, and cry, ' Stop!'"

" That's very good indeed. Present both pistols."

Mrs. Grantley did so.

" Now go on."

" Your money or your life!"

" Bravo! Bravo! That's good!" cried King, quite enchanted.

" Your watch!" continued Mrs. Grantley; " your watch! Thank you. Your rings! Thanks. Ah! I see a lady. There is no cause for alarm. I am Gunpowder Dick, who never hurt a woman, nor ever will; but I must trouble you for your ear-rings and necklace."

" Nothing could be better," said King; " you'll be an ornament to the profession. You were born to be a highwayman!"

" And now "——

" Now we'll suppose you have got your booty; and now you'll bow, and retire a little way from the carriage; and now you'll say "——

" Then I say," interrupted Mrs. Grantley, " instantly give me the will and the papers you have in your pocket, or, I swear to you, this moment is your last."

She now presented her pistols at Tom's head, and the highwayman was transfixed to his seat with surprise.

" What do you mean?" he at length asked

" What I say. The papers, or you perish!"

"Come, come," cried Tom; "we have had enough of this play, now."

"No, we have not," said Rosalie. "I performed in your play in a manner which pleased you; and now you shall perform in mine in the manner which best pleases me. The papers or your life! I give you one moment only to decide."

She paused.

Tom moved not.

"Enough," said Mrs. Grantley; "you refuse, and you die!"

"Furies!" cried King, taking out the papers, and throwing them down. "Put away that weapon. There are the papers."

He threw them on the floor, and Mrs. Grantley immediately put her foot upon them.

"And now," she continued, "get into yonder cupboard."

"Yonder cupboard?"

"Yes. In!—this moment!"

Tom would have hesitated, but the weapon pointed at his breast made him hasten to obey.

In another moment he was in the cupboard, with the key turned upon him.

"So far, so well," thought Rosalie; "but where is Sam?"

Mr. Pattypan at this moment popped his head into the chamber.

"I wonder whether I may venture in," thought Pattypan.

He was answered immediately.

Mrs. Grantly thought him another of the band of thieves, and cried out,—

"Villain! advance another step, and I fire!"

"Don't don't," cried Peter; "I've only just escaped from one danger below; don't let me tumble into another up here. I'm as harmless as a turkey. Oh, Lord! I'm out of the frying-pan and into the fire!"

"Who are you?"

"I'm only Peter Pattypan, the pastrycook. I don't mean any harm, so pray don't fire."

"Ha!" cried Rosalie; "that is well. We are in great danger."

"That voice!" said Pattypan; "why, it's Mrs. Grantley!"

"Yes, yes," said the lady; "I am Mrs. Grantley; here to save my unhappy husband. Where is he?"

"I'm sure I don't know."

"I must seek him."

"If you'll take my advice, you'll stay here. It's an awful place down below."

"But my husband? Can nothing be done for him?"

"He's all right for the present. I saw him in the kitchen as I came up the stairs."

"Yes, yes; but he may be in danger. What can be done?"

"Well, I'm not able to do much, and you can only do about the same. But an idea strikes me. Your father is off for the watch. I'll get round the parapet into the next house, and admit them that way."

"Do so," said the lady; "and here! Take this pistol, and act for the best."

"I'll do the best I can," said Peter, darting from the apartment.

He had not long been gone when Rosalie heard footsteps on the stairs.

She had not returned to her place of concealment many moments when Turpin, Jack, and Mr. Grantley entered the room.

"What keeps Tom?" asked Turpin.

"Why, he's not here!" said Jack.

"Of course not," cried Mr. Grantley. "By Heaven, you have deceived me. You have no will!"

"I have," said Turpin; "and it is here."

He went to the trap in the floor, and raised it.

"Gone!" he cried; "how's this?"

Before anyone could move or speak, Tom King commenced knocking with might and main at the cupboard door.

"Heaven and earth," said Jack, "there's some one in that cupboard."

"Who's there?" shouted Turpin.

"Let me out, let me out!" cried King.

"It is King. Open the door, Jack."

Rann did as he was desired, and King rushed into the chamber.

"We are betrayed," he cried; "let us away. There is no knowing the danger by which we are surrounded."—

"But the will"—

"Has been taken away by some youth."

"Indeed!" said Jack; "then there's only one thing to do and that's to cut."

"No," cried Turpin; "I'll not lose this man yet. He has the five thousand pounds about him, and I mean to have it."

Turpin here drew his knife.

"If that's your game," said Jack, "I'm off. I'll not be a party to any violence. He came here under a promise of security, and secure from violence he shall be for me."

"Fool!" cried King, "help to get the money."

"My word was given that he should be unharmed, and if I can't prevent you from harming him I can at least walk away, and thus keep my word."

Uttering this speech, Jack left the chamber.

"He is gone," said Turpin; "and now for the money. Surrender it," he cried to Grantley, "or you die!"

"I deride your threats," said Grantley. "I am a man and can protect myself."

"That we shall see," said Turpin. "Now, Tom, upon him!"

They rushed upon Grantley, and a terrible struggle ensued.

Grantley fought bravely to release himself and save his life, but after a few efforts he was overpowered by his two adversaries, and thrown to the floor.

In another moment the knives of the assassins would have been at his throat, but Mrs. Grantley rushed from her hiding-place, and presenting her pistol at the highwaymen, dared them to advance.

"Strike at your peril!" she cried. "Beware, or I fire!"

"By heaven!" cried Tom, "it's that cursed Dick. Now, Turpin, at him while I manage this fellow. That's the boy who has the will."

Turpin advanced, and Rosalie attempted to fire upon him, but she had not strength enough to pull the trigger, and with a bound King was upon her, and striking her a violent blow on the forehead, knocked her to the earth.

"Villain!" cried Grantley, "you have murdered a poor defenceless woman!"

"Good God!" said the highwayman, bending over the prostrate form, "it is a woman. What is to be done?"

"Done!" shouted Turpin, "nothing but to secure this fellow in the cellar, and fly with the will. Take it—quick!"

King drew the will from Rosalie, and ran to the assistance of Turpin, who had pinned Grantley by the throat.

The poor fellow, on recognising his wife, and seeing her so brutally treated, became powerless, and submitted to be dragged from the room by the two highwaymen, who hurried him down the stairs as fast as they possibly could.

CHAPTER XVIII.

JACK'S ESCAPE WITH MRS. GRANTLEY FROM THE ATTIC WINDOW.

JACK had only retired to the adjoining attic.

On seeing Grantley carried down the stairs, he sprang into the front apartment, and locked the door.

The first thing his eye fell upon was Mrs. Grantley, bleeding and insensible, upon the floor.

"Hillo!" he cried, springing towards the prostrate woman, "what work is this?"

He raised the poor bruised head, and gazed upon it.

"By heaven!" he said, "a woman! This is too bad—too bad! Who could have done this? King? No; he would not injure a poor defenceless girl. It must have been Turpin; and if so he had best look out, for I'll repay this act with interest. What do I see?"

He gazed more intently on the poor white face, over which the crimson blood was streaming.

JACK'S MARE AT LENGTH FALLS EXHAUSTED.

"Why I know those features. I've seen them somewhere, and very recently. Yes — it is the wife of the man they are attempting to rob. What is to be done? They will not allow her to leave the house, and to remain here is death to her."

He looked about the room.

In one corner he saw a jug of water, and this he brought to the poor woman, and bathed her bleeding brow with the care and gentleness of a kind nurse.

At length she revived.

Her first act was to place her hand on the pocket that had contained the papers.

They were gone!

The poor woman uttered a shriek and sprang to her feet.

"The papers!" she cried, "the papers! Where are they?"

"What papers?" asked Jack.

"Oh," said the lady, "you here? Then you have them. Oh, if you are a man, give them to me!"

"I have no papers," said Jack; "and would to heaven I had had no share in this night's business, for it is one that little suits me."

"Do not prevaricate," cried Mrs. Grantley. "The papers, I say!"

"I tell you I have none."

"Was it, then, a dream? No, no. I remember all—how I possessed them; the appearance of my husband; the struggle, and the fearful blow."

"By whom given?"

"The younger man."

"Tom King?"

"The same."

"Then he shall pay dearly for it. If anyone has the paper of which you speak, 'tis the men who were here. I know nothing of them."

"But on them depends my husband's fortune and his honour. The will!—the will must be ours."

"*And it shall!*" said Jack; "mark me. It is I, Sixteen-String Jack, who makes the promise, and I never break my word. I do not like the business, for I am no common thief who preys upon rich and poor indiscriminately—who seizes booty regardless of aching hearts and ruined homes. I'll none of this, and rather than descend to it, will starve in the streets. You *shall* have your will."

"Thanks, thanks. I can believe you, for there is truth in your eye, and earnestness in your voice. I will trust you."

"You cannot do better. But there is no time to waste in talk. We must escape."

"But my husband?"

"Never have a fear for him. They will only rob him. Murder is too serious a thing, even for Knaves'-acre, particularly on a night when the hawks are abroad in such numbers. I will look to him anon. Now I can only devote myself to saving you, for you have most to fear in such a den."

"Let us, then, fly," said Mrs. Grantley, moving towards the door.

"Stop!" cried Jack; "not that way!—it is more than your life is worth."

No. 6.

" What, then, is to be done ? "

" We must escape from the window."

" Impossible ! "

" Not at all," said Jack. " I've accomplished more difficult tasks than that."

" But we are so far from the ground."

" We are ; but I'll render the descent more easy."

Jack now approached the bed, and stripped off the blankets.

Drawing his pocket-knife, he commenced to cut them into strips. These he knotted together with great speed and dexterity, and in a few minutes he manufactured a ladder which touched the ground.

" Now," he said, " trust yourself to me and have no fears."

Fastening one end of his ladder to the bed, he dropped the other into the street, and slung himself through the window.

In a moment Mrs. Grantley was hanging to his neck in mid-air, and, grasping the rope with both hands and feet, he quietly, but quickly, slid to the ground.

" Now," he said to the trembling woman, " whither will you go ? It is not well for me to be in the streets to-night ! I will see you safe, at all hazards."

" I will not quit the spot until I am convinced of the safety of my husband."

" Do not trifle," said Jack, with great earnestness ; " you are safe now, but I will not say how long you will be so if you remain here. I will answer for the safety of your husband if I cannot effect his freedom. Fly you must, for, with your knowledge of what progresses in that house, your life is not worth an hour's purchase, if caught by one of its inmates. Now, will you fly ? "

" I fear I must."

" Yes ; you must, indeed ! You can do no good, and had best trust in Providence for the safety of your husband."

" I know not where I can seek a shelter."

" Think. Have you no friends here ? "

" Not one."

" Impossible ! There must be some one who will keep you in safety till the morning."

" Oh ! I have bethought me of the confectioner's house in Holborn. Perhaps they will receive me. But Peter is here."

" No matter ; let us seek his home. Anywhere rather than this fearful spot."

Rendering Mrs. Grantley all the assistance in his power, Jack sped with her along the street, and out of Knave's-acre.

He was but barely in time, for, as he disappeared, King and Turpin burst in the door of the attic from whence he had taken Mrs. Grantley, and peered anxiously about for her.

" Confusion ! " cried King ; " she is gone. How could she have flown ? "

" Oh ! the window," said Turpin ; " look here ! She has made a ladder of the blankets ! "

" Then all is lost. She will give information to the watch, and we are caught."

" We had best fly. We have Grantley's money, and he is safe with a cracked head in the cellar."

" Fly ! " said King. " How are we to fly ? "

" How ! why, by the door, to be sure—how else ? "

" Yes ; and tumble into the hands of the fellows who, ere this, are on their way here to nab us."

" No matter. Come on. Better fight them in the street than here."

" You are right. Let us cut at once."

They were about to rush to the door, when the boy, Sam, entered and locked it after him.

" Who are you ? " demanded Dick.

" Samivel, the confectioner's boy," replied that worthy ; " don't yer know me ? "

" I remember him," said King ; " a promising young gallows-bird ! "

" Yer don't say so," said Sam. " Now that's not a kind speech, Mr. Tom King."

" Psha ! Get home to your cakes."

" Now, no cheek, but just listen to me. I vant to know vot's become of my friend, Mr. Grantley ? "

" Do you ? Then you'll want to know a long time if you rely upon me to tell you anything about him."

" You'll alter your mind presently."

" I doubt it."

" But I don't."

" Bah ! No insolence. Let us pass."

" Look here, Mr. Tom King," said the boy, unlocking the door, and holding the handle in his hand ; " coming in through the attic vinder of the next house is old Millhurst, and about a dozen of the vatch. Now, if yer don't tell me vere Mr. Grantley is, I'll jist jump in and tell 'em vere *you* are, and then you'll be nabbed. Now, there's lots of time for both of yer to escape through that vinder if no alarm is given, but I promise yer an alarm *vill* be given unless yer tells me vot's become of Mr. Grantley."

" Hang it," cried Turpin ; " the boy looks in earnest. Tell him."

" I hear a noise in the next room," cried Tom.

" Now then," said Sam, " yer've got just a second. Vill yer tell me or not ? "

" And you will take them off the scent, if I tell ? " asked King.

" And no mistake," replied the boy.

" Well, then, he's in the cellar, and there's the key."

He tossed it to Sam.

" Right," said the boy, escaping through the door ; " you can go."

As soon as he had closed the door, Tom King sprang to the lock and secured it.

" Now," said Turpin ; " to get out of this terrible hole."

Sam rushed into the adjoining attic as the first of the watchmen appeared at the window.

CHAPTER XIX.

SAM ASSISTS IN RESCUING GRANTLEY FROM THE JEW'S CELLAR.

" Now then," cried Sam to the officers, as they hastened along the parapet, " look alive, or they'll all be off."

" Who are you ? " demanded the officer.

" Who is he ? " repeated the confectioner ; " I'll tell you who he is. It's my boy Sam ; but how the young vagabond came here, I'm sure I can't tell. It puzzles me."

" I should think so," said the officer. " You're not the only master who gets puzzled at the appearance of his boys at this place. Why, bless you, nine-tenths of the young varmints of London know these houses as well as their own homes. It runs in the blood of 'em, I suppose. But it's no use wasting words here. Where's this person—Grantley ? "

" In the cellar," replied Sam.

" How do you know that ? "

" Because I've watched and found it out."

" Well, and where's his wife ? for this gentleman says Mr. Grantley was followed here by his bride."

" Quite correct," said Sam. " She's gone."

" Gone ! How ? Which way ! "

" As to how," said Sam, " it vos through the vinder ; and as to vich vay, it vos by a coil of blanketing, of vich a rope vos made for the purpose."

" And how could a lady do this ? "

Sam was about to reply that it was by the aid of Sixteen-String Jack ; but reflecting that, from all he had seen and overheard, Jack had made a sacrifice of life and liberty to save her, he determined not to mention him ; and so he simply replied,—

" I vosn't here to see."

" Oh, it's no use wasting more words," said the officer. " Just draw your pistols, boys, and come down into the lower rooms. We're strong enough to take the whole gang if we wanted to."

" Yes," said another officer ; " but I don't think you'll find many of the gang here to take. But how about the Jew ? Must we have him ? "

" Not this journey," said the chief of the watch. " He'l

useful to Harding and the others, and we mustn't interfere with him."

"Very good. Then he's safe, for all I care."

"Now then, no crawling; let us go down with a rush."

A rush was accordingly made; and as the officers reached the foot of the stairs the front door was beaten in, and a second detachment of the watch rushed in, headed by Mr. Millhurst.

"Upon 'em!" cried that gentleman, in a state of great excitement; "upon 'em! Beat 'em down. Come on, men!"

He mistook the officers who had effected their entry by way of the attic window for some of the gang of thieves, and cheered on his men to attack them.

In the darkness some blows were actually struck before the parties recognised each other.

After a slight conflict and a great deal of rough language had been expended, the two parties of officers now joined forces and marched into the kitchen. Very fortunately for the Jew and his party, the poisoning scene, in which Peter Pattypan had taken so conspicuous a part, had driven the majority of the hangers-on from the house; and, as we have seen, the three highwaymen made their escape just in the nick of time.

"Where is Mr. Grantley?" demanded Mr. Millhurst of the Jew. "Where is my son-in-law, you old thief?"

"My! Hear that, now! Me an old thief! My! my! That is too bad. Oh, vot a dreadful thing it is that people should be allowed to break into the house of a quiet, respectable old man, and insult him like that! It's dreadful!—it's dreadful!"

"Oh, shut up your cant, you old raven," said one of the officers. "We know your game, so don't try on the snivelling dodge with us. Where is the gentleman brought to your den by those three gallows-birds?"

"Oh my! my! That the good shentlemen should think that gallows-birds came to roost in the old man's nest! It's too bad! It's too bad!"

"Will you shut up that row and answer?"

"Vot am I to answer?"

"The truth. Where is this gentleman; or, rather, where is your cellar? for we know that that is the place where the gentleman is."

"My cellar! Oh, it can't be! Nobody vould be so vicked as to put a shentleman avay in the old man's cellar and make people believe he vos a party to evil goings on. I couldn't believe there's so much sin in the world."

"Poor, innocent old fellow!" said the officer, with a sneer. "It's very hard, no doubt; but you needn't hesitate another moment if you don't want a walk this cold morning as far as Newgate. Now, where is your cellar?"

"It's here," said the Jew, pointing to a door at one end of the kitchen; "but I've lost the key."

"And I've found it; so you needn't trouble on that head."

The officer held up the key given him by Sam while descending the stairs, and the Jew looked at it in amazement.

"Vhy, how did you get that key from Tom?"

"Oh, oh! You begin to know something at last, I see. You can't imagine how King gave up the key? You'll find out more mysterious things than that before we've done with you."

The officer fitted the key in the lock, and, with two others, descended into the cellar; and in a few moments returned, assisting Grantley (who had been violently beaten over the head) between them.

"How came you here?" demanded the officer of Grantley.

"I was brought here under false pretences."

"What were they?"

Grantley was about to answer, when the thought of his position burst upon him and sealed his tongue.

"I must not answer."

"You must, if you require justice done and these fellows apprehended."

"I will not answer," said Grantley. "Suffice it to know that I was under the impression that certain papers of importance to me would be given me here in consideration of a sum named."

"And have you received the papers?"

"No. I have been robbed and ill-used by those who brought me here, but have not had the papers I was promised."

This much, and this much only, would Grantley say.

He dared not repeat the scene which had occurred upstairs.

The officers, seeing his determination, pressed the matter no further.

"You can go, sir," said the man; "but you act very stupidly in not being more explicit, in o der that justice may overtake those who have placed you in this position. But that is not my business, and so I wish you good night. You are sure this gentleman's wife is clear of Knaves'-acre?" continued the other, turning to Sam.

"Ah, my Rosalie!" cried Grantley. "Where is she?"

"What!" said Mr. Millhurst, "my child in this place?"

"She vos here," said Sam; "but she's clear off now."

"My child here!"

The old man repeated these words over and over again, as if he could not realise the fact they conveyed.

"Yes," said Peter, "she followed with that rascal Sam in order to save her husband; and it strikes me she did it."

"She's a perfect duck," said Sam, in ecstasy; "you should have seen her trot along that 'ere precious parapet."

"No more words," said the officer; "we will see you all safe out of this place, and then leave you."

Turning to the Jew, he continued,—

"You've got off rather luckily this time, but you'd best take care; your time is coming, my friend."

The Jew was silent. The thoughts of the body of the burglar were running in his mind, and he dreaded lest Peter should mention the subject; but that worthy was too full of the scene passing before him to remember anything of what had passed.

So without more words the whole party went into the street and the fence closed the door upon them.

"A bad night's vork," he said, as he went back to his kitchen, "a very bad night's vork. I'm an awful loser by it. No revard, no monish, no custom, no nothing, and my beautiful boys all frightened avay. It's too bad—too bad. I shall break my heart—I know I shall. My! my! It's awful sad —awful sad!"

He went back to his kitchen, and as he was about to enter it he stopped, and, an idea striking him, murmured,—

"But I know vot I'll do. I'll send them all to bed, and *never a vun chop shall they have!*"

With this awful threat of vengeance, Moses, somewhat composed in spirit, rejoined his few remaining guests, to talk over the events of the night.

* * * * * *

"Whither are you going?" demanded the officer of those under his protection, as he hastened with them from the Acre.

"I am going to my home," said Mr. Millhurst; and then turning to Grantley, he continued, "Sir, I am sorry to say that we part now and for ever, unless by to-morrow you make clear the mystery which overhangs this day's proceedings. I am insulted! My child's prospects blighted in having joined herself in marriage with one who will henceforth be looked upon with that suspicion which must attach itself to you. I regret this much, but I cannot do other than I have stated will be my course. So now I have only to say farewell!"

"Sir—sir, you surely will not leave me thus?" cried Grantley. "Believe me, I have acted in this matter for the best."

"That may be so; but until full explanations are given in public I cannot again call you son and friend. So good morning."

With this Mr. Millhurst walked away, and the watch, dividing their forces, went off in different directions.

Grantley was then left with Peter and Sam.

"My head!" cried Grantley, grasping his head between his hands, "oh, the pain will drive me mad! But I could bear all but his words."

"Oh, nonsense!" said the kind-hearted little confectioner;

" do not mind him ; he's only passionate and hasty, and to-morrow will regret having spoken thus."

" No," said Grantley, " I cannot thus persuade myself. He appeared to be terribly in earnest. Would that it could be otherwise."

" Think no more of it, my dear sir, and in the morning all will be well again."

" And now I must go home."

" In your present state such an act would be foolhardy," said Peter ; " do not think of it, but honour me by accepting a bed at my house until it is daylight, and a proper conveyance can be found for you."

" But Rosalie ? "

" In all probability we shall find Mrs. Grantley at my house. It is not likely she would return to her own under these circumstances."

" True," said Grantley ; " at all events I will go with you as far as Holborn ; and if my wife is not there, I can then hasten home."

" Let me assist you," said Peter, " lean on me ; and Sam, you dog, get the other side of Mr. Grantley, and lend your arm."

CHAPTER XX.

THE MEETING OF JACK WITH MRS. MALVERS.

JACK, in a comparatively short time, brought Mrs. Grantley to the door of Pattypan's house in Holborn.

The housekeeper and Mrs. Malvers were sitting up for Peter ; and hearing Jack's loud knock at the door, both ladies concluded that the confectioner had returned, and ran down-stairs to admit him.

The surprise of Mrs. Malvers on recognising Jack, and what appeared to be the poor, fainting boy, who bore him company, may readily be imagined ; whilst Jack in turn, exhibited very marked signs of astonishment in recognising the lady.

" What brings you here ? " demanded the woman he had rescued from the scaffold, extending her hand kindly.

" It is a long tale," said Jack ; " may I enter and relate it ? "

" Certainly," said Mrs. Malvers ; " come to my apartment. Whom have you with you ? "

" Mrs. Grantley."

" Mrs. Grantley ! Good Heavens ! the lady who was married to-day—and in that strange dress ! What is the meaning of this ? "

" I will explain all in a few words," said Jack ; " but just let me assist this poor lady to your room."

On coming in contact with those of her own sex, and the fierce excitement of the night over, the poor young lady fell into a fainting fit, and Jack had to carry her up the stairs.

" Poor soul," said the lady, " how pale and ill she looks ! Pray relate what has happened to her. I cannot rest until I know."

Jack thus urged, told as briefly as possible all he knew of the singular adventure of Mrs. Grantley.

" How strange you should have brought her here ! How singular are the ways of Heaven ! "

" What mean you ? " asked Jack.

" I mean that I know more of this matter than any of you. The confession of my cousin has placed it in my power to relieve the anxiety of this lady, and place her happiness beyond doubt."

" You speak in riddles."

" I have no doubt you think so. But listen ; there is another will, a later one, bequeathing all to Mr. Grantley."

" Indeed ! "

" Ay, indeed ! "

Mrs. Malvers then related to Jack the substance of her interview with her cousin.

" So the will is in the old attic at the Red Rose," said Jack, when Mrs. Malvers had ceased talking. " If so, I will have it from its resting-place, and place it in Mr. Grantley's hands ; but let me entreat you not to hold out any hope of its recovery

to the lady, for I may fail to find it, and disappointment would be a sad blow to her."

" It would, and therefore I will observe your advice, and maintain a strict silence, although I cannot believe that you will fail."

" There is a chance that I may do so, and therefore act with caution."

Mrs. Grantley now recovered her senses, but was over-whelmed with confusion at being found in a costume so singular and unwomanly.

Mrs. Malvers, observing what was passing in the mind of the young lady, at once conducted her from the room, for the purpose of offering her a change of dress.

They had no sooner gone than Mr. Grantley and Peter arrived. Their surprise at finding Jack in the house may very readily be imagined.

" You did not expect to see me," said Jack.

" Villain ! " cried Mr. Grantley, " begone. How dare you enter here ? "

" I am going," said Jack, somewhat nettled at this speech. " I am going, and I should not have dared to enter here, but for the purpose of placing your wife in safety."

" My wife ! "

" Yes. I rescued Mrs. Grantley from the house of the old Jew, and I conducted her here. I see, you think me as bad as those in whose company you found me, but I assure you it is not so. For a time I was led away by them and lent them my assistance ; but as soon as I found them dealing treacher-ously I turned from them, and determined to aid you. The lady you'll find with your wife will tell whether I am to be trusted or not. Mark me, Mr. Grantley ; I am now in your service, and I will do my best to see you righted, and restore your peace and happiness. I do not ask you to think better of me until I prove worthy of your confidence. Good night."

Mr. Grantley bowed, and Jack left the room.

In a few moments he was heard descending the stairs, and then the street-door closed, and he was gone.

" To think," said Peter, " to think that a highwayman should ever have entered my house ! I shall never get over it."

Mrs. Malvers now re-entered the room.

" Where is Jack ? " she asked, after being introduced to Mr. Grantley by Peter.

" Jack ? " repeated Peter, " is that the Jack that saved you ? "

" The same," said the lady, " and a poor, devoted fellow he is, although his calling is one of so terrible a nature."

" But my wife," said Grantley, " where is she ? "

" You will find her in the next room."

Grantley left the room and entered the apartment where his wife sat weeping.

" Rosalie," whispered the husband.

The voice roused the poor lady, and springing to her feet with a cry of joy, she was enfolded in her husband's arms.

" I feared you would not escape from that terrible place," she said, " and the thought almost distracted me. How did you evade them ? "

" I was rescued by your father and a strong body of the watch, dear Rosalie."

" Indeed ! I am glad of that. I would rather my father found you there than another."

" Yes, Rosalie ; but your father has turned his back upon me ; I am now no more to him than the stranger he passes in street."

" Do not believe it," cried Mrs. Grantley ; " I know my father better ; he will be friendly again to-morrow."

" He will be friendly with me no more."

" How do you mean ? "

" Rosalie," said Grantley, " you know all. You know why I left you last night—why I flew to Knave's-acre with those men ? "

" Yes."

" Your father wanted me to explain my conduct, and clear up the mystery which enshrouded my acts. I had not the courage to do so."

" Oh, why not ? "

" Because I was doing a wrong."

THE WILL-SEEKERS BAFFLED.

"A wrong!"

"Yes, Rosalie—a deep and terrible wrong. I was seeking to gain possession of a document to which I had no right. I was guilty of the intention of committing a fraud—for I had thoughts of destroying my uncle's will, and thus defrauding the institution to which he bequeathed his property."

"Oh, why did you dream of doing this?"

"Because I loved you, Rosalie. Years I have fought for you—years I have struggled on in the hope of becoming worthy of you. He gave you to me at last, in the belief that I was a rich man. Had I gone to him and said, 'Trouble has come upon me, and I am a beggar,' would he have still said, 'Take my child?' No; he would have spurned me, as he has done before, and I should have been a broken-down, broken-hearted man. And I thought of you too, Rosalie. I knew you loved me as dearly as I loved you, and I knew you would suffer as I suffered; so I paused. The temptation was too strong for my honesty, and I fell. But I am punished now. They have robbed me of all, and I shall be a beggar. Yes, Rosalie, the money your father gave me to-day is in their hands, and I am penniless."

"It is sad—very sad!"

"It is! It is! Oh, fool that I was, to turn from the right path, and sacrifice my good name!"

"Do not upbraid yourself," cried the wife; "you did what you thought was for the best; and if you have erred, it is only that which nine out of ten would have done in your case. No matter now—think no more of it. The world is before you. Begin again, and fight your way upward manfully. Atone for the past by your goodness in the future."

"But the stain is on me—the stain is on me, and it will not be wiped away."

"Nay, nay; there is yet time to retrieve your fault, and place yourself right with the world."

"I do not see how."

"The means are simple."

"No, Rosalie; before to-morrow night those terrible men will have placed the will in the hands of the trustees of the institution to which the property is left, and my escapade in Knave's-acre will be made public by the watchmen. The public will draw its own conclusions, and I shall be a blighted man."

"Not so. These men will not go to the institution with the will until they have tried you again, and endeavoured to draw more money from you. Therefore, do you go to the trustees to-morrow, and tell them all you know of the existence of the will, and your determination to relinquish all the property, without placing them to any trouble to prove their claim and title; thus you will be enabled to look the world in the face again and hold up your head among honest men."

"Your advice is worthy of you, dearest, and I will be careful to follow it to the letter."

"Then there is no further cause for trouble."

"No further cause! Heaven defend us! No cause for trouble, and you lost to me!"

"What mean you? Am I not your wife?"

"Yes, dearest; but I am not base enough to drag you with me into the depths of poverty to which I must now descend. Return to your father. He will treat you kindly, and you will continue to enjoy the luxuries to which you have been so long used. I will not stand in the way of your happiness."

"Grantley," said the lady, "you are cruel to me now, and I do not deserve it. I am your wife, and I would have you remember the solemn obligations I undertook yesterday morning at the altar, before God and man. There I linked my fate to yours—bound up my happiness with yours, and swore to be yours—for better, for worse, for richer, for poorer—until it pleased God to break the bond by taking us to Himself. Remember this, Grantley, and tell me if you think so meanly of me as to suppose I would leave you in the first trouble that has come to you. I am no fair-weather wife—no partner of the sunshine only of your existence. I am yours, Grantley, for ever, whate'er your fortune; so speak no more of my return to my father."

Grantley was affected to tears, and could say nothing in answer to his wife's passionate speech.

"There," continued the affectionate, right-thinking woman, "do not give way to grief; our troubles are but light, after all."

"With you to share them, they are nothing,"

Husband and wife now returned to the group they had left in the front room.

There was sunshine in their faces, and they made glad the hearts of those who saw them.

"Are you about to return home?" said Peter, "or will you for the night accept the poor accommodation I can offer?"

"We have no home, my good friend," said Grantley; "we have lost all, and are now beggars. Will you now renew your hospitable offer?"

"I can't understand it," said Peter; "but if you tell me you are in trouble, and want my poor help, it is yours as long as you will accept it. I do not forget, and I hope I remember gratefully."

"I know you," said Grantley, "for you are a good, kind man, and deserve well of all mankind. I must test your kindness to the full, for, as I have said, I am now homeless, penniless. I would not willingly be a burthen to you, for I am strong, and can work; but my wife is helpless, and for her sake I must claim your hospitality."

"For her sake you may claim all I've got, and have it; for she is a true lady, and in my humble way I love her as dearly as if she were my own child."

Mrs. Malvers longed to tell them something of the will, just to dispel a little of their sadness; and she in all probability would have done so, but that she remembered the words of Jack, which compelled her to remain silent.

"It is hard," she said, "to raise the cup of bliss to their lips, and then dash it down again; so I will say nothing, and pray that Heaven may give them patience to bear this great trial."

CHAPTER XXI.

THE CITY OF LONDON ORPHAN ASYLUM.

LONDON, at the date of our story, did not abound in charitable institutions, as it does now. Men had not yet awakened to the fact of the great good they could do, and philanthropy slumbered.

In its day, the City of London Asylum for Orphans was considered a very noble and very admirable institution. It was devoted to the uses of fatherless and motherless girls born within the limits of the City.

It was a City institution, devoted to City children, presided over by City officers, and supported by City men.

The idea of this institution originated with an old gentleman of the City, who died immensely rich, leaving one child, a girl, who married against his will, and whom he permitted to starve, bequeathing his vast wealth to the foundation of a home for orphan girls; perhaps thinking that the place might one day prove serviceable to the children of the child he had discarded.

Be that as it may, the institution was founded, officers were appointed, a board formed, trustees elected, secretaries and other salaried officials appointed, and six-and-twenty orphans duly elected and put into the costume of the institution, which consisted of a very hideous blue-serge gown, a large white apron, and frilled night-cap of awful dimensions.

Having done this much for the orphans, the trustees, the board, and the salaried officials prepared to make themselves comfortable.

The board was to meet once a fortnight, and discuss matters of business after a splendid dinner, and thus make itself comfortable.

The secretary was to have a fine office and a fine salary, and make himself comfortable. The matrons and governesses were to be provided with homes and salaries to make themselves comfortable; and, in fact, everybody was comfortable except the orphans themselves, who complained, in the most barefaced manner, that the serge gown was too cold for the winter and too hot for the summer, that the caps tore their faces, and that it was impossible for them to keep the great white aprons clean.

They also said, and stuck to it, that boiled beef four days a week, and salt pork the remaining three, did not agree with their constitutions, and affirmed, with the greatest effrontery, that to this source was due the awful attacks of scurvy which broke out among them.

The trustees said such base ingratitude was shameful, and that *they* never heard of such a thing.

The secretary quite agreed with the board, and dauntlessly asserted that *he* never heard of such a thing.

And the matrons and governesses swore by the secretary, and said that if it were their last words, and they were going to be hung for it, they would assert with their last breath, that *they* never heard of such a thing.

And so things went on comfortably!

Every now and then another City man would pop off, and leave the whole, or part, of his property to the institution; and it flourished.

The board fattened perceptibly. The secretary purchased a carriage.

The matrons and governesses grew sleek, and were reported to be putting away a nice little fortune, each of them.

And the orphans looked very discontented with their blue-serge frocks, white aprons, and night-caps; and still went on asserting that the scurvy was due to the salt beef and pickled pork, and not to their own nasty, wilful, and good-for-nothing dispositions, which of course was palpable to everybody. It was board-day—the day after the wedding and misfortunes of Mr. Grantley—and the board was assembled in all its majesty to discuss the affairs of the institution.

Mopsworth was the chairman, and he was supported by nine City men, who tried to assume an air of gravity and importance, which, however, degenerated into burlesque, and rendered them ridiculous.

It was twelve o'clock.

"Now," said the chairman, "Mr. Skinwell will oblige us by reading the report."

Mr. Skinwell, a rather flashy gentleman, in an elaborate and embroidered waistcoat, rose to read the said report.

He read through rows of figures and strings of memoranda, and at last came to the balance at the banker's, which was announced to be £7540 3s. 4½d., a fact which was received with great satisfaction by the board generally.

"And now," said the chairman, "what other business is there?"

"In the next place, sir," said the secretary, "I must trouble you with my own private grievances, if you will oblige me by listening."

"We are all attention."

"To begin, then, I must apprise you that in consequence of the enormous increase of the work of the secretaryship I have been forced to call in the assistance of practical accountants; secondly, sir, I have had to enlarge my offices to accommodate them; thirdly, they have entailed on me an expense of one hundred pounds; fourthly, I see no possibility of that expense ever diminishing; and fifthly, I must beg of the board to remember that my position will not admit of my expending these sums without the prospect of reimbursement; and therefore I have to claim the attention of the board to the fact that the salary of the secretary is inadequate, and should be raised at least three hundred pounds per annum."

" Having heard the report of the secretary, gentlemen, what do you say? Can we entertain the application?"

There was a murmur around the table, and then one puffy old gentleman said aloud " that in his opinion, the secretary ought to be supported."

The motion was then put, " that the salary of the secretary be increased two hundred pounds per annum."

Carried *nem. con.*

Now, Mr. Skinwell is there anything else?"

" Two trifling matters, sir; the first is simply this: the matrons and governesses have to find their own tea, sugar, and candles, and they complain that they find it impossible to do so without great inconvenience. They, therefore, beg that the board will allow them their tea, sugar, and candles."

" What expense will this entail?"

" One hundred and twenty pounds per annum."

" Now, gentlemen, what do you say? Can you entertain this application?"

The puffy old gentleman here rose again, and said that " no woman as was a woman could do without creature comforts, which they were, tea and sugar "—and he was about to add " and candles;" but remembering that tallow was not an article of consumption in England, he continued, " and it's too bad to think that people who had to live on one hundred and ten pounds a-year could find themselves in candles;" and, therefore, he thought the matrons and governesses ought to be supported.

They were supported, and the extra one hundred and twenty pounds required was immediately voted.

" And now for the other little matter."

" It's one with which you are already acquainted. The orphans complain that they get no milk and sugar, and that the bread is poor; and they further say that they attribute the ravages scurvy is making among them to the saltness and inferior quality of the beef and pork supplied. I need not add that they ask for a change of diet."

" Infamous!" said the chairman. " No one ever heard of such a thing! The idea of orphans daring to ask for milk and sugar, and hinting that fine wholesome beef and pork produced scurvy. It's too bad—too bad!"

The puffy gentleman, in a fit of indignation which stifled his eloquence, was here understood to say that, " in his opinion, the orphans ought *not* to be supported."

And they were not supported, and still had to be content with their delicious salt meat, and endure the evils of their malignant skin disease.

" And that's all?" asked the chairman of the secretary.

" And that's all, sir."

" Well, now, I think we may go to dinner, conscious of having done full justice to the orphans Providence has been pleased, in its infinite mercy, to place under our charge."

To this beautiful speech the board muttered an approving " Hear—hear!"

A movement was about to be made to the dining-room, when a porter announced that a gentleman wished to appear before the board.

" What is his name?" asked the chairman.

The porter handed in a card.

" Mr. Grantley," said the chairman, glancing at the bit of pasteboard; " I know Grantley of the City—a very wealthy and highly-respectable young man. Show him in."

Grantley was shown in, and briefly told his tale.

The amazement it created can very readily be imagined.

" I knew not of this matter until last night," said the young man, " so I could not come to you before. I now place the matter in your hands."

" Yes; but if these dare-devil highwaymen do not produce the will we have no claim," said Mopsworth.

" Enough that I have seen it," said Grantley. " I know my uncle has left all he did possess to the institution; and I, therefore, relinquish all my claims to it, and am here to arrange for the immediate handing over of the whole."

" Very good and very honourable," said Mopsworth; " but it is impossible that we can take possession just now. Let us induce you to hold this property in trust for us until some arrangement can be made. Let me see, Mr. Grantley, you have no private income, I believe?" inquired the chairman.

" No, sir; the act of my uncle leaves me a beggar."

" Dear me—dear me—how sad!" continued the sensitive Mopsworth; " but it is fortunate for us, for we can now offer you a sa'ary to undertake the management of the affair for us. Knowing the business of your late uncle, I am assured we should realise more by retaining it than by its sale; so if you will oblige us by becoming our manager—at a salary of, say a thousand a-year—we should esteem it a great kindness."

" It is a favour I scarcely dared to ask," said Grantley, overjoyed at this unexpected good fortune.

" Well, then, the matter's perfectly understood. You are our manager, and at a salary of one thousand per annum. Dear me! to think that my late respected acquaintance should have left his wealth to this noble institution. Dear me! But we will now to dinner. Mr. Grantley, you will dine with us?"

" I thank you—no. I must return to my wife."

" Well, then, some other time."

" I shall be most happy. And now, good-day."

" Good day. Come and see Mr. Skinwell to-morrow."

" I will do so," said Grantley, as he took his leave.

" Wonderful thing, to be sure!" said Mopsworth. " So the old fool has died, and left all his money to the Orphan Asylum. What a confounded old lunatic!"

" What an idiot!" cried the others, in a strong chorus.

" Well, now, cook," said Mopsworth, " what is there for dinner?"

" There's nice turkeys, two hams, a sirloin of beef, pigeon and game pies; before which, sir, you will have turtle soup and a fine turbot."

" Ah! that's good," said the old man, smacking his lips, in anticipation of a treat.

" And, oh! I forgot to mention, sir, that there's a splendid round of *salt beef* among the joints."

" *Salt beef*, sir!" said the chairman; " *salt beef!* Why, it's not fit for pigs! Don't let me ever have to tell you again about salt beef. Pitch it into the ash-pit; or, stay—give it to the orphans; it won't hurt them."

CHAPTER XXII.

JACK SEEKS THE WILL.

REPULSIVE as the exterior of the Red Rose beer-house undoubtedly was, the interior was decidedly worse.

In every respect it was a low house. It was low in reputation, and low in the company that used it.

Thieves and rogues of every description harboured there, and the place was open day and night for their reception.

The neighbourhood was to the hunted felon what Alsatia was to evil-doers of old.

It was a harbour and a refuge, into which stainless men dared not penetrate.

The watch only ventured within its precincts in strong forces, and then only with caution and at hours when they knew the worst characters to be far away.

Into this neighbourhood, on the night after his rescue of Mrs. Grantley from the Jew's house, Jack Rann penetrated, for the purpose of seeking to unfathom the mystery of the will supposed to be hidden in the chimney of the old attic of the Red Rose.

As a matter of course, he left his mare at home and came on foot.

Well muffled in his cloak, he came unnoticed, and approached the door of the house without molestation.

He knocked once.

" Who's there?"

" It is I, Jack Rann."

" What, Sixteen-String Jack? All right."

In a moment the bars were drawn, and the door opened for the admission of the highwayman.

" Why, Jack, what brings you into the Minories?"

" I'm hunted out of my quarters, and so have come here for a night's lodging. Can I have it?"

" Have it! In course you can. Ain't we proud to be able to accommodate the gallant Jack?"

" Thanks; and now let me go to bed."

" Go to bed, Jack! why, it's not midnight."

" I'm tired out."

" Well, but there's some of the boys in the big-room. Won't you come in and drink a glass or two with them?"

" Not a glass, not a drain. I'm ill and weary. Let me go to bed."

" Well, so you shall," said the landlord; " so you shall; but we're dreadfully sorry to lose your company as soon as we've got it. However, you shall have the best room in the house, Jack, for old acquaintance sake. Here, Tom, show the bold Jack to the best bedroom."

" Where is the best bedroom?" demanded Jack.

" On the first floor."

" Well then, I shan't have it," said Jack. " I want to sleep; but very little of it should I get in your best bedroom. No, no; the attic's the place for me. Show me up."

" What, the bold Jack sleep in my attic! I wouldn't hear of such a thing."

" But I insist."

" Well, but it ain't fit to be slept in. It ain't a been used since the poor feller as is in the condemned hole for murder slept in it."

" So much the better."

" You're determined to have the place, then?"

" That or none. I have it, or I go."

" Well, you wilful rascal, have your own way. Bother the fellow; I can do nothing with him."

" I'm to have the attic, then?"

" Show him up, Tom; but he'll get no sleep in that place."

" I don't want any," thought Jack; but he merely said, " I'm glad you will give me my own way."

" You're a funny dog," said the landlord.

" I am," said Jack. " When I have a fancy in my head I generally carry it out."

" You do, as everybody well knows."

" Well, good night."

" Good night, and good rest."

Jack mounted the stairs, and was left at the door of the attic by the boy whom the landlord addressed as Tom.

" There's your candle," said Tom; " and now I'll leave yer. Mind, it's an awful place for rats."

" They won't disturb me."

" Won't they! The feller that slept here last told another story."

" Yes, my friend," said Jack, closing the door, " but I don't intend to sleep here."

He waited until the boy had descended the stairs, and then bolted the door.

" I'll wait till they get a little more noisy," said Jack. " They may hear me now."

He did wait, and at last the mirth of those below was at its height.

" Now's my time," he said.

He then stooped over the grate, and drawing a stout crowbar from his pocket, commenced to tear away the stone-work of the chimney.

Through hitting upon the wrong spot in the great chimney, Jack had torn out a tolerably large heap of stones before he came to the hole he sought.

At length he found it; and, putting in his hand, he drew forth a tolerably large and heavy box.

He had no sooner deposited this on the ground than he was disturbed by a loud knocking at the door of the attic.

" Come what will," said Jack to himself, " no one must enter here. Now then," he continued, aloud, " who's there?"

" It's I, Reuben; let me in."

" Not to-night."

" I say let me in!"

" What is it you want?"

" Why, I want to know what all this infernal knocking is?

It sounds as if the whole house was coming down; and as I don't want to have my house torn down without knowing the reason why, I've determined to see what you're up to."

" Get away with you," said Jack; " there's no knocking here, and I want to go to sleep."

" It won't do," said Reuben; " open the door."

" I will not open the door."

" Then I'll break it open."

" You had best not do so, Reuben. I'm a desperate fellow, as you well know; and I've made up my mind not to be played with to-night; so don't tempt me to do that which I should regret."

" A fig for your regret! Something tempted you up into this dismal old attic, and that something we mean to know as much about as you do; so open the door."

" I'll not do so."

" Then look out, for we're coming."

" I'll once more advise you to go downstairs peaceably."

" And I'll once more advise you to open the door."

" Get away, Reuben; get away."

" I speak to you for the last time."

" It's useless."

" Then down with the door, Tom. Now, together."

There was a great crash, and the old door came rattling down from its hinges.

Reuben, who dashed in first, produced a lantern, and turned it full upon Jack, who stood with his back to the grate, and with the box at his feet.

" Hillo!" cried Reuben, " what's that?"

" It's mine," cried Jack; " mine," and so do not attempt to place your hand upon it."

" Whatever is here belongs to me," said Reuben, turning his lantern full upon the box. " Hillo!" he continued, " that's the box the fellow that's to be banged brought here."

" No matter," said Jack, " it belongs to me just now, and I'll defend it with my life."

" Ho, ho! my boy; that's it, is it? Now, I'm sure there's something in the box worth having. If you defend it with your life, it must be worth looking after; so stand on one side."

" I'll not do so."

" We're two to one."

" Were you forty to one, I would still defy you. I will have the box, so do not tempt me."

" No more jaw," cried Reuben. " Upon him, Tom, and seize it!"

" Well," said Jack, " I've warned you. If you advance another step, you see what you have to meet."

He presented a couple of pistols at their heads as he spoke, and the men drew back for a moment.

" Now," he continued, " do you feel inclined to take the box?"

" Yes," cried Reuben, " at all risks. Come on, Tom."

" Now!" shouted Tom, springing forward.

" Now!" cried Jack, levelling his pistol, and firing full at the breast of the landlord's assistant.

" Oh!" cried the ruffian, staggering back, " I am shot. I am killed."

Reuben now tried his luck, but Jack was prepared for him, and he, too, fell, pierced by a ball.

Without a moment's delay, Jack sprang to the door with the box, and, dashing past those whom the sound of pistols had attracted, rushed down the stairs, and forced his way out of the house.

Running with all his might, he soon got clear of the Minories with his supposed treasure.

But now that he had it, he scarce knew what to do with it.

He dared not enter a strange house with it, he would not venture to the Jew's den, and he was in fear lest he should fall across the watch, and get taken into custody.

" By Jove!" he said, " it will never do for them to catch me now; but how I'm to get free of them I'm sure I don't know."

The words had scarce passed his lips, when in the distance he saw the glimmer of a watchman's lantern.

He was now in Lombard street.

MURDER OF THE OLD WICKET-PORTER.

To fly was to be discovered, to stand still was to be run against by the approaching bearer of the lantern.

Jack knew not what to do; but, in the emergency, stepped into the first doorway he came to.

Shrinking into the shadow of the overhanging porch, he cowered against the door, and, to his surprise, found that it gave way under his touch.

"Fortune favours me," he said. "I will step inside until the watch has passed."

Acting on the thought, he entered the house, and closed the door after him.

The passage was perfectly dark, so that he could not see an inch before him.

"Hang the things!" he muttered, "this is awful. If I got into any trouble, I could not defend myself and the box too. What shall I do?"

He had no time to reflect, for at that moment some one rushed out from a door near at hand, and fell into his arms.

"It's all right," he heard a voice exclaim. "Here, take this."

Something heavy was placed in Jack's hand.

"Now," continued the voice, "meet me in two days at the old Ferry House. Go to the Heath to-morrow, at twelve. The old boy crosses in his carriage. He has the document; get it from him at all risks."

"That voice!" said Jack to himself; "where have I heard it?"

The figure swept past him, opened the street door, and was the next moment speeding away down Lombard street.

"That voice, that voice!" said Jack again; "it's as familiar to me as my own. Ah, I know now. It was Malvers. How strange that he should be here at such an hour, and how much more strange this meeting! What can be in this parcel he has given me?—and what did he mean by going to the Heath to-morrow? It is evident he mistakes me for some one else. Well, it's fortunate, that's all."

Next moment Jack saw the street door opening again, and a figure steal into the passage.

"This is the real Simon Pure," thought Jack, "but he comes five minutes too late."

"Now then," said the new comer, "arn't you coming to-night."

Jack, mimicking the voice of Malvers, answered,—

"I'm here."

"Well, did you find the bag?"

"No."

"Ah! How's that?"

"Because it is not where I thought it was."

"Humph! A nice mess we've made of it, then."

"I don't see that."

"Don't you. Then I do. What's to be done?"

"He crosses the Heath to-morrow night," said Jack, at a venture.

"The deuce he does! How did you learn that? Has Tom left word?"

"He has."

"Well, then, he's a trump; and if he isn't, say my name is not Dick Turpin."

"Oh! thought Jack, "your name is Turpin, is it? I thought I knew you, dark as it is."

No. 7.

"Well," continued Turpin, for it was that worthy, "there's a great point gained. What time does he cross the Heath?"

"At an hour after midnight."

"Then I shall be there."

"Just too late," added Jack, chuckling to himself. "Now we've finished our business," he said aloud. "Get away; it won't do for us to be seen together. Good night."

"Good night."

The door was opened and shut again, and Dick Turpin was gone.

"Well," said Jack to himself, "this is about the most singular adventure I ever met with; but it may turn out a lucky one, after all. But it's no use to waste time here, or I may get caught. Now to see if the coast is clear, and then for a hard run to Holborn. I must reach the shop of the little confectioner and deposit this box there, or I shall lose it; and it's by far too precious a treasure to be lost as soon as won."

He opened the door softly, and finding the street deserted, stole quietly forth, and hurried away towards Holborn by the nearest and less frequented route.

CHAPTER XXIII.

THE OPENING OF THE BOX—THE DISAPPOINTMENT—THE MYSTERIOUS BAG—ITS CONTENTS—A CLUE TO THE WILL.

AFTER a sharp run Jack reached the house of little Peter Pattypan, and although it was nearly two in the morning hesitated not to knock boldly at the door.

In a few minutes Peter put his head out of an upper window, and demanded to know who knocked.

"It's a friend," said Jack; "a friend who desires to see Mrs. Malvers on matters of the utmost importance."

"This is a peculiar time in the morning to wish to see a lady on business, isn't it?"

"It is; but, I pray you, hesitate not to admit me. Matters of importance depend upon my at once seeing the lady."

"I've heard your voice before," said Peter; "but I can't recognise you. Nevertheless, I'll call Mrs. Malvers and let you in. But no tricks, you know; I'm well armed."

For full a quarter of an hour Jack kicked his heels in the doorway, awaiting the appearance of Mr. Pattypan.

At last our hero had the satisfaction of hearing the bolts of the door shot back, and seeing the light stream through the chinks and keyhole.

Immediately afterwards he stood face to face with the confectioner.

The little man was habited in a large white flannel dressing-gown, and on his head he wore a nightcap almost as tall as himself. In his hand he carried a gigantic old horse-pistol, which time and a damp wall had rusted past recovery.

"Hillo!" cried Peter, starting back in alarm as he caught sight of the highwayman, "hillo, there! Thieves—robbers! They're here again. Where's the watch?"

"Hush, for heaven's sake, or you'll ruin all!"

"I mean to ruin all. I'm not going to be slaughtered like a lamb. Where's the watch? Why don't this dangerous weapon go off of itself and kill somebody?"

In spite of the torture Jack endured from fear that the outcry of the confectioner would alarm the watchman at the head of the hill or the neighbours, he could not help laughing at the comic agony of the figure before him. The little man retreated backward on tip-toe, quaking with fear, ready to sink into the earth.

His lamp and pistol dropped at his side, and he looked the incarnation of distress.

"Fear nothing," said Jack, following our little friend into the passage, and carefully closing the door; "I'm friendly to you and yours. Do you not know me? I saved Mrs. Malvers."

"Oh, so you did," said Peter, regaining some of his confidence. "At first I thought you might possibly be one of the worst of the three villains I had the horror of meeting at poor dear Mr. Grantley's."

"I am not the worst, as you shall prove before long. But now show me where I may find Mrs. Malvers; it is important that I should see her without delay."

"I called her before I came down. Go upstairs into the front room, and I will follow you. But as you are a man and a Christian, don't shoot anybody, and pray respect the plate. There ain't much of it, but it's all family relics, and, as such, valued beyond its worth."

"Oh, man alive," cried Jack, impatiently, "I wouldn't touch your plate if a ton of it was in my path. The friend of Mrs. Malvers is my friend, and his property is sacred."

"That's a very beautiful sentiment," said Peter, following Jack up the stairs; "in fact, it is the most delightful sentiment I've heard for a long time. You're a good young man, although the most abominable rogue I ever met."

"What?"

"No offence, sir, no offence. Pray don't knock your head against the ceiling."

They entered the front room indicated by Peter, and here Jack deposited his box and the bag of which he had become so mysteriously possessed on a table, and told Peter to set down his light. Peter had just placed his lamp on the table when Mrs. Malvers rushed into the room.

"You have it," she cried, as her eye fell upon the box; "you have not failed!"

"Hey?" said Peter, mystified at this outburst.

Jack glanced uneasily at the little man, and Mrs. Malvers, seeing that he wished him gone, said,—

"Pray withdraw, my good friend. This is a matter which concerns me alone."

"Hey?" said Peter; "what, leave you without protection, and in company of so desperate a character! I couldn't think of it."

"Pray do. I am safe with Rann; he is my good friend, and I fear not to be with him."

"But I'd rather not withdraw. He may turn desperate and blow your brains out before you know where you are. Pray let me remain."

"Nay, nay; I have nothing to fear, and would rather be alone."

"Oh, if that's the case, I'll go; but, nevertheless, I think it's a dreadful thing—and, if he should turn desperate——"

"Begone!" shouted Jack, getting angered at this pertinacity of the confectioner, "begone, or I shall indeed grow desperate."

"There, I knew he would; let me call the watch. Look at the fire in his eye. I'll alarm the house."

"Pray, pray, withdraw, and rest satisfied that no harm will befall me. This is a matter of vital importance to more than one beneath your roof; so I pray you leave me."

"Very well," said Peter; "I'll sit on the stairs until you call me, but I'll leave you the pistol in case of danger."

The confectioner deposited his harmless old pistol on the table, and slowly withdrew from the room.

As soon as the door was closed, Mrs. Malvers resumed,—

"Is this the box from the old inn?" she asked.

"Yes," said Jack, "and it has only been obtained by violence and bloodshed."

"Heaven forbid!"

"It is too late to pray Heaven now. They would oppose me, and I could not afford to lose my prize."

"And the will?"

"I have not yet opened the box."

"Let us, then, do so. The will! Oh, how I tremble lest it should not be there!"

"I will soon see," said Jack, drawing a large clasp-knife and wrenching off the hinges. "Now for it."

The cover flew off, and a heap of papers lay before the gaze of the two persons.

"Quick!" said Mrs. Malvers; "search for it."

Hurriedly all the papers were drawn from the box; one by one they were turned over and examined, and at last the box was empty.

There was no will!

"It is not here!" said Mrs. Malvers, hoarsely.

"Then you have been deceived."

"Yes; but why should Austin have deceived me? What reason could a dying man have for such conduct?"

"I cannot think. But one thing is patent—there is no will."

"It must have been purloined."

"How? By whom?"

"Oh! I know not; but the box *must* have been tampered with, for certain am I that when Austin last saw it the will was there."

"It is possible," said Jack, taking up the box and examining it.

"Yes," he said, "this box has been tampered with. The lock has been forced; but when or how, I cannot say."

As he sat down the box, something in it rattled at the bottom.

Jack put in his hand, and drew out a small signet-ring.

As Mrs. Malvers looked upon it, she uttered an exclamation of surprise, and started back.

"Do you know the ring?" asked Jack.

"Yes," she said, "too well. It belongs to my ill-starred husband!"

"Your husband!"

"Yes; I can swear to the ring."

"Then it is your husband who has stolen the will."

"In all probability. He is evil enough for that, or worse."

"You say truly. He is, indeed, evil enough for anything. Oh, that I had had a suspicion of his handiwork to-night, and when I had him alone in that passage, I would have torn the will from him, though it had been secreted in his heart."

"How? Have you seen Malvers to-night?"

"Yes."

"And where?"

"In a house in Lombard-street. He placed this bag in my hand, mistaking me for another, and bade me stop some one on the heath to-morrow night, who had a deed of which I must possess myself."

"Explain."

Jack briefly related the whole of his adventure in Lombard-street.

"It is very strange," said Mrs. Malvers; "very strange. But open the bag; its contents may throw some light upon this mystery."

Jack here tore open the bag given him by Malvers, and from it took a packet of money and the following letter:—

"44, Lombard-street.

"DEAR MALVERS,—I herewith leave for you the promised sum of one hundred guineas, in part payment of the debt I owe you. The will is incontestably that of the old merchant, and it reverses the one bequeathing the whole of his estates to our Charity. You left it with me as security for certain moneys lent and certain assistance rendered, but at the time I little thought it would ever be of the value it has since proved. I grieve that you have met with and taken into your confidence those fellows who possess the will bequeathing the property to the Asylum, for I cannot trust them. Give them the enclosed money, or any part of it, and make the best bargain you can in order to obtain the will, which we must have at once. It is useless to them, now that fool Grantley has told the board all about it; so they had best give it up without bother, or as sure as fate the board will have all the thief-takers in London after them, and their doom is inevitable.

"I am, yours truly,
"MORGAN SKINWELL."

"What can this mean?" said Mrs. Malvers, as Jack finished reading the letter.

"It means that there is some diabolical plot afoot," said Jack, "and that we have the clue to it."

"Yes, but I cannot unravel the tangled skein."

"But I can. This letter, and the message, supposed to be given to Turpin, is but a bait to tempt him to the heath to-morrow night, in order that he may fall into some trap laid for him. This Skinwell appears to have something to do with the Asylum?"

"Mr. Grantley told me he was the secretary."

"Well, he is a villain, and is in league with your husband.

For what purpose I know not, unless that it be to defraud the Grantleys. Turpin has the first will, and they wish to force it from him; he is, therefore, to go to the heath to-morrow night. I have, at least, counteracted that part of the plot."

"How?"

"I imitated the voice of your husband, and misled him."

"To what purpose?"

"I scarcely know, for my plans are not matured. It is enough for the present that I know the will is in existence, and that I have a clue to the one who holds it. The rest must be left to time and circumstances."

CHAPTER XXIV.

THE MEETING BETWEEN SKINWELL AND MALVERS—EXPLANATIONS AND PLANS.

WHEN the unhappy Austin secreted his box in the chimney of the attic of the Red Rose, he little thought that the eyes of his quasi-friend Malvers were upon him, and that his cupidity led him to determine on searching the secret receptacle on the earliest opportunity.

Soon after Austin was made prisoner, Malvers found an opportunity of returning to the Red Rose and secreting himself in the old attic, for the purpose of prosecuting his search.

Knowing better than did Jack the exact locality of the box, he removed a few of the bricks of the fire-place, and, without trouble, found that which he sought.

Forcing the lock with the skill of a finished burglar, he tumbled over the contents of the box.

The major portion were old and useless deeds; there were a few rings and other articles of jewellery, a little money, and the will of the eccentric uncle of Grantley.

This he at first threw back into the box, merely withdrawing the valuables which most struck his fancy.

Whilst examining these, or in all probability whilst placing on his fingers the rings he had found, the little signet he wore became disengaged from his finger and fell among the papers unnoticed.

Cursing himself for wasting so much good time to so little purpose, he was about to reclose the box and place it back in its hiding-place, when his eye fell again upon the will.

"I may as well have it," he said, "it may one day be useful."

He then withdrew it, replaced the rifled box, and left the attic.

Some time passed, and Malvers hung about the dens and haunts of thieves, awaiting the execution of his wife and making preparations for flight.

Day by day he became more and more addicted to drink, and at last he fell into the habits of a confirmed sot, and nothing could draw him from the gin-shops of the most disreputable parts of London.

At length he became known as Blind-drunk Hackett—the name he had assumed—and he was looked upon as fast sinking into a grave, or at least becoming a fit subject for the madhouse.

The escape of his wife and its accompanying incidents did not tend to make him any better, and he was at the verge of death from illness and starvation when the wonderful story of young Grantley, and the manner in which he resigned his great fortune, reached his ears.

As Grantley had disguised nothing, it soon became patent that the will of the merchant was in the possession of either Tom King or Dick Turpin.

Gradually the soddened brain of Malvers became conscious of these facts, and he remembered the will he had snatched from young Austin's box.

At first he thought he would bargain with Grantley, but hearing some accounts of certain dishonourable acts of Skinwell, the secretary of the Asylum, he thought he could do better with him, and so determined to put his case plausibly before him.

Before he had an opportunity of doing this, however, chance

threw him into the company of Turpin, at one of the houses frequented by thieves.

"Well, Mr. Turpin," said the drunkard, "the world says you've been stealing wills."

"Well, then, the world lies," said Turpin, "and you have no right to repeat the world's scandal to the face of the scandalised man, and if you were not drunk, I'd give you a lesson in holding your tongue."

"You're very good; but you needn't be so precious proud over nothing; you know you have the will, and I know it; but then I know you havn't *the* will, and so what matters it?"

"What do you mean?"

"Why I mean that there was another will, made after that which gave the orphans the heap of money—the will bequeathing all to young Grantley."

"There's no such document," said Turpin.

"Oh, isn't there, though? I thought there was," said Malvers, with a drunken leer. "I really thought there was, and that *I* had it in my possession."

"You?"

"Yes, my friend; do you see anything extraordinary in that?"

"Much."

"Indeed! Well then, I don't."

"But touching this will; you said"—

"I said nothing at all, so don't ask any questions. Get away; but don't pride yourself on holding a trump card in that bit o' waste-paper: for waste-paper it is, take my word for it."

Turpin tried to draw the drunkard into further conversation on this theme. He gave him more drink and tempted him by every art of which he could think; but it was all in vain—Malvers was dumb; nevertheless he had said enough to induce Turpin to follow him night and day, and endeavour to drag more out of him.

But it was a failure; Malvers could not be induced to say another word on the subject.

One night, having well primed himself with brandy, Malvers staggered from the Minories and made for the house of Skinwell, in Lombard-street.

It was late, and the clerks had all gone away.

The one servant was out on an errand, and Skinwell was alone.

Consequently, when Malvers knocked at his door, he had to open it himself.

"Can I see Mr. Skinwell?" said Hackett.

"I am Mr. Skinwell. What do you require?"

"Oh, you're Skinwell," said the sot; "well, I require a few minutes' conversation with you."

"This is no time, nor are you in a fit condition to converse; I am to be found here any morning if you have any business with me."

"I just have business with you, and I sha'nt come here in the morning."

"Get away, fellow, or I'll thrust you into the street and call the watch."

"Call the watch, for all I care. They won't hurt me half so much as they will you. Now do it."

"What is it you require?" demanded the secretary.

"That's more like business," said Malvers, "much more, only you might as well ask me inside."

"Tell me your business."

"Well, I've called concerning that will affair, in which young Grantley's mixed up."

"Ah, what have you to say about it?"

"Am I to come inside or not?"

"Certainly; this way."

Malvers staggered into the house, and the door was closed.

In a moment he was seated in a luxurious chair in Skinwell's office.

"Now, may I ask you to relate what brought you here? Have you any clue to the will?"

"*Which* will?"

"*The* will; there is but one. Are you making a fool of me?"

"No, my fine friend; but it strikes me you're making a fool of yourself. You say there is but one will"—

"Yes."

"Well, I say there's two."

"Two. Impossible!"

"Not a bit of it. One will, the *first*, is a document in the possession of two highway robbers, bequeathing all the money Grantley's uncle died possessed of to your institution. The *second* will, in my possession, revokes all former wills, and bequeaths all the money to Grantley himself. What d'ye say to that?"

"I can scarcely believe my senses."

"I should say you couldn't. Now what d'ye propose doing?"

"Propose doing!"

"Yes, propose doing. I want to know, in as few words as possible, whether I am to sell the will to you or to Grantley?"

"Let me think."

"It can't want much thinking of."

"It does; one moment."

A whirlwind of thought flew through Skinwell's brain.

Since the first hint of the old merchant's property and gigantic business being left to the Asylum was uttered, the mind of this silly man had been at work to devise some plan for getting the whole affair into his own hands.

He saw that if he could but oust young Grantley, he could make money in heaps out of the bequest, and to do this his fertile brain was at work night and day.

He had gone into matters with Grantley; he saw how, if he had but the reins of management he could pull them so as to jerk money into his pocket at every turn, and he mentally determined that at the first opportunity Grantley should be dismissed from his post, and thus secure to himself the coveted position.

His plans for this had become matured, and he was glorying in the dismissal of the young man who had acted so well, when Malvers entered his house and astounded him with the information of a second will.

For some moments Skinwell sat as one in a dream.

Should this second will really exist, all his plans would be destroyed, and his castles in the air fall to the ground, a heap of ruins.

If he could secure the will, it would be worth his while to do so. He looked to the handling of the merchant's property, and the business he had bequeathed to the Asylum, to furnish him with a splendid income, and he asked himself whether he should sacrifice all in a moment, or whether he should treat with the man who was capable of securing to him the prize he so coveted.

He looked at Malvers, who, raising his eyes, asked—

"Have you made up your mind?"

"I do not know," said Skinwell; "I do not know what to say to you. I am dumbfounded."

"More fool you. Is it worth your while to possess this will?"

"It may be. What do you want for it?"

"Ten thousand pounds."

"Then we need converse no further. I have no such sum."

We will not trace this conversation further. We will not give the details of the protracted interview, but will simply state that after hours of warm talk on both sides, the wily Skinwell succeeded in inducing his drunken companion to join him in his plans against the Grantleys, and, by destroying the will, to secure to themselves the management of the estate in the interests of the Charity.

After a deal of persuasion Malvers agreed to this. "For," said he, "ten thousand pounds would, perhaps, soon go, and I should be none the better off when it was gone; but if I join in the plans you propose, I shall secure a living of some kind or the other for life. So it's a bargain."

"And you will destroy the will?"

"Not if I know it. The will gone for ever, I should have no security for your acting honourably by me. But as long as I hold it you must come down handsomely; and so the matter's settled."

" Not yet," said Skinwell. " What proof have I that you really hold any will at all ? "

" What proof? D'ye think I should be fool enough to say I held it if I didn't ? "

" I don't know anything about that; but I shall treat no further with you until I have seen the document. I have been a fool to go so far."

" Have you? Well, then, you shall see the will."

" Produce it."

" Produce it! Why, you don't think I've brought it here with me; do you ? "

" Why not ? "

". Why not! What! Take the lamb into the wolf's den? Oh no, that's not the way I was taught to do business."

" Then if not here, where is it ? "

" Don't you trouble yourself in the least about *where* it is. Let it be sufficient for you that *I* know where it is, and that I can put my hand upon it whenever I want it."

" I will see it before I treat with you any further."

" Very well, then; meet me at the ' Red Rose ' in the Minories, to-morrow night, or rather to-night, for it's morning now, and I'll show you the will. That will do, won't it ? "

" Yes."

" Then you'll come ? "

" I will."

" That's right. It's a splendid place. Lots of fun—fine singing and dancing—the Bouncing Bodger in the chair."

" So I should imagine."

" So you would imagine ! No, you wouldn't imagine anything like it, unless you have been to the ' Blind Weasel;' that's the only house of entertainment that can be compared with it. They're both without a rival."

It boots not to tell how these men separated, and how they met again and again, until they became fast friends.

This may be readily imagined by the reader.

The arrangement between the villains was soon made, to their entire satisfaction; but there was one who watched them narrowly, who looked on with anything but pleasure at the bond of friendship he saw thus securely cemented. And that was Dick Turpin.

The highwayman saw that his chances of making further use of the will were growing remarkably small; and it may, therefore, be supposed that he looked at Malvers with anything but the eye of friendship.

And Malvers, on his part, certainly had no affection for the robber; in fact, he feared him.

He had, in his drunken moments, revealed to Turpin the fact of his possessing the second will; and he lived in dread lest the highwayman should attempt by force to gain possession of the document.

Turpin set on his friend King to try and tempt the drunkard into parting with his treasure, but it was useless.

Malvers was firm; he had secreted his document, and it was useless to search for it.

Times out of number the drunkard's pockets had been ransacked. His steps had been dogged at night; his sleeping chamber and his haunts searched by those well calculated to discover a secret panel or trap wherein the document could be found; but all in vain. There was no trace of it !

So troublesome did the two highwaymen become, that Malvers one evening stole to the house of Skinwell, and told him that his life was not safe.

" Something must at once be done, for I dread violence."

" I do not see what I can do," said Skinwell. " These men are bold and courageous. It is useless to war openly with them, for no good can come of it."

" No, no; we must do nothing openly. But does there not occur to you some plan of disposing of them ? "

" I can think of none."

" Some trap must be laid for them. It is well known that they possess the will bequeathing the Grantley property to the Asylum."

" Yes; it is a fact known to the whole of England."

" Well, you are the man who must, perforce, get rid of them. It all rests with you."

" I do not see that."

" But I do. The trustees of the charity require the will. They are anxious to possess it, and would pay handsomely for it, not being aware of the existence of the later deed. What, then, so easy as for you to talk them into expending a few hundreds on Harding, the Jew thief-taker, for the purpose of bringing them to justice? What matter is it to you whether they get the will or not, as long as we secure them in Newgate, and by that route send them to the gallows ? "

" True."

" Well, is your intellect any brighter now ? "

" I think I see my way clearer; but still there are many difficulties to sweep away."

" Oh, if I were only the man I was ! If my brain did not fail me ! If I could but think as I used to be able, I would clear away the difficulties as though they were so many spiders' webs. But I cannot do it now, and am obliged to come to you. But now that I am forced to trust to you don't let me be deceived—don't fail me. Pray brighten up, and rid me of those dogs, who are ready to spring upon me and tear me to pieces."

" I am thinking how it can be done. Do you think you could bring them to me ? "

" To what purpose ? "

" No matter. Could you bring them here ? "

" Doubtless."

" Then I *can* see my way clear. I will find pretences for employing them, and by a skilful series of manœuvres, with which I will not trouble you, I will induce them to think that I hold the will, and that I am not so careful over it but that by a bold stroke they might gain possession of it. Leading them by this string, I will draw them into the clutches of Harding, and then "——

" And then let them look to themselves. It's not often that escapes from the cells of Newgate are effected."

" You are right."

Thus it was settled that Skinwell should attempt to dispose of the two highwaymen.

Without a suspicion, Turpin and King walked into the trap laid open for them, and in a few days they became the favoured guests of Skinwell, whom they soon dubbed a real jolly good fellow.

The cunning man of business so completely blinded these people by his affectation of confidence and continual display of simplicity of character, that the highwaymen began to congratulate themselves on being in a fair way to gain possession of the will, which they supposed their new friend to possess.

Time passed, and at length came the night of Jack's adventure in the attic of the old inn in the Minories. For that night the following plan had been laid :—

It was arranged that Skinwell should be absent from his house, but that Malvers should be there to meet Turpin, and lead him to the heath on the night following.

Malvers informed Turpin that he should have some money left out by Skinwell, in part payment of the debt he owed him for the will. On hearing this, Turpin, always greedy for money, pricked up his ears, and asked Malvers if he felt inclined to purchase the first will; to which, of course, Malvers replied that he did, well knowing at the same time that Turpin had no intention of sparing that document.

Turpin then arranged that if Malvers would give him one hundred guineas that night, he would at some distant time hand the will to him.

He must have taken Malvers to be a complete fool to suppose him capable of being gulled in this manner, and it suited Malvers to let him entertain that opinion.

The plan of action to be observed by Malvers was, as it were, to incautiously let drop hints to the highwaymen that Skinwell had gone across Hampstead-heath to visit the chairman of the board of guardians of the charity, who was to return to London on the following night, bringing with him certain sums of money to be deposited next day in the interests of the charity.

What actually took place is before the reader.

The mistaking of Jack for Turpin in the dark passage, the handing him the bag and money, and Jack's interview with Turpin, are incidents which were given in the preceding chapter.

To describe what followed will require a new chapter.

CHAPTER XXV.

JACK DETERMINES TO ASCERTAIN WHO IS TO CROSS THE HEATH—THE AMBUSH—BIRDS IN A TRAP—THE POST-CARRIAGE—THE ATTACK, AND THE DEATH OF THE POSTILION.

JACK RANN could not rest after his interview with Mrs. Malvers. His brain whirled with excitement, and although he sought his couch as the day dawned, after a night passed in labour of no light nature, sleep visited not his eyes.

He rose after a few hours of restless tossing and mental agony, and proceeded to prepare for another night of toil and excitement.

His first care was to visit his mare, and see that she was all right.

Finding this to be the case, he turned his attention to his weapons, and put them into perfect order.

Having completed all his arrangements, he anxiously awaited the coming of night; and as he paced his little chamber, in one of the dens in Knaves'-acre, he thought the day would never terminate.

Long and anxiously he watched the falling shadows, but it appeared to him that they gathered slower than usual.

He thought he never remembered so clear an evening and so long-lingering a sunset, although in reality the air was murky and the mantle of night fell over the great city rather prematurely.

But to the anxious watcher time lags, and the hours seem to crawl.

Jack found it so.

But at last the long-prayed-for time arrived, and the distant clocks warned him that he should now to horse.

The pistols were finally examined, the last touch put to his costume, the gay bunch of sixteen ribbons were fastened to the long boots, and the knight of the road was prepared for his nocturnal work.

"Would that I could have slept," he said. "Oh, would that this dreary, dreary sensation would vanish, for I am in no humour for this night's work."

He stole to the stable, and there found his mare awaiting him.

A rough-looking man in the garb of an ostler held her head. Jack carefully placed his pistols in the holsters, and then enveloped himself in a large cloak.

"It's a fine night, Master Jack," said the man, "a fine night, sir; and the heath will be as light and as cheerful as if daylight instead of moonlight was a shining."

"You're right, Tom—you're right."

"Good luck to ye, Master Rann."

"Good night," said Jack, tossing the man a coin, and riding away.

Jack rode slowly away on the Hampstead road, and in half an hour gained the open country. Before him was the heath, then as lonely and desolate a spot as one would care to traverse.

It was a favourite haunt with Jack, and the very sight of it went far towards raising his spirits and dispelling the gloom that had been so long gathering upon him.

It was a splendid night; the moon rode high in the heavens, and, as the ostler expressed it, "the heath was as light and as cheerful as if the daylight instead of moonlight was a-shining."

Far away over the barren waste stretched the furze and purple heather.

All was still and calm; but the night air was sharp and frosty, and made the blood tingle through the veins.

Jack's steed was full of fire and pranced about proudly.

Had the highwayman but known that behind a certain clump of bushes lay concealed the thief-taker Harding and two of his assistants, the possibility would have been that he would have experienced a still further depression rather than a rise of spirits.

No sooner had Jack appeared on the heath than the hawk's eye of the Jew fell upon him.

He, however, imagined him to be Turpin, whose arrest he was there to effect.

"Ah!" screamed the Jew, cocking his pistols, and then rubbing his long, bony fingers until the knuckles cracked again; "ah, my friend Dick, vot a flat you must be to come here upon such a vild-goose chase! Ha—ha! The longer you live the bigger fool you get. To think that such a clever dog as you vos some two year ago should be done like this! It makes me laugh. There never vos anything so funny. I do declare it's peautiful—peautiful!"

"Hold your row," muttered one of the assistants, "hold your row, can't yer? Dick's a shy bird, and if he hears your croaking he'll be off. Once give him a chance of putting Black Bess into motion, and our chance is gone."

"Yes," said the other. "he'd trample us under foot, and then be off like a flash of lightning and leave no trace of his flight. But Harding will make a fool of himself; it's no manner o' use to attempt to stop him."

"Not a bit—not a leetle bit. I like my joke, I do, and I can't and von't keep it down. But don't be afraid—Dick Turpin von't hear me."

That was very possible, seeing that Dick Turpin had not yet appeared on the heath.

"Won't hear you!" remarked one of the assistants, "won't hear you! Why you'd be heard a mile off, with that ugly voice of yours. It's worse than that of any aged raven I ever came across."

"Is it? Vell, yours ain't so peautiful."

"It's christian-like, at all events."

"Yes, and that's the bitterest thing you could say about it," said the Jew.

"Oh, hold your jaw," said the assistant thief-taker; "it's not worth saying a word about."

"All right, ma tear," said the Jew, in a conciliatory tone, "all right. Ve von't quarrel about it—not ve. My tear life! How cold it is in this place! The dew has soaked through my cloak, and I'm dripping vet. Oh, if it should freeze, I shall be bound down to the ground, and have to vait until it thaws again."

"A good job, too," said the assistant.

"Oh, vould it be a good job? Vot vould you do, I shou'd like to know, if I vos frozed to death?"

"I should get on pretty well, for I s'pose the Newgate people would put me into your berth."

"And a nice mess you'd make of it. Vy, you've no more caution than a mad bull. It's not the lion, but the fox, that makes the best thief-taker. You're in your right place, so don't go for to make any mistakes."

"Well, you've no small opinion of yourself. The 'nonsuch' I should think you called yourself."

"And a very good name, too. Yah! The 'non-such'—th't's a peautiful name, ma tear."

In conversation like the foregoing, with an occasional snarl and a little conciliatory wiping off of the roughness produced thereby, the three thief-takers passed the time, keeping through all a sharp eye upon Jack, who continued moving to and fro on the heath, but never coming sufficiently near the Jew and his myrmidons to occasion recognition.

An hour was in this manner expended, and then the faint sounds of the distant clocks borne on the breeze reached the ears of the watchers, and told them that the hour of action was come.

Jack, as he heard the sounds, leaned forward in his saddle, and listened for the sound of approaching wheels.

The Jew's sharp eyes marked the action, and he said,—

"Ah! Listen, my poy! You'll hear fast enough. But ve must contrive to get nearer to you."

There was no occasion for a movement, for Jack set his steed in motion, and cantered lightly over the heath to the very spot where the Jew and his friends lay concealed.

Seeing him approach, the three men threw themselves on their faces, thus failing to discover who was the real hero of the night.

There was a pause of a few moments, and then Jack's quick ear caught a sound as of the distant rumble of a carriage.

"Now," he said, "now for the revelation of this mystery. I dread some evil, but I am determined to prosecute this search to the utmost. Yes—Grantley shall be saved from the ruin into which he has fallen."

He threw off his great cloak, and freed himself for action.

Once more he looked at his pistols, and then, finding all was right, he stooped over the neck of his steed, and said,—

"Now for it, pet—now for it. Steady and true."

The gallant animal seemed to thoroughly appreciate the importance of the situation, and with one nod of her graceful head, as if to express her comprehension of what was expected from her, she stood as still as a statue by the road side.

Another minute, and a great rumbling post-chaise, drawn by two horses, under the guidance of a fashionably-accoutred postilion, drew near the spot.

Like a dart from a bow, the mare sprang to the side of the carriage, allowing Jack the opportunity of hitting the postilion a blow on the head with the butt-end of his pistol.

The man did not fall from the saddle, but the blow was of sufficient force to make him stagger—to completely daze his vision.

Jack in a moment drew the rein of the horses, and then rode up to the side of the carriage, and, pistol in hand, shouted to its occupant to deliver his money and papers.

The traveller was Skinwell, and, as a matter of course, anticipating the attack, he received the highwayman with a loaded blunderbuss.

"Who and what are you?" demanded Jack.

"And who and what are you?" cried Skinwell, seeing that his antagonist was not Turpin.

"I'm Jack Rann, or Sixteen-String Jack, if you prefer that title; and I'm a knight of the road—or, in other words, a highwayman."

"Then, Mr. Jack Rann," cried Skinwell, "I've nothing for you, except the ball in this blunderbuss; but, as I don't want to harm you, I'd advise you to ride off at once."

"Not until I am satisfied that you have not about you that which I seek."

"What do you seek?"

"I'll tell you. It's the will—the second will—made by the man who, in his first, left all his property to the Orphan Asylum, of which you are the secretary."

"Indeed! If that's the case, we are enemies—so take this."

Skinwell fired, but Jack, with the greatest dexterity, avoided the muzzle of the weapon, and the ball flew into the air.

At the same moment Jack dashed the butt-end of his pistol into the face of the secretary, and laid him prostrate at the bottom of the carriage.

"Now for a search," cried Jack.

But at that instant he received a blow on the back of the head that knocked him out of his saddle, and completely stunned him.

In an instant the bridle of his mare was grasped by one of the Jew's assistants; but she plunged violently, and could not be held down.

Unfortunately for the postilion, he at that moment dropped out of the saddle from faintness, and fell to the earth.

He was no sooner prostrate on the ground than the highwayman's mare broke from the thief-taker's grasp.

She gave a terrific bound in the air, and, horrible to tell, her hind hoofs struck the head of the prostrate man, and in a few seconds his career was ended.

The mare stumbled over his body, and rolled heavily to the earth.

This gave the thief-taker another opportunity of securing her. She at once found that she was mastered, and ceased to start and plunge.

"Goodness gracious!" screamed the Jew, looking at Jack, "my eyes! this ain't Turpin at all."

"Who is it, then?"

"Vhy, Sixteen-String Jack! Hurrah! It's a bad night's vork in von respect; but good enough in another. Ve shall get the revard, and still stand a chance of nabbing Dick Turpin."

"What's to be done?"

"Bundle him into the carriage vith Mr. Skinwell and put the darbies on him vhile he's insensible. You, Bill Manks, jump on the horse, and ride to the old stable, a mile on the Hampstead side of the heath. Chuck him in; and here, take the reins of the mare and carry her off along with yer."

"Why not go at once to London?" asked Bill Manks.

"To London!" said the Jew. "There, I know you'd make a good thief-taker, you vould. Vhy, you donkey, isn't Dick Turpin on the London road by this time, and vouldn't he knock out yer brains and rescue Jack in the twinkling of an eye? No London to-night. The stable vill do very vell for the occasion; so off vith yer. There ain't a moment to loose."

The corpse of the postilion was thrust in with the wounded men, and the door slammed to.

Bill Manks obeyed his orders with the greatest alacrity, and the carriage was soon rolling back again in the direction in which it had come.

CHAPTER XXVI.

THE JEW IN ECSTACIES—AN HOUR LATE—DICK TURPIN A PRISONER—A TRAMP ACROSS THE HEATH—THE STABLE.

"OH, this is the best night's vork ve ever made," cried the Jew, dancing with glee. "Jack a prisoner, and Dick coming into the toils. The government revards and the heavy price paid by Skinwell for the capture of Turpin, vill make a heap of money."

"Yes, but you're not likely to make a heap of money if you stand capering there, instead of lurking behind yon furze-bushes!"

"Ah, that's true. Ve mustn't frighten avay the birds; let 'em come into the trap—let 'em come into the trap."

"Yes, governor; it's all very well to say let 'em come; but Dick's an old soldier, and the chances are that he won't come. Besides, one mounted man's worth more than two on foot; so what d'ye think of doing?"

"Think of doing! Ah! that must be settled speedily. Vot's to be done—vot's to be done?"

"It's no use to spring out on him, and risk a hand-to-hand encounter. If we do, he'll get the best of it."

"That's so."

"Well, the only thing to be done is to shoot him down."

"But suppose ve kill him?"

"Well, it's only a brutal highwayman the less, and we sha'n't have much on our consciences."

"Just so; it vosn't the conscience I vos thinking about, but the loss of money. If ve kill him, ve only gets half the revard ve'd have if ve get him alive."

"That's so."

"Vell, vot's to be done under the painful circumstances? You vouldn't like to try to haul him down."

"Not with half a regiment at my back; for as safe as eggs are eggs, I should be under the heels of that infernal mare of his at the very first attempt."

"Oh, that mare's an awful thing; she's got quite as much sense as a human being, and knows a thief-taker as vell as her nosebag."

"Just so, my friend; and she isn't going to try the strength of her heels on my body this journey."

"Vell, I s'pose there's nothink for it but to shoot him down; but it's a pity—it's a pity. He'd be quite an ornament to the gibbet."

"So he would. But there's no help for it; Dick Turpin won't be taken alive."

"Vell then, he must be taken dead; only I think ve could

knock him off vithout quite killing him. You're a good shot ? "

" Tolerably good."

" Vell, you'll fire at some part that's not vital ; you von't hurt him more than you can help ? "

" I shall fire at his head. It'll be a kill-or-miss game with me, for I know Turpin too well to go in for half-measures with him."

" Oh my ! vot a dreadful brute you are, to be sure ! I never did see such a blood-spiller in all my life ; it's awful to think of—it is, it is ; quite awful ! "

" Bah ! " was the remark of the assistant ; "a little blood-letting does no harm, and it's only the faint-hearted as would shrink from it."

" Vell, I'm not faint-hearted, but I don't like blood. It's an awful thing, and vhen I've seen it, I think of it at night-time. It haunts my dreams and makes me uncomfortable ; that's vot it does. No, no ; save me from blood ; it's a bad thing, a bad thing."

" But I'd like to know what we'd do if we shrunk from it."

" Ve'd do pretty vell. It's only just this, after all—miss once and catch the second time."

" Nothing of the kind ; once bit, twice shy. Your burnt child seldom likes to play with the fire."

" Ah, and your killed child never has the chance. D'ye see that ? "

" Very good logic ; but it won't pay now-a-day to be over particular. For my part, I'd stop at nothing."

" Until something at last brings you up vith a round turn for ever. Vell, you stick to the bull-dog bisness, and I'll try my own fox-like movements."

" With all my heart."

Half an hour of anxious waiting at last terminated in the appearance of a horseman on the heath, coming from the London road.

" At last," said the Jew.

" At last," muttered the assistant ; " now to be sure about this flint."

" Don't kill him, if you can help it."

" Silence, you old fool, and if you haven't pluck enough to fire, give me your pistol ; I'll warrant I'll make better use of it than you will."

" Take it," said Harding, " and I'm precious glad to get rid of it."

He handed his weapon to his companion, who at once proceeded to put it into proper order.

Carefully arranging the flint, he laid the weapon on the ground close to his right hand, and so arranged that he could grasp and discharge it the moment after the first was rendered useless.

*   *   *   *   *   *

" I don't know about this game to-night," said Turpin to himself, as he walked leisurely along the carriage road across the heath. " It strikes me I've made a fool of myself, after all. Why didn't I have the money promised to me ? and why should I come here to get the will from this Skinwell without the aid of Tom King ? I can't see through it. If Tom knew of Skinwell's intention of crossing to-night, and that he would bring the will with him, nothing would keep him away. However, I'll keep my eyes open, and woe be to him who tries to run me into danger."

He placed his pistols at full cock, and set Bess in motion.

The mare was fresh, and attempted to play some skittish tricks ; but Dick, unfortunately for himself, was in no humour for this, and curbed her with an austerity that at once proved to Bess his determination to stand no pranks.

So the mare hung her head and walked on with the docility of a lamb.

Had Dick allowed her to continue her antics, he would, at all events, have bothered the aim of the thief-taker, for the mare was at all points of the road at once, and the chances were many against a true aim being taken at a man's head.

As it was, the mare crept on slowly towards the fatal spot.

Chance, too, drew her to that side of the road nearest the men in ambush.

Another three minutes, and Dick was in line with the thief-taker's pistol.

The fellow took a deliberate aim at the highwayman's head, and then fired.

Dick uttered a yell of pain and fell to the earth, but not before another bullet had penetrated his right shoulder.

Instantaneously the officer was at the mare's head, and the Jew was bending over the prostrate body.

" You've killed him. It's all over vith the poor poy. Mind, I didn't fire. Don't say I did it, that's all."

" Oh, don't fear ; I don't want anyone to share in the glory of the act."

" Glory ! Much glory there is about it. Poor Dick, poor Dick ! The world's vell rid of a nuisance."

Harding raised the head of the fallen man, and proceeded to search for the bullet wound.

He pulled off the hat, and saw that the ball had not penetrated to the brain ; but striking the strong-made hat on the side of the left temple, had run in a slanting direction across the head to about an inch behind the ear, and at that point had pierced the hat and made its exit.

The second bullet lodged deep in the shoulder.

" Well, what d'ye make of it ? " asked the Jew's assistant.

" I make of it that he is not going to die this time."

" Humph ! I'm sorry for it."

" And I'm precious glad, for I shall have the full revard, and the satisfaction of knowing that the blood of Turpin is not in any particular on my hands."

" I s'pose you'll say that when you see him dangling with a rope about his neck in front of Newgate ? "

" Yes," replied the Jew, " I shall. It'll be the law that vill have the responsibility of killing him then. It's nothing to do vith me."

" Well, no matter ; dead or alive, he's our prisoner at last, and now put him on the back of the mare. It may be that he's taking his last ride on her."

" I doubt it. He's not the poy to be killed by a trifle, and it vouldn't surprise me if he got over this and lived to pay you out for the trick. More extraordinary things than that have happened."

" Oh yes ; pigs might fly ; but they never were seen to do so."

" Ah ! you're a hard-hearted rascal ; but come along, help the poor child on the mare."

Turpin groaned as he was lifted from the ground.

" Ah," said the Jew, " you'll groan more before ve get to the stable."

They held the wounded man on the back of his faithful mare, and set off in the direction the carriage had taken.

As the Jew had predicted, Turpin groaned in the most distressing manner during his journey.

The wound in his head gave him excruciating pain, and his shoulder became stiffened and increased his agony.

The very torture he underwent served to bring him to his senses, for in a few minutes he opened his eyes and looked up at his captors.

" Well, Dick," said the Jew, " how d'ye feel ? "

" Oh, don't torture me more than you have done ; I'm in an agony of pain."

A cold perspiration broke out on the poor fellow's brow, and he fairly shrieked with the pain he was undergoing.

They shifted his position, and tried to make him ride easier, but nothing could soothe the torture he was undergoing, and in a few minutes his brain reeled under it, and he became delirious.

" Poor poy, poor poy ! " said the Jew. " Ah, he'll escape the hangman now, or I'm much mistaken."

" Your money or your life ! " cried Dick. " Stand and deliver ! Dick Turpin never took ' no ' for an answer. Steady, Bess ; now then, your purse—no, no, I don't care about that, after all. It's the will I want. Now, Skinwell, hand it over, or it'll be the worse for you."

" He thinks he's stopping Skinwell's carriage," said the Jew.

" More fool he," was the remark of his companion.

JACK SETTLES ACCOUNTS WITH TOM KING IN THE CHURCHYARD.

"Out with it!" cried Turpin, struggling to an extent that made it necessary for the Jew to get on the back of the mare and hold him on. "Out with it; I'll take no excuse; you thought to do me, but now I'll do you. Ha! ha! you'd make a fine thing out of it, wouldn't you, and swindle Dick Turpin? But you can't, you can't. I'll crush the very life out of you, I will, I will."

"You'll crush the life out of *me*," said the Jew, struggling with his prisoner. "My tear life! but this is an awful position —an awful position. Vot shall I do?"

"Hold on," was the answer of the assistant.

"It's very good to say hold on; but just you try and do it."

"I'd rather not. This suits me best."

"Oh!" said the Jew, as Turpin sank back into his arms, exhausted from his struggles and loss of blood; "ah! thank goodness, he's quiet at last."

"Yes, quiet at last. Perhaps quiet for ever."

"And perhaps not. Men vith constitutions like his don't die of trifles."

"Two 'pistol-bullets, one in the head and the other in the shoulder, can't well be called trifles."

"Not in the general vay, but there's no knowing vot some people can endure."

"You're right; but I hope Turpin will die. I don't want see him live, even for an hour."

"Ah, you brute! But here ve are at the stable."

They had crossed the heath, and taken a road to the right. A ride through a long, green lane brought them to a little valley of meadows. In one of these stood an old stable, with a thatched roof. It had been long built, and formerly belouged to a farm that had stood in the neighbourhood, but which had long since gone to decay.

It was a substantial place, and, saving its thatched roof, was quite capable of standing a great deal more wear and tear.

Outside this building stood Bill, holding Jack's mare, and Mr. Skinwell, seated on an old log, and holding his head with both his hands.

He started up when he saw who had arrived.

"Hillo!" shouted he; "what's this?"

"By Jove!" cried Bill; "they've nabbed Turpin."

"Yes," said the Jew, springing off his horse, and assisting the insensible highwayman to the ground, "ve have caught Dick Turpin."

CHAPTER XXVII.

THE INTERVIEW IN THE STABLE—THE DEPARTURE OF SKINWELL FOR LONDON—THE JEW AND JACK'S MARE— THE ESCAPE THROUGH THE ROOF AND FLIGHT TO LONDON.

"So," said Jack, as Dick Turpin was thrust in at the stable-door, and fell prostrate at his feet; "so they have you, too, have they, Dick? Well, they're in luck's way to-night. Poor fellow," he continued, stooping and raising the head of his quasi-friend, "you have been roughly handled. My crack on the skull has been nothing compared with yours."

He proceeded to loosen the scarf about Dick's throat and then went to a corner of the stable where the rain had formed a little pool.

No 8.

Scooping up some water in the hollow of his hands, he dashed it into the face of the insensible man, and repeated this again and again, until there was some sign of returning animation.

"Rouse ye, rouse ye, Dick," cried Jack. "What's the matter, old boy?"

"Who's that?"

"Don't you know me? It's Sixteen-String Jack."

"Ah! where am I?"

"Under old Harding's lock and key, my boy; in some outlandish stable or other."

"And the mare?"

"I've seen nothing of her."

"I hope they'll take care of Bess."

"I hope so too. How did you manage to be taken?"

"My brain is so confused that I can scarcely tell you, Jack. But I think that I was fired at from behind some furze-bushes by that fiend, old Harding."

"I thought you would have escaped them after they had got the best of me, but it seems that there was no such luck for you."

"Oh! fool that I was, to be gulled into coming to the heath! I should have thought that there was a trap set for me into which I could not help falling, but the hope of obtaining that cursed will blinded me to all danger. But I am speaking of that of which you know nothing."

"Don't be too sure of that, Dick."

"What! do you know of the second will?"

"Yes, and it was to get possession of it that I was on the heath to-night."

"What's that, Jack? I didn't think you were the sort of fellow to interfere with another's game."

"And neither am I, Dick; but you have behaved ill over this affair, and all that you have got to-night serves you right. After having passed your word to Grantley to give up possession of the will at the Jew's in Knaves'-acre, you ought to have done so, and washed your hands of the business. You had his money, and that was enough."

"Well you are a nice fellow to preach in that style, when you were actually out for the avowed purpose of getting hold of this second will, in order to make money out of it."

"No, Dick; you mistake me altogether. I was out to get possession of the will, in order that I might give it to the man from whom it had been unjustly withheld. Oh! Dick, Dick, the misery you have occasioned in that family!"

"Well, I don't care. He shouldn't have cut up so rough all at once."

"That's no excuse. You ought to have given him the will, having promised it to him, and there's no manner of excuse for you. Dick, I'm ashamed of you, and I say again, all this serves you right."

"I suppose it does, Jack—I suppose it does; but it's an awful mess to be in. I feel as if I should never be a man again,'

"You'll be right enough by to-morrow."

"I hope so; but don't talk to me any more to-night, old fellow. You've made me thoroughly ashamed of myself, and my head's twisting with pain. Could you fling a little more of that cold water over me?"

"Yes, I'll do all I can to help you, my lad."

Jack again poured water over the head of Turpin, and then wiped away the blood and bandaged up the wound.

This relieved the sufferer immensely, but the pain in his arm still continued.

On ascertaining this, Jack opened the sleeves of the coat, and, after bathing the wounded limb, placed it in a sling, and made the sufferer as comfortable as he possibly could.

"I think I could sleep," said Turpin.

"Do so, old boy," said Jack. "A nap will do you a world of good, and you'll wake up as fresh as a kid."

He placed a heap of straw under his friend's head, and then walked away from him.

He, however, returned again on the instant.

"Dick," he said.

"Well, Jack?"

"Have you been searched?"

"No."

"Look at my hands."

"It's so dark I can't see. What is it?"

"I've got the darbies on."

"Ho, ho! and you want 'em off."

"I think, if anything is to be done, I can do it better with them off than on."

"So I should say. Feel in my right pocket."

"All right," said Jack, diving his hand into Dick's capacious pocket; "here's a key. Have you strength enough to use it?"

"I'll try."

Dick raised himself slightly, and applied the key to the lock of the handcuffs.

He turned it, and at length set one of Jack's hands free.

"All right," said Jack; "I'll manage the other, old lad; do you try to sleep."

"You mean to cut, Jack?"

"Yes, if I get the chance."

"Well, good-by, and success to you. I would'nt lie here if I only had strength enough to move. Good-by, and good luck to you. When I'm in Newgate think upon me sometimes, and tell all my old friend that I didn't give in like a cur. Say you saw the two wounds they gave me, and explain that Dick Turpin didn't lay himself down and throw up his liberty until he hadn't the strength of a kitten."

"And do you think that Sixteen-String Jack is black-hearted villain enough to go to London with any such message? Do you think that he'd show his nose among friends again, after leaving Dick Turpin in the clutches of the ravens when he had a chance of carrying him off with him? No, no, Dick; that isn't the way I do things."

"You're a good fellow, but don't endanger your chance of escape to save me. It's fool-hardiness to risk your liberty in the hope of getting me off. My chances are few; yours are many. Fly if you can, and don't think of me."

"You may as well preach that logic to a stone wall as to Jack Rann. Call it what you will, Dick, I'll not be talked out of it. We both go or we both stay. So say no more about it, and try and get a little sleep; it gives strength and you may want yours soon."

"True, Jack, true. Bless you, my boy; you're a good fellow, and I respect you."

"Get some sleep, get some sleep," said, Jack, walking away.

A drowsiness soon fell upon the wounded man, and in a few minutes he was oblivious to all that was passing about him.

Jack went to the window of the stable and looked out.

It was a solid structure, was that window. Large iron bars traversed it, and on looking at it Jack muttered, "Not that way, at all events."

He then went to the door.

It was a massive piece of oak, and seemed well secured on the outside.

"Deuce take it!" cried Jack; "the place is as strong as a Newgate cell."

He again went to the window and listened.

The parties on the outside were moving.

"Now," said the Jew, "Bill will mount the post-horses, and take Mishter Skinwell to London in the carriage."

"All right," said Bill.

"And then," continued the Jew, "you'll just run round to Newgate and get a dozen officers to come vith you, so as to take these fellows safely through the streets of London."

"I'm down to the move."

"And don't be long. It's light at seven o'clock, and ve must be at Newgate before that."

"All right."

"It's perfectly understood, then?"

"Oh, yes, perfectly."

"Then jump in, Mishter Skinwell. I am glad to be able to congratulate you on having vun of the birds."

"I'm delighted at being able to congratulate myself, my friend. But don't rest until you have the other fellow. Remember, five hundred pound for him."

"I'm not at all likely to forget that."

"Well, then, I wish you good morning."

"Good morning and a pleasant ride to you."

"It won't be a very pleasant one, with this cracked head of mine. The jolting of the carriage will shake me to pieces."

"I wish," muttered Jack, "that it would do so, you old thief."

Immediately afterwards the carriage rolled away from the neighbourhood of the stable—Skinwell, snugly ensconced inside, and Bill acting as postilion, in the place of the unfortunate wretch who now lay stiffening in his gore.

"Yah!" said the Jew, turning to his companion. "I'm almost frozed to death. You havn't a drop of brandy have you?"

"Not a drain."

"Vot a pity! Vot a pity!"

"It *is* a pity; for it's a bitter morning, and lying so long on that heath ain't made us any better able to stand it."

"Not a bit—not a bit. Oh, how my teeth do chatter!"

"Walk about, then, and keep yourself warm."

"It's all very vell to say valk about and keep yourself varm, but how is it to be done? I am almost frozed to the spot."

"So am I."

"I'm precious glad of it," said Jack. "You'll be the less able to stand what I'll give you if I get out of this."

The Jew and his friend continued chattering, and Jack paced up and down the stable, seeking some mode of escape.

At length he turned his eyes to the roof. Through the spaces in the thatch he saw the beams of the waning moon.

"That's my way out," he said; "but how am I to get up there?"

The roof was all five feet above his head, and he could find no mode of reaching it. The thatch was supported by wooden beams, which ran the whole length of the stable.

"If I could but reach them, I should be all right," he said.

He walked to the end of the stable, and then carefully felt the wall. Waving his hand about within an inch or two of the stones, he at last struck it against a large nail.

"Whew!" he said, "that's the thing. If there was only another."

Seizing the nail in his left hand, he raised himself up, and felt about the wall with the right.

There was another nail, and Jack grasped it.

"Fortune's in my favour to-night," he said. "I shall get out of this, or my name's not Jack Rann."

In another moment he had seized the beams of the roof.

Grasping them with both hands, he pulled himself up until his head touched the thatch.

Finding a place for his feet on a beam that traversed the stable, some two feet from the thatch, he was enabled to tear it away with his right hand while grasping the small beam with the left. In a minute he had torn away sufficient to pass his body through.

He was now in the open air.

The voices of the Jew and his assistant now fell distinctly on his ear.

He looked down and saw that Harding was engaged in patting his own mare on the neck.

"Why doesn't she trample him under her hoofs?" thought Jack, as he looked angrily down.

"Isn't she a beauty?" asked the Jew of his man.

"Yes, she is."

"I think I shall keep her for myself.'

"Do you?"

"Yes. It's a pity she should fall into anybody's hands, and I alvays vanted a good horse; so I'll stick to her."

"Not if I know it," thought Jack.

"Oh, Jack vouldn't much like to see me patting his mare, vould he? He's so jealous of her."

"I should think he was. He thinks more of her than of himself."

"Vell, he'll have the satisfaction of knowing that she's in good hands. I'll make him a promise, before he's scragged, to take the greatest care of her."

"You're very good, but I'll save you all that troubl ," thought Jack.

While the Jew was yet patting the mare, Jack drew from his pocket the heavy handcuffs he had relieved himself of, and holding one of them in his right hand, he crawled along the thatch until he reached the edge.

Unobserved, he let himself down by the wall, and then dropped to the ground.

The Jew and his man started forward, but before they could recover from the surprise into which his sudden appearance had thrown them, they were each greeted with a terrific blow on the head from the heavy irons, which had the effect of laying both the men on the earth.

Not content with this, Jack struck them again very heavily, and then they lay without life or motion.

"That's done," said Jack; "and now for the key of that door."

He drew it from the Jew's belt, and sprang with it to the door.

In an instant it was opened and he entered.

"Dick," he cried, "Dick! Hillo, lad! where are you?"

"Hillo! what is it?"

"Here? quick as lightning. The door's open. Can you walk?"

"Such words would make a cripple walk," cried Dick, jumping to his feet. "Hurrah! Where's the Jew?"

"On his beam-ends, together with his friend. I took the liberty of knocking these irons about their heads."

"That's a brave Jack; and now to fly."

"Yes, off we go."

Dick staggered out after Jack, and in a moment the latter was off to a distant tree, to which was secured Turpin's mare.

"Come, Bess," he cried, "your master's waiting."

He loosened the rein that secured her, and ran with her to the stable.

To hoist Dick into the saddle, and place the reins in his hand, was but the work of an instant.

He then rushed to the spot where his own mare stood, and with a shout of joy sprang upon her back.

"Now," cried Dick; "which way?"

"Any way but the road to London."

"Why?"

"Because in an hour a dozen constables will cross the heath, to convey us in triumph to town."

"Much obliged to 'em, but we'll save 'em all the trouble."

Dick was now all alive. Save that he could not move the injured arm, he experienced but little inconvenience from the rough usage he had met with. His sleep had refreshed him, and he felt strong again.

"Poor old fellows!" said Jack, throwing a glance of mock sympathy to the men he had overthrown so unceremoniously; "poor old fellows! How stupid they will look when they find the birds have flown."

"I should think they would. And now for a long and strong gallop until bright day makes us come to a halt."

"I'm with you."

Next moment they were flying away from their temporary prison as fast as their splendid steeds would carry them.

CHAPTER XXVIII.

MR. GRANTLEY'S WAREHOUSES—THE NEW CLERK—SKIN-WELL'S VISIT—BAD NEWS.

A MERCHANT'S offices and warehouses in the City of London during the last century were not the towering palaces, full of architectural beauties and elegant marks of the decorator's art, we find at the present day.

Old, dingy buildings, hidden under the shadow of a little church, unknown to all but old citizens, were frequently the places where the merchant princes conducted their affairs—affairs of little less importance than those which now demand such magnificent buildings for their transaction.

Mysterious labyrinth as the City still is to those who know it not, it was, at the time of our story, a still more intricate and objectionable place to get into.

The hand of improvement had not then swept away the grim old alleys that shut out the light of day.

Courts wherein the grass grew, and which appeared to be some solemn old monastery, of which the ticket-porter at the entrance was the guardian spirit, had not yet disappeared.

The lanes and strings of "buildings" had not been brushed off to make room for the great streets with the great shops; and the wonder was, how those who trusted themselves in such a neighbourhood ever came out again.

"Maggot's-court" was the name given to the place wherein the business of Mr. Grantley was conducted.

It lay—we are afraid to attempt to say precisely where it lay—but it was somewhere in the neighbourhood of Thames-street, and was approached through a number of lanes and alleys, and lay close by a churchyard, which at that time had quite a rustic appearance, and reminded one of the time when the Salters' or Grocers' Company, or some other worshipful body, passed through it in imposing procession to worship in the church which threw its shadow over the old headstones and tombs. It was a quaint little churchyard, and we are of opinion that if our readers were to go in search of it now they would doubtless light upon it. But we still decline to make an attempt to point out its exact locality.

The best way to find it would be to enter Thames-street boldly, and having got on a distance of say half-a-mile—it doesn't matter at which end you entered—turn away from the river, wander about without any particular aim, and the probability is it will be lighted upon in a comparatively short space of time.

Having found the church, bear away to the right of its yard and then descend some steps; there be will sure to be some steps to descend. Well, having descended the steps, look about for a little, low archway, raised at the time, say, of the Tudors; it can't be missed. There! it is found, and now peep in.

It is difficult to see into the interior, but the eye first lights upon a roughly-paved courtyard, between the stones of which is quite a verdant crop of grass.

Having sufficiently admired the grass, bend low, and you will find that it grows in a little triangular yard, surrounded by buildings whose peculiarities are that they look to have been modernised to suit modern purposes, and that those purposes are the requirements of trade.

In the archway—we will drop the present tense now—was a quaint little man, dressed in rusty grey. It was a withered man, and his clothes and his face spoke of days gone by.

Over his grey suit he wore a natty white apron, and on the front of the apron was a porter's badge.

This was the guardian of Maggott's-court, and his name was Adam Lord.

Adam Lord and his wife lived somewhere in the court; it was idle to speculate where, but it was somewhere, and that was sufficient.

The clerks of the office knew where the spot was, and so did Mr. Grantley, for he frequently visited it when Adam or his wife fell sick; but the strangers and the world in general could never fathom the mystery.

Adam was porter to the firm forty years, and during the whole of that period had never been beyond Thames-street.

He boasted of this, and used to say that "that was a thing which very few men in the world could credit themselves with."

His world was Maggot's-court.

The inhabitants thereof were the clerks and mercantile men who visited the place, and the king was Mr. Grantley, than whom Adam could not be brought to believe a greater man ever breathed, without it had chanced to be his uncle, who occupied the throne at Maggott's-court before him.

When the reverse of fortune came to Mr. Grantley, some of the clerks endeavoured to make Adam comprehend it, but the attempt was futile, and they gave it up in despair.

Two days before the morning of which we are now about to treat, that respectable individual, Malvers, dressed with great care and neatness, stepped into the court, and passing Adam with extreme contempt, sought out Mr. Grantley's office.

He was admitted, and at once stated his business.

"You see, Mr. Grantley," he said, "I am a friend of Mr. Skinwell, and having plenty of leisure time on my hands, have determined to devote it to furthering his interests, and in bettering my own position. The fact is, I am far from being a rich man. In short, I am a poor gentleman, and must not be particular as to how I put money in my purse. I made application to my friend Skinwell, when I heard of the singular manner in which this concern fell into the hands of the Charity, and he at once agreed to the request I made"—

"And that request was"—

"That he would be kind enough to find nice snug employment for me within the precincts of Maggott's-court."

"Indeed."

"Yes, indeed; and here I have a letter of introduction to yourself, which you will now favour me by reading."

Grantley accepted the letter from Malvers, and leisurely read it.

It ran as follows :—

"Mr. Grantley, Sir,—You will please find employment for the bearer hereof, Mr. Montague, a highly respectable individual, whom I feel a pleasure in making known to you. You will please make him a sort of head or confidential clerk. In fact, place him next yourself and oblige,

"Truly yours,
"WALTGRAVE SHINWELL."

Grantley looked troubled as he read the words.

Malvers noted this, and asked him if the letter contained anything to annoy him.

"Nothing at which I can feel annoyed, sir," replied Grantley ; "but something at which I feel hurt."

"Dear me. And what may that be?"

"Simply this. Mr. Skinwell asks me to make you head clerk, and place you in a position near myself. To do this, I must displace an old, valued servant. It is that which hurts me."

"A very proper feeling; but perhaps something can be done to make him think but little of the matter. If his salary is not affected"—

"Oh, sir, you do not know Matthew Peterson. He has been here since boyhood, and the position he holds has been the aim of his life. Beyond this office he has no thought. The books of the firm are to him the sole pleasure of life. His position as confidential clerk is as dear to him as our honour is to us. If he is displaced, it will break his heart."

"Dear me! How extremely absurd! Can nothing be done to appease him?"

"Nothing."

"Well I am sorry for it. But I know of no remedy."

This was spoken in a tone of cool insolence that disgusted the young merchant, and he only regretted that his being a servant there prevented his rising and kicking the fellow from the room.

From the first moment, Grantley felt a deep and terrible dislike to the man before him, and he would fain have dismissed him from his presence.

"But," he reflected, "we are on terms of equality here—both servants of the same master. I am powerless."

"Well, Mr. Grantley," said Malvers, "I think we have no more to say to each other. I shall be at my post to-morrow. Meanwhile make old Peterson listen to common sense, and persuade him into the belief that he will be far more happy without responsibility than with it."

Grantley replied not, and the visitor left.

"Better," said the merchant, when Malvers was gone; "better tell poor Matthew at once. It will be well over."

He rang a bell which lay on the desk at which he sat, and in a few moments an old man, looking for all the world like another and better bound edition of the ticket porter, entered the office.

Of course he had not the white apron and badge ; but independent of these appendages, he looked the counterpart of Adam.

"What is your pleasure, Mr. Grantley?" asked the old man.

" Sit down. Matthew ; I have much to say to you."

" If it is all the same to you, sir, I would rather stand."

" As you will, Matthew. Now listen to me, and promise that you will not feel hurt at what I am about to say."

" Is it anything serious, Mr. Grantley—you look so wretched ? "

" It is serious, Matthew ; but more so to you than to me. You saw the gentleman who has just left me ? "

" Yes, sir."

" Well, Matthew, he brought with him a letter from the secretary of the Asylum, asking me to place him in the place you now hold. See, here is the communication."

He handed Skinwell's scrawl to the old man, who took it with trembling hands and glanced over it.

' And I must leave," he said, " I must leave, after all these years of service—after all these years, and never one holiday ! That is too bad, too bad. It will be the death of me."

" No—no, Matthew ? it is not so bad as that. You are not to leave, but simply to take one step lower on the ladder, and hand over your trust to another."

" Is not that dreadful ? Is not that dreadful, Mr. Grantley, after all these years, after all—all these years ? "

" It is sad, Matthew—very, very sad indeed ; but there is no help for it ; and after all, it is not a matter to grieve so much about. Look at me—to what am I not reduced ? A few short weeks ago I was master of all ; but now I am, like yourself, only a servant. Is not that hard to bear ? And yet I do not complain."

" You set me a good example, Mr. Grantley—a very good example indeed ; but there is a difference between us. To you the world is open, and you may—you doubtless will - rise once more to the position you have lost ; but what hope is there for me ? Look at me, Mr. Grantley—sixty-five years of age and failing fast ! What hope have I ? I am thrown down never to rise again, it is too dreadful for me to bear, too dreadful."

" Never mind, Matthew, never mind ; bear up against it and hope for the best."

Matthew stood silent and dejected for a few moments, and then, turning to Mr. Grantley, he asked when the stranger was coming to take possession of the books.

" To-morrow," said Grantley, " to-morrow, Matthew."

" Very good, sir, very good ; he shall find them ready for him. There's not an error in them from first to last, and they will do credit to any man. I shall not be ashamed to place them in his hands."

With this the old man left the office, and went into his own little box.

There he busied himself with his books, and although occasionally absent in mind, he never took his eyes from the rows of figures before him.

At last he went out into the clerks' office.

" Mr. Smith," he said, " be kind enough to hand me your books. Mr. Rogers and Mr. Mason will do the same in a couple of hours."

" What sir ! " said Mr. Smith, tumbling off his stool in astonishment, " my books *on a Thursday ?* "

" Yes, sir ; the fact is the books must all be made up to-night."

" To-night ? Such a thing never happened before since I have been in the firm."

" Never, Mr. Smith, never within my recollection ; but we have no alternative now."

" And what has happened, to bring this about, if I may make so bold as to ask ? "

" You may, Smith, you may. We have known each other a number of years, and have always been on the best of terms, so that which affects me will at least interest you. Know then, my friend, that to-morrow I am to be superseded."

" Superseded ! "

All the clerks raised their heads, and gazed at the old man in blank astonishment.

" You don't mean to say you are dismissed ? "

" No, not dismissed ; but some friend of the new proprietors has stepped in over my head, and I am no longer to hold the position of head clerk."

" Well," said Smith, " I don't like making use of harsh language. It's not in my way, but I will say it and stand to it, such conduct is a burning shame, and the new proprietors, whoever they may be, ought to be kicked for their conduct ; and now they may find some one to supersede me as soon as they think proper. There ! "

Mr. Smith became very red in the face, and resumed his seat in a great rage with everyone in general, and the new proprietors in particular.

" You must not use hard words," said Matthew ; " we must not have that, friend Smith ; you forget that the gentlemen have a right to do as they think proper, and that we have no right to question their acts."

" A right to do as they think proper ! So they have—a legal right. But what *moral* right is there ? That's what I require to know. Who has done so much towards making the firm what it is as you have done ? Who has toiled and toiled nights and days together, so frequently and so disinterestedly as you have done ? And now, after having spent all your life in amassing a vast fortune to thrust into their greedy maws, they turn round and recompense you by kicking you out of the position you have earned for yourself. It's disgraceful—disgraceful."

" So it is," said the others, in indignant chorus ; " so it is—disgraceful."

There was rank mutiny in the office, and Matthew trembled, lest, in the heat of their indignation, they should make a mistake in the books, and thus cast discredit on the firm.

Thinking that his presence only acted as fuel to fire he left the place and shut himself up once more in his own little box.

Next day the new confidential clerk arrived, and jauntily took up his position. He introduced himself to the clerk, asked for his " friend Matthew," and demanded the books.

Matthew called him into his own office, and there addressed him.

" This was my office," he said " it is now yours. I have arranged my books in proper order, and you will now be able to keep them without any difficulty. I do not think you will find one little point requiring explanation, for I have done my best to make all clear."

" And you suspect I am going to bother myself with all these trumpery old parchment-bound records of sales of silks and satins, and other flummery. Bah ! you are mistaken ; my position here is a merely honorary one. Let those who like it do the work ; for my part, I am content to look on. So here, Matthew, take your books and bundle off with them—I will manage without them. The only thing I want from you is this snug little box of yours, where I can enjoy myself comfortably. So get away with you."

He piled all the books—ledgers, day-books, cash-books, and all—in old Matthew's arms, and sent him off with them.

Great was the surprise in the outer office, when the old man related what had transpired between him and the new " confidential ;" and still greater was the surprise and consternation, when, at a more advanced hour of the day, the head of the office was seen, through the window of his box, puffing away at a long pipe and in a state of semi-intoxication.

These facts were communicated to Mr. Grantley, who, in great indignation, sought the office of the new-comer, and in no very polite terms delivered his opinion of his conduct.

" Look here, young man," said the would-be clerk, " I am here of my own choice, and you're here on sufferance ; therefore, I'm your better, so far. You may be manager and I may be clerk, but that shan't be sufficient reason for your ordering me. I'll do as I like ! I'm here to look after you all and to keep you in order, not to glue myself to a desk and scribble away rows of figures from morning to night ; so say nothing about my conduct, or it may be the worse for you."

Grantley saw that he was powerless to argue with the man, and so left him ; communicating to the clerks that, although he deeply regretted the presence of such a man, he was powerless to dispose of him.

Never had such a scene been witnessed in that house before, and all the *employés* left at night, gloomily reviewing the incidents to which they had been witnesses, and prophesying the downfall of the business very speedily if something were not done to prop it up.

Next day Malvers was at his post again, and made no further attempt than he had done on the preceding day to conduct the business entailed on his position.

At mid-day Mr. Skinwell visited Grantley, as he said, " just to see how things were progressing."

" They progress but very poorly, sir," said Grantley, " and are not at all likely to improve while Mr. Montague holds a position here."

" What do you mean ?"

" I mean that the man who spends the time of his employers in drinking and smoking while he should be attending to their interests, is not likely to materially benefit any establishment, particularly that of a merchant, where the example of sobriety, diligence, and gentlemanly behaviour cannot be too fully placed before the *employés*."

" And how does my friend fail ?"

" By getting disgracefully drunk, and turning his office into a common pot-house."

" And does Mr. Montague so far forget himself ?"

" He does, indeed."

" Well, I *am* sorry for that, and am glad that you have so clearly put the matter before me. I will see him at once and make him explain his conduct."

" If he can. I have spoken to him, and have been insulted for my pains. I do not think you will fare any better."

" Oh, it's a mistake—a mistake ; nothing more, my dear sir ; I will soon rectify this, believe me."

Skinwell left the manager, and sought the room of the new managing clerk.

He found that individual, seated before a desk that should have been covered with books, but which was, instead, occupied by bottles and tobacco pipes, enjoying his pipe, and applying himself diligently to a bottle before him.

" Well," said Skinwell, " this is a nice game isn't it ?"

" What do you mean ?"

" What do I mean ? Why, I mean that this proceeding of yours is a nice way to augment our interests ; is it not ?"

" Don't see but what it is."

" You do not see but what it is ?"

" No."

" Well, I must tell you that it is ruin for both. If this honest fool, Grantley, puts the case before the board, we shall both fare the worse for it."

" Hang the board ! what do I care ?"

" Nothing, perhaps ; but I have all to care."

" Well, then, care away. It's nothing to do with me."

" It shall have to do with you, and that you shall find ere long, my fine fellow.

" None o' your nonsense. You ain't got the will, you know ; so what's the use of talking ? I'm master, for I have the document ; so no more of your jaw, and just allow me to do as I think proper."

" I say you shall not."

" And I say I will."

" So it has come to open war, has it ? Well, war be it. Hark, ye drunkard ; I'm as desperate a man as yourself, and now I'll tell you what I have determined on doing. I will speak of this second will to the board, and thus secure to this man, Grantley, the wealth we have sought to appropriate ; for on the slightest hint of the existence of such a document, the gentlemen whose servant I am, would hand back to him the property he so generously gave them without the production of the deed that entitled them to it."

" You would not dare do this."

" Put me to the test."

" Nay ; but old fellow, why should we quarrel ?"

" Rather ask why should we not quarrel ? Is it not terrible that just as we have all in our grasp, you must turn round, and by your wretched drunkenness dash our plans to the ground and bring ruin upon us ? Is it not past endurance ?"

" Well, but you know I didn't mean anything wrong."

" Didn't mean anything wrong," said Skinwell with marked contempt. " Look at the position in which you have placed yourself. You who should have been circumspect in your actions to the last degree ; you who should have set the example of sobriety and attention to all the house ; look at yourself. I find the office converted into a tap-room ; bottles and pipes occupying the places of ledgers and day-books, and tobacco smoke making the air heavy with its fumes. It is unbearable, unpardonable conduct."

" Oh, nonsense ; look it over this once ; it's not likely to happen again. I'll *try* and do better."

" Try ! You must assure me you will do better, or I carry my threat into execution, and render you powerless and a beggar."

" Well ; I will do better ; so say no more about it. And now, what has happened since we parted ? You crossed the heath all right, didn't you ?"

" Well, it entirely depends upon what you call all right. I had my head smashed."

" I imagined you would."

" Did you ? Then I didn't, or I'd have seen the heath cursed before I would have gone near it."

" But you trapped Jack and Dick Turpin I heard ?"

" Yes ; safe enough."

" That's a good job. I suppose they are safe in Newgate ? "

" I suppose so."

" What ! Didn't you see him there ?"

" No."

" Well, I should have done so had I been in your place."

" If you had had your head broken, you would have done precisely what I did."

" Perhaps I should, perhaps I should not. Well, it's a nasty thing to have one's skull cracked ; I know it from experience ! But have you not yet seen Harding or his fellows ? "

" No, they have not come near me."

" Isn't that strange ?"

" I am inclined to think so. Three days have elapsed, and I have neither heard from nor seen them."

" I can't make that out."

" I am in the same position, but I mean to go to Harding's house now, in order to see what he means by his conduct."

At this moment a clerk entered the office, and informed Skinwell that some one wished to see him.

" Who is it ?"

" I do not know sir ; but I think the gentleman is Hebrew."

" Indeed. Show him in."

The clerk withdrew, and in a few moments Harding, with a large cloth bound tightly over his brow, entered the little box of the confidential clerk.

" Excuse me for following you here," said the Jew ; " but it's my fate ! I thought I had best see you before I went to my home. I've just returned to London."

" Indeed ! and where have you been ?"

" I can hardly tell you, where I have been, ma tear ; but it's just half over England."

" Wherefore ?"

" Oh ! its a long and a very sad story. Them boys—them awful boys ; they escaped—they escaped."

" What ! the highwaymen ?"

" Yes, them naughty boys. They escaped—they escaped ; and just as I had them so snug, too."

" Good God ! How did that happen ?"

" I'm sure I haven't no more notion than a babe unborn. Vun vos half-dead, and the other had on the bracelets, and yet they got clean off—clean off."

" What a misfortune !"

" I should think it vos. Ain't it hawful, ma tears ?"

" Well, go on with your tale. What did you do, finding them gone ?"

" I couldn't do anything, no more could my mate ; for the dreadful boys bound us hand and foot, and ve had to vait until my men came from London to release us. And look at my head, my tears ; that's the effect of their hard knocks."

" Oh ! hang their hard knocks."

" It's all very fine for you to say hang their knocks, but I'd rather hang *them* for their knocks. Vell, gentlemen, I sent all my fellows avay in different directions to try and find the young villains, and I've been after 'em myself I can't tell you vere I haven't been, but I know all the midland counties have seen me during the time that elapsed since we parted at the old stable. Oh my! oh my!"

"And you have lost all trace of them? They have evaded you?"

"Vell, not quite. I got upon the track, but my horses couldn't keep up with theirs. At every village vhere ve inquired they had gained upon us; so knowing you wouldn't mind the expense, I put two of my best hands on horses bought for the purpose, ma tears—bought for the purpose. And they're upon 'em now; they must be hunted down."

"That's well. And this fellow King—where is he?"

"I'm upon him; but buying the horses *for you*, ma tears, has used up all my money, and that's vot I come here for. I called at your office and found you had come here; so I set off after you, knowing that the urgent nature of the business vould be sufficient excuse for disturbing you."

"You did well. What money do you require?"

"Vell, I don't vant to be more extravagant than I can help; so I'll say two hundred guineas, ma tear."

"It is exorbitant!"

"And I paid von hundred pounds, ready money, for two horses in your services! My!"

The Jew looked remarkably astonished and very indignant.

"And if you did, will they not fetch the money again?" asked Skinwell.

"Not a penny of it, ma tear—not a penny of it. Against them horses catch Black Bess they vill be ridden to death."

"He speaks truth," said Malvers; "I know very well what Turpin's nag is."

"Well," said Skinwell, "I see there is nothing left for me but to comply with your request."

He sat down to his desk, and wrote an order upon his banker for the sum demanded by the Jew.

The Hebrew greedily pocketed the cheque and left the office, promising early news of the pursued and the pursuers.

"Humph!" said Skinwell, when he had gone; "a nice game this! Two of the greatest fiends in Christendom at liberty, and working against us!"

"Two! what has Jack to do with it?"

"Simply this. He told me on the heath that he knew of the second will, and demanded it from me."

"Hang the hound! He seems to know of everything in Christendom. He is the dark shadow that crosses my path. He is the rock ahead, and my evil genius. Curse him; I hope they will not let him slip through their fingers."

"Fear nothing; they will have him. If money can hunt him down it shall be expended. It will be long ere I forgive him the knock on the head he gave me."

"And I will never forgive his forcing from me that which has compelled me to hide my head like a hunted stag—that which has brought me to be the drunken wretch I have become."

"Say no more now. His time will come."

"It shall."

Malvers ground his teeth and hissed these words through his tightly-compressed lips.

"And, now," said Skinwell, "before I go let me warn you to throw off this drunkenness, and assume the character you have to play here. If you are not careful, this young fellow will best us after all."

"I will be more discreet in future."

"Remember, to you is entrusted the task of playing him out of his management here. To do this you must keep the brain cool, and the nerves well-strung."

"I am to be trusted. Fear nothing. I have been a fool, but you shall not have to complain again."

They separated, and the new manager commenced his work of reformation by sweeping away his bottles and pipes, and calling for his cash-box.

"At least," he said, "cash affairs will interest me—particularly if there is a balance in hand that can be easily appropriated."

CHAPTER XXIX.

THE LONG RIDE—REPEATING THE VERSES—EXHAUSTION OF JACK'S HORSE—AND THE CONFLICT IN THE GREEN LANE.

THE highwaymen well knew the sort of people they had to deal with, and did not place themselves in any fancied security.

They judged rightly that the Jew would leave no stone unturned to overtake them and make them prisoners; particularly after the treatment they had given him.

Turpin's naturally vigorous constitution served him on the pinch, and to his rude health and spirits might have been traced his almost miraculous recovery from the two severe pistol wounds he had received.

He rode strongly and well, but his wounded arm gave him considerable trouble.

Jack was all fun and gaiety.

His spirit rose to a boisterous point immediately he felt his gallant steed bounding under him.

"Hurrah!" he shouted to Turpin, ever and anon, "hurrah for the road, Dick. We've a long ride before us, old boy, and Heaven only knows when we shall bring up."

"I know it. Bloodhounds are on the scent, and if we would avoid them we must exhaust them."

"Yes, for there's no shaking them off by trickery. No, no! trust old Harding and his boys for that! They would stick to a fellow like grim death, as long as nature lasted out to serve them."

"You're right. It's not the first time they've had the pleasure of chasing me."

"Well, it's to be hoped it won't be the last."

The beautiful animals dashed gaily along the road, and throughout the first day they scarcely slackened speed for more than half an hour, until the sun had set.

That night the friends made their couch under the shelter of a haystack, keeping watch in turns, and their steeds ready for a further burst if the emergency required.

They were not, however, disturbed, and ere the sun rose they were off again; whither they knew and cared not.

Early in the day they stopped a carrier's cart bound for some market town, and helped themselves to as much edibles as they required, tossing the astonished proprietor a gold coin in payment.

The men broke two or three fresh eggs in the mouths of their horses and then swallowed a like quantity themselves.

A little way-side brook served to quench their thirst, and like giants refreshed, they resumed their flight.

"I say, Dick," said Jack, after a few hours' riding, "I wonder where we are."

"I haven't an idea; we must have come some fifty or sixty miles."

"More; nearer seventy."

"Well, we're in the midlands somewhere, and that's all I know or care."

"True, boy, and the same here; but I think we may venture to double."

"I think not; we had best go on until dark and sleep somewhere. To-morrow we may be in a better trim to face about."

"Very well; but I wish we had asked that carrier where we had got to."

"I never thought of it. But no matter, on we go."

They went on, and at length drew rein.

It was pitch dark now, and they meant putting up for the night.

They again sought the shelter of a haystack.

There was one in a field some hundred yards distant from the spot in the road where they had stopped.

"That's our bed for the night," said Jack; "so we had best retire at once."

"All right, my boy. Shall we have to dismount and open that gate, or will the nags clear it?"

"It's a rasper," said Jack; "but we'll give them a try at it."

Dick Turpin immediately put Bess to the test, and the noble mare flew lightly into the field beyond the road.

Jack followed, his mare behaving in the same gallant manner.

"I say," said Dick, "there's a village yonder. Arn't we too close to it?"

"Not a bit. Who will disturb us now? And mayn't we be astir again before they come forth from their cottages?"

"Well, as you like; but I don't care so much about these close quarters."

No more was said on the subject, and in a few minutes the steeds were secured and the friends seated under the haystack.

"Now, Dick," said Jack Rann, "you go to sleep first. You're weakest, and want most rest."

"I don't deny it," said Turpin; "but a short spell will do for me."

It was fated to be a very short one.

Turpin closed his eyes, and was soon fast asleep; whilst Jack gazed up into the clear vault above, and gave way to thought.

At that moment his mind wandered back to days of yore. He pictured his childhood, and called up from the depths of memory reminiscences of those days of innocence gone for ever.

He also thought of his poor old mother, who had not died until his name was infamous throughout the land.

He remembered her look of horror when the intelligence first reached her that her son was a thief.

He thought of all this, and the tears coursed down his cheeks.

Alas! for the dark side of the picture.

Those who dream that the lives of those criminals whose names figure in the pages of history, whose acts of daring shine out boldly, and whose romantic adventures are as "familiar in our mouths as household worlds," were all gaiety, sunshine, and excitement, could never have pictured one of them in the position in which Jack Rann was now placed.

The clear blue vault of Heaven above him, nature hushed into mysterious silence around him, and *a voice speaking to him of the depths of his heart.*

It was then the horrors of his life burst upon him in all their hideousness.

It was then he felt what a pitiable thing he was; and it was then he wished that he had chanced to have been the humblest tiller of the soil, the veriest wretch that hugged his rags in starvation and poverty, rather than the brilliant, world-famed *thief* he was.

Not all the good he had done could appease his conscience then; and he started to his feet, and in anguish cried aloud—

"Oh, God! how I wish that I could be a better man!— that I knew how to set about reforming my life!"

He could see no chance of this.

He was hunted down, and before him he could only see the gallows.

Startled at the sound of his own voice, he resumed his seat on the hay; but just as he sat down a sound reached his ear that drove all thought save that of imminent personal peril from his mind.

In the distance he heard the sound of galloping horses.

He listened again.

Yes, there was no mistaking it.

Horses were approaching rapidly.

"Dick, Dick," he whispered, shaking his friend.

"Hillo! What is it now?"

"Listen."

Dick rubbed his eyes and shook off all traces of sleep, and bent his ear in the direction indicated by his friend.

"What do you hear?" asked Jack.

"Nothing."

"Listen again."

"Hillo! There's horses coming up the road we left, and at a thundering pace, too."

"Well?"

"Well!"

"It's the officers."

"Never a doubt of it."

"They've dropped on our friend the carrier—I'll stake my life on it—and he's put them down to our route, or they would never ride like that."

They drew the horses away behind the haystack, and then, throwing themselves on their faces, they awaited until the approaching parties should be nearer.

The moon was shining brilliantly, and they could see distinctly all who passed on the road.

Their horses stood as still as graven statues, and they awaited the coming of the horsemen in breathless expectation.

Another moment, and two horsemen passed on the road, within a hundred yards of where they lay concealed.

"They're the two officers, sure enough," said Jack; "and now, my boy, we are fairly in for it."

"No doubt of it! I see how it will be. They will ride on to the village, make all the inquiries they can, and find out that we have not passed."

"The result of which will be that they'll immediately guess we are in the neighbourhood. Deuce take it! we are in a sad scrape."

"So I perceive. There they go. They have turned down the lane to the right, which will lead them straight into the village. Now, there's nothing for it but to fly, as if the fiend were at our heels."

"Right! Now for it."

They sprang upon their steeds, and flew across the fields like the wind.

Comparatively few seconds elapsed ere they were once more dashing bravely over the road by which they came, imagining that the officers were riding in a contrary direction.

It was not so.

Some distance from the village was a toll-gate, and at this spot the officers had to draw rein.

"Hey!" they shouted, "now toll-keeper, look alive, and let us pass through."

It was all very well to invite the toll-keeper to look alive; but at that moment he was sound asleep and dreaming of things more pleasant than turning out into the cold night air, for the purpose of unbolting his gate to late travellers.

"Hey! hey!" shouted the men, "come, old tortoise, ain't you going to get out o'bed to-night?"

The toll-keeper now popped his head out of his bedroom-window, and demanded what was wanted of him.

"Want!" said the men; "why, we want to pass through, to be sure."

"And who are you?"

"The king's officers of justice—that's all; and if you don't get down without delay, you'll have to take the consequences of detaining us."

"I'm coming," said the man; "but I didn't expect anyone at this hour; and it's so seldom that we meet strangers, that I was for a moment confounded."

"All right, but do make haste."

In less than a minute the toll-keeper appeared in the road, bearing with him a lantern.

He opened the gate, and the men were about to pass, when one of them turned and said to him,—

"How long ago did two horsemen pass through?"

"What kind o' horsemen?"

"Two fellows in scarlet, mounted on blood mares."

"I've never see'd two such people since I kept the toll-bar."

"Hey! what!" said the other; "no such people passed?"

"No."

"But you might have been out of the way. Your wife might have passed 'em through?"

"No; that couldn't well be, because seeing as how I've got no wife, or anybody else, to do my work for me."

"But hang the things!—they must have passed through. There's no other road, is there?"

"There's a road t'other side o' them hills, but its four mile off."

"Oh, they wouldn't have gone that way. It's too far off the track."

AN UNEXPECTED VISITOR.

"Well," said the second horseman, "if the old man is right, we've been doubled. Now, are you certain?"

"Oh! I couldn't be deceived," said the toll-keeper.

"Well, if you're deceiving us, you'll take the consequences, that's all. We're after two notorious highwaymen, and if they slip through our fingers through you, I wouldn't like to stand in your shoes."

"Well, all I have to say is, that unless they jumped the gate—and it's a twinger to get over—they never came this road."

"Then there's nothing for it but to turn back again."

They therefore turned their horses' heads, and, bidding the toll-keeper "Good-night," began to retrace their steps.

"This is a lively thing," said one to the other. "Curse 'em; I thought we must have had 'em at that village."

"I expect we're done."

"So do I. It would be a surprise to me if we came up with 'em again."

"Well, all we can do is to keep our eyes open. There's naught else, unless we fall across some traveller who has chanced to drop upon 'em."

They cantered on for about half an hour, when the sound of hoofs struck on their ears.

"Hillo!" said one to the other, "if I'm not mistaken, that's a horseman."

"Yes, and coming clean down upon us."

They drew rein, and walked their horses slowly.

In a few seconds they were met by a frantic horseman, divested of coat, hat, and wig, and riding as if for life.

They stood in his path, and made him pull up.

"It's all over with me now," said the traveller; "it's all over, and I give up the ghost. They've taken my money and my clothes, and now you had better take my life and have done with it."

"Hillo! friend, what are you talking about? Money and life! How came you in this state?"

"No matter; I'm a ruined man, and I don't care a fig. Do what you like with me—I ain't particular. B'ow my brains out, or cut my throat—it's all one to me."

"Hold that row," said one of the officers; "we are no cut-throats. What has happened to you?"

"Oh, I'm sure I don't know. To think that I should have travelled this road so many years without being molested, to at last fall into the clutches of such scoundrels!"

"Into whose clutches? Why don't you answer? We are king's officers."

"Are you? I'm very glad of that. I thought you might be some other blackguards."

"You're very complimentary. But no matter. Tell us your story."

"Well, gentlemen—since you are gentlemen—I'll tell you all about it. You see I was cantering along, thinking of nothing in particular, when what should I hear but the sound of horses' hoofs. Being in the habit of meeting people from the village yonder—to which, by the way, I was bound—I took no notice, and goes on quietly enough until I came close to two horsemen. 'Stop!' cried one, and I stopped accordingly. 'Nonsense, Dick,' says the other, 'this is not the time, and we may shortly have the officers upon us.' 'That's as may be,' said the one called Dick; 'but,' he continued, 'it's not my way to

No. 9.

let anybody pass me; and if all the fellows connected with Newgate were at my heels, I'd have my pull at my man; so let us see the contents of those capacious pockets.' I now saw that my men were robbers, and I was about to set Dobbin into motion, when that blackguard Dick caught me by the collar of my coat and pulled it from my back, leaving me shivering in the cold. I made a grab at it as it went, but it was no manner of use; Dick had it; and knocking off my hat and wig with the end of his pistol, told me to ride like mad, or it might be the worse for me. I needed no second invitation, I can assure you; and giving Dobbin his head, I rattled along as fast as his four legs could carry me."

"Good!"

"Good!" said the poor little ill-used traveller; "but I think it's bad, very bad, sir, and no mistake about it. My coat contained five-and-twenty guineas; and I may as well go home again now, for I've no money to spend at the fair in the village yonder."

"Well, you're to be pitied, my friend—much to be pitied; but still, you've the satisfaction of knowing that you've been robbed by Dick Turpin and Sixteen-String Jack, the very princes of the road."

"Have I, though?" said the man. "Well, I shouldn't have thought it."

"I don't suppose you would. But we can waste no more time with you. If we capture your friends, you may rest assured that you will find your coat and money at Newgate."

"Oh, hang the coat and money!" said the man; "I don't care about it. Robbed by Dick Turpin and Sixteen-String Jack! My life!—it will be something to talk about for the remainder of my days."

He set spurs to his horse and rode off, the officers following his example.

"We are right once more," said the officer. "Well, this is a slice of luck."

"Yes, indeed, but I never thought Dick Turpin would have been such a fool as to leave such a scent behind him as this. He must have been cracked. Why, a child would have known that we should turn and follow."

Hour after hour they rode, and at length daylight came.

It was a damp, foggy morning, and the impress of horses' hoofs was plainly marked on the wretched country roads. Ever and anon the officers stooped forward and anxiously scanned the ground in search of the trail of the fugitives.

Hour after hour they rode, and watched and listened attentively; and thus time progressed, until the hour of eleven had come and gone.

They now arrived at a spot where three roads branched off.

"Hillo!" said one of the officers; "this is a puzzler, and no mistake. Now, which is it to be?"

"Let us dismount, and seek for some traces of them."

They did so.

Taking the reins of the horses in their hands, they made a close examination of the ground; and after some difficulty, found recent traces of the hoofs of two horses.

They were visible in the road to the right.

"That's the road we came," said the officer. "It is on the homeward track."

"And that's their road, as safe as possible. Where should they go, if not back to London? It's the only place in which they can enjoy even comparative safety."

"You are right, and I'll stake my life these are their marks. So come along."

They remounted and spurred their horses forward. They were fine, fleet steeds, well calculated to perform the task required of them, and as yet they exhibited no signs of distress.

Forward they went, and still the marks of the horses' hoofs were visible, and reassured the officers that they were on the right scent.

On and on, and at last the hour of mid-day tolled from some distant church.

"If we don't overhaul them by sunset," said one to the other, "it will be a bad job; for under the cover of night they may again, and more successfully baffle us."

"Well, I agree with you; but it's no manner of use to try and get more out of the horses; they won't stand it much longer at this pace."

The horses now exhibited strong and unmistakeable signs of distress. They were in a perfect state of lather, and their stride seemed to fail.

"It's no use losing them, even if they drop under it; for it's now or never."

"You are right. Better kill the horses than lose the men. Go on again."

They once more spurred their jaded steeds, and they nobly answered; but the fire seemed to be fast fading out of them.

"I begin to give it up as a bad go," said one of the officers; "one half hour more, and we are beaten."

They were in a road bordering a little wood in a semi-circle.

The turn in front of them would reveal an extensive tract of country.

On they rode, still forward, each moment telling more fatally upon their horses.

It seemed as if the assertion of the officer was to be verified, and that another half hour would indeed tell in a fatal manner upon their steeds.

They now almost reeled, and snorted violently, as they attempted to keep the pace their riders required of them.

On, on they went, and the bend of the road was reached.

Before them lay a flat country, through which they could see, winding away into the misty distance, the road they were pursuing.

They strained their eyes and endeavoured to catch a glimpse of those of whom they were in pursuit.

"If they ain't to be seen now, we may as well give it up as a bad case, and ease the horses."

"Hurrah!" burst from the lips of his companion, as he strained his eyes into the distance, " hurrah!—see there—see there!"

On either side of the road was a tolerably large hedge, and this seemed to grow narrower in the distance.

Just visible above this protection, in the extreme distance, could be discerned two moving objects.

"By Jove! we're upon 'em now; that's the boys, or I'm a Dutchman."

"Go on—go on. We'll have 'em now.

Highly excited at the prospect of a successful termination to the chase, the men lashed their jaded steeds into the semblance of a gallop, and then urged them on by every means in their power. They shouted and coaxed—they raved, and lashed, and patted them—and the noble beasts continued to strain every nerve.

They were bathed in steam—a froth started from their mouths and nostrils, and the veins seemed to be doubled in size on their arched necks and well-formed limbs.

Still on; the riders were relentless. It was a matter of life and death to them. The steeds were as naught. Before them they saw the prize they coveted, and nothing could keep them from grasping it.

Leaving them to keep up the chase, we will see how it fared with the pursued.

*   *   *   *   *   *   *

Jack never ceased remonstrating with Dick Turpin on the folly of stopping the traveller.

"It is fatal to us," he said, "fatal, fatal! If they are following, this man will surely put them on the right scent, and then it will be all over with us."

"Oh, nonsense—can't we trust in our horses?"

"Yes; but there's fish as good in the sea as ever came out of it."

"By which you mean that these fellows are as well mounted as ourselves."

"The possibility is that they are."

"I can't conceive that. However, it's no use talking now. What's done is done, and can't be helped. So let us forget it."

"I never shall; for in all my experience, I do not remember such folly"

"Oh, bother! I couldn't resist the temptation, and that's all about it. If you talk for a month, you'll make no more nor less out of it."

They rode on in gloomy silence.

Jack's heart misgave him, and he would fain have parted company with his companion. It was beyond his patience to endure such a wild act as Dick had been guilty of, and it quite upset the equilibrium of his temper.

"It's too bad—far too bad," he kept repeating to himself, "and nothing can justify it; but I mustn't leave him. He is weak and wounded, and if he should be taken I should never forgive myself."

Sulky with each other, they maintained a deep silence until they entered the road in which their pursuers caught sight of them.

"By Jove! it's all over," said Jack, looking back and catching sight of the officers; "they are upon us."

Dick gave utterance to a loud and prolonged whistle.

"That's the boys, sure enough."

"Now, I should think you are quite aware of the folly of your act?"

"Yes, Jack, yes; but it's no use talking. Let us try what the mares will do. They've been hard pressed, but I do think they will pull us out of this difficulty."

"I can't flatter myself that such will be the case, for my poor old girl is jaded to death."

Bess seemed to be the freshest of the two. Indeed her powers of endurance were almost supernatural.

Although tired and reeling, her wind did not fail her, and she appeared able to last for several hours.

"It will all depend upon the horses now. If theirs are the best, there is nothing for it but to give in."

"Yes, there is."

"I don't see any other course."

"Well I do. There's fighting to be done, and in that we may not come off second best."

The steeds of the pursued and the pursuers were now taxed to the utmost, and they seemed to go stride and stride, without lessening the long gap between them.

The officers would rise in the saddle and cry to each other, "Not an inch do we gain." And the robbers would turn their heads and cry angrily, "They are still upon us; no shaking them off."

In this manner a distance of some four miles was traversed.

The leaders now descended a steep hill, at the bottom of which was a junction of roads.

Jack and Turpin had as much as they could do to keep their steeds on their legs in the descent of this hill.

They had almost accomplished the task.

They had all but gained the flat beneath, when Jack's mare stumbled.

He tried to pull her up, but she reeled and threw him to the ground, falling heavily on her side.

"It's all over," cried Jack, seeing how vainly his beloved steed struggled to regain her feet; "it's all over. Fly! Dick, and save yourself. See! they are upon us."

"Jack," cried Turpin, "don't think I'm capable of such an act. If it hadn't been for you, I should have been in Newgate by this time; and had it not been for my folly, in all probability we should have been riding away unmolested. Therefore, don't think I'm cur enough to leave you."

"Go, go," cried Jack; "one's enough for them. It's madness for both to be caught."

"I won't stir. Bess has plenty of stuff in her yet. Jump on her back and come with me. If they catch the mare, I'll eat 'em."

"I won't move. Go, Dick, go!"

"Not without you."

"This is madness. Two minutes more, and they will be upon us."

"I don't care—I'm as obstinate as yourself. I'll not budge without you."

"Madman," cried Jack, becoming highly excited, "save yourself. I will not imperil your safety; besides, I will not leave my mare while she has a spark of life in her."

"Good!" cried Turpin, springing to the ground; "you're a true one, you are. I like you all the better for sticking to your steed. She's a beauty, and worth fighting for; and I'll stand by her, too."

They grasped hands in silence.

Next moment the officers appeared on the brow of the hill.

"Here they come; and if they take us, it shan't be without a fight for it."

They drew their pistols, and cocked them deliberately.

"Now then for it."

The officers paused on seeing the antagonistic position of the robbers.

"Hillo!" said one to the other; "they mean showing fight. What's to be done?"

"Follow their example," briefly replied his companion.

They drew their pistols and cocked them.

"We must do our duty, and the reward mustn't be missed under any pretence. So come on."

They walked their horses slowly down the hill, and levelled their weapons.

Jack and Dick Turpin did the same.

"Now, then," said one officer to the other, "no throwing away a charge. Be steady, and let them fire first."

"And if they won't?"

"Well, get within range and chance it; but, mind, no flukes."

They still kept steadily on, and, when within pistol-range, drew the rein.

There was a pause of a moment's duration.

"Now," cried one of the officers to the highwaymen, "you are our prisoners."

The men answered with a derisive shout of laughter.

"Hadn't you better take us first?" asked Jack.

"We intend to do so in our own good time. But, first, I call upon you to throw down your arms and surrender yourselves."

"That's just what we thought you would do," said Turpin; "and it's just what we won't do."

"Well," said the man, "we shall fire."

"And so shall we."

The four weapons were raised simultaneously, and each aimed at the breast of his antagonist.

They were discharged together. The four shots rang out as one.

A cloud of dust, and then a groan.

Jack had fallen!

Seeing this, the officers threw away their pistols, and, drawing their staves, rushed upon Turpin.

He was but one, and on foot.

His antagonists had all the advantage, and in spite of his brave resistance, he was borne to the earth and secured.

"Hurrah!" shouted the officers; "the game's our own."

They were about to apply themselves to securing their prisoners, when the clatter of a horse arrested their attention.

Looking up, they beheld a gallant horseman almost standing over them.

Before they had time to rise to their feet, the horse of the newcomer was upon them, and had trampled them down.

In a moment the rider had dismounted, and, dealing each of the officers a severe blow on the head, laid them senseless.

"Hillo!" cried Turpin, looking up, "if I'm not mistaken, that's the brave boy who never left a friend in trouble—Tom King."

"It's the same," said King, assisting his friend to his feet; "and what's the matter with poor Jack?"

"He's had a taste of one of their leaden pills."

They now stooped and raised Jack, who was bleeding freely from the breast.

They tore open his shirt, and saw that he had received a severe wound. The bullet had, however, only penetrated the flesh, without injuring any vital part.

They staunched the blood, and set him on his legs again.

Jack gazed about him wildly, and for a few moments could not comprehend the position in which he was placed.

Gradually, however, he discerned what had occurred, and, on

Tom King presenting his hand, grasped it warmly, and gratefully thanked him for his timely rescue.

"By Jove!" said Turpin, "it was a near touch, and I never dreamt of your arrival. If you hadn't come, Newgate and the gallows would have been our doom. But what brought you to us so opportunely?"

"I have been after you since the night you were mad enough to seek the heath. I dreaded some such mischance as this, and could not rest until I had found you. I have been to all the places where I thought it would be likely you had flown, but it was all unavailing. Last night I stumbled on the track of these fellows who now lie at your feet. I tracked them through the night, but lost them until this morning, when I once more chanced to drop upon their route. Heaven be praised! I came up in time to save you."

They now turned their attention to Jack's mare, who, having had a tolerably long rest, recovered her wind, and stood on her legs once more.

"I thought it was all up with the mare," said Jack; "and if it had been, I should have dropped broken-hearted! Poor old girl, she is the best friend I ever had."

"Ah! she's worth twenty dead ones, and will serve your turn for many a long day to come."

"And now what is to be done with these wretched hounds? See, they are opening their eyes once more."

"What is to be done with them!" repeated Turpin; "there's but one thing to be done with them, and that's to tie them, back to back, to the direction post yonder, and there let them stay until some one comes to release them."

"Oh! gentlemen," said the officers in a breath, "you wouldn't do such a thing; we are sure you wouldn't."

"You are sure of no such thing, you wretched hounds. To the post you shall be tied, and if you don't like it, we will give you something else that will be still less palatable."

"Oh! gentlemen, have some mercy; we didn't mean any harm, indeed we didn't."

"I suppose not," said Turpin; "you never do. But come on, no nonsense; to the post you will be tied!"

The men still continued to protest against this treatment, but it was without avail. They were dragged to the direction post and firmly secured thereto, back to back.

The three highwaymen then mounted their steeds, taking the precaution to lead away with them the splendid horses recently ridden by the officers.

"Now," said Tom King, "remain there my fine fellows, and repent of your sins. You will have sufficient time, for the probability is that no one will traverse this road again until to-morrow."

"It's too bad of you," said the officers; "too bad, and you're only joking. Come, let us go free, and we will promise not to molest you again."

"You're very moderate, but such shrewd officers as you must be kept out of the way of temptation; and we couldn't for the world be parties to your discredit. Good-day."

The officers looked at the robbers with imploring eyes, but the three jovial rascals merely shook their hands jocosely as an adieu, and then rode away.

In a very few minutes they were out of sight, and the unhappy limbs of the law were left to contemplate the ridiculous figure they cut.

They could only think, with the highwaymen, that in all probability they would remain where they were until the following day.

CHAPTER XXIX.

TOM KING AND DICK TURPIN PLAN A ROBBERY—SKINWELL'S GOOD FORTUNE—HOW THE HIGHWAYMEN ESCAPED FROM THE MANOR-HOUSE.

Two months have passed away since the events recorded in the last chapter.

It is summer-time, and all the earth is gay, and in the full glory of pure sunshine and zephyr breezes.

The trees are clothed in their bright coats of green, the fields are golden, the hawthorn in the hedges perfume the air, and all is gay and happy.

Two months have passed since Turpin and Jack had their marvellous escape from the officers.

Two months fraught with cares and trials for some of the characters in this our drama—with happiness and bliss to others.

During the period over which we have passed in silence, the new head clerk conducted himself in the office of Mr. Grantley with exemplary care, as far as the world could perceive.

His hours were regular and his habits decorous. The only exception that could be taken to him was that he exhibited a too marked anxiety to relieve himself from all trouble, and a too palpable love of handling the money of the firm without giving anything like a satisfactory account of it.

To Grantley he was civil, but they never became intimate, the young merchant having conceived an unconquerable aversion to the man, and disliking the manner in which he appropriated the cash of the firm.

On this subject he more than once spoke to Skinwell, but that individual laughed off matters by assuring Grantley that his excessive carefulness over the interests of the firm led him into suspicions for which there was not the slightest foundation. He was satisfied, he said, and therefore no one else had any right to raise objections.

Grantley was thus silenced, but not convinced.

He set down the man who was thus patronised by the secretary as a villain, and nothing could divest him of the impression.

Meanwhile all the cash profits of the firm were paid over to Skinwell, who, no doubt, had a fine picking out of them before he accounted for them.

To him was deputed the sole management of the affairs of the great estate, and he continued to turn this authority to his own ends.

One thing only checked him, and that was the presence of the young merchant.

The integrity with which this careful servant watched over the interests of the firm was most extraordinary.

Night and day he was at his post, managing with as much care as if for himself.

Thus the business prospered, but Skinwell was discontented.

He wished to sweep the merchant from his path, in order that he might grasp more; but he found this no easy task, for Grantley gave him no opportunity.

In spite of the care with which Malvers watched for an opportunity for pouncing down upon him, there was none to be found; and the two villains had to bite their lips and await their time.

Grantley had continued to live with Peter Pattypan.

As a matter of course his house at Hackney was taken possession of by the trustees of the charity.

They at first proposed to sell it, but Skinwell persuaded them out of this, and by a skilfully arranged plan induced his employers to allow him to rent the place.

They were only too glad to get a tenant of this kind; and so Skinwell took up his abode in the manor-house, and thither his friend and companion, Malvers, would repair, and remain as long as he thought proper.

Mrs. Grantley did not seem to feel the reverse of fortune that had come upon her, and by her bright smiles contrived to lighten the heart of her husband, who was not, however, capable of looking upon things as cheerfully as herself.

He could not forget that he had brought his wife to poverty.

He well remembered that he had made her father set his face against her, and this saddened him and kept the cloud lingering on his brow.

Mrs. Malvers would watch them attentively for hours together, and grieved that she had failed to make them happy.

Jack she had never seen since the night on which he had become possessed in so mysterious a manner of Skinwell's money.

She could only conclude, therefore, that he had failed, and dared not meet her.

And thus matters progressed, when we again take up the thread of our narrative,

* * * * * *

It was a magnificent night in the month of July, and two well mounted horsemen might have been seen riding gaily from the metropolis towards the little village of Hackney.

They were no others than Turpin and King, the highwaymen

We are privileged to mount their steeds and ride unseen behind them; so we can mark their conversation.

"It's so use," said King to Turpin, "I say it's no use to hesitate. Jack seems determined to do the over-honest in this case, and take that will of Skinwell's, or his friend, whichever of them holds it, to Grantley, and place him in possession free of cost. That won't suit us."

"We have no interest in the people, if he has; and so we must act independently of him, and try and possess ourselves of the document without his knowledge."

"Yes; you have said that before."

"Well, Dick, I will say it again and again, until you are convinced that I am right. It's too good a chance to be thrown away."

"The chance is good enough, but it's this I look at; Jack is a good friend, and he ought not to be put out of the way when we can avoid it. If he has this notion of righting young Grantley, why let him do it—that's all. I half promised to stick to him in the matter, and, I tell you plainly, I've a mind to do it."

"Listen to me, Dick Turpin. Jack is only a friend; we are something more. We are bound together by ties of the most terrible kind; oaths registered above have made us one, if not in thought, at least in action. We are sworn to aid one another in all things, without questioning the advisability of the proceeding. I have aided you and faithfully kept my part of the compact; I now, for the first time, solemnly call upon you to keep yours. I say to you that if we get possession of this will, our fortunes are made; and I am sick of this life, and would gladly relinquish it. By holding the will I can do this; and, therefore, I look upon it as a golden opportunity that must not be lost; so you must and shall aid me."

"Say no more; I am with you; but I shall never be able to look Jack in the face again."

"Nonsense; he is a Quixotic fool, and will only lead you into danger if you think of him. The gallows is staring him in the face. I would avoid so unpleasant an end."

"Well, you expect to be enabled to do this by finding the will of this uncle of the merchant Grantley."

"Yes; with this in my power, I will bleed this Skinwell to death, and make him pay for thrusting me down as he has done. A curse upon him! I have an awful score to wipe out with him one of these days."

"And so have I. I shan't forget the hunting he gave Jack and me for three or four days over a strange country, in which we more than once nearly came to grief.

"Well, either he or that companion of his holds the will. I know they have it about them, and I know it is to be had by a bold dash for it. They are now both at the Manor House at Hackney, once the property of this same young Grantley."

"The place at which we first met him?"

"Yes, Dick, the same. Well, that house must be entered, and its occupants frightened out of the will; or if needs be, knocked on the head. I have determined to have the will this night, and I will do so if I have life and your assistance."

"What makes you so certain that these men carry the will about with them?"

"I tell you they are so jealous of each other that they dare not place the document in any receptacle, for fear of losing it. Neither would hesitate to rob the other, and so I am assured that the one who has the will carries it about his person."

"And they are both here at Hackney?"

"Yes."

"Well, we shall soon know: for see, yonder glimmer must be the lights of the Manor House."

A short ride brought the friends to the Manor House. They concealed their horses in a small coppice that skirted the gardens and lawn, and at once made for the house.

"What plan do you mean to pursue?" asked Turpin, as they stole along the garden and approached the building.

"I have not yet made up my mind, but it is certain that the pair of them must be trapped and searched."

"Do you think they have retired for the night?"

"I'm sure I don't know. By the lights flashing about I should say that they were as yet awake."

"Had we not best wait for another hour or two?"

"Why?"

"Because it is easier to cope with them in their beds; besides, the servants will not be enabled to fly to their assistance so readily."

"That is all very well; but I want to see them together, to hear them speak, to watch their actions. How else shall we get a clue to the will?"

"True, true."

"Now no further talk on the subject; but let us have immediate action. See, yonder, the windows almost reach the ground; it will be easy to enter at that point."

"I'm with you."

They crept along without the slightest noise until they reached the terrace that faced the lawn. This they mounted, and still keeping as much in the shade as possible, approached the windows and peeped in.

The apartment was slightly illuminated. On the table were the remains of a meal, and the number of empty bottles scattered about betokened a very uproarious kind of feast.

"No one there," said King, "and the shutter is open. Come along. We shall get no better chance than this."

They, without much trouble, succeeded in opening the lattice, and entered the apartment, as they thought, unseen.

It so happened, however, that Skinwell, feeling giddy after his deep libations, invited his friend Malvers to take a turn round the grounds before retiring; thus by a single stroke of good fortune, avoiding a meeting with the two desperadoes who entered the house with such evil intentions.

Chance led the secretary and his friend to a clump of trees and bushes, from which a sight of the terrace could be obtained.

Here they kept up a maudlin conversation, the purport of which was that Grantley should be sacrificed as soon as possible.

Drink, it appeared, had not quite destroyed their cunning, for with brains soddened with wine they framed a complete and devilish plot for the ruin of the young man they had already so much injured.

"Look here," said Malvers, "I have it now."

"What have you now?"

"Why, a plan for ridding ourselves of this honest ass."

"Let us hear it."

"Well, here it is. To-night I handed over all the cash to Grantley, at his request, in order that he might make up the quarterly balance-sheet for the trustees."

"Well?"

"Well, in my cash box were notes and gold to the amount of fifteen hundred pounds."

"I do not see your drift yet."

"I will make all clear presently. The cash box was placed in his possession by me. I can swear to that; the amount I can also swear to. Well, I saw where he placed the box, and took the precaution to get an impression of the lock of the safe."

"Well, well?"

"It takes but a few hours to get a duplicate key made at the shop of a locksmith of my acquaintance. And what's so easy as to enter the office to-morrow night, to abstract the cash, and to leave all as secure as left by Grantley himself?"

"But if he banks the money or returns it to you to-morrow morning?"

"I'll take good care he does nothing of the kind."

"Well, so far so good; but if Grantley protests that he knows nothing of the money after it is missed, I don't see how we can fasten guilt upon him."

"Don't you fear. I've a plan! Grantley always carries notes about him, and I have seen him leave his pocket-book about carelessly whilst he has gone on business to the Docks and other places. If I were to take from my box two or three notes and place them in his case, abstracting therefrom others to the amount, do you think he would discover his mistake until he was fairly in the toils?"

"Well, your plan certainly begins to look comprehensive; but these notes—how can you convince people that they are the ones you handed him amongst your cash?"

"How? Do you think I was stupid enough to hand over my money without copying the numbers and dates of all the notes?"

"Good. I begin to see your plans."

"Well, ar'nt they good?"

"Very good. Under the circumstances I don't think they could be better; but—"

"Well—another but?"

"Yes; another and another, if I think proper. But, I say, I doubt if you could induce a magistrate to convict upon such evidence as you could bring."

"I'm of your opinion. We do not want a magistrate to convict; we only want the trustees of the Asylum to dismiss him."

"You are right. It is impossible to catch him tripping, so this is the only course open to us. It only requires to be neatly worked out in order to prove successful."

"Leave all to me. I am sure to bring the affair to a satisfactory termination. Such work is in my line."

They were about to return to the house, when the eye of Skinwell fell upon the terrace of the house.

"Look, look!" he said to his friend.

"Hillo!" said Malvers; "there are two fellows getting in at the dining-room window."

"Yes; and mark them. Have you not seen them before?"

"Never."

"Look again."

"Why, by Jove! I do think I know them. It's Turpin and Tom King."

"Yes, yes. What can they want here?"

"What can they want here? Why, you or I. Both of us, perhaps."

"Wherefore?"

"Because they know that the will must be in the possession of one or other of us, and they mean to have it."

"You don't say so."

"But I do; and so we had best look to ourselves."

"What have I to fear? I have not the will."

"True; but you will not tell them it is in my possession, and thus ruin both?"

"I don't know what to do."

"Your brain is unsteady—your heart fails you. If you do not pluck up some courage you are lost."

"Lost, indeed."

"Come, be a man. Let us think a moment. I have it."

"What will you do?"

"Listen. Are the servants in bed?"

"Some of them. My man, at least, waits up; and, doubtless, the butler has not yet quitted his pantry."

"Very well, then. Run round to the back of the house and arouse the servants, but keep them quiet. Get two stout horses saddled, and let the grooms be ready to mount, them if necessary. Arm them as you best can, but, above all, don't lose a moment."

"And what will you do?"

"My plans are clear. These fellows have horses hereabout, and I must secure them as I best can. Without their steeds they are at our mercy."

"Right. I will endeavour to play my part to your satisfaction."

"Away, then. And mind, no disturbance."

They separated.

Skinwell crept cautiously round to the back of the house, and Malvers ran swiftly to the coppice we have mentioned. There he found the horses of the robbers. Catching them by the bridles, he hurried them away by the carriage road to the stables of the house.

During the time occupied in doing this, Skinwell had managed to arouse his household.

He simply told the men that he believed there were robbers in the house, and bade them prepare to effect their capture.

"They may escape us and get into the open country," he said to the grooms; "therefore, mount two fleet horses, and be prepared for a chase."

The men were delighted at this unexpected bit of excitement, but had they known who the persons simply described as "robbers" were, the possibility is that they would not have hurried in the work, for King and Turpin had that sort of reputation which led men of peaceful inclinings to avoid collisions with them.

In a few minutes all was arranged, and the *denouement* anxiously awaited.

We will return to the two highwaymen.

They entered the dining-room, and, after waiting to see if any one approached, quitted the apartment, and stole through all the others on that floor.

"They're not here," said Turpin, "we had best hide until later in the night."

"They must be somewhere about the house. Let us go up-stairs."

"I don't think it advisable."

"But I do. Not a moment is to be lost. I shall search the upper apartments."

Turpin would have again remonstrated, but King ran up the stairs.

"Hang the fellow," said the less hot-headed of the two; "he is sure to get into some trouble or other."

Turpin was right, for they had no sooner set foot in the corridor above than one of the female domestics rushed from a room, and confronted them.

Finding herself in the presence of strangers of so remarkable an appearance, she uttered a loud scream and ran back again.

"Confusion!" cried King; "she has alarmed the house."

"Yes," said Turpin, "I hear footsteps below. What's to be done?"

"Fly. Hang it, I have made an ass of myself."

"If you had taken my advice you would never have come here."

"It is too late to utter vain regrets. Come—are you ready?"

"Yes."

"Well, then, let us make for the window by which we entered. You may find some of these fellows at the foot of the stairs. Dash through them, and get to the window at all risks. The coppice is to the right; make for that."

They literally flew down the stairs. At the foot, as King had imagined, were two or three male servants, awaiting their appearance.

Drawing their pistols, they used the butt-ends in opening a passage for themselves, and in a few seconds found themselves at the window of the dining-room.

As they prepared to spring through Skinwell entered the apartment, and levelling a pistol, fired.

Turpin dropped, slightly wounded.

In an instant two or three men rushed upon him and bound his arms.

King escaped, and ran with all his might to the coppice.

"Ah! you may run," said Skinwell, looking after him. "You may run, but it's of no avail. Set them after him."

The word was passed round to the mounted grooms to go in pursuit, and ere King had reached the coppice they were flying after him.

"The horses gone!" he cried, staring about him; "the horses gone! Fool that I have been!"

His first impulse was to run, but the sound of horses approaching assured him of the folly of this proceeding.

He stood like a tiger at bay and faced his pursuers.

On they came, and when they were within pistol shot he discharged his weapons full in their faces, but without avail.

He then threw down his weapons and folded his arms doggedly on his breast.

"Come on," he said; "come on. You can take me if you will, for there's no use in resistance."

"You're a sensible fellow," said one of the grooms; "a very sensible fellow. Who are you, and what were you doing here?"

"I'm Tom King; your master knows that well enough. As to what I was doing here, that is my business, and I don't choose to communicate it to ignorant lacqueys, so question me no further."

"Oh! you're Tom King, are you?" said the grooms. "Well, its something for us to say we've done what half the London thieftakers couldn't do—that is, make you surrender yourself a prisoner. But we're bound to say that had we known who you were we shouldn't have been so eager to follow you."

"I'll stake my life on that," said King, as they walked him back to the house.

*　　*　　*　　*　　*

The wound received by Turpin was but a very slight one, and being immediately attended to, caused him but little inconvenience.

"Well, Dick," said Malvers, to the fallen highwayman, "you seem to have made a mistake to-night."

"Yes; but it was none of my seeking."

"Oh, you preferred being led by your friend King to using your own discretion?"

"Ah! had he listened to me, I shouldn't have been here now."

"I suppose not. You were always the most sensible of the two."

"At all events, I knew how to keep out of danger. Well, I hope they won't catch Tom, though he has let me into this mess."

"And I hope they will. In fact, I know they will; for he cannot stand against such cattle as is sent after him."

"Ah, you don't know of what sort of stuff our horses are made."

"Oh yes, I do, or I shouldn't have taken the precaution of locking them up in the stable."

"Black Bess and King's horse locked up! Then it's all over with him."

"I should think so! But don't trouble yourself; the horses are in very good keeping. Hillo! what is that noise?"

At this point Skinwell entered the apartment wherein Malvers was keeping guard over Turpin, and marshalled in the triumphant grooms, holding between them Tom King.

"There you are, you nice pair of beauties, prisoners at last, and no thanks to that fool of a Jew."

"Ah, you may crow now," said King, looking with contempt at Skinwell. "Every cock has full licence on his own dunghill; but my time will come yet."

"Your time, my friend, has come; think not that I will lose sight of you again until you swing on the gallows."

"Bah! that for your boast," cried King, snapping his fingers.

"You will see," said Skinwell, "you will see."

"Take care that you do not see and feel too."

"No more of this," said the secretary, growing warm, "no more. Take them away, and let them cool their heels in the coach-house; I don't think they will get out of that in a hurry; more especially as I shall take the precaution of binding them hand and foot to the wall."

The robbers only sneered at this threat. They were callous now, and their dogged obstinacy exhibited a contempt for punishment and for life itself, marvellous to witness.

Under the escort of a strong body of servants, they were conveyed to the place indicated by Skinwell.

It was a building adjoining the stables, and from its massive gates and locks really looked very like a prison.

There was but one window, and this was a small one, some feet from the ground, strongly secured by large iron bars, between which only a small boy could squeeze his body.

The highwaymen were conducted to this place and secured to a strong post, just under the little window.

They were bound so securely, that to move hand or foot was an entire impossibility.

"See how you like that," said Skinwell, gazing at his prisoners. "You will find that a sort of imprisonment not easily shaken off, I'm thinking. And now make up your minds to remain there until to-morrow, when I'll have you conveyed to Newgate, under an escort that you are not likely to evade."

Neither of the robbers replied, and in a short time they were left to their own reflections.

"Curse them all," said King; "we're in for it this time, and no mistake. Turn as you may, these ropes will never let go their hold of our limbs. Oh, if I could but free my hands."

"It's useless to wish any such thing. The job's too well done for that."

"It is, it is; more's the pity. Oh, Dick, it's not for myself I care; but the thought that I have dragged you into this mess drives me distracted."

"Psha! What matters it for one more than another? I don't mind, for something tells me my time is not yet up."

"I'm not afraid of Newgate," said King; "but it is a lamentable thing to reflect on being brought up by a couple of inexperienced yokels, after having done the very best of the London men."

"So it is, Tom; but it will all come right in the end."

They had no further consolation to offer one another, and so engaged themselves with their own thoughts.

After a few moments thus occupied, a sound, as of the flapping of wings, over their heads, roused them.

"What is that?" asked King.

"I'm sure I don't know, unless it's bats."

"Very likely."

There was another pause, and then the flapping of wings recommenced, accompanied by a loud and long-continued cooing.

"Pigeons," said Turpin, briefly.

"Yes; they come in through that hole over the door. Oh! I should like to be at that hole. In ten minutes I'd make it large enough to pass the pair of us through."

"Wishing again! What folly!"

Once more they relapsed into silence.

An hour passed slowly and gloomily over, and once more there occurred something to startle the prisoners.

The little window became completely darkened, and the moonlight was shut out of the coach-house.

The robbers held their breath.

There was a sound as if some one was pressing his way through the bars.

They strived to look up, but they were too firmly bound.

"Ugh!" they heard a sharp but not unmusical voice exclaim; "ugh; that vos a squeedge, and no mistake. Now for it."

Catching the bars in his hands, the owner of the voice lowered himself suddenly on the heads of the prisoners.

"Hillo!" they shouted in a breath.

"Oh, my eyes!" said the voice, as the body from which it emanated dropped to the ground in affright. "Oh, my eyes: I'm in for it now. Oh! if you please, sir, I didn't go to do it, I didn't—it vos all a mistake, it vos."

"Who are you?" asked King.

"Hey!" said the voice; "hey! Don't I know who that is?"

"How should we know whether you know us or not?" asked Turpin.

"Hillo! vhy, it's Turpin and Tom King."

"It is."

The owner of the voice here drew a dark lantern from his pocket, and flashed in the faces of the highwaymen, at the same time revealing the outline of his own form.

"Why, I've seen you before," said King; "you're that foolish confectioner's boy Sam."

"In course I is. Vhy, vot can you have been up to here, to get in this mess? My eyes! but they haven't forgot to tie you up!"

"I should think they hadn't."

"Vell, how did you get into this pickle?"

King briefly explained.

"And now," said Turpin, "will you tell us what occasioned your visit?"

"Pigeons," said Sam.

"Pigeons!" echoed his hearers.

"Yes, pigeons. Them blessed carriers have been running in my head day and night ever since I came down here to the marriage breaksuff, and this evening I couldn't stand it any longer. 'Come what may,' I says to myself, 'I'm bound to go down and try to get some o' them pigeons.' I asked Mr. Grantley to give me some, and says he, 'They're no longer mine, boy, or you might have the lot.' Well, thinks I, if that's the case, there's no harm in taking a few of 'em; for if they ain't your's they're nobody's; and so I determines on coming down and taking my chance."

"And you mean to say that you have come all the way out here for the purpose of trying to get a few worthless pigeons?"

"Worthless! My eyes! but you know a lot about it, you do. My! there ain't such carriers as these in all England. You should see their beaks. My! but they're stunners."

"The fellow's pigeon mad."

"Yes, I just am. I don't think there's anything like 'em in the vorld except rabbits. They're my particklars, too, they are. Vell, I hung about until I see the old boy who has been a valking round this place take his hook quietly, and then, says I, 'Now's my time,' and so I clambers up to the little vinder and squeedges in; for you must know I've been here before, and know my vay in."

"Well?"

"Vell, and instead of pigeons I drops upon you, and I must say a very pretty mess I finds you in."

"No matter; thanks to the pigeons, you're come; and now, without more ado, cut these cords."

"What for?"

"What for! Why, to set us free, to be sure."

"And vhy should I set you free?"

"For the sake of old times and old acquaintanceship."

"Vell, I vill say that vhenever I vent to the old Jew's crib you treated me vell. But yer see I cut all such friends as you now, for Mrs. Grantley has put before me in a very forcible manner the fact that if I vent on as I vos a going on, the possibility vould be that I should end my precious career on the gallows, and so I've reformed. No beer, no spirits, no short pipes now. Oh no; I'm gone in for 'Honesty is the best policy,' and pigeons."

In spite of themselves, the robbers could not help smiling at this peculiar manifesto on the part of Sam.

"Come," said King; "you're a good boy and I'm glad to see that you have given the old Jew the slip, for he only leads youngsters into dangers. But for all that, there's no earthly reason why you shouldn't cut these cords. If we saw you in this plight, don't you think we'd do the same for you?"

"I suppose you mean escaping?"

"Not a doubt of it, if we only get the chance."

"Vell, that's not the sort o' thing I ought to take part in; but I haven't the heart to cut and leave you in the mess; so here goes."

He drew a clasp-knife from his pocket, and commenced sawing away at the cords of the prisoners.

In a short space of time he had completely cut through the bonds, and the two men were free.

In the greatest glee they sprang away from the post to which they had been so long confined, and dancing with delight they fairly hugged their liberator.

"You're a brick," said Turpin; "and if ever I get a chance to serve you, see if I won't do it."

"Vill you, though?"

"That I will."

"Vell, if you should fall across a nice lot of pigeons"—

"Fall across them! Why, I'd fly after 'em to please you!"

"That's wery good o' you and now I'll take my leave. I say, if you should be caught again, I hope you von't say a vord about me, for I vouldn't have Mrs. Malvers to know of my night's vork for all the vorld."

"All right."

"Wery vell, then, I'll vish you good-night."

Sam scrambled up to the window, and forc his way between the rusted iron bars.

"I say," he said, putting in his head, as he was descending into the yard. "I say, be careful there. I see a figure lurking about in the shadow of the house."

"All right," whispered the highwaymen, and the next moment Sam was gone.

The iron bars of the window were fixed into a framework of wood, and this had, with the damp, and long exposure to the air, become partially rotten.

"Now," said Turpin, putting his hand into his long boot, and drawing out a formidable knife, "now, Tom, stoop down and let me stand upon your back whilst I cut away at the e window-sills, for by that means we must esaape."

"Hush!" said King; "footsteps approach."

"Nonsense; it is but the boy retreating."

"Hist! I say. Listen now."

"By heaven, you are right. They are coming to see that we are all right before finally retiring."

"What shall we do?"

"Here, let us stand close to the door and let them enter. Whoever they are, we can, doubtless, master 'em, if we can but fall upon 'em without their seeing us first."

"You are right. Hark! they are at the door now."

King was right. They were at the door.

Distinctly the prisoners heard the key turn in the lock, and the great iron bar removed.

Then the door swung slowly upon its hinges, and two men entered, the foremost bearing a light.

They advanced some three steps, and had their backs turned upon the highwaymen.

Acting simultaneously, the two friends sprang upon their visitors with crushing force, bearing them heavily to the earth.

The light of the lantern revealed the familiar visages of Malvers and one of the grooms.

"A word," said Dick, raising his knife; "one syllable, and this is buried in your throat."

The eyes of Malvers started from his head, and his face was drawn into a ghastly spectacle, from the horror he experienced.

Kneeling heavily on his chest was Dick Turpin, his knife glittering at his throat.

His companion was in the power of King, and saw that he was helpless.

There was an unseen witness to this scene, and that was the boy Sam, who had seen Malvers and his companion approach, and had returned to see the result of their visit.

"Spare me, spare me!" cried Malvers, as soon as he could find breath to speak. "Oh! do not kill me."

"What would you not have done to us?"

"Oh! do not threaten me with death. I am penitent. I will do all you would ask of me."

"Will you give up the will?"

"What will?"

"What will! There's but one of which I should care to speak, and you know that one well enough."

"Indeed, I have no will."

"What! Dare you lie now?"

The knife was raised once more.

"I do not lie; indeed—indeed, you may believe me."

"Then who has it?"

"Skinwell."

"Where is it concealed?"

"I cannot say."

"A lie! You know full well. Come, I'll force the words from you with the knife."

"Don't, don't. Put away the knife, and I will tell you. He carries the will about with him, and sleeps with it under his pillow."

"Good. You shall conduct us to his chamber, and woe betide you if we go on a bootless errand."

"That's right Dick," said King, who had now bound his man with some of the cords that had lately encircled his own limbs, "stick to that, and we shall have the will."

JACK'S DISCOVERY IN THE BARN.

"Nonsense, nonsense," said Malvers; "you do not mean to make me assist in robbing my benefactor."

"You're capable of doing that, and worse; so none of that cant and hypocrisy, Come, rise and show me the way to the chamber of Skinwell, whilst Tom prepares the horses."

"Indeed, I dare not go there; I cannot."

"Then I am convinced that the will is not there."

"It is, it is," said Malvers.

"It is not, and you know it."

"Come," said Tom King, leaving his prisoner, and walking to the assistance of Dick; "let us search him."

"No, no," cried the affrighted wretch; "no, no, do not do that—do not. Indeed, I have nothing about me."

"Then you can't object to being searched Come, no resistance, or death will be your fate."

They searched him from head to foot, but there was no sign of parchment in any of his pockets.

They were about giving up the thing as lost, when King tore open the fellow's shirt.

Hanging about his neck was a kind of chest-protector, made of soft skin, and tied so tightly as to be entirely imperceptible to the touch.

"What is this?" said King.

"That is nothing. Do not touch it—do not touch it, I beg and entreat you."

"Your entreaties are as nothing. Come, let us have it."

Seizing the skin violently, King tore it from the body of his foe.

"Here," he said, rumpling it in his hands; "hark, Dick; there is parchment here. Ha! ha! at last we have the will, and Skinwell and yourself are in our power."

They bound the two men to the post they had so lately occupied, and tying a handkerchief over the mouth of each, left them, and stalked into the stable-yard.

In the lock on the door of the coach-house they found a bunch of keys.

"They belong to the groom," said King, "and consequently will open the stables. If we can't find our own steeds we will have others."

They ran in the direction of the stables, and, as chance willed it, they opened the very one in which their own noble animals awaited them, ready bridled and saddled.

To spring upon their backs and dash out of the stable-yard was but the work of an instant.

There was another individual who quitted the precincts of the Manor House by another way at the same moment.

It was the boy Sam.

"Vell," he said to himself, "vell! I vonder vot vill it vos ! I vish I knew more about it. *I'll not let it drop!*"

CHAPTER XXX.

TOM KING'S LETTER TO SKINWELL—PLAYING A DANGEROUS GAME—SIXTEEN-STRING JACK HAS A LONG TALK WITH SAM—THE PLOT TO DISHONOUR GRANTLEY—THE PURLOINED CASH-BOX—THE MURDER AND THE WITNESS.

THE astonishment of Skinwell on discovering what had been the result of Malvers' visit to the prisoners may be readily conceived.

The secretary raved and stormed for hours, and could not be appeased.

' The will gone ! We are bowled out beggars—convicted felons ! Oh ! what will be the end of this ?''

" Psha !'' cried Malvers; " cease these childish ravings, and think.''

" How can I think ? In a few hours the will and the history attached to it may be in the possession of Grantley.''

" May be ! Ah ! may be ; but the chances are that it will never come into his hands.''

" How ? ''

" Does not your sense tell you that these fellows will reflect now much more they can make out of you than him ? Depend upon it, before the day is out, you will have some proposition from the fellows.''

" I doubt it. And even if I have, can I league myself with such wretches ? Can I associate myself in a criminal partnership with two notorious highway robbers ?''

" Well, you might do worse; at all events for a time. For my own part, they are just the sort of people I should like to work with, for the possibility is that the connection would be but a short one. A pistol-shot or a hempen cravat may end their career so suddenly and with such advantage to one's self.''

" You are right. It might have been worse. Ah ! if they will only keep the secret.''

" Fear nothing. Go to your office the same as usual, and I will go to mine. Depend upon it you will find that I am right. You will hear of these fellows before long and in the manner I have mentioned.''

Skinwell took the advice of his friend, and after breakfast on the morning after their encounter with the robbers they rode to London together, and went about their several avocations as if nothing whatever had happened.

Malvers was right.

Before mid-day Skinwell received the following letter :—

" You see we have won the fight, although you struggled so hard for victory. Fortune has favoured us, and the will is in our power.

" Are we to hand it to Grantley, or will you pay us for keeping it secret ?

" We want money, and if you are prepared to advance it to the amount required by us we will serve you faithfully.

" Why should we quarrel over this matter ? There is enough in the estate for us all to share handsomely; and so no hesitation, but extend the hand of fellowship, and let the past be wiped away from our memories.

" We await your answer. If you mean to row with us come to-night to the Red Rose. Your friend will show you the way; and, as earnest of straightforwardness, bring with you £5000. That is the sum we shall want in our preliminary arrangement.

" The future course can be marked out afterward.

" We shall expect you at nine o'clock. Do not fail.

" Yours in good faith,
" Tom King, for self and
" Dick Turpin.''

" Confusion !'' cried the secretary, as he read this letter. " Confusion ! What am I not reduced to ? What terrible fate hangs over me ? These men, these devils, will either bring me to the gallows or drive me mad, mad, mad !''

He seized his hat and set out for the office of Malvers, in order that he might lay the letter before him and receive his opinion thereon.

    *   *   *   *   *

It was about the same time when Sixteen-String Jack—muffled and disguised beyond recognition—knocked at the side-door of Peter Pittypan's establishment in Holborn and demanded an interview with Mrs. Malvers.

The door was opened to him by Sam.

" Hillo !'' said that worthy, who looked all the worse for having no rest the previous night. " Hillo ! What brought you here ?''

" Here, come inside and shut the door. I've something to say to you.''

" To me ?''

" Yes, to you. Are you in a hurry to see the lady ?''

" No. Unfortunately, I have nothing very particular to say to her.''

" Vell, if that's the case you may as vell come into the bakehouse and listen to me for a few minutes. I've somethink to tell ye that will amuse ye, I'm thinking ''

Jack followed Peter's dutiful apprentice into the bakehouse, and, standing before him, asked him the nature of the communication he had to make.

" Vell, you know—but hadn't you better take a seat

Jack did not see anything to sit upon.

" Vell, on second thoughts, you had best stand up ; flour don't, as a rule, improve the appearance of black clothes.''

" Now, what can you have to say to me ?'' said Jack, impatiently.

" Vell, to commence again. You know Turpin and King ?''

" Of course I do. Was it to ask me that you brought me here ?''

" No, it vosn't ; but don't be so impatient. Vell, you do know Turpin and King and so that's settled. You vouldn't believe that I met 'em in the country last night, vould you ? ''

" Met Turpin and King in the country ?

" Yes ; at Mr. Grantley's old house at Hackney.''

" You are jesting ?''

" Never more serious in all my born days.''

Jack suddenly evinced more interest in the words of the youngster.

" Yes,'' continued Sam ; " and under peculiar circumstances. I'll tell ye how it was.''

" Do.''

" You know I'm awful fond of pigeons ? ''

" Yes, yes.''

" Vell, I knew there vos some stunners at Grantley's old place, and I thought last night that I'd have a few of 'em, and so set out for Hackney. Ven I vos there at the vedding breaksuff, you know, I marked their roosting-place—an old coach-house—the only entrance to vich vos a little vinder, through vich I could barely squeedge.''

" I am all attention.''

" Arrived at Hackney, and getting, without much difficulty, into the stable-yard, I squeedged myself through the vinder, and who should I come down upon but King and Turpin bound hand and foot to a post.''

" Indeed !''

" Yes ; they had been made prisoners during the day, and vere awaiting the morning to be took off to Newgate, like lambs to the slaughter-house I released 'em, and took my leave vithout the pigeons; but after I had got a few paces from the stable, who should I see but two men a coming ou from the house, and carrying a lantern vith them. ' Now,' said I to myself, ' there vill be some fun in that coach-house, and so I'll go back and have a peep at it.' Sure enough, the two men vent straight to the coach-house, and opening the door, valked in—like flies a going into the spider's veb. I mounted to the vinder, and vot should I see but Turpin and King, vith the men under 'em, holding knives to their throats and threatening vith death if they squeaked. Vell, the vun that Turpin handled appeared to be a sort o' swell in his vay, and Dick stuck to him until he frightend his vits out. It appeared he wanted a vill from him.''

" A will !''

" Yes ; for he continued to ask him vere it vos concealed; and the other fellow said at first that he didn't know, and then that it vos under Skinwell's piller, and all that kind o' thing; vhen Tom King pulls open his shirt, and sings out that he had got the document,''

" Indeed ! Are you sure ?

" Quite sure. ' Vell,' I thought to myself, ' this is a rum start,' and I couldn't forget it; for, d'ye see, there's so much talk o' vills in this house, that the least mention o' vun brings a feller up vith a rou d turn ; more especially ven it's mentioned in connection vith the fellers that have turned poor Mr Grantley out of his property.''

" You are right, boy, you are right. Oh, you little dear,

the benefit you have conferred on Mr. Grantley by telling me this; you can but little conceive the good you have done!"

" Hey! vot the deuce d'ye mean?"

" I mean that you have put me once more on the track of the holder of the document which restores happiness to the Grantleys, and which I thought was lost to me for ever. But not a word of this to anyone, not a syllable; for if we raise any false hopes, it will perhaps break their hearts. Good-bye."

" You're not going?"

" Yes."

" But Mrs. Malvers?"

" I'll see her when I have better news to give her. Adieu."

" But vhere are you off to?"

" To hunt down the oppressors of the Grantleys."

Jack was gone.

At the promised hour Skinwell and his ally sought out the disreputable haunt mentioned in the letter of the highwayman, for the purpose of ratifying the bargain proposed by King.

On meeting with Skinwell, the new head-clerk explained to him the success with which he had plotted the ruin of Grantley.

" It is all right," he said, " it has turned out just as I wished—nothing could be better. I opened his safe unseen and changed the notes without detection. He is now completely in our power."

" You forget that the most difficult part of the undertaking has yet to be accomplished. The taking of the cash-box."

" Leave all to me! I know what I am about, and will not fail."

" I trust to find that you have kept your word."

" I shall be certain to do so."

They walked on in the darkness down into the depths of the Minories and entered the house appointed for the meeting.

What avails it to dwell upon the scene?

Why should we recount the fierce retorts, the oaths, the haggling, and the mutual recrimination of that meeting?

It was a scene of violence and wretched depravity.

We will hasten it over, merely pausing to relate that, after a struggle for supremacy, Skinwell had to give way to the demands of the highwaymen, that the money was paid, and secrecy and mutual interest sworn to.

They then parted, having cemented the bond of fellowship in crime.

Finding their way out of the Minories, the secretary and Malvers parted near London-bridge.

The former hastened to the place where his carriage awaited him, and the latter went about his work of crime at the warehouse of Grantley, or rather of the trustees of the City of London Orphan Asylum.

It was a beautiful moonlight night, and as he passed through the little churchyard against which the offices of " the firm " lay, the old tombstones stood out in bold relief, and the dewdrops hung in pearl-like clusters to the boughs of the old willow trees.

Myriads of stars sparkled in the bright blue canopy of heaven, and all was still and serene.

In the bosom of one less hardened in crime than Malvers such a night and such a scene would have had the effect of turning him from the work he had in hand; but no thought of heaven, no reflection on death crossed the mind of the reprobate.

He had assisted in the murder of one nearly related to his own wife; he had tried his best to fix the terrible guilt upon her; he had sunk down into the depths of degradation, and he earned his daily bread by crime.

He envied not the repose of those good old citizens who slept peacefully beneath his feet.

Their lives passed in honesty and peace, their deaths, calm and Christian-like, their repose sweet and uninterrupted beneath the shadow of the ancient church, whose bells had rung in their ears from infancy, whose minister had guided them in their onward path, and soothed their last moments, had no more for him.

He was a dark, bad man.

His back was turned towards heaven, and sin held possession of his soul.

He could not pause to think lest repentance should come and unnerve him.

Onward he went on his wretched path, and he bore on his brow the sign of a God-forgotten man.

Onward through the churchyard he crept.

He reached the steps leading to the spot where the little archway led to the grim old warehouses and offices.

The wicket was locked.

" That's a difficulty very soon overcome," said he, thrusting a key into the lock. " There, it is well I took the precaution to take casts of all these keys, for they certainly take good care of the old place a night."

He gently re-closed the door, and walked under the shadow of the old houses to the offices.

Again he had recourse to his keys, and in a few moments he was within.

He re-locked the door, and then turned on the light of a dark lantern.

By its aid he threaded the labyrinth of desks and found the private room of Grantley.

" So far, so well," he said; " but hang it, how dark and dismal it is, and how wretched I feel here. What woman's fears are these? Courage; there is work to do, and it must be done without shrinking."

He advanced to the safe, and making use of a key of peculiar construction, which he drew from his bosom, the great door opened, and he laid his hand upon the cash-box.

" I have it," he muttered, " I have it, and all is well."

The door of the safe was closed and he was about to leave the office, when his eye lighted upon certain articles that lay upon the table.

Malvers turned the light of his lantern full upon them.

They were a penknife, a pocket-handkerchief, and two or three letters addressed to Grantley.

" They belong to Grantley," he said; " as usual, he is careless of everything that has no interest to the firm. Well; they are of no use to me, let them lie where they are."

He was about to leave them when some other thought struck him, and taking up the articles he placed them in his pocket.

He now left the place.

Stealthily as he came, so he retraced his steps.

The door of the offices was closed, and he left behind him no sign of the entrance and departure of a burglar.

His work was done in consummate style, and it would have puzzled the most acute observer to have found the slightest trace of his presence.

All went well until he reached the little archway, and here, standing in his path, and holding a lantern full in his face was the old porter.

Malvers started back aghast at this sudden and unexpected apparition.

" What shall I do? He recognises me! A curse upon him! I had forgotten that he lived here."

It is always so with the criminal, he always forgets one point.

Cleverly as he may do his work, well as he may wipe out the traces of his presence, there is always that one point forgotten that leads to his detection and conviction.

Escape for a while may be possible—years may elapse before the day arrives; but it will come, and the terrible all-convincing " one point " starts forward, and guides the hand of justice in the execution of its work.

The point in this instance was the presence of the old porter. Malvers had not given him a thought, and here, as he was escaping successfully, the old man stood in his path like an accusing spirit, and demanded his business there.

" Ask no questions, dotard," said the clerk. " Can I not come and go when I please? I am managing clerk at this place now."

" No one ever came here at this hour before. I have known the firm, man and boy, these"——

" Oh, curse your reminiscences; I don't want to know them."

" You have a cash-box under your arm ; it's Mr. Grantley's box. I know it well."

" Confusion! detected, trapped ! Then there is nought for it but his death. It is none of my seeking. Meddlesome old fool that he is, to thrust himself in the way of danger."

Malvers dropped the box, and sprang upon the terrified old man.

" Fool," he cried, at his fingers grasped the throat of the honest old man, " fool, you have sought your own death; receive it from me !"

He dashed the old man to the earth, and then placed his knee upon his chest, and made his fingers meet over his throat.

There was but one faint struggle, and then the old man was dead.

But there was no compunction in the face of his murderer. No; he was too hardened to think of aught but that he had effected—aught but his own safety.

And so the old man lay under the archway, with the pale moonlight streaming down upon him, and his murderer picked up his booty, and prepared to unlock the wicket.

Cautiously he peered forth.

All was still, and the little alley appeared to be empty.

" 'Tis well," he cried; " I can go forth in safety."

As he spoke, a sudden thought struck him.

" *The things I took from Grantley's desk !* "

The idea was prompted by the fiend himself.

Malvers took from his pocket the articles that he had snatched from the young merchant's office, and then walked away.

" It must fix the guilt upon him !" he cried, " aye, upon him ; and I shall have full sway at the old place now."

As he moved away, a figure started from the opposite side of the way, and rushed to the little wicket.

It was a boy, whose costume plainly bespoke him the apprentice of a baker and confectioner.

" Hillo !" he said; " you're out again at last, are you, my old boy ? I've vaited a long time for ye. Let's see vot yer've been up to."

The boy thrust open the little wicket which in his haste Malvers had forgotten to lock, and peeped into the archway.

" Hillo !" he cried, " hillo, there ; get up."

He saw no sign of life in the old man he addressed, and advancing towards him, endeavoured to lift him from the ground.

Then he saw that he was dead.

" Murder, hey ? Vell, I'm arter ye, my boy."

He dashed through the wicket, and ran through the church-yard in the direction Malvers had taken.

The boy was none other than Sam, the apprentice of Peter Pattypan, the confectioner of Holborn.

He had been set on the track of the murderer by Sixteen-String Jack.

CHAPTER XXXI.

JACK SETTLES ACCOUNTS WITH TOM KING IN FULHAM CHURCHYARD — THE DUEL—THE INTERRUPTION — THE WILL FOUND AND THE FLIGHT TO LONDON—MRS. MALVERS ACCOMPLISHES HER WISH.

TOWARDS night, on the day of the meeting between Jack and Sam, the apprentice, Jack, acting on some information he had received, sought out the young pigeon-fancier, and told him to track the man he had seen used so ill by Turpin and King.

" Do not leave him for a moment. I suspect some foul play is intended Mr. Grantley, and to you I entrust the task of seeking out the plot."

" I'm there," said Sam, delighted at being employed in a manner so congenial to his tastes, " vhere's the shop ? "

" If you mean where are you to meet the villain, behind a tombstone in —— Churchyard at an hour before midnight, and there await him."

" I say, vot a lively billet !"

" Are you afraid ? "

" I'm not afraid of nothink. Vot d'ye think o' that ? "

" Well, I think you are a tolerably courageous boy, and I know I can trust you ; so be at your post, and mind you stick to the fellow like a bloodhound."

" I'll never leave him if vunce I set eyes upon him. But vot's yer game ? "

" I'm upon the track of Tom King. I want that which he shall this night yield up to me."

" All right; as long as you means right by Mr. Grantley, I'm vith you through thick and thin. But, my eye! von't there be a shine vith the guv'nor if he finds that I'm out again to-night ! Maybe I didn't get a vigging this morning ven I valked home !"

" No matter; you must risk all in the cause of Mr. Grantley. Do we understand each other ? "

" And no mistake."

They parted.

What was the success of the boy's mission we have partly seen ; but we must leave him now, to follow the footsteps of Rann.

What he had heard led him to believe that King, after settling affairs with Skinwell and his friend, projected a visit to a little villa beyond the Bishop's-walk at Clapham, wherein lived one he had made up his mind to rob.

This intelligence came from Turpin, who, after all, could not find it in his heart to break faith with Jack.

" He is pursuing the most straightforward plan, and I detest this trickery and skulking. I'll tell Jack all, and let him act for himself. I can lie neutral and see them play it out, and I hope that the most deserving will win."

It was about an hour after his parting with those he had so cleverly tricked, that Tom King set out on the road to Putney.

He was habited in a great black cloak, and rode a strange horse ; but Jack knew him, and at a distance followed him on his errand.

The road to Fulham in those days was not bound in by shops and streets of fashionable dwelling-houses as it is now.

After passing Hyde-park, the houses became very few and straggling, and the road lay in the open country.

The night was, as we have before said, a brilliant one, and the horse of the highwayman cantered merrily along the road.

A quarter of a mile behind him rode Jack Rann, bent upon obtaining from King the document he bore about his person.

A ride of little more than an hour brought the men to the little mean village of Fulham.

Here Rann drew rein, and allowed King to get a good lead of him.

He saw Tom pull up at a little public house, called the Bells, and here his horse was left.

The dusky figure of the robber could be marked in the bright moonlight stalking away towards the old churchyard of Fulham ; and, as he passed through the little wicket, Rann advanced.

He marked the outline of the man he had dogged, fading away in the distance, and then he dismounted from his mare, and securing her to the little gate, he entered the churchyard.

" Here," he said, " here among these old tombs, I will await his coming, and here we will settle our accounts. Fitting place! for assuredly one or other of us will fall. We are both desperate men, and the strongest and most skilful will prove the victor."

It was a splendid old churchyard ; full of antique tombs and monuments, and with beds of choice flowers tastefully laid out and well-tended.

It was approached at each end by a wicket—the one leading into the village, the other opening on the path leading to Bishop's Walk ; so called because it was the path to the palace of the Bishop of London.

Stately trees bound in the bishop's garden, and overshadowed the path to the churchyard.

The church itself - a fine old edifice, simple in its architectural arrangements, grand in its age and memories—lay nestled in a corner, and stood grandly out in the moonlight, throwing its shadows over the pathways.

The trees whispered as they were stirred by the gentle breeze, and in the distance was heard the ripple of the Thames, as it flowed sluggishly on.

Close at hand was the old wooden bridge, on which flickered the sickly oil lamps, and across the water, conspicuous in the bright moonlight, was the little town of Putney, in solemn repose.

Such was the spot in which Jack awaited the coming of King.

Time flew on, and two o'clock came without bringing with it Tom King.

Jack began to despair of his coming.

" If he should have taken another road ! "

This thought began to haunt the watcher, when a shadow approached the wicket at the further end of the churchyard, and a pedestrian approached.

" At length," cried Jack, " at length he is here."

He shrank away behind a large tomb, and awaited the approach of King, who hastened along the path with rapid strides.

He was within a pace of the tomb behind which Jack was hiding, when that worthy sprang forward and confronted him.

" Stop ! " he cried.

" Hillo ! " said King, stepping back and placing his hand on a pistol, " hillo ! what is this ? "

Don't you know me ? "

" Why, yes ; it's Sixteen-String Jack. Whew ! What a fright you gave me ! Well, Jack, what brought you to Fulham churchyard to-night ? "

" I came to see you."

" To see me ? Couldn't you find me in London ? "

" Yes ; but I chose to follow you here."

" What, in the name of fate, are you after ? There is something in your manner and voice that seems strange to me. I can't comprehend you."

" You will before we have done."

" That sounds like a threat."

" The sound matters little to me."

" Come, Jack, you are mad ! This is not the language friends should use to each other."

" It may not be the language of friends, but it is the language of plain, straightforward business, and that is all I have to do with you, Tom King ; for you are no longer a friend of mine."

" Psha ! let me pass ; you are either drunk or mad, and in either case I wish to hold no talk with you."

" I am neither drunk nor mad, and you must listen to me. Now without further preface, I will tell you why I have followed you to this place. You have wronged an honest man, and I have come here to right him."

" What do you mean ? "

" I mean that you have played Grantley false, after his having placed infinite trust in you. You tricked and robbed him, and are now plotting with villains to keep him steeped in poverty and wretchedness. It is to crush your infamous plans that I have sought you on this spot at this time."

" Indeed ! "

" Yes, indeed ! You bear yourself boldly ; you think, perhaps, to awe me, but I have a will as strong as your own, and I am come here with the fixed determination of risking my life in doing justice to those you have oppressed and bowed down in sorrow. I want from you the will you have concealed about your person."

" The will ! "

" Yes ; the second will of the old merchant, bequeathing the whole of his wealth to Grantley."

" Psha ! you rave. What do I know of your Grantleys and wills ? "

" Seek not to evade me by a lie, Tom King, I tell you there is a document in your bosom that I must and will have ; so produce it."

" Since it is come to that," said King, growing furious, " I own I have the will ; but I tell you to your teeth that it shall not pass into your possession."

" I have sworn to have it, and I will keep my oath."

" Since you are thus obstinate, there is nothing for it but this "

As he spoke, he placed his hand in his belt and drew forth a pistol, which he hastily cocked and presented at Jack's head.

Rann was as quick as himself, and his weapon was levelled at the same time.

" You see, I am prepared to meet you even, at that game.

" Come, drop your pistol, and don't be a fool," said King

" I have no wish to fire, but I shall do so if you refuse to hand me the will."

" Listen to me, Jack. You shall share in the game—there's only Turpin and I in it—and you shall have your third. Will that satisfy you ? "

" Nothing will satisfy me but the will. Am I to have it ? "

" No."

" Then turn and step back five paces, and I will do the same. As soon as we have measured the distance we face about and fire."

" This is direct madness. Why should we kill each other ? "

" I have spoken."

" Since it must be so, I am prepared. Come, count five paces."

They turned their backs upon each other and commenced walking the five paces.

" One ! "

" Two ! "

" Three ! "

" Four ! "

There was a loud report, and a shot whistled close to Jack's ear.

With a yell, King fell.

The next moment Jack was at his side.

With hasty hand he tore open the vest of the highwaymen, and snatched from a deep pocket a parchment which a glance sufficed to tell him was the will he sought. There were voices close at hand, and, starting to his feet, Jack turned and fled towards the gate.

As he passed through, several men, coming from the direction of the river, rushed upon him, and he had to battle his way through them.

Endowed with the strength of a lion, he soon dashed his assailants on one side, and then, springing upon his steed, galloped away on the London road.

As soon as the men recovered their senses, and regained their feet, they dashed into the churchyard, and there found the body of Tom King.

" There's been murder and robbery done here. Quick—get some horses and foller that feller. Quick, quick, or he'll gi' us the double."

The men ran back again to the wicket, and no sooner were they in the road than two horsemen from Putney rode up.

" What was the meaning of those shots ? " demanded one.

" There's been murder going on in the old churchyard yonder. The feller as did it has just rid off on the London road. Arter 'un, arter 'un, and bring 'un down."

" It's lucky we came up just now. We're officers."

" Then you couldn't 'a come in better time. Go like wind. He's well mounted, and nothun' short of a clipper will catch 'un."

Two men now brought the body of King from the churchyard, and the officers, drawing from their pockets small lanterns, turned their light full upon his face.

" As I live," shouted one, " it's Tom King, the highwayman."

" Tom King ! " shouted the men in a chorus.

" Yes, Tom King," continued the officer. " Did any o you catch sight of the fellow that's ridden away ? "

" Yes, we all saw 'un."

" How was he dressed ? "

" We don't know."

" What, was there nothing peculiar about him ? "

" No."

" Yes, there was," shouted one who had not before spoken. " There was just this peculiarity about him : as he knocked me down I caught at his boot, and *this* came off in my hand. ' *He held up a bunch of many-coloured ribbons !*

" Oh ! " said the officers, " we know now who it was.

"Do 'e, though? And who was it?"

"Sixteen-String Jack."

With this the men du bed spurs into the sides of their steeds, and galloped away at a frightful pace.

Something seemed to tell Jack that he was followed, for he rode at a tremendous pace, and never eased his mare a second.

Great, however, as was the prowess of his steed, those behind him were not a whit worse mounted, and ere long the clatter of hoofs rang in his ears.

There was but one thought in his mind. He was possessed by but one fixed idea, and that was to reach the house of Peter Pattypan.

"The will in the hands of Mrs. Malvers," he thought, "and all will be well."

Forward he dashed, and his mare answered gallantly to the sound of his voice.

It seemed to him but a few moments' ride from the churchyard to Hyde park Corner.

A few brief moments, but still moments of intense agony; for behind him, nearer and nearer, came the clatter of the horses following him.

Nearer and nearer. Still onwards he dashed.

Now over the rough stones of London.

Street after street was passed, and still he pressed forward.

At length the well-known shop on the hill met his gaze, and he spurred on his mare to the door.

During the last five minutes of the ride he had ceased to hear the sound of the hoofs behind him.

He sprang to the ground and approached the door.

All was still, and in the distance he could distinctly hear the patter of horses' hoofs again.

Wildly he beat at the door of Peter's house, and then turned to face his pursuers.

The noise of their horses' hoofs rang still more clearly on the hard stones of Holborn, but as yet they were not in sight.

"There is hope yet," cried Jack, as he raised his hand to the knocker once more.

He was about to repeat his summons, when the door opened and he sprang into the passage.

"I knew it was you," said Mrs Malvers, who had opened the door, "I knew it was you, Rann, for throughout the night something whispered me that you would come."

"Close the door," said Jack; "I am pursued."

The door was closed and locked on the instant.

"Come with me to the upper apartments; there is a light in the front room."

"Quick, then, or they may be upon me."

"Of whom do you speak?"

"I know not who they are, but men are in pursuit of me."

"What brought you here?"

"What should bring me here, but the one thing you and I have most at heart?"

"The will?"

"Yes, the will."

"Is there, then, hope? Have you any trace of it?"

"Behold it!"

Jack drew from his bosom the parchment, and placed it in the hands of Mrs. Malvers.

She grasped it eagerly, and was about to open it, when the light of the lamp fell upon it.

It was stained with blood.

Shudderingly she let it fall from her grasp.

"Nay, do not heed the blood," cried Rann; "it is that of a villain and traitor. He deserved the death I gave him."

"I dare not touch it."

"Do not hesitate. For God's sake, secure it. Has not enough already been risked for its possession? Can you afford to let it slip again?"

"True, I am a weak-hearted fool to hesitate. I will secure it at once."

"Where is Mr. Grantley? It were best in his possession."

"He is from home. We have been expecting him many hours, and he has not arrived."

"Indeed. Then lide it where you will, but be sure and place it in safety, for once gone it is gone for ever."

At this moment there was a great knocking at the door of the house, and it appeared as if the whole fabric was shaken to the foundation.

"What is that?" said Mrs. Malvers.

"It is the men who are tracking me."

Here Peter and his servants, accompanied by Mr. Grantley, entered the room.

"What is the matter?" cried Mrs. Grantley, in extreme terror.

"Hillo!" said Peter; "here's that highwayman again. I suppose it's his friends at the door, who want to rob and murder us all."

"Look!" cried Mrs. Malvers, unfolding the will, and flourishing it under the eyes of Mrs. Grantley. "Look, dearest—a second will, bequeathing all to your husband. See, you are restored to happiness through Rann."

Mrs. Grantley gazed at the will in amazement, and ran her eyes hastily over the words.

There was no mistaking it. The plain, indisputable document restored her husband to wealth and the position from which he had been torn.

The fact was more than she was capable of bearing, and bursting into tears, she sank, insensible and exhausted, into the arms of the women.

"Mr Grantley's wealth restored!" cried Peter. "Well, I'll have my tongue torn out if ever I say a word against a highwayman again as long as I live!"

"Hark!" said Mrs. Malvers, opening the door, and listening; "hark! they are forcing the street door. What is to be done? They will assuredly capture Rann."

"I'll blow their brains out first!" cried little Peter, in a fever of excitement. "Capture Rann, the saver of Grantley! They had better not try it on."

"Listen! the door seems to give way. What is to be done?"

"What is the distance into the street from this window?" asked Jack.

"Sixteen feet," replied Peter.

"Very well," said Jack; "go you to the door and keep them in conversation for a few minutes, and I will effect my escape this way. Fetch me a sheet."

"I'll do as you bid me," said Peter; "and take my word for it, they don't come in until you are gone, if they send me to Newgate as an aider and abettor."

"So far so good," replied Jack. "Do you fetch me the sheet," he said to Peter, who straightway ran to fulfil his orders.

Peter slowly descended the stairs, and walked to the street door.

"Hillo!" he shouted, "who's there? and why do you disturb me with your riot?"

"Open, in the King's name; we are officers."

"And wherefore should I open to you?"

"Because you have within your house a robber and murderer named John Rann, upon whose head a price is set, and whom we demand you at once to deliver up to us?"

"Get away with you," cried Peter; "you talk like madmen; there is no such person here."

"You lie! We have tracked him to the very door, and here stands his horse."

"I tell you, you labour under an error, and beg of you to go away."

"Not without Rann. Will you open?"

"Not without sufficient reason."

"We have given our reason for our demands; and if you do not comply with them, we will tear down your door."

"Well, you've tried very hard to do that during the last five minutes; perhaps you had better continue the amusement."

"Come," said one to the other, "lend your weight here, and let us have this door down; this fellow is playing with us."

Peter was in a great state of excitement, and listened to the blows that fell in a continuous shower on the door, in an agony of hope and fear.

The door held out bravely, but nothing could withstand the

tremendous blows that were dealt it. At length it creaked and groaned, and its hinges were giving way from their sockets.

Just as the little confectioner was about to give up in despair. Mrs. Malvers glided down the stairs and stood at his side.

Peter started.

"Lor'!" he said, "how you did startle me!"

"Open the door," she said, without heeding his remark; "all is prepared for his escape."

"Through the window?"

"Yes."

"All right, then. Hillo!" he cried, "since you appear so determined on entering the house. I'll open the door; but I warn you that I'd have justice for this annoyance."

"Open on the instant."

"Very good; I'm opening as fast as I can."

He slowly withdrew the bolts, and unlooped the chain.

In another moment the men dashed into the passage.

"Come along," cried one, "there are lights in the room on the first floor."

"Forward, then."

"Oh, yes, forward," cried Peter; "and much good may it do you."

With a rush, the officers dashed past Peter up the stairs.

They paused at the door of the front room, in which they suspected was hidden their man.

The door was tried.

It was locke

"Burst it open, Geoffery! or by the fiends he will escape," exclaimed the leader of the runners.

In a moment, with a crash, the door was torn from its hinges.

The officers, with a yell, rushing into the room.

Cries of rage and fury escaped their lips.

The bird had flown.

Sixteen-String Jack was gone.

CHAPTER XXXII.

THE FLIGHT FROM LONDON—THE MOONLIGHT RIDE—THE MEETING WITH THE STRANGE HORSEMAN—"MONEY OR YOUR LIFE"—ARRIVAL OF THE RUNNERS—A RACE AND A RUSE—EXULTATION OF SIXTEEN-STRING JACK—THE CANTER THROUGH WILLESDEN—THE LONE FARM-HOUSE —THE WHITE FIGURE IN THE MOONLIGHT—THE STRANGE DISCOVERY IN THE OLD BARN.

WHEN left by Mrs. Malvers, Jack had completed all his preparations for a descent from the casement, and as the officers were admitted into the house he slid down the sheets and table covers he had fastened to the window, and stood in the street. To knock down a man who held his mare by the head, and vault into the saddle, was with our hero the work of a moment, and as the enraged runners made their appearance at the open casement with a loud shout of triumph the daring highwayman gave his bonny steed the reins, and with the swiftness of thought was borne from the spot.

It was a lovely night.

The moon shone bright and clear in the blue vault above.

The hour a late one, there were but few passengers in the streets

Faint shouts were borne to his ears on the wings of the wind.

It was the cries of his pursuers.

The officers were on his track.

A warm glow darted through the frame of Jack, who patted his bonny steed, and urged her on in the race.

To him, a race for life.

"Hillo! away, Meg, lass! show them what you are made of! Ha, ha, ha! the will in the hands of Mrs. Malvers will to-morrow be in possession of Edwin Grantley. I have fulfilled my task. I swore to place the precious document in its owners' hands, and Sixteen-String Jack never breaks an oath or forgives an enemy. I would to Heaven poor King had fallen by

any hand but mine; but 'twas not to be; he brought his fate upon his own head. 'Twas written, nor I nor he could reverse the page of destiny."

Moodily reflecting upon the events of the night and the scene in the churchyard, Jack rode on—nor heeded that the shouts of his pursuers sounded every moment plainer and plainer on the air.

He was lost in reverie.

Tom King, he who had been a friend, had fallen by his hand.

Though he deserved his fate, yet did Jack lament his death.

At length, roused by the cries of his foes now ringing loudly in his ears, he pressed the sides of his steed, who again started off at a terrific pace.

Excited by the race, Jack halloo'd loudly, as his bonny mare dashed on.

The shouts of the officers growing fainter and fainter in the distance.

Jack, who had taken to the north road, had now left London behind him some four or five miles.

Open country was before him—thickset hedges lined the road, whilst here and there a tall poplar or grim-looking wych-elm reared its height up in the air.

The moon, bright and lustrous, cast a silvery radiance on all around.

Bathing all alike in a flood of light.

Like an electric flash, the highwayman passed along the road.

The hedges and trees flitting past him as his brave steed bounded on.

Wildly he shouted as he was borne onwards.

A hamlet was reached and passed, a quarter of a mile beyond was a roadside inn, the few lights in the windows of which were no sooner seen than they were lost.

With the speed of a whirlwind, Sixteen-String Jack dashed along the road.

His bosom heaving with the excitement of the race.

But what is this? another horseman on the road, but coming along in the contrary direction! A loud shout escapes the lips of Jack.

Who, with his usual impulsive daring, has resolved to waylay the traveller whom he is about to meet.

The clatter of the hoofs of the horses ridden by his foes, sounding in his ears, deters him not.

"I'll do it! in spite of them. So ho, Meg, lass!" ejaculated Jack, tightening the reins, and drawing her in, as the traveller drew near, "So ho, lass! We must halt for a moment; my purse is empty, and must be replenished, and, by the devils, not a hundred runners at my back should stop me in my present project. Humph, the traveller is here!"

The stranger now cantered up, and would have passed the highwayman, but was prevented by the latter drawing in his steed, so that the road was blocked up.

"Stand aside, scoundrel, and let me pass."

"Sorry to trouble you, old fellow, but there is a toll here."

"A highwayman?"

"Just so—you have hit it."

"I think so, scoundrel, take that!" The traveller, an elderly man, of some fifty years of age, snatched a pistol from his pocket and fired at Jack.

There was a loud report, followed by the sound of a heavy blow.

Ducking his head, and avoiding the bullet, Jack, with a curse, sprang from his own steed upon the stranger's, and dragged him from his horse to the ground.

"So ho! easy does it. Yours was a bad shot, my flower. You fired too high—it's no use struggling, I am bound to skin you, after your ungentlemanly conduct"

"Villain! thief! ruffian! highway robber! You shall suffer for this!"

The traveller, foaming with rage, struggled furiously in the grasp of Jack, who, holding him in an iron grip, rapidly relieved him of his valuables.

"Help, help, help!" The cries of the enraged traveller sounded shrill and clear in the night air.

The answering voices of a party of horsemen echoed his cries for aid.

Jack, pocketing the articles he had taken from the person of the stranger, gave a look back, and at one spring vaulted into the saddle.

A party of six were dashing along the road at their utmost speed. The steam from their horses curling and wreathing like smoke in the air.

A loud hurrah and shout of triumph burst from these men as they gazed upon the figure of Jack.

The voice of the foremost horseman rang loud and shrill in the lone spot, as he shouted—

"There he is, lads. Twenty guineas to him who lays hands upon Sixteen-String Jack! Upon him! Secure him!"

"Will you have me now, or when you get me?" exclaimed Jack, with a laugh of scorn, giving his mare the rein, and dashing from the place.

Oaths and curses escaped the lips of the officers, as their man disappeared in a turning of the road. Paying no attention to the entreaties and cries of the enraged traveller, the runners, giving their horses the spur, dashed onwards in pursuit of the flying highwayman.

On reaching the bend in the road, the enemies of Jack caught sight of him as he was careering along at a headlong pace, that bid fair soon to leave them far behind.

With oaths and curses of savage fury, they goaded on their exhausted steeds, till the wretched animals were ready to sink from exhaustion.

"If we don't come up with him soon, curses on him, he will escape us," muttered the leader of the runners, digging his spurs into the flanks of his horse, that were already streaming with blood.

"He has got a fine mount, Mr. Anstey," exclaimed one of the men, "that mare of his would carry him to the devil, no matter how long the road."

"There's only one as can match her in speed, Jenkins," ejaculated another of the officers.

"And that one, Gregson, is—"

"Bonny Black Bess, the steed belonging to Dick Turpin. Were it not for their fine pieces of horse-flesh these knights of the road, Messrs. Turpin and Jack, wouldn't so often escape falling into our hands, and so bilk the stone-jug."

"Right you are, Gregson," replied his companion, then nodding to their leader, who was some few paces in advance, he added, "but see, we are lagging, we must give our beasts the spur. Why, the fiends, we shall have Anstey yelling at us for a couple of laggards."

Giving their poor beasts both whip and spur, the two officers now joined their companions, who were a trifle in advance.

The runners had now reached the foot of a steep hill.

All beheld the highwayman's horse toiling slowly up the ascent.

The moon shining brightly over head, made all as light as day.

Jonathan Anstey, the leader of the runners, pointing with his whip, to the form of Jack, exclaimed—

"Hark you, lads! now's our only chance, let us come up with him ere he gains the summit of the hill, and by —— he is ours." A fierce oath issued from the lips of the officer, as he, with whip, voice, and spur, urged on his panting steed.

"It arn't no use, Anstey, our beasts can't do the hill! There, curses on it, mine is down!"

The horse of the man who was speaking, in toiling up the ascent, missed her footing, and fell to the ground, her rider narrowly escaping a broken limb in the fall.

With oaths and curses the leader of the officers, grown angry in the fruitless chase, jumped off his steed, and followed by the rest, led it up the hill.

All adopting this mode, running by the side of their exhausted beasts, soon gained the top of the ascent.

The leading runner and his men now gazed into a kind of hollow below.

The moon cast her pale silvery rays upon the scene.

A bright and beautiful one.

But the men brought to the spot in pursuit of the highway-man noted not the loveliness of the night, or the beauty of the country.

Wild with rage and disappointment, they sprung into their saddles and tore down the hill, on reaching the bottom of which all was silent and lonely; far ahead, they perceived the road in its devious course, winding like a serpent, but their man, the highwayman, whom they had so pertinaciously and vengefully followed from Holborn, was nowhere to be seen.

Sixteen-String Jack had disappeared.

Oaths and curses of furious disappointment escaped them, and then, with one impulse, they all gave their steeds the reins, and with wild shouts dashed off along the road.

Scarce had they left the spot ere Sixteen-String Jack, with a loud exultant laugh, crept from beneath a little bridge that crossed a brook by the side of the roadway, and then giving a shrill whistle his bonny mare Meg bounded from behind a hedge that grew at the end of a piece of meadow land some quarter of a mile from the highway. Reaching her master, the dumb brute, with a joyous neigh, rubbed her head against his face, seeking evidently his caresses.

"Ha, ha, ha! that was cleverly done Meg, my girl, we have sent them on their wild-goose chase, and I'll swear they won't draw rein this side of twenty miles. Ha, ha! Jonathan Anstey, you will find it a difficult task to cage Sixteen-String Jack. Now then, my bonny girl, we will canter on to Willesden; it will be but half an hour's ride, and then we will put up at the 'Cat and her Kittens,' kept by my old friend Jem Lutterworth 'Tis some time since I have seen my old chum Jem, so forward, lass, and may our foes ahead have a good race in their chase of a myth! Ha, ha, ha!"

Again laughing at the idea of how he had outwitted his pursuers, our hero, who had sprung upon the back of his mare, cantered from the spot, nor drew rein till he was near the pretty little village of Willesden.

About to gallop on, Jack now pauses as he observes some horses drawn up in the roadway, near the centre of the village.

Willesden, consisting of some two dozen tenements, was distant from where he had drawn up his steed perhaps some five hundred yards.

The horses he beheld he immediately guessed belonged to his enemies.

"Here they are on their back track, Meg, and curses on them, they have stopped at the inn of my old pal, so the 'Cat and her Kittens' is no place for us at present," muttered Jack, who, irresolute what course to pursue, remained gazing at the village before him.

To return to London would be to be again hunted by the officers, who would be certain to gain tidings of him on the road.

There was no hiding place at hand, not a tree or a hedge that would conceal him and his mare.

Jack was nonplussed.

For a few moments he remained undecided how to act.

Every instant there was the chance of the officers leaving the inn.

At length, with a glance at the road before and behind him, Jack proceeded towards the village.

He had discerned two horsemen approaching from the London road, and in a moment made up his mind what course to pursue.

It was one that well accorded with his daring adventurous spirit, and usual scorn and contempt of danger.

Jack foresaw that a return to London was impossible.

The officers would soon leave the inn, and danger, and strong chance of capture, would face him on either side.

The advancing horsemen, warned by the runners, would bar his path.

And made captive, bound and fettered, he would be dragged back.

Back to a cell within the dreary prison house of Newgate.

There was only one line to adopt.

One of daring, and full of danger.

It was to pass through the village.

Slowly and cautiously that he might not be heard.

TURPIN'S ATTACK ON THE RUNNERS.

Fortunately, on the side of the road opposite the inn there was a smooth piece of sward extending near the length of the village.

Upon this green carpet of verdure Jack led his sagacious mare, who, as if instinctively aware of what was required of her, stole cautiously along, her hoofs emitting no sound upon the soft sward.

Jack's heart beat tumultuously as he arrived opposite the inn.

He could hear loud voices within.

An oath escaped his lips, as a man appeared issuing from the door.

With a curse, Jack drew his pistols from his belt, and prepared for a conflict.

Another moment, and they will be upon him.

The stranger horsemen are rapidly approaching the village with their assistance. The runners will be able to secure him.

He is hemmed in on every side.

An exclamation of surprise escaped Jack.

The man who made his way out of the inn, on perceiving him, gave no alarm, but hurriedly made his way across the road.

"By all that's good, I thought so—dreamed it, Jack. Tip us your daddle and hasten off, and then return in an hour, and the best the Cat and her Kittens can give shall be yours."

"What, Jem! The deuce; how is this?"

"Hush! this is no time for parley. Your foes let out to me of whom they were in search. I suspected you had tricked them on the road; 'twas like you. I also was sure, since you had taken this road I might expect a call. But, away, or by the devils you'll be nabbed, Jack."

With a bound the landlord of the roadside inn gained the door, as one of the officers appeared.

"Hillo! what's up? I hear horse's hoofs!" exclaimed the man.

"Yes; I've been watching them," replied Jem Lutterworth, the landlord, who, drawing the officer's arm in his, pointed to the two travellers, now within a quarter of a mile of Willesden. "You see those two fellows."

"Well, yes; I guess I aint blind."

"Do you know who they are?"

"Can't say. It can't be our man, the Stringer, cos Jack is too downy a bird to walk into a trap like that."

"But it is him!"

"The devil!"

"Yes, and the other in his company is Dick Turpin. I know them both."

The runner waiting to hear no more, rushed back into the inn. The landlord looking behind, perceived that Jack had ridden out of sight. A smile crossed his features as the posse of officers rushed out pell mell, and clambered on to the backs of their steeds. In another moment they were rushing at break-neck speed to meet the strangers.

The proprietor of the Cat and her Kittens, not waiting to see the result, hastened into the house.

"Get ready the darbies, Bolt; and you, Mac Nabem, get on the off side. They can't escape us," ejaculated the excited leader of the runners.

In another moment there was a desperate melee in the roadway. One of the travellers, the foremost horseman, with a loud shout fired a pistol at the officers as they dashed up.

No. 11.

"Hold! What's your game? Are you all mad?" exclaimed the other stranger.

"Help! help! Give it the ruffians! These are doubtless other members of the gang, companion of the villain who robbed me an hour back."

"Jonathan Anstey, the Bow-street runner, and the rest of his men drew back in amazement. The strangers whom they had attacked were no others than the man whom Jack had robbed when escaping from the officers, and a runner who had been left on the road behind them.

Return we now to our hero.

After successfully passing through the village, Jack, again giving his mare the reins, cantered at a dashing pace along the the road.

He had left Willesden some two miles behind him, when he was startled by observing a female form hurrying wildly along the road.

The bright rays of the morn made the wanderer of the night look like some spectral form.

Without covering to the head, the white figure hurried on. As near as Jack could discern, it was the form of a young girl that so strangely appeared before him.

Patting his mare upon the neck, the sagacious beast gave a bound, and like the wind, rushed along the road.

There was a shrill scream upon the night air, and the white, spectral-looking form with mad speed turned a corner of the road, and disappeared from the sight of the highwayman. In a few seconds, however, Jack had reached the spot where the strange appearance had vanished.

But the only thing that met his gaze was a lone farm-house, a large board in the front of which informed the wayfarer that it was to let.

It was a lonely, desolate-looking building, the out-houses and barns apparently falling into decay. All alike looked drear and dismal.

Perceiving no signs of the strange form that a few minutes before had flitted from his sight, Jack dismounted from his horse and prepared to inspect the outbuildings of the farm.

His curiosity was aroused.

A strange impulse led him to try and unravel the mystery of the young girl's disappearance.

Convinced that the wanderer was not far off, Jack determined to institute a thorough search ere he left the spot.

Dismounting, he made his way to a large gate that he found was nearly off its fastenings. Pushing his way through, he now stood in a courtyard or space that had evidently formerly been used for cattle.

Straw, manure, and other rubbish yet lay strewn upon the ground.

At the end of this open space stood a large barn, and beside the barn some stables and two or three sheds.

Some hundred yards back lay the farm, a large, white building, that looked ghostly and dreary in the rays of the moon.

Making his way across the fore-court, Jack at length stood by the barn.

A sudden darkness now fell upon the scene.

The moon that had been shining so brilliantly the early part of the night, now disappeared behind a thick canopy of clouds.

The wind rising, sighed and moaned dismally round the lone farm, the rude gusts seeming as though singing a dirge upon the deserted tenement.

A sudden chill passed over the frame of our hero.

Fear, Sixteen-String Jack knew but by name.

It was not that feeling that now weighed upon him it was a nameless one, caused by the desolate nature of the place—a kind of awe or horror of he knew not what.

The thought that it was a supernatural form that had led him to that lonely farm once crossed his mind, to be immediately dismissed.

Had he not heard a shriek ring upon the air as the figure dashed away from his sight?

No, it was a human form, and Jack determined ere he left the spot to fathom the mystery that was connected with it.

Perhaps it was an unhappy girl flying from some persecutor who had perchance wrought her ruin.

It was a sombre, dreary looking place, was the lone farm.

An involuntary shudder crept through the frame of Jack as he stood there by the barn, listening to the sighing of the wind, and gazing up at the old house now scarce discernible in the thick darkness.

Stumbling forwards in an endeavour to find a door leading into the barn, Jack now happened upon a lantern that lay upon some straw at his feet.

Picking it up, he found to his joy that it contained a small piece of candle.

With some flint and steel he had in his pocket, he soon procured a light.

Lantern now in hand, he at length discovered, not a door, but an opening fastened up with shutters, that were rotten and half removed from their hinges.

Jack, wrenching these aside, thrust his head through the opening, and holding the lantern forwards leaned in, and cast his eyes over the barn.

A cry of astonishment escaped him.

The yellow flash from the lantern disclosed a strange scene.

He found that he was looking in, not upon the barn itself, but a kind of stable, attached to or parted off from it.

Upon a heap of straw in a corner of the rude shed or stable Jack beheld a lovely female form.

The same, doubtless, that had so strangely appeared to him upon the highway.

Making his way through the open space, Jack presently stood by the senseless figure of a lovely girl.

So still and calm was that female form, that at first, with a shudder, the highwayman imagined he was gazing on a corpse.

Kneeling down, and placing his hand upon her bosom, to his joy he found that the spark of life still existed in the pale, cold, and silent form.

Strangely interested in the young girl who had so mysteriously crossed his path, our hero drew forth a flask from his vest, and placing it to her lips, impatiently awaited the result.

Breathlessly he watched the lovely countenance of the senseless girl.

Very beautiful was she.

In all his adventurous career never had Sixteen-string Jack met with one so fair and lovely.

A strange thrill darted through his veins as he held her in his arms.

But no thought of harming the hapless girl entered the brain of our hero.

He would have dashed out the brains of any who had offered to lay rude hand upon that helpless form.

With his eyes fastened upon her lovely features, impatiently he watched her return to consciousness.

It was a strange scene that, in the rude stable adjacent to the old barn.

By the senseless body of the lovely girl knelt the figure of the highwayman.

With enraptured gaze he leant over the fair girl.

Never before had his eyes lighted upon such youth and beauty.

Lost to all, he could have gazed for hours on that lovely face.

With her dark chesnut hair hanging in dishevelled tresses over her marble brow, and upon her beautifully rounded shoulders, she lay in the arms of the highwayman, looking like a being, not of earth, but some lovely, ethereal form, wrapped in a deep repose.

Her features, of the Grecian type, were dazzlingly fair; long, dark lashes, rested on her beauteous face; her finely pencilled eye-brows, of the same shade as her hair, set off the pure, dazzling complexion of the young girl; her lips, slightly apart, revealed a set of pearly teeth anon. As consciousness once more returned, her cheeks flushed up with colour, her eyes, of dark blue, bright and sparkling, opened, and turned in wonder and alarm upon the face of our hero. Then, with a wild shriek, she tore herself from his arms, and starting to her feet, glared, first at the form of the highwayman, and then at the place in which she found herself.

"Where, where am I?" she gasped; then drawing her

hand across her brow, she again turned her eyes upon the person of Sixteen-String Jack, who, in mute admiration, remained rooted to the spot, gazing upon the beautious vision before him. "Where am I? Oh! 'tis all a hideous dream. My father's threat!—my imprisonment!—the offer of release at the price of becoming the bride of the villain, Lester!—my escape from a fate far worse than death! All, all! recur to me! But where—where am I now? That strange form—this place! In my dream methought I sought refuge from my foes at the farm of Mathew Ashford. The shouts of my pursuers rung in my ears. I remember my wild flight—a refuge, a shelter, gained I know not how. All, all the rest is a blank; and now, surely, I dream, and am still the victim of some fearful vision!"

"No, dear girl, you dream not."

"Who—what are you?" The terrified girl gazed wildly around, as in a whisper she addressed her companion.

"A friend."

"A friend?"

"Aye, on my soul, yes!"

"How came you here?"

"I was led hither by a phantom form that I beheld without."

"And that form?"

"Was yourself."

"You tell me I dream not. Cans't tell me where I am? Do I still live! Or am I a wretched, doomed being of another world?"

There was a wild, dazed look, a maddened expression, upon the young girl's face, that alarmed the hghwayman.

"You live, dear girl, and I swear to you, whate'er your peril, whoe'er your enemies be who have pursued you thus, that I will make them rue the hour they persecuted you, and drove you thus to seek refuge upon the lone highway."

"I believe you, stranger! There is that in your manner convinces me of your truth!" exclaimed the young girl. "I know not where I am, scarce remember how I came hither, but trust to your honour to lead me hence."

"In safety, yes! where'er you wish!" exclaimed Jack, who would have perilled his life to save that of the unprotected girl, whose beauty and distress had won his pity and his admiration.

For the first time in his chequered career, the bosom of our hero was filled with emotions akin to love.

Yet, had any one told him the real state of his feelings he would have laughed them to scorn.

He had always made it his boast that he would never yield to the gentle passion.

A half terrified look stole over the face of the strange wanderer of the night, as her companion stepped forward and seized her hand.

Reassured by his gentle and respectful manner, she however followed him to the door of the barn, that Jack discovered by the glimmering of the morning light that stole through the crevices.

With little difficulty forcing it open, they presently stood in the fore-court that ran parallel with the high road.

The early light of morning now shone upon the scene.

Jack with joy perceived his faithful steed standing patiently and immovable at the gateway through which he had forced himself an hour before.

The sagacious, fond brute gave a loud whinnying as she caught sight of her owner, and pawed the ground impatiently at his approach.

The sun, scarce risen from her bed, threw but a dim, pale light upon the earth.

The old farm-house, looking little less drear than in the shadows of the preceding night, the mysterious stranger, as she caught sight of the building, clutched at the arm of her companion for support, and glaring wildly round, exclaimed in accents of horror,—

"Oh, take me hence! 'Tis indeed to the farm of the wretched Mathew Ashford that my frenzied steps led me last night. I now remember all. They told me the poor, old man was dead, but I believed them not; yet is there in this deserted building

evidence that ruin or death has been at work. But, see! see, stranger! yonder comes Silas Vaughan, my father's accursed adviser, he to whom I owe all my woes. Oh, save me! save me from him! Oh, in mercy let him not drag me back!"

"Not if I know it! Not if he were one of Satan's whelps, should he harm you whilst I had a hand and eye to serve you. Tremble not, dear girl, the hump-backed hound shall tear my heart out ere he drags you hence."

Pity at the poor girl's distress, and anger at the threatening gestures of the stranger, roused the devil in the breast of Sixteen-String Jack, who, with his left arm supported the fragile form of the mysterious maiden, and with his right hand grasped a thick cudgel he had snatched up on observing the approach of an uncouth, wild-looking dwarf, that with all speed was rushing forward, mounted upon a grey cob.

"The devil on horseback, as I live!" shouted Jack, laughing loudly, as the stranger drew up before him.

The introduction of a fresh character, playing a prominent part in this history, must be reserved for a fresh chapter.

CHAPTER XXXIII.

SILAS VAUGHAN AND THE HIGHWAYMAN—THE DEMAND, THE REFUSAL—TREACHERY OF THE DWARF—A PISTOL SHOT AND A STRUGGLE—THE CRY FOR HELP—THE PATROL—TERROR OF DORA ANNERSLEY—A MELEE AND ITS RESULTS—BRAVERY OF SIXTEEN-STRING JACK—THE MARE AND HER DOUBLE BURDEN—A SHORT RACE—THE ARRIVAL AT THE HAUNTED MILL—THE SECRET CAVE BY THE OLD MILL STREAM, AND STRANGE MEETING WITH AN OLD FRIEND.

"Eh! eh! eh! ha! ha! my pretty Dora. So we have tracked you then at last! But ere nightfall you shall be lodged in a safer, surer prison than thy father's roof—a prison built for such mad ones as you, my willful Dora. You shall be borne off to a mad-house! Eh! eh! eh! do you hear? I, Silas Vaughan, will take you there."

"No, I'm damned if you do, you misbegotten whelp of the devil!"

The chuckle on the lips of the hideous dwarf, who now sprang from the back of the cob, changed to a vindictive growl, as, glaring from beneath his pent brows, he hissed between his set teeth,—

"Eh! eh! eh! Who will stay me?"

"I will."

"Eh, eh, eh! indeed! Look you, stranger, in handling the serpent take care it does not sting. What is she to you?"

The horrible-looking dwarf here pointed to the pale, shuddering girl, who now clung to our hero for protection.

"This much, my friend of the hump, that I hold her under my charge, and curse me if you or the devil himself shall tear her from me."

"Oh, oh! I see she hath cast the glamour of her charms upon thee. Poor fool! you will risk death for her smiles, and eh, eh! death shall be your portion if you longer refuse to give her up. I am her parent's trusted servant; by him am I commissioned to bring her without delay back to that roof the shelter of which she fled from last night. Give her up, then, mad fool, or by the fiend below, you shall find I can bite as well as bark."

The dwarf here pulled from his bosom a pistol, and coolly cocked it before the highwayman.

A smile of scorn and contempt crossed the features of Sixteen-String Jack as he listened to the horrible-looking creature before him, and beheld the action that accompanied his threats.

A strange, wild-looking creature was the dwarf, Silas Vaughan.

Scarcely human did he appear in his deformity and ugliness.

Standing not more than four feet in height, the wretched being had a huge hump on his back. With scarce any neck, his head appeared sunk between his shoulders; his arms, of prodigious length, reached to his knees; his huge, bony hands opening and shutting as if grasping at the air; his forehead, low and receding, was covered with shaggy tufted locks of coal-black hair; his eyes, deep sunk in his head, were nearly hidden by his heavy beetling brows; with huge mouth, large projecting teeth, high cheek bones, and yellowish complexion, the man resembled more a hideous being of another world than a human creature.

Struck with his frightful ugliness and deformity, Jack for a few moments could do nought but gaze on in wonder and astonishment at the object before him.

But when the dwarf, with a malicious scowl upon his hideous face, drew forth a pistol and levelled it at him, Jack, with a curse, started forward, bidding the half senseless girl who had hung upon his arm have no fear—that all the fiends from below should not take her from him.

"Put aside that barking-iron, you son of the devil, or by heavens, I'll crack your skull with as little hesitation—"

"Eh eh eh! Try it! You will find the head of Silas Vaughan a nut hard to crack."

There was an eldritch scream or yell from the lips of the hideous being, followed by a loud report.

About to rush upon the monster before him, Jack, catching his foot in a stone, stumbled and fell.

The fall saved his life.

Another second and he would have had the bullet from the pistol of the man Silas Vaughan crashing in his brains.

With a cry of rage Jack rose to his feet, and bounding upon the dwarf seized him in his grasp.

A fearful struggle now ensued.

Low gutteral ejaculations escaped the lips of Silas Vaughan.

Deep breathed curses issuing from the mouth of Jack, who, to his surprise, found that the dwarf possessed a strength quite equal if not superior to his own.

Wildly they struggled and wrestled in each other's grasp.

The air ringing with the loud shrieks of the distracted girl, who, in trembling, shuddering horror, watched the contest.

With his long arms wound round the body of our hero, Silas Vaughan twisted and writhed like a serpent, trying to throw the agile highwayman off his feet.

But Jack well evaded the other's efforts, and at length by an exertion of strength, lifted his adversary bodily from the ground, hurling him from him with fearful violence to the earth.

About again to grapple with the half-stunned wretch, Jack was deterred by catching sight of a couple of patrols, followed by two or three strangers, rapidly making their way to the spot.

It will be remembered the scene of the encounter between Jack and the strange enemy of the young girl took place just outside the gateway leading to the farm.

This was close to a bend in the road, so that any one coming from the London direction would only be seen when close to the vicinity of the farm-house.

Perceiving there was little time to lose, and that the odds were against him, our hero with the quickness of thought, caught the trembling girl, Dora, in his arms, and placing her upon the saddle of his mare vaulted behind her.

"Away, bonnie Meg! my girl. If ever you loved your master, serve him now," shouted Jack, at the same time gently touching his mare on the flank.

Though carrying double, the noble beast was about to dash away when she was restrained by the hand of Silas Vaughan, who, with a cry for help, clung tenaciously to the reins, despite the kicking and plunging of the horse.

"Help, help, help! oh, oh, oh! I have them."

"Then mind you keep them," replied Jack, giving the wretch a blow on the head with the butt of a pistol, that caused him with a scream of agony to let go his hold of the reins.

But the patrol and the others were now upon him.

"Let him not escape," cried a voice; "secure him, officers; 'tis Sixteen-String Jack!"

"Tear him from the horse!"

"Send a bullet through his skull!"

"Yield yourself a prisoner," exclaimed one of the patrols; "it's no use, Jack, the odds are too many for you this time."

"Liar!" cried Jack, furious at the thought of relinquishing the unfortunate girl to her foes, and battling wildly with the officers and the two strangers.

The shrieks of the unhappy girl, the cries of the officers, the reports of pistols, rang loudly on the air.

Hampered and impeded in his movements by the form of the poor girl, who now clung wildly to him, the chances were against Jack, who, with a shudder, began to fear he would fall a prisoner.

For himself he cared not.

But for the poor pallid victim who wound her arms round him in agonising despair, he would have sacrificed his life.

An end now was put to the scene.

A strange but providential one for our hero.

One of the patrols had succeeded in securing the reins of the highwayman's steed, and holding them firmly prevented the horse from bearing her master off.

The dwarf, Silas Vaughan, staggering to his feet and perceiving that the knight of the road was overpowered by numbers, drew a pistol from his vest, and with a malicious chuckle fired at the helpless form of the man whose blood he had sworn to have.

His malice, however, defeated its object.

Instead of stretching Sixteen-String Jack a corpse it released him from his foes.

The ball from the pistol of Silas Vaughan lodged in the brain of the patrol who held the mare in check.

The highwayman's steed, finding herself at liberty, like lightning bounded from the spot.

The wretched officer, without a groan, falling to the ground, his skull fractured by the bullet intended for Jack.

A loud defying shout burst from the lips of Jack as he was borne off.

A shout that was echoed by cries of rage and fury from his enemies.

Who a few moments afterwards were dashing along the road in pursuit.

The clatter of the horses' hoofs sounded clear in the ears of the highwayman.

Borne to him on the still morning air.

His foes were well mounted.

He had but the start of a few yards.

They would soon be upon him.

Slight as was her weight, yet would the bonny mare in a long race feel the increased burthen of the young girl.

A shudder ran through the frame of Jack at the thought of the beautiful girl he held in his arms falling into the power of her enemies.

He would perish rather.

A feeling of delicious joy filled his bosom as he held the beautifully rounded form of the unhappy Dora in his embrace.

He could hear the beating of her heart, could feel the pulsations of her heaving bust as it pressed to his bosom.

Her soft, plump, and beautifully rounded arms were clasped about his neck.

He wished at that moment that the race might last for ever.

At length he is recalled to himself by an admonition from those behind that they are close upon him.

A loud report rings upon the air.

And as he is borne along the road, a peculiar whiz or whistle sounds close to his head.

It is a bullet from the pistols of his foes.

Whiz, whiz! thup, thup!

Jack is conscious that he is serving the purpose of a target to those in his rear.

Feelings of rage and fury fill his bosom.

He dare not turn upon them.

He is not alone.

The life of the beautiful being he holds in his arms may be sacrificed in a hand to hand conflict.

There is nothing to be done but to keep on.

Until his brave steed gives in.

And then?

Jack bit his lips with fury as he thought upon what might happen.

His bonny mare, however, gave yet no signs of distress, whilst one of those behind him had thrown its rider.

This caused a delay.

Five minutes were invaluable to Jack then.

Whilst his foes were seeing to their comrade his brave steed dashing on.

A narrow lane is reached.

Jack without hesitation guides his brave beast down it.

It may open upon a means of escape.

He may be able to baffle his foes.

They are now hidden from his sight.

He reaches the end of the lane before he detects the sound of their horses' hoofs following again in his track.

With a cry of joy Jack now catches sight of a shelter from his enemies.

A by-road runs across the end of the lane.

A little way down this road stands an old ruined mill.

With an exultant shout and thrill of joy, Jack recognises the old building.

At the last moment, when about to give way to despair, a means of hiding from his pursuers opens to him.

With encouraging words, he urges on his now panting steed.

He can hear the shouts of his foes in the lane he has left behind him.

A few moments, and they will reach the road along which he now frantically urges on his brave and exhausted mare.

A narrow path turning off the road, leads to the ruined mill.

The old pile looks sweetly romantic, in the yellow light of the morning sun.

The bright rays of the golden orb fall full upon the ruined mill.

Reaching it ere his pursuers appear, with a prayer of thankfulness, Jack guides his panting steed through a large opening in the front of the mill.

Scarce has he passed in, ere he hears the clatter of horses' hoofs upon the roadway leading to the lane.

His enemies are close upon his track.

Jack, now alighting from his horse, lifts from her back the form of the young girl, Dora, and merely murmuring the words "Follow, Meg, follow," passes out of the mill by an opening at the back, similar to that by which he had entered.

They are now behind the mill, and of course hidden from sight of those in the front.

Jack at once makes his way to the dried-up bed of the stream, the waters of which at one time fed the mill.

At the further end of this course, now overgrown with wild vegetation, and under the brow of a hill, there stood the trunk of a huge willow.

Blighted, like the old mill, and fallen into decay.

The whole front of this trunk was broken in, leaving a space sufficient for the entry of two men.

To this blighted and decayed willow, Jack led Dora and his steed.

He can now hear the voices of their pursuers.

They will presently gain the mill.

"Quick, quick! follow me, dear girl, and fear not," exclaimed Jack.

Darting into the hollow trunk of the old willow, Jack, in a few seconds, opened what appeared, to the eyes of the astonished young girl, a door.

"Hasten through, dear girl, and fear nought. I have yet to secure my bonnie mare."

Without hesitation the terrified girl passed through the dark cavity at the back of the tree.

In a moment after, followed by Jack, leading his sagacious steed, who, at the voice of her master, unhesitatingly entered the passage, bending down her head and partly crawling through on her knees.

Once through the opening at the back, the horse was able to stand upright.

All was darkness.

Black, inky darkness.

Not a ray of light penetrated this secret haunt.

Praying his companion to have no fear, for that now they were safe, Jack at length procured a light, by means of some flint and steel, and igniting a piece of taper he procured from a secret recess, revealed the strange hiding-place fully to the eyes of the young girl.

Gazing round with eyes of wondering surprise, she discovered that they were in a large cave.

In the centre was a rude table and two stools.

The cave had very evidently been used as a hiding place by some one on a former occasion.

With a smile Jack listened to the cries of those without.

The voices of their pursuers being borne plainly to their ears.

Observing a look of alarm steal athwart the features of his companion, Jack, in a low voice, exclaimed,—

"Have no fear, dear Miss Dora; all danger now is at an end. Our foes know not of the existence of this secret cave. Only one other is aware of this hiding place—and that other is a friend, now in London; we might remain here in safety for hours, nay days, and be not discovered. Be not alarmed, then, at the barking of those bloodhounds without, we are now safe from their fangs; they cannot reach us here."

"And how—how, my preserver, can I repay the perils you have gone through for one you never saw before?" murmured the young girl, clasping the hand of our hero in hers, and bedewing it with tears.

"Nay, think not of it, dear girl. I were a base scoundrel and unmanly villain, had I acted any other than I have. But dare I ask why you are pursued so relentlessly by that son of the devil, with the boy on his back, he who calls himself Silas Vaughan? By the fiend his master, I will yet make him rue the hour he crossed my path."

"Oh! beware of him, he is a fearful man!" ejaculated the poor girl, in a voice shaking with terror.

"I fear him not; and by the mother that bore me, I'll give him something to remember me by, before I have done with him. But now tell me, dear girl, where am I to convey you when we leave this cave?"

"I know not."

"Have you no friend?"

"Alas! no."

"No one to whom you can fly in your distress?"

"No one!" Choking sobs here almost choked her utterance.

A thrill of joy darted through the frame of Jack, who was strangely pleased at the news that the young girl had no friends to whom she could fly for a refuge.

The brain of the daring highwayman was in a whirl.

Young, of an impassioned temperament, free, generous, and, despite his calling, of noble nature, all his sympathies and best feelings were aroused for the welfare of the unfortunate girl who had so strangely crossed his path.

The unfortunate girl, about whom there hung a fearful mystery, was one formed to kindle all the nobler passions of a youth such as our hero, who never before had seen a woman for whom he would have given his faithful steed.

But now he would have sacrificed life itself for the beautiful Dora—she whom he had saved from a fearful fate.

Finding that his fair companion did not revert to the cause of her distress, Sixteen-String Jack pressed her not again upon the matter, but resolved in his mind, what his next step was to be.

The young girl was flying from a terrible fate.

Its nature she did not explain.

Beyond what she had stated in the barn, that she was to be given as a bride to a man whom she loathed and detested to such an extent that death were preferable to a union with him, Jack had heard nothing.

"What was to be done?" he asked himself, as he stood by the side of the unhappy girl in the secret cave.

We have seen that, despite his being a knight of the road, Jack was possessed with a spirit of honour that would have led him to blow his own brains out ere he had offered insult to his beautiful charge, or left her to the mercy of her foes.

Jack was aroused from the reverie into which he had fallen by a soft hand being placed upon his shoulder, whilst the sweet voice of his companion ringing, in his enraptured ears, like the notes of a silver bell, exclaimed,—

"You are silent, my preserver; you are thinking how else you may serve one whom you have already snatched from a fate worse than death. Ere we part I will make you acquainted with my sad history, but let me pray you not to trouble your thoughts with my future course. Guide me from this place and hasten to your home."

"You know me not, Dora, dear girl, if you think I would leave you thus. No, before the day is over, I will place you in a sweet retreat, where harm can reach you not, and where you may remain until you decide on your future actions, or wish to see no more the man who to serve you would give up life."

Jack spoke fervently and warmly to the young girl, whose hot tears he felt falling on his hands as he held her in his arms.

Had it been that the taper, now burnt out, had still been alight, by its faint flicker Jack would have noted the flushed face of his charming companion and her look of joy as she clung to him, ejaculating,—

"How, in what way, can I prove my thanks for this kindness at the hands of one to whom I am a stranger, and whose name even I know not."

"My dear girl, my name is,"—Jack paused; he dared not make her acquainted as to who he really was. A cold chill darted through his frame, as he pictured to himself the horror of the innocent girl, should she discover that it was to a highwayman, a knight of the road, that she owed her safety and placed her trust in. "My name is Alford—Jack Alford!" he at length exclaimed, adding, "but do not, sweet girl, talk of thanks for that that I have done; the course that I have pursued would have been adopted by any man deserving the name, who might have met you in your distress. And now tell me, dear one, who it is I have had the happiness to serve."

"My father," ejaculated the young girl, with an involuntary shudder, "my father is a Mr. Mark Annersley, of the Blue Bells, a manor and estate situate on the North road, about three miles from the White Farm, where we met."

"And the creature, Silas Vaughan, who—what is he?"

"A wretch! a villain of the blackest dye! A man who holds a terrible sway over all the actions of my cruel parent."

"Has he been in your family long, dear Miss Annersley?"

"I know not. I ne'er saw him till a twelvemonth back, then, when I arrived at the manor on leaving school, I for the first time beheld the wretch, Vaughan, the sight of whom caused horror and aversion in my breast."

"Did you not let your parent know of this?"

"I did."

"And what said he?"

"He told me that I must conquer my dislike for that for the future Silas Vaughan would be a member of his household, and was a true and trusted servant."

"Strange, that a man of your father's position should have such a blot of humanity about him. There is some secret in this, dear girl, that you know not," exclaimed Jack; "but tell me, have you heard no remarks from the mouths of your relatives who may have visited your parent's house.

"My father sees no one; nor have I sister, brother, or mother, to aid me in my wrongs."

"No matter, dearest girl, you have now met with one that will be all of these—that will in your cause shed his heart's blood; but tell me, dear girl, if I remember rightly, was not the cause of your flight a threatened marriage with a man whom you held in your hate?"

"It was so! I will tell you all upon a future occasion. But hark! By heavens! they have found the secret of our hiding place! We are lost!"

The hand of the poor girl clasped in Jack's turned icy cold, as the murmuring of a voice sounded from without.

Jack, with cool determination, drew his pistols from his belt, prepared for action upon the least symptom of surprise.

There was a strange thumping noise without. It was apparent to Jack that somebody was tampering with the tree.

A low, smothered curse fell upon his ears.

In his converse with Dora Annersley, Jack had noted not the flight of time, nor had listened to his enemies, whose voices for some time sounded plain and clear as they searched the old dried-up bed of the mill stream.

It was evident they were yet without.

They were determined to watch the lone spot, where their victims had so mysteriously disappeared.

Tap, tap, tap.

The young girl clung in wild terror to the arm of Jack.

Tap, tap, tap.

Followed by a heavy blow without, that threatened to crash in the secret door.

But the contrivance had been executed with care.

It required no slight force to break in that secret door.

That could be made secure by those within the cave by means of a bolt and a spring.

Tap, tap—followed by loud audible curses.

A loud report suddenly sounds without, and a bullet, with a crash, tears through the door.

With a whiz, passing the head of Jack, and lodging in the walls of the cave.

Things are getting serious.

Drawing, with his fair and trembling charge, from the vicinity of the secret entrance, Jack meditates as to what course he shall pursue.

Crash—again a bullet tears through the wood.

At the danger of his life, Jack now, bidding Dora remain at the back of the cave, makes his way to the door; drawing back the bolt, and touching the spring, he, with pistols in hand, stands awaiting the moment that those without will force their way into the cave.

He has resolved to fight his foes.

Two lives he holds in his hands; the other he may conquer in a struggle.

He fears that a longer stay in the cave will avail them not.

His enemies evidently have learnt the secret of its existence.

'Tis no longer a secure hiding place.

The minutes pass by, but there are no signs of those without.

All is still and quiet.

Nought sounds upon the ears of the highwayman save the sighing of the winds without.

What does it mean?

Have his foes gone?

At length, unable to bear the torture of suspense, and determined to know the worst, Jack cautiously opens the door.

At first a burst of light into the cave blinds our hero.

A loud curse and ejaculation of surprise then fall upon his ears.

Looking up, Jack perceives the figure of a man standing in the hollow of the old willow.

A face and form well known to him stands at the entrance of the cave.

It is Dick Turpin!

"What, Dick!"

"Why, Jack! curses on it, it's you, then, who have kept me out of the old tree cave."

"So then 'tis you, Dick! Confound it, do you come here for ball practice?"

"Jack!"

"Yes, it is Jack, and you have been trying your hardest to put a bullet in his skull. But what brings you here to the old tree cave?"

"I may ask the same question of you."

"Oh! I have been pursued by the Philistines, and remembering this retreat, made my way hither in the nick of time."

"Hem! have you seen anything of King?"

A dark cloud gathered over the features of Jack. Hiding his momentary confusion, and not wishing at that moment to acquaint Turpin with what had happened, he exclaimed, in a hurried manner,—

"No, no, no, Dick, I have not. Why do you ask?"

"Oh! I merely wished to know. He was to have met me at the 'Green Tree,' in Westminster, but disappointed me."

A heavy frown rested on the brows of Turpin.

Well Jack understood the cause.

He suspected Tom was playing him false respecting the booty to be shared from the proceeds of the will.

He little knew the hand of death had fallen upon the wretched highwayman—his friend.

Jack, lost in a bitter reverie, and with sorrow remembering that 'twas his hand that had laid his comrade low, stood with folded arms at the entrance to the cave, forgetful of the presence of another, and lost to the remembrance that in the cave, just concealed from the eyes of Turpin, was his companion, Dora Annersley.

A cry of astonishment arouses him.

With a loud laugh, Turpin, pushing by his companion, is about to pass into the cave.

Jack intercepts him.

" Stand back, Dick ! "

" Nonsense, Jack, 'tis all right, you sly dog ! I see you have a petticoat with you, but I'm mum—I'll tell no tales ; but, damme, let us have a look at your hidden beauty."

" Dick ! Dick Turpin, hear me ! "

There was something in the tone of Jack's voice that had its effect upon the highwayman. Drawing back, he waited to hear what his companion was about to say.

" Dick, we are pals ! You know me. You will believe me, when I swear to you that the young girl now concealed in the cave, was, till las night, a total stranger to me. I strangely crossed her path when she was in fearful peril at the hands of villains, who, by the fiends, shall rue the day that they interfered with Sixteen-String Jack. Followed by the enemies of this girl and by the officers, I with difficulty escaped. I am about to convey my unfortunate charge to some safe retreat, but let me beg you, Dick, neither by word or action, to let drop who and what we are."

" All right, Jack," exclaimed Turpin, grasping his hand, " I'll put a stopper on my mouthpiece ; I'm not one to sell a pal. But, however, let us away ; but ere I depart I have something to do in the cave ; a little deposit for a rainy day I placed there months back I now require ; do you, with your fair friend, await me at the ruined mill. I will be with you immediately."

" Very well, Dick, but do not delay, for I wish to be gone."

Leaving his companion standing by the tree without, Jack entered the cave.

With a cry of alarm, he lifts the young girl up in his arms and darts out into the air.

Answering not to his call, Jack had discovered her stretched senseless in their hiding place.

With glances of amazement and admiration, Turpin cast his eyes upon the lovely form that Jack held in his embrace.

" By Heavens, a beautiful creature, Jack ! Where did you meet her ? "

" At the White Farm, on the road to Willesden ; but do you hasten to the mill, Dick, and bring with you my mare."

" All right, Jack ! I'll be with you in a moment. Bess is in the mill ; in ten minutes we'll be off and away."

Dick, making his entrance into the darksome recesses of the old tree cave, disappeared, whilst Jack, with the insensible Dora in his arms, hastened to the old ruin close at hand.

Alarmed and agitated, Jack chafed the soft white hands of his helpless companion in his, till at length, with a sigh, her beautiful eyes opened, and cast upon him a look of such thankfulness, that the heart of our hero bounded in his bosom.

Terrified at the murmuring of voices without the cave, not knowing if her preserver had fallen into the hands of their foes, added to the terrible excitement of the past few hours, had caused the poor girl to relapse into one of those fits of insensibility in which he had first discovered her at the White Farm.

" Be not alarmed, this is a friend," he exclaimed, as Dora started up from his embrace, glaring wildly at Turpin, who, leading the mare Meg, at that moment entered the mill.

With a reassured look, the beautiful girl upon this extended her hand to the highwayman, murmuring as she did so praises of Jack.

" I owe him my life, my more than life. He has saved me from a fate which would to me have been far worse than death." With her hands she here covered up her lovely features bedewed with tears, and pallid with the sufferings she had gone through.

" Nay, think not of it," ejaculated Jack, confusedly averting his face from the glance of his friend, upon whose features he observed a significant smile.

" Would that I had been able to do you service," ejaculated Turpin, turning to the young girl, who had now extended him her hand ; but glad I am my friend has been enabled to rescue you from peril, and be assured he needs not thanks for such a service ; you will always find my friend Jack—"

" Alford ! " ejaculated our hero, with a meaning glance at his friend.

" One that will go through fire and water for those in whom he takes an interest."

" I owe him a service that never can be repaid," murmured the young girl, casting a look of thankfulness on Jack.

" Stay, I beg you, Miss Annersley, speak no more on the subject ; and now, if you are sufficiently recovered to bear the fatigue, we will mount and away."

" I am ready, but, pray you not to neglect ought for me. Once in London I may elude those who will search for months for the missing one. whom they would condemn to worse than death." A livid pallor here stole over the face of the trembling girl as she recalled to her mind some painful remembrance of the past.

" Oh, fear not, dear girl ! " exclaimed Jack ; " I that have torn you from your foes will still defend you from them ; but come, we will away. Dick, do you lead on and I will follow."

" Whither are you bound, Jack ? " exclaimed Turpin, as he mounted his mare.

" Well, I know not."

" Do you propose to make straight for the Long Village ? " (London.)

" I know not where to go," muttered Jack, who, with the young girl sitting beside him on his horse, made his way slowly along the road leading from the old mill.

" Well, I think, Jack, that town would be the best place."

" I don't know, Dick, I do not think I shall return to London for a few days."

Jack by no means feared his companion, yet he did not wish to make his way to London in company with Dick, ere the latter had become aware of what had happened respecting Tom King and the will, now safe in the possession, Jack presumed, of Edward Grantley.

" Where do you think of putting up, Jack ? "

" I have not given it a thought."

" Well, it's necessary that you do so, quickly. I think I know a place where yourself and Miss Annersley would meet with every convenience."

" How far from here, Dick ? "

" Oh ! three miles, not more."

" Close to Willesden, then ? "

" Yes."

" I fancy I know the house you would recommend."

" Possibly."

" Is it not Jem Lutterworth's ? "

" The same. The Cat and her Kittens will afford you every accommodation."

" I am aware of it."

" Then you will halt there ? "

" Yes, Dick, for to-day, at all events."

" Very good. I shall ride up to town, for I have business I must see to."

" When do you imagine you will return ? "

" Oh, late to-night or early to-morrow."

" Very good, then I'll await your arrival, Dick, ere I think of leaving the inn."

Giving their steeds a gentle admonition, to quicken their pace, the two friends were soon bounding along the high road in the direction of Willesden. The cheeks of the lovely girl seated by the side of Jack, flushed with the exercise, and anon turned of a livid pallor as they dashed by the lone farm-house.

Jack, with a smile, pointed out to Dick the spot where he had had to struggle with the officers, at the same time casting a glance of joy upon the fair features of his companion as they hurried on, reaching and passing that part of the road where he had first discovered her flying form in the white moonlight of the night before.

Ever and anon casting a glance of deep admiration upon the fair girl sitting beside his friend, Turpin engaged in listless converse to pass away the time. True to his promise to Jack, he gave no clue in his conversation to the business of himself or his companion. Giving his name as Richard Palmer, he stated that he was a commercial traveller on a large scale. A grim smile here crossed the features of Jack as he listened to this avowal of his friend, who by his easy manners and unceasing converse, however, kept the unfortunate Dora from dwelling too much upon the terrible incidents of the past night.

At length they halted at the Cat and her Kittens, which, situate in the centre of the little village of Willesden, was the cosiest, neatest, and most cheerful inn on the road for many miles.

Here alighting, they were shown into the house by the bluff, jovial, rubicund visaged, landlord, who, with a wink at Jack, exclaimed,—

" All right, no one here ! But as I do expect visitors," he here cast a meaning glance at the two friends, " why, I'll show you into the blue parlour. That's a room where no one, I'll answer for it, will venture to disturb you ; and for the pretty lady, if she will condescend to sit with my daughter, Jane, why she may be as comfortable and retired in the snuggery, as I term my private chamber upstairs, as though she were in one of the secluded rooms in the Tower."

They had now arrived at a large parlour at the back of the bar, into which they had been led by their host.

Expressing her thanks, and with joy accepting the offer of the worthy landlord to retire with his daughter, Dora Annersley, with a grateful glance at her preserver, now left the chamber in company with a bouncing, rosy cheeked, plump young maid, of some seventeen years of age, who by her merry cheerful manners soon won the confidence of the friendless girl, who, save the stranger by whom she had been aided the night before, had not a friend on earth.

A strange wayward fate was Dora Annersley's.

Strangely mixed up, too, with that of Sixteen-String Jack.

Worn down with the fatigues and reaction upon her frame of the wild scenes through which she had passed in a deep, heavy, sleep, in an upper chamber of the old inn, she was ignorant of a wild hurry, noise, and disturbance in the lower part of the house, that succeeded their arrival.

Half an hour after she had retired with the daughter of the innkeeper, the two friends, who were seated in the bar parlour, were startled by a loud noise below.

A moment afterwards, Jem Lutterworth, the host, rushed in upon them, exclaiming,—

" Off with you, lads, to the blue room. The grabs are even now without the doors."

Jack and Turpin started to their feet with oaths and cries of rage.

" Where are the horses, Jem ? "

" All right, Dick ; safe in the castle."

" But curses on it, I want to get to London."

" You can't go now, Dick, unless you want to give yourself up to the Philistines."

Followed by Jack and Turpin, the latter terribly annoyed that he could not for a time leave the house, the landlord hurried from the parlour down a dark passage, and reaching a flight of stairs, bidding them hasten after him, ascended with more agility than it might have been supposed he could exert. Arriving at the summit, he opened the door of a large dining-room ; crossing this they passed through a smaller chamber, in one corner of which stood a large portrait of a cavalier.

The sound of hurried feet, loud voices, mingled with oaths and curses, ascended from below.

" Jack, you know the trick ; get into the blue parlour with all speed, for the parties below are going on anyhow in my absence. I will visit you as soon as I can."

Hurrying away, the two friends were left alone.

" Well, Jack, they are pretty warm on our track."

" Yes, Dick, but they won't nose us out of this place."

Touching a spring that was let into the frame of the huge painting, that, the size of life, rested against the wall, Jack, to the astonishment of his friend, revealed a sliding panel, through which, stooping down, they both made ther way.

Closing to the door, which fastened with a loud snap, they found themselves in a small but comfortably furnished chamber.

The paper on the walls, the coverings of the furniture, all were of a deep bright blue.

" The blue parlour, Dick."

" So I perceive."

" A fine hiding place from the enemy."

" Yes ! any exit beside the way we came ? "

" No ! and the spring fastens from without."

" The devil ! then we are prisoners ? "

" Till Jem comes, yes."

" But, damn it, suppose Jem don't come."

" Oh, he will be with us right enough."

" But an accident might happen."

" Well, we should then burst the door."

" Could we do so ? "

" Of course we could. But hark ! By the devils, there he is ! "

There was a noise in the other room, and the secret panel lowly opened.

A white, ghastly-looking face appears.

Pale, livid, as that of a corpse.

A cry of astonishment escapes the lips of Turpin, who rushes to the secret door.

Jack, with surprise and horror, starts back, glaring wildly at the ghastly looking face.

It is that of his friend, Tom King !

CHAPTER XXXIV.

THE RETURN O HACKNEY—THE PRODUCTION OF THE WILL — RAG OF SKINWELL — THE GRANTLEYS AND THEIR FOES—SUDDEN APPEARANCE OF ERNEST MALVERS —THE SERPENT'S STING—THE TERRIBLE ACCUSATION— THE STRUGGLE—TRIUMPH OF MALVERS—SAM AND THE WATCHMAN—THE DYING CONFESSION—THE UNEXPECTED PROOFS—SEIZURE OF THE MURDERER AND RELEASE OF THE INNOCENT.

AT an early hour of the morning following the night of Jack's escape from Peter Pattypan's, Edward Grantley, in company with his wife, Peter, and Mrs. Malvers, started for the Manor House, at Hackney.

It was about nine o'clock that the little vehicle, in which Grantley had driven down, drew up at the door of the Manor House.

The early morning sun cast its bright rays with a golden glow on all around.

The birds winging their way about the grounds, merrily twittering their joyous notes.

The flowers, their petals glittering with dew drops, resemble so many rich gems, in the golden rays of the orb of day.

With pride and pleasure Edward Grantley gazes round upon the scene.

A bright and joyous one.

All looks happy and joyful in the rosy hue of the lovely morn ; the dew glittering like crystals on the buds and leaves, the many-coloured convolvulus with its beauteous shades of purple, greet the eye as it alights upon the walks of the Manor House.

And at length, after his many trials, Edward Grantley can call the rich estate his own.

Can surround his young wife with luxury and wealth.

She who for him had given up so much.

With surprise and dismay, Skinwell appears at the door.

Something tells him that the will, giving to Grantley the estate, is in his possession.

The highwayman has played him false.

THE ESCAPE FROM THE IVY MANOR HOUSE.

With glowering brow the old man demands the business of his visitor.

"I have come to take possession of the house. My solicitors will be here anon; should you resist my authority here, Mr. Skinwell, it may be worse for you. I have heard of matters lately, that redound little to your credit."

"You come here as heir-at-law, Mr. Edward Grantley?"

"I do."

"Hem! of course you have no objection to state to me the nature of the power you hold, that enables you to step into the possession of the estates despite our pleasure."

"Oh dear no! Mr. Skinwell" making his way to the hall, followed by the exultant Pattypan, together with Mrs. Malvers and his wife. Grantley beckoned Skinwell to join him in the library. Arrived there, and carefully closing the door, Edward, with compressed lips and flushed brow, exclaimed,—

"Now, Mr. Skinwell, we are alone."

"Ye—es, alone," murmured Skinwell, nervously.

"Mr. Skinwell, secretary to the City of London Orphan Asylum, you are a black unmitigated villain!"

With a bound, the irate Skinwell started from his seat.

"Sir! sir! sir! I'll have you to know those epithets are actionable. You pauper! you miserable wretch! You—you—you—" speechless, and choking with rage, Mr. Skinwell staggered back into his seat.

"Calm yourself, sir, and remember that 'tis now in my power to have you thrust from this house at a moment's notice."

"You must first prove to me that the law will give you the power."

Though he was pretty sure that Grantley, by some means, had gained possession of the will, yet did the villain grasp at the last chance of retaining the estate.

"What gives you the power of retaking the property from the hands of the Asylum, eh! eh! eh! tell me that, Mr. Grantley?" Mr. Skinwell gave utterance to a kind of giggle or chuckle, as he for a moment observed a sudden pallor cross the features of the young man.

With a spasm of terror, Grantley had, upon putting his hand to his vest, missed the will, but with an exclamation of joy, he now remembered he had placed it in his pocket-book. Taking the precious document from its hiding-place, Grantley exposed it to the eyes of the enraged Skinwell, who, with a curse, immediately recognised the valuable paper.

With a yell of fury the enraged secretary bounded upon the astounded Grantley, and endeavoured to snatch from his grasp the will that had already cost so much misery and crime.

There was an exclamation of rage and surprise from the lips of Grantley, followed by the sound of a heavy blow, as with his clenched fist he sent the villain secretary to the other end of the apartment.

"Scoundrel! thief! you shall suffer for this!"

The enraged Grantley, who now guessed that to the wretch before him he owed his being kept from the possession of the will giving to him the estates, was about to call to Peter and the servants to kick the villain from the house, when he was startled by the sudden appearance of Ernest Malvers, and a crowd of officers hurrying across the lawn.

With a grim smile Skinwell observed the advancing crowd,

No. 12.

Perhaps all was not yet lost.

There was a smile upon the features of Malvers that spoke triumph, rather than despair or alarm.

With a chuckle Skinwell awaited his coming.

They crossed the lawn, and the foremost of the officers knocked loudly for admission at the outer door.

A moment afterwards there was the sound of loud voices, in angry contention.

The rush of many feet up the stairs.

" In the library, first door to the left," exclaimed a voice.

There was a moment's silence. Then a rude bang at the door.

With alacrity, Skinwell hurried by Edward Grantley, and threw it wide upon its hinges.

Ernest Malvers at once made his way into the chamber.

Followed closely by some half-dozen officers, two of whom immediately went over to the amazed Grantley.

There were dark, stern looks upon the faces of all.

Looks of serious and deadly import.

As though they had arrived upon some fearful errand.

With wild amazement depicted on their features, Mrs. Grantley and the wife of the villain Malvers entered the room, the latter, with a shudder, starting back as her eyes fell upon the wretch her husband.

For a moment there was a deep silence in the apartment, broken at length by one of the officers, who, tapping Edward Grantley on the shoulder, exclaimed,—

" You are Edward Grantley, I believe ? "

" That is my name."

" You have lately acted as clerk at an office in the City ? "

" I have."

" Well, that office was broken into last night, and a robbery was committed."

" Well, sir ? " the news scarce affected Grantley, who saw that more was to come; a grim smile upon the features of Malvers and the wretch Skinwell causing him to shudder as he cast his eyes upon them, and warning him of danger.

" There was not only a robbery, but murder was done last night at your office," ejaculated the officer.

" Murder ? "

The cry was echoed by all in the room.

" Aye, murder, Mr. Grantley, and by the side of the victim was found these articles. Do you know them ? "

The officer here held up to view the handkerchief, penknife and letters, deposited near the dead body of the murdered porter by his assassin.

A shudder stole through the frame of Edward Grantley, as he gazed upon the hideous proofs held up before him ; his face turned the livid pallor of the grave, as he leant forward, and in a tone of voice, a little above a whisper, ejaculated,—

" Those articles are mine ! "

" Of course they are, and he is the murderer," exclaimed Skinwell, eyeing his victim with a malicious stare.

" Silence ! Mr. Grantley, upon these proofs of circumstantial evidence, it is my duty to make you my prisoner, on the charge of murder."

The officer here placed his hand on the shoulder of the dazed and maddened Grantley, who, in a wild and frenzied voice, cried out,—

" No ! no ! no ! on my soul, I am innocent of the foul crime you would impute to me ! I am the victim of a base plot. The web of an infamous scheme to ruin and bring destruction on my head enwraps me. Nay, take off your hands, I'll not be taken ! "

Wildly the young man struggled, as the officer and two of his men seized him in their grasp.

Malvers and his villain coadjutor, the wretch Skinwell, gazed unmoved upon the scene.

Loud piercing shrieks rang upon the air, from the lips of the young wife, who beheld with madness her beloved partner struggling in the hands of the officers.

" Away with him lads. On with the darbies," (handcuffs) shouted the leader of the men.

" Help ! help ! help ! you shall not tear him from me."

The young wife, throwing her arms round the neck of her husband, impeded the actions of the officers.

" Away with that mad woman ; bear her hence."

" On with the bracelets, Owen."

" Hold ! stop yer little game. Vot are yer arter ? "

All started back, as Sam Snike burst into the room, accompanied by a watchman. " Hold ! I'm come to put a stopper upon as nice a little plot as vos ever hatched by two willains in human form. In the first place, seize that ere cove ! He is the murderer of the old vicket porter, and no other, and I and the watchman here can prove it. Oh ! you precious beauty, how does yer feel, old cove ? "

Sam here, having first directed the attention of the officers to the villain Malvers, began to indulge in a kind of cellar flap or street dance round and round him, and then wound up with a jig and a war-whoop before the alarmed and amazed Skinwell.

" What does all this mean ? " exclaimed the officer.

" Lock him up ; the young cur is drunk ! He has lost his wits ! " shouted the enraged Malvers.

" My vits are sharper nor yours vos last night, muster thief and murderer, vhen yer dropped this ere knife, vith vitch yer stabbed the poor old vicket porter, and this here bunch of skeletons, vitch I found along vith the vatchman here. Oh ! the knife is his'n ; there's his name on the handle."

" The lad is right. This looks suspicious. Mr. Ernest Malvers, you are my prisoner."

" Curses ! this is folly. Am I to be arrested at the word o such a thing as that ? "

" Don't go on like that, old cove, or you'll hurt yerself. Remember, Muster Malvers, gnats can sting, and I'm blowed if I don't sting you this time. Cheer up, Muster Grantley, he'll be hung, and I'll go and give a jig at the foot of the gallows. Vot a lark. Ain't I done him up brown ? "

In vain were the curses and struggles of Malvers. Handcuffed by the officer, he was carried off.

Edward Grantley, with Sam, and the watchman who had accompanied him to the manor, following with the officers to attend before a magistrate.

A complicated and villainous plot was then laid bare.

The wretch Skinwell, in fear and terror, turned evidence against and betrayed his companion, not proof against a circumstance that was brought forward to prove the innocence of Edward Grantley, and trembling to be implicated with him in his crime.

It appeared that when first discovered by Sam Snike, the poor old wicket porter was not dead, the name of his murderer being scrawled upon a piece of paper stained with his own blood, ere he breathed his last ; and this was done in the presence of the watchman. This, together with the knife of Malvers, found on the ground, and the skeleton keys, cleared Edward Grantley of the foul charges, apart from the betrayal of his comrade by the villain Skinwell.

That night Skinwell and Ernest Malvers lodged in Newgate.

Edward Grantley, reinstated at the manor house, in joy and thankfulness breathed a prayer to the One above, who had snatched him from the fearful peril that had encompassed him.

CHAPTER XXXIV.

THE DEVIL'S PUNCH BOWL IN OLD WESTMINSTER—A FLASH KEN AND ITS VISITORS—CHURCH-YARD DICK AND BURKING BILL—THE PROPOSED BURGLARY—SUDDEN APPEARANCE OF THE STRANGER—THE CONSULTATION—THE COMPACT OF CRIME.

At the time of which we are writing Westminster was very different to now.

Wondrous changes have been effected by the hand of time.

The Alsatia of Whitefriars had disappeared, but old Westminster, at the period at which our story is laid was a wild and in many parts open spot.

The old Mint, the Minories, Field-lane, and other resorts of crime were, a century ago, flourishing and frequented by all the vilest outcasts of London.

Many dens of crime were there in old Westminster.

One of which, known to be frequented by the most daring

criminals, was alike avoided by the wandering stranger and the officers of the law.

Only when in strong numbers did the latter venture within the precincts of the Devil's Punch Bowl, as it was called.

Tothill-street, at the time of our life romance, was all open fields, whilst that part of Westminster lying near the river was in many places flooded by the tides.

At the end of a dark, narrow, ill-lighted street, in which there was, perhaps, never more than two or three oil lamps, giving out a sickly light, stood the Devil's Punch Bowl.

It was a large, old fashioned tenement, nearly all built of wood.

The strong, black, oaken beams could be seen from without, as they ran from end to end of the building.

Small casements, consisting of diamond-paned pieces of glass, the leadwork of which was in many parts torn and broken away, gave an air of thorough antiquity to the old house.

Standing some three stories high, its roof hung right over the upper casements.

The back of this building looked out upon the river, then a glistering, silvery stream, not as now a receptacle for all the filth of a great city.

In front of the inn a blighted oak reared its decaying trunk in the air.

Grim, sombre, and ghastly looked the old tree, as it stood there in its decay, its naked boughs and bare trunk weathering many a winter's storm.

From one of the strongest limbs was suspended the sign of the house before which it stood.

The Devil's Punch Bowl.

A red flagon or bowl upon a black ground.

It was a dark, murderous looking building, was the Devil's Punch Bowl House.

Even in the summer sun it looked dismal, drear, and sombre.

A halo of crime appeared to hang about the place.

On the wild dark nights the winds from the river roared and screamed shrilly round the old inn, the sign creaking, swinging, and groaning, like some disembodied spirit in the storm.

But loud peals of laughter would sound from within.

The winter's storm kept not away the guests of the Devil's Punch Bowl.

No matter if the elements were fair or foul, there was always a large assembly of visitors at the Bowl House.

On the night of the day that saw the return of Edward Grantley to the Manor House at Hackney, there was more than a usual number of visitors at the Bowl, as the frequenters called it.

The night, for the time of year, was a chilly one.

The wind sharp and keen, blew in strong, fitful gusts about the old inn.

Soughing, moaning, screaming, and whistling among the naked boughs of the blighted oak.

Entering the low door of the old house, as the Abbey clock of Westminster boomed out the hour of eleven, a tall, powerfully built man, made his way along a dark passage, and reaching the bar, before which stood a motley crowd of members of both sexes, cursing, swearing, and drinking, asked a fierce-looking negro, who was serving the customers, if a companion had called; receiving an answer in the negative the man made his way from the bar, returning the nods of various associates as he passed along.

Leaving the noisy crowd behind him, the visitor, who appeared well-known to all, walking along a passage that ran beside the bar, passed two or three doors on his right and left hand, and halted at one that faced him at the end of the passage; opening this, he descended a flight of steep, winding stairs, at the bottom of which was another door. Here he gave three hard knocks; a few moments elapsed, and it was opened by a stout, ill-featured, ruffianly looking man, who, nodding his head as the summoner passed through, exclaimed—

"All right Burker, the lads are in the kitchen."

"Churchyarder aint here, is he?"

"No he aint passed the trap (*door*) to-night, Bill."

"Tell him I'm here, when he comes."

"All right, Bill, I'm fly."

The man now, leaving the door-keeper, made his way down a long, narrow passage, lighted at either end by an oil-lamp, the faint glimmer from which but feebly served to show the way.

At the further end of this underground corridor or passage was another door, from the other side of which came the hum of many voices.

Rapping loudly with his knuckles on the panel, the door was instantly thrown open, and the man made his way into a large room that appeared from its size to run the entire width of the house.

It was a strange scene in the underground chamber of the Devil's Punch Bowl.

There were at least thirty or forty men congregated in that huge kitchen, for such indeed it was.

The ages of the visitors varied from eighteen to forty.

All the features of the guests of the Bowl House were stamped with low cunning, depravity, and crime.

In the centre of the room was a large table the legs of which were fastened to the floor.

A cloth, any colour but the original white, was laid upon the table.

Iron plates, to which knives and forks were hanging by chains, were being placed round the table by a sallow faced, sickly looking, humpback.

A dirt begrimed urchin of perhaps twelve years of age, was carrying round a basket from which he took great hunks of coarse bread, placing them beside the plates.

Huge cans of ale and porter, with various kinds of spirits, were brought into the kitchen.

Supper was about to take place in the old Bowl House.

Supper was the grand meal there.

The visitors, absent all day, sat down at night in that huge kitchen and eat a meal that would have laid most men on a sick bed, so large was the quantity of everything that was consumed.

It was a strange assemblage that gathered together in the kitchen of the Punch Bowl.

House-breakers, highwaymen, footpads, resurrection men, pickpockets, and impostors and criminals of every grade, were collected in that underground chamber of the flash ken.

In one part of the kitchen a fellow was dancing and stamping about, who had just before taken off a wooden leg.

In another corner, a thin, cadaverous looking creature, was bathing his arm with warm water to wash off the acids he had placed upon it in the morning to give his flesh the appearance of a scald or burn.

Another fellow, with pinched features, and of hungry starved appearance, who had sat by one of the bridges all day, with a board before him on which was chalked, " I'm starving and in want" was busy unwinding some wrappers from a limb he gave out had been crushed by machinery, the leg, when the fastenings were removed, appearing shrunk and shriveled from being constantly bandaged.

Sitting near him was another who had really lost a leg in a fracas with some officers. This man, dressed as a sailor, would take his post by London-bridge, and with a highly coloured daub of a wreck among icebergs, depicted how he had lost his blessed leg in the frozen ocean.

Opposite to this fellow was a man, who in the day might be seen in the streets following a dog, with a placard pinned to his breast on which was scrawled, ' Pity the poor blind."

Begging letter writers, cadgers, pimps, loafers, and fogle snatchers (*pickpockets*), all were there, herded with men whose trade was murder and every species of crime.

The table now being covered with huge joints of beef, roast and boiled, legs and shoulders of mutton, toads in-the-hole, beef-steak pies, fowls, and every description of food, there was a general fall to.

There was no ceremony by the guests at the Punch Bowl house.

At supper every one helped himself and ate his fill.

It was just as the clatter of the knives and forks mingled

with the discord of the many voices in the huge kitchen, that a man, standing some six feet in height and thin in proportion, made his appearance at the door.

Of fierce, forbidding looking features, this man's aspect was increased in horror by his thin, hollow cheek and sunken eyes.

Thin, snaky locks of black hair hung over his brow, whilst his complexion was that of a resuscitated corpse; the nose, sharp and prominent, stood out from his cadaverous features. But the eyes of this strange and hideous object was the most remarkable thing about him: deep sunk in the head and covered by thin black brows, they shone in their sockets like little beads of fire.

Bright, black, and piercing, and shifting round; taking everything in at a glance.

To this man the visitor, who had arrived some little time before, and who had left word for his companion to join him in the kitchen, now stepped forward.

" You are late, Churchyarder."

" Better late than never, Burker."

" Did Mulberry tell you anything about the lay?"

" No! merely said summat was up, and you wanted me."

" All right, Dick, we will leave the kitchen and have a chat in the parlour above."

" Right you is."

" Any news of Bony?"

" Yes, he's lagged," answered the other, following his companion from the kitchen.

" The devil! Then he's safe for a lifer, unless he can escape from the stone jug."

" It was his blowen (*female*) that nosed upon   him. Ah, if she were mine wouldn't I give her my mark if I slipped the clinkers (*fetters*)."

" By — so would I, Dick!" replied the other with a fierce oath; " but here we are at the parlour. We'll have some of your favourite brew, whiskey hot, and then to business."

Ringing the bell, upon the appearance of a slatternly wench, the man named Burker, gave the order for the liquor in question, and seating himself beside his tall, gaunt and hideous looking comrade, exclaimed—

" Yer an't busy, Dick?"

" No! Bill! there's nothing doing."

" I thought so! that's why I sent Mulberry to tell yer to call, as I fancy I can put summat in yer way."

" Is it a snatch?" (*to steal a body.*)

" Yes, Dick!" replied the other with a smile, " but it's a live subject, not a stiff un."

" What the — do you mean, Burker?"

" Why this: that it's to carry off a gal."

" Hem! Is there much gilt hanging to the job?"

" Oh, yes; the party as puts up the lay pays a dose of swag."

" Where does it come off?"

" At Putney."

" When?"

" To-night."

" Any one in it asides you, Burker?"

" Only Mulberry."

" And you want me to join?"

" Yes, we may have a tough job."

" If I goes with yer, in course, we shares the shiners."

" Of course."

" The crib you have to crack is at Putney, you say."

" Yes, it's an old house guarded by a savage dog, and tenanted by a rough old fire-eater, formerly in the army."

" Oh! then we'll have our work."

" Well, yes."

" In course you'll take a doctor (*a piece of poisoned meat*) with you for the dog."

" The very thing I shall do."

" You'll collar the gal?"

" Yes."

" While I sees to the old man."

" That's the card, Dick; you hit me where I want yer."

" Just so, Burker. I can tell what's what; it ain't the first time we've worked a lay together."

" Well, I'm on with yer, Bill, like beans."

" I knowed you would, Dick."

" When do yer start, Bill?"

" When I'm paid the deposit down for the crack."

" Is the bloak to meet you here?"

" Yes."

" Will he come?"

" Will a duck swim?"

" But he mightn't like the crib. The Devil's Punch Bowl ain't got a very good character for swells."

" Oh, this chap is a fine cove. I've done one job for him afore."

" Then, in course, it's all right."

" As a trivet—and by blazes, here he is."

A tall stranger, muffled up in the folds of a military cloak, at that moment entered the room.

Glancing at the two men seated at the table, he held out a piece of dirty pasteboard upon which was scrawled, " Bill Burker, Bowl House, Westminster."

" Yes, that's me, Captain!" exclaimed the stoutest ruffian rising to his feet.

" I am here to my appointment, are you prepared to carry out what I desire?"

The stranger, disguising his voice, spoke in a low tone to the two men, the while he kept a scrutinising glance fixed upon the death's-head countenance of Churchyard Dick, for whom a more appropriate cognomen could not have been found.

" I have only been waiting yer arrival, captain."

" 'Tis well; who is that you have with you?"

" My pal as helps me in the job."

" Knows he the danger of the task you have in hand?"

" Yes, captain."

" And is prepared to join you?"

" Yes! we only waits orders."

" Very good; 'tis now near twelve."

" Just about it."

" In a good trap you may get to Putney by two."

" Yes, captain; and a very nice hour for a crack that'll be."

" Well, you can ride down at once; you have a vehicle, I suppose?"

" Oh yes, captain, with as fine a piece of horseflesh as ever trotted in harness."

" Very good; now here are notes for fifty pounds, do the work well and efficiently and the other half shall be doubled. You understand?"

" Perfectly; a hundred a-top of this, instead of fifty?"

" Exactly! now what time may I expect to see you at my residence?"

" Well, let me see," mused the burglar. " Say I and my mates gets to Putney by two; if all goes fair and square, we are away from the crib in half an hour arter that; consequently we gets to your crib at Wimbledon by three o'clock, or thereabouts."

" I may expect you then at the Ivy Manor House by that hour?" ejaculated the stranger.

" You may, captain, and not be disappointed. And now, Dick, we had best be off. Go tell Mulberry all is settled, and let him get ready the trap."

The stranger now, drawing his cloak closer round him, and bidding the ruffian whom he had employed not to make a bungle of his task, withdrew from the room, and ten minutes afterwards was threading his footsteps along the dark thoroughfare at the end of which was situate the Devil's Punch Bowl.

Ten minutes after the departure of the muffled stranger a light cart drew up at the door of the old inn, and the man Burking Bill and another, followed by his tall horrible looking companion, Churchyard Dick, whose real name we may premise was Dick Church, and whose loathsome calling was that of a resurrectionist, got into the vehicle and immediately drove off.

It was a dark dismal night.

Cold and drear enough for autumn or early winter.

Instead of the middle of summer.

Puffing away at some pipes they had placed in their mouths at starting, the three men for some time dashed along the road, merely exchanging a word or two.

An hour passed by.

London, left for some time behind them, was now replaced by the open country.

Vauxhall and Wandsworth-road, then all bare, bleak, and open fields, were passed by the burglars and companions in crime.

A few houses here and there standing solitary and alone were the only habitations on the road.

At length Wimbledon is reached.

Still the vehicle, with the three ruffians bent on rapine and crime, dashes on.

Putney-heath is crossed.

Cursing, and giving utterance to horrid oaths, the companions drive the cart down a long dark lane that opens out on the high road to the little village of Putney.

"Well, Bill, this ere's better than that cussed heath."

"Right you are, Mulberry. Whew! how the infernal wind whistled over the cussed place."

"I thought it would cut us in two," said the man Dick Church, with a curse.

"Rather a difficult matter with you, Dick," said the man Bill Burker, with a laugh.

"How so?"

"Why, you're so cussed thin the wind wouldn't know where to take yer."

"You're sharp to-night, Bill."

"I'm not the only sharp un out, Dick."

"No, that cussed wind is a proof of that; but, curses on it, how far are we from the crib?"

"Why, here we are."

The burglars now drew up by the gates of a large house, the grounds of which faced the lane down which they had come.

"They call this Cold-Blow-lane, and cuss me if it aint cold, too," exclaimed Burking Bill, jumping from the cart.

His companions with oaths and curses joined him, and the three presently stood conferring by the gates of the house it was their intention to break into.

"Have yer got the doctor ready for the dog, Bill?"

"Yes, it's all right, Dick."

"Barking irons primed?"

"Yes."

"I suppose I'm to slit the weazand (*throat*) of the old man if he raises an alarm?"

"Curses, yes! This is too good a plant to be sold."

"Plenty of wedge (*plate*) I suppose, Bill?"

"Heaps, Mulberry; and curse yer, look sharp and get it out—easy does it, sleek the trap (*fasten the gate*) and follow me. I've been here afore to-night and taken an inventory of the grounds and the building. Kious! (*be quiet*) and we'll soon do the trick."

Like three dark phantoms the burglars and midnight marauders made their way towards the house that loomed in the darkness before them.

It was a wild kind of night.

The wind screamed and roared through the branches of the giant oak and stately beech.

The clouds in black heavy masses hung over head.

The grounds surrounding the lone house at Putney were large, wooded, and extensive.

Fir Tree Grange was well known by the residents in the little village of Putney.

It was a grey, weather-beaten old manor house.

All the inhabitants of the old building were locked in slumber as the three burglars approached, and anon halted by the grey storm-beaten pile.

"Hist! hold the glim, Mulberry, while I see to the blinkers here (*shutters*)."

The three burglars now stood beneath a casement that opened out upon the lawn they had crossed a few moments before.

It was a wild scene, those marauders breaking their way into the house, grouped there at the window like three dark phantoms.

The wind roared with unrestrained fury round the old grange.

Holding a dark lantern up to the window by which they stood, and drawing back the slide, a dull yellow flicker was thrown upon the spot.

The ruffian Burker, with some implements he drew from his pocket, began to force the shutters of the casement.

First placing a piece of brown paper covered with pitch over a sheet of glass, he pressed against it, the pane falling out without noise.

The shutters now remained to be seen to.

With a peculiarly shaped and sharp instrument the housebreaker cut a square hole out of one of the panels of the shutters, and on its removal endeavoured to force his arm through.

A curse escaped his lips.

"What's up, Bunker?"

"Can't yer sleek the trap?" (*force the shutter*).

"Curses, no."

"Why?"

"'Cos it's sheeted with iron."

Oaths and curses of disappointment escaped the lips of the burglars.

"What's to be done, Bill?"

"Cuss me if I knows, Dick."

"Aren't we better try the back?"

"It's our only chance, Mulberry, so come on."

The three ruffians now left the front of the manor, and winding their way among the thick shrubbery, at length paused before a side door that was at the end of a narrow passage lined on either side with holly bushes, the leaves of which rustled and shook in the raging wind.

"Here we is."

"Right and tight."

"We mounts this wall."

"And in a brace of shakes we finds ourselves all among the kitchen stuff."

"Mulberry, just cut back and see if the drag and the horseflesh is all right, and when yer comes agin we shall be in the crib."

"Right you are, Bill." The burglar at once made off, whilst his companions, scaling the wall by the door, were presently standing at the back of the house.

Groping along, the light of the lantern flashing like a Will-o'-the-wisp in their path, the burglars at last halt beside a large door.

"This ere is the entrance to the slavies hall; hold the glim, Dick, while I sleek the gate" (*open the door*).

A few minutes passed away, the two dark figures, like birds of ill omen, standing motionless by the door.

The wind soughed and moaned on over the old grange.

All is silence.

Save the roaring of the blast, nought can be heard.

The sleepers in the old house slumber on, unconscious of peril.

The two dark forms still stand by the door in the garden.

Amid the pauses of the howling winds a strange rasping, grating noise might be heard.

At length this ceases.

There is a low, muttered converse between the burglars.

Deep breathed curses escape their lips.

Anon they are joined by another.

"What, not yet in the crib, Bill?" exclaimed the new comer.

"No, curses on it."

"Why, how's that?"

"The door, like the shutters, is sheeted with iron."

"The devil."

"Well, let us take a look round; it won't do to be floored, no how."

Again the three men hurry on, cursing and giving utterance to horrible imprecations of rage and fury.

They now reach the back of the old manor house.

Casting his eyes up, an exclamation of satisfaction escapes the lips of the Burker.

"Dick Mulberry, it's all right, the crib's as good as cracked, and I only hopes arter we've cracked the nut we may find a good kernel. Look here, Dick, yer see that ivy?"

" Yes, running right up past that casement on the first floor. I sees your move, Bill, and a good un too."

" One on us must make our way up, prize open the window, get in. go below, unlock the door, and let the others in."

" Beautiful, Bill! Spoken like a horacle."

" But who's to go up the ivy ?"

" Why, Dick's the only one on us, Mulberry, as can manage it neat."

" And Dick's the cove as will do it, though it's rather out of his line, seeing as he generally transacts the churchyard business; but, howsomever, here goes."

The burglar now made his way quickly up the thickly-growing ivy, that flourished and grew in wild luxuriance up the walls of the manor at the back.

His dark figure was scarce distinguishable amid the thick mass of leaves as he worked his way up, his companions eagerly watching him from below.

Anon he pauses at the casement some twenty-five feet or more from the ground.

For a moment his dark figure appears fully revealed, leaning out from the mass of thickly growing ivy.

There is a sudden gust of wind that screams shrilly as it careers over the house, but above the howling of the blast there is another sound.

The crash of broken glass.

A moment afterwards the casement is thrown up, and a figure leans out.

The burglars below sinking down, are unobserved in the darkness that enwraps all around.

Whilst the ruffian above, flattening himself against the wall, is hidden by the thick ivy.

A large wild looking object now with a blind whirl dashes at the window.

With a curse the figure of a man at the casement disappears, shutting it to.

Whilst the huge bat that had startled him, with its leathern wing outspread, whirls down into the grounds below.

The wind roars on—time passes.

But all is still and quiet in the manor house.

The burglars stir not.

Half an hour elapses.

The bell of the little clock tower on the roof with dull clang gave out the hour of three.

A thin grey light in the mass of heavy clouds in the east gives warning of the approach of dawn.

With a curse the two men now rise and dart from the garden as their quick ears detect the opening of a door.

In a few moments they are in the house.

" Who was that at the window, Dick ?"

" One of the slavies, Bill."

" Did yer get into the room all right ?"

" Aye! and left him snoring like a devil."

" A good thing for him, Churcher, that he didn't wake agin."

" Yes, 'cos if he had, why—"

" You'd have slit his weasand " (cut his throat).

" Just so."

" But kious (softly), here we is in the butler's crib ; now Mulberry, while me and Dick goes up stairs, do you make the most of your time and collar the wedge (plate), we'll join yer with the gal, hurry from the crib, trot off to Wimbledon, and the job's done."

" Right you is, leave me to look arter the swag, Bill, I'll pretty soon have it out o' here into the trap."

Leaving their companion below, the two men, first drawing a pair of thick woollen hose over their boots, made their way up the stairs to the chambers above.

" Where does the gal sleep, Bill ?" exclaimed the house-breaker who followed behind his companion.

" Next to the room in which dorses (sleeps) the old man," replied the Burker, in a whisper, as they softly stole up the stairs.

" That's awkward, Bill."

" Yes; but you must quiet the old bloak if the girl should pipe an alarm."

" All right, Bill, I'm there."

" Kious (be quiet), here we are."

The two men now halted in a corridor upon each side of which were three doors.

" Which is our side, Bill ?"

" The left."

" What doors ?"

" First and second."

" Well, in yer goes to yours, while I drops into the other, and if the old bloak wakes why I shall drop him one, that's all."

With a dark look of savage ferocity the ruffian here drew from his pocket a long glittering knife.

For a few minutes these daring marauders stood in the corridor.

The silence of the place was suddenly broken by a sharp clicking sound.

As of the unlocking of a door.

Then the two dark forms of the burglars disappeared. One into one chamber and the other into the next.

Entering the first chamber, the ruffian, Burking Bill, is startled by observing a night light.

For a few seconds he stands motionless, then, his eyes gleaming with joy, he treads softly and hastily up to a dressing table upon which rest some beautiful jewels; a diamond necklace, earrings, and bracelets, are all swooped up by the robber and thrust into his pocket.

" By ——, a fine swag, the nobbiest lay I've ever had, so help me," murmured the ruffian, who now stepped cautiously up to a bed, the silken hangings of which hid the sleeper from view.

With drawn breath the burglar pulls back the curtains.

An exclamation of surprise and admiration escapes him.

Lying in the bed, one of her plump round arms thrown out upon the counterpane, is a young and lovely girl.

Young and beautiful, very beautiful is she.

Of the brunette class, her beautiful skin with a rich olive tint is smooth and soft as velvet, her person, admirably formed, is partly revealed by the covering that enwraps her, its folds falling closely and in abandon as she lies asleep, her firm round polished and richly developed bust heaves tumultuously at every breath ; a sweet smile hovers over her lovely features, whilst her ruby lips, slightly apart, reveal her even, close, and pearly teeth ; rich ringlets of dark brown hair in wavy masses lie strewn upon the pillow, serving as an admirable frame to set off the beauteous face of the young girl.

" By the devils she is a stunner !" muttered the villain burglar, lost in admiration as he gazed upon the lovely sleeper; then remembering the object of his presence there, with a grim smile he drew a large silk handkerchief from his pocket, and passing it under the head of the lovely girl, with the speed of thought had wound it round her mouth ere a cry could escape her lips.

Struggling violently, the poor girl was torn from her bed, and, wrapped in the coverings, was borne in a moment from the room.

In the corridor without the burglar was joined by his comrade, who, with a chuckle, emerged from the other chamber.

The hapless girl, stricken with terror. ceasing her struggles, remained clasped in the arms of the Burker.

" Got the petticoat all right, Bill ?"

" Yes, damn it, every thing goes well and first rate. I've collared some splendid sparklers out of the room. Got any swag, Dick ?"

" Curses, yes, a fine ticker set with stones; but come, we will be off ere our luck turns agin us. I wonder how old Mulberry is getting on."

" Right enough, I'll swear he has got a tidy dose of wedge out by this time."

The two men, with chuckles and oaths of satisfaction, hurried down the stairs.

" Go on, Burker; what the —— are yer staring at ?"

The burglar with the young girl in his arms had paused at the bottom of the stairs.

His companion now, with a start, beheld the cause of his strange hesitation.

Glaring upon them in the darkness of the hall below were two fiery eyes.

Eyes that gleamed in the dark like balls of fire.

They had forgotten the dog.

A low growling noise fell upon their ears.

Oaths of horror and alarm escaped their lips.

" Curses, the dog ! "

" By the fiends, it's all up."

Transfixed, the two ruffians remained at the bottom of the stairs, gazing with horror at the gleaming balls of fire before them.

For a few moments there was nought but a low growling noise from the dog, but at length the silence was broken by a rough voice in the hall, exclaiming—

" How now, Churchyarder and Burker, what is yer arter ? what's your game ? "

Scarce had these words escaped the lips of the ruffian, Mulberry, when the dog, with a bark that rung through the house, sprang upon the two men that stood upon the stairs.

" Away with the gal, Burker, leave the cussed brute to me."

There was a scuffling of feet, and fierce struggle in the hall of the house, followed by the loud report of a pistol.

The dark figure of the burglar bearing the young girl in his arms then dashed along the hall, and, unfastening the bolts of the door, threw it open, with a curse, rushing into the garden without.

The alarm bell now rang with dull clang upon the air.

All in the Fir Tree Grange were aroused.

Loud voices and cries of alarm rung through the house.

After a fierce encounter the two burglars left the dog with its skull beaten in lying at the bottom of the stairs, and, followed by some pistol shots from the weapons of two men that rushed after them into the grounds, managed at last to effect their escape.

There was grief and sorrow at the Fir Tree Grange the morning of the burglary.

For the only child of Colonel Howard, the owner of the Grange, had been carried off.

And could not be traced.

The ruffians who had borne off their prey left no track behind.

Colonel Howard and his daughter never met again on earth.

In after years the lovely Clarissa Howard recalled with a shudder the night of her abduction from the Fir Tree Grange.

CHAPTER XXXVI.

THE SCENE AT THE CAT AND HER KITTENS—THE THREE FRIENDS—THE REUNION—THE OATH—THE RUNNERS AND THE HIGHWAYMEN—THE ENCOUNTER—THE ESCAPE OF THE COMPANIONS—HURRA FOR THE ROAD !—THE MEETING— CAPTAIN LESTER AND SIXTEEN-STRING JACK—THE THREAT —THE VOW OF VENGEANCE—THE DEPARTURE OF THE THREE FRIENDS—THE HALT AT THE DESERTED HOUSE— THE DARK SHADOW ON THE STAIRCASE—A MYSTERY.

UPON the sudden and mysterious appearance of his friend Tom King, who he thought had perished at his hands in the churchyard at Fulham, Sixteen-String Jack was so startled that for some two minutes he stood speechless, glaring at what he thought was some shadow from the other world.

" Tom King ! "

" Yes, Jack ! old fellow, 'tis indeed your old pal ! nay, you need not stare so, Jack, I'm no immaterial being of the other world, but your friend, safe and sound, wind and limb," said King, with a slight laugh, partly closing the door of the secret chamber, and approaching his companion.

" What the devil does all this mean ? " ejaculated Turpin, glancing at his friends in surprise.

" Oh ! only that Jack takes me for a ghost, Dick ; " then, seizing Jack by the hand, he placed his mouth to his ear, exclaiming in a whisper, " Forget the past, Jack, not a word to Dick—mum," then, with a significant wink, he drew back and began to explain the reason of his sudden appearance in the blue chamber.

" You must know, my dear pals, that in an encounter with a gent the other night whom I attempted to ease of some superfluous cash, I was sent to grass by a leaden pill from his barking iron." (Tom here gave a significant wink at Jack.) " When I fell I thought all was over with me, for the bullet, as I imagined, had pierced my chest. But I was mistaken ; upon recovering from the senseless state into which I had fallen I found myself reclining on a rude table in a little chamber of a roadside inn on the way to Fulham. About to utter an exclamation of surprise, I refrained, for upon unclosing my eyes I discovered the forms of two Bow-street runners. From what they said to each other I learned that I was considered as dead. ' It's all up with Tom King,' said one ; ' Yes, replied the other, the rascal has cheated the hangman ;' both then left the room, and as they closed the door, with a strange dizziness in the head, I staggered from the table on which I had lain to the ground, and made my way to an open casement. 'Twas broad day. A beautiful breeze was wafted into the chamber, which helped to revive me, and remove the feeling of faintness that oppressed me. Upon opening my vest I now made a wonderful discovery." (Tom here looked hard at Jack.) " I found that the bullet I fancied had entered my body had merely torn up the skin, first indenting itself in this medal" (here King drew a large silver piece from his pocket, the centre of which was flattened in,) " that for a whim, to please a dark-eyed little Spanish girl, I have for some time worn by a ribbon round my neck. The bullet, after lodging against this resistance, glided off, tearing through the flesh under my arm ; the concussion of the ball it was that stretched me senseless on the ground. You may be sure I lost no time in vacating from the inn, but short as that time was it served to reveal my actions to the runners, who, with a loud whoop, were soon upon my track, hunting the man who a short while before they had imagined was a corpse."

" A novel chase, Tom."

" Yes, Dick, and a damned disagreeable one for me, as I felt very queer on my pins, and was aware that, if captured, I should very speedily be placed in the stone jug."

" How did you effect your escape, Tom ? "

" Why, by a ruse, Dick. I doubled on them, let them get a-head, and then retraced my flying steps. I was, however, through this incident unable to meet you, and what is more, whilst insensible, lost the paper I had in my bosom relative to that little matter upon which we were to have met."

" The devil ! "

" Never mind, Dick ! perhaps it is as well. I think that affair was rather out of our line," here Tom, with a smile, glanced meaningly at Jack, who, with surprise not unmixed with joy, heard that his friend had escaped death at his hand, and also evidently regretted the business about the Grantley will.

" But what brought you here, Tom ? "

" I was about to make my way to the old tree cave by the ruined mill, Dick, but was met on the road by a greasy-faced farmer, who, although 'twas broad day, I couldn't resist from making pay the king's toll."

" Ha ! ha ! ha ! devilish good, Tom," said Jack, recovering his usual bouyant spirits, " and did the old grazier refuse to tip ? "

" Oh, no ! I eased him of a flimsy (a note) for fifty goldfinches (guineas), but was interrupted by a whole posse of runners. Upon their showing head I put White Wizard or his metal, found myself hard pressed, put up at the ' Cat and her Kittens,' Jem housed my steed, told me some pals were in the blue room, and left me as my pursuers arrived. I at once made my way hither, and to my surprise lighted upon my dear old friends, Turpin and Jack. And now let me hope, dear pals, for the future we may thoroughly understand each other ; let us no more be at odds as we have been over that cursed will of the Grantleys. Why should we, three knights of the road, disagree ? Let us band together—swear one never to cross the others, and as union is strength we may safely levy contributions on society to pay our expenses whilst we run the race of life."

"Tom you are a noble fellow, nor shall Dick be deceived in any way as to the past," despite the warning frowns of his friend, Jack now explained the meeting in the churchyard at Fulham, its results, and also how he had secured and placed the will in the hands of its proper owner. "And now, dear pals, I for one, am ready, heart and hand, to swear always to hold your interests as my own. Let us then, as Tom has advised, for the future work together, and when one is in trouble let him find a true pal in those who are free, and ready to aid him in the time of danger. Let us take an oath, we three knights of the road, to remain from to-day, fast, firm, and true, one to the other."

"With all my heart, Jack," exclaimed Turpin.

"Bravely said, Dick!" ejaculated King.

Standing then in the centre of the little secret chamber of the old inn, clasping each others' hands, the three highwaymen then swore an oath of friendship, which they in after years, during their chequered and dangerous career, never failed to remember.

"Now, dear pals, a bumper round," exclaimed Jack, pouring out three goblets of rich red wine.

Holding high their glasses, with their faces wreathed in a smile of joy and good feeling, each then gave his toast.

"To the King!" said Jack, with a laugh, "and may he never find his subjects refuse to pay their mite to the treasury for his support."

"To Bonny Black Bess, and may every knight of the road secure as faithful a stead."

"Well said, both! my toast is, A dark night, a full purse, rosy wine and ruby lips: and may we never fail to secure them all!"

"Bravo Tom, no heel-taps! down with it."

At a draught each then drained his glass, but scarce had they placed their goblets on the table, when they were startled by voices in the chamber adjoining the blue room.

"Well, look here, Mr. Jem Lutterworth! It's all very fine, but we know our men are here, and we intend to have them."

"Do you mean to insinuate that 'The Cat and her Kittens' is a house of refuge to knights of the road."

"That is just what I do mean, Mr. innocent Jem; you are a downy card, but you don't come the blind over Jonathan Anstey."

"I assure you, Anstey, I haven't seen anything of those whom you seek."

"Gammon."

"Upon my honour."

"Your honour! Devilish good. You never had any."

"Well, we can't quarrel on that point, thief-taking Jonathan! And when you catch sight of a highwayman at 'The Cat and her Kittens,' it will be good for sore eyes."

"Very well, Jem Lutterworth, we shall see."

"Well, I hope you may, as I don't like a visitor to leave my inn disappointed."

"Oh, go to the devil!"

"Thank you, Newgate Jonathan, I'd rather not."

"Well, get us some drink."

"Certainly, with the greatest of pleasure, where will you take it?"

"Better room down stairs, gentlemen."

"We prefer to remain here."

"Very good," the friends, who had heard every word of this converse between the landlord and his guests, now turned and gazed with looks of annoyance into each others' faces.

"Dick!"

"Tom!"

"Jack!"

"This is awkward."

"Rather."

"What's to be done?"

"Can't say."

"We are in a trap."

"Something like it."

"Caged."

"Just so."

"Well, Jack, you are good at getting out of a scrape, what do you advise?"

"I don't know what to advise Dick, at the moment; we are safe here, in the blue room."

"Yes, Jack, and I wish we were safe out of it."

"All in good time, Tom! patience is —"

"A virtue! right Jack, but as the gal said, I ain't got any virtue."

"Well, wanting it, Tom, you must bite your thumbs and kick you heels till we get out of this."

"A pleasant alternative."

"Very."

"Well, never mind, pals, we've some of Jem's best wines, so we'll drink confusion to all Bow-street runners."

"We must spare the bottle, Dick."

"The devil, Jack! For why?"

"Because when the wine is in—"

"The wit is out. Oh, yes; but what the deuce has that to do with our getting jolly in this little snuggery?"

"Because, Dick, we should speedily convert it into anything but a snuggery."

"How?"

"What the devil's he driving at?"

"Why, look you, my dear pals; if we make the least disturbance we shall be heard by our friends in the other room."

"The devil. So we shall."

"I never thought of that, Dick."

"Nor I, Tom."

"Well, I'm longer in the head than you my lads—I did."

"But what the —— are we to do, Jack?"

"Wait, Tom, till the enemy retreat."

"But, damnation, they may stop for hours."

"Well, we must wait."

"I'd sooner make a bolt out on them and end the matter."

"It won't do, Dick."

"No, Jack is right; if we leave the secret chamber now whilst the grabs (officers) are in the next room it will never serve as a hiding place at a future time."

"Very true, curses on Anstey and his myrmidons, we must wait."

"That's the only thing we can do, Dick, but hark, Jem has returned," placing their ears to the thin partition that divided the secret chamber from the other room, the companions now listened to the discourse of Jem Lutterworth and the officers.

"There is the wine, gentlemen, and fine stuff it is; been in cellar fifty years."

"Pity your carcase ain't been with it."

"Thank you, Mr. Bolt! I think after that I'll make a bolt of it."

"Stay, Lutterworth, one word with you."

"Fifty if you like, Mr. Anstey."

"You say that master Tom King ain't here."

"No."

"Nor his pal, Dick Turpin?"

"I ain't seen them."

"Well, of course, it would be rude to doubt your word, Jem."

"On my honour."

"Well, never mind the honour; we'll believe you."

"Thank you."

"Oh, no thanks, and as our men are not here, Jem, why ——"

"You'll go, gentlemen?"

"No, Lutterworth, we'll wait till they come."

An audible curse from the lips of the landlord and a shout of laughter from the runners now fell upon the ears of the three friends.

"Damn that fellow Austey, he is too funny for me! I'll put a bullet in his skull before I've done with him " muttered Turpin.

"I'll pay him my respects, Dick, if I see a chance at any time."

"Ditto, pals, I owe him one," said Jack.

VILLAINY DEFEATED—CONVICTION OF MALVERS.

Again the friends listened to the converse of the officers who over their wine, recounted the different adventures that had befallen them from time to time, ever and again chuckling as they recalled to mind how they had been instrumental in dragging many a poor victim to the fatal Tyburn tree.

The highwaymen in the secret chamber gave utterance to deep breathed curses, as they listened to the officers.

Unable to leave their hiding place, they were compelled to hear the converse of their enemies.

Three hours passed away.

Still the companions with untiring patience, but with compressed lips and knitted brows, stood by the wall of the blue room.

A low muttered converse, that the friends could not catch the purport of, was now carried on by the thief-takers, who were presently heard to quit the chamber in which they had been regaling.

"They are gone, Dick."

"Curses on them, yes, Tom."

"Now then Jack, let us be off."

"Hold, Dick, be not too hasty, their departure may be but a ruse."

"Damn it, are we to stop here a century?"

"No, Dick," replied Jack with a smile, "only till Jem comes to tell us all's right."

"But he may be an hour before he can get to us."

"Well, we must wait."

"No, Jack, curse me if I do."

"I'm of Dick's opinion, Jack; let us chance it. I've an appointment with a pretty little petticoat to-night. I must get to London and change my apparel ere I can meet her."

"Well, I've no female in the way, only I'd like to be with my bonny black Bess," ejaculated Turpin.

"And I with the sweet Dora Annersley," murmured Jack to himself, who, as the image of the lovely, friendless girl recurred to his mind, forgot all caution and was as eager to get out of their hiding place as either of his companions.

"Well, Jack, are you coming?"

"Aye, Dick, have with you; but let us see to our barking irons, in case of accidents."

"Right, Jack, mine are ready for use." Turpin, glancing at the locks, replaced the weapons he had pulled from his belt.

"And mine," said Tom.

"All ready," said Turpin, who took the lead.

"All right; get out as quick as you can, Dick."

Needing no second bidding, Turpin, pushing the panel, that had not been securely closed by King on his entrance, followed by his companions, stepped out of the blue room that had served them in such good stead.

Closing the secret door behind them the three friends advanced to the centre of the apartment, left a few moments before by the officers.

With a chuckle Dick made his way to the table, and taking off it a pair of handcuffs placed them in his pocket.

"I'll also on them on the wrists of the amiable Anstey if I see a chance, one of these days," exclaimed Turpin.

No. 13.

"A good joke that, to clap the darbies on their owner," ejaculated Tom King with a laugh.

"Hush! make no noise pals, but let us see how the land lies before we show head." Jack, with cautious steps, now made his way from the room, followed by his friends. In a few minutes they were all three standing on the top of a flight of stairs at the bottom of which was a short hall or corridor, with the bar parlour on one side and a room for common visitors on the other. At the end of this little passage was a door opening out to the front of the bar.

"Now then, come on, Jack, the grabs are gone, it's all right," exclaimed Turpin, pushing past his companion, who was standing hesitatingly at the top of the stairs.

Before Jack had time to recall him he was half way down, Tom following close behind.

"Ha! ha! ha! Anstey's done again, sold a pup, we've done the trick," shouted Dick, who now, with a loud laugh, opened the door on his left and entered the room set apart for chance visitors to the house.

"How do you do, Dick? Ah, Tom King, delighted to see you, gentlemen. You see it's not us but you who are sold; not I but you, Dick Turpin, has been sold the pup. Jonathan Anstey as you see, has done the trick. Seize them lads! On with the darbies."

With a curse King had started back, as he had discerned the figures of four or five officers in the room into which Turpin had made his way.

Nothing daunted or taken by surprise, Turpin, who had been calculating his chances whilst the thief-taker was talking, now coolly pulled a pistol from his belt and fired at a runner, who, though disguised, he well knew to be one of the most wily and cunningly ferocious of his class. Knife in hand, the runner staggered back with a curse, gasping in a voice choking with blood and rage, for the bullet had entered his lungs.

"Seize them Anstey! Hell! devils! let them not escape."

With a rush, the officers bounded on Turpin, who was about to retreat from the spot.

Tom, finding Dick was seized by the runners, turned back, he having reached the foot of the stairs, and was soon with his companion engaged in a desperate struggle with their foes.

Oaths, curses, and imprecations echoed through the room, the table overturned with a loud crash, adding to the din and babel of sounds.

"Shove the bracelets on 'em."

"Stun them with your staves, my men."

"Don't let them escape."

"We have them now!"

"Then mind you keep us," shouted Dick Turpin, who suddenly taking his hands from off the shoulders of one of the runners with whom he was struggling, gripped them tight round his oins, and by sheer bodily strength lifted the man off his feet, hurling him with a crash to the floor.

"One rubbed out who's the next?"

The words had scarce left his lips when he was seized upon by the leader of the thief-takers, the man Jonathan Anstey. This officer was a powerfully built, herculean man, and in point of strength, far the superior of Turpin.

Wildly the highwayman struggled.

But the contest was unequal.

He was speedily overpowered and borne to the ground.

Whilst oaths and curses of impotent fury escaped him.

King, engaged in a desperate strife with two of the runners in one her corner of the room, could lend no aid.

Another moment and Turpin would have been manacled, but as the officer was about to thrust upon his wrists the iron fetters, he was stricken to the ground by a fearful blow at the back of the head.

"By the fiends, just in time! I thought you had cleared out Jack."

"What, and left my pals in the hands of the grabs? No fear, Dick. Down with 'em."

Excited and angry, Jack now dashed wildly at the runners, who were struggling with Tom, whilst Turpin coolly slipped the handcuffs he had in his pocket upon the wrists of the half-senseless Anstey.

It was a strange scene, the conflict of those three men with the merciless runners. Hunted down by their foes the highwaymen now turned upon them and administered fearful punishment with their clenched fists and butts of their pistols.

"Let them have it, Jack."

"Give that fellow a tap on his domino box, Tom."

"Look out, Dick!"

The warning, given just in time, caused Turpin to start aside, and avoid a blow from a heavy life preserver, wielled by one of the runners.

Anstey, partly recovering the effects of the terrible blow he had received at the hands of Jack, with curses of impotent fury, glanced wildly upon the struggling figures before him.

Loud shouts, oaths, and cries for help echoed through the room.

There was a trampling of horses' feet without the inn.

With a look of alarm upon his rubicund features, Jem Lutterworth now dashed into the room.

Catching Jack by the arm, in a whisper he exclaimed,—

"Off and away, Jack! There are some more of the cursed runners without, headed by a wild looking imp of Satan that lives at the Blue Bells who swears he saw you enter here."

"Ha! curses! 'tis the wretch Silas Vaughan. Jem! As you value life, let that monster glean no tidings as to the presence of the poor girl whom I brought hither. I will return to-night; do you place my lovely charge in the secret room, so she will be free from harm."

"All right; she's safe enough in my hands, Jack."

Those few words between Jack and his friend Lutterworth were given in a hasty whisper, as hurling the officers aside, they had dashed out of the room followed by Turpin and King.

The runners, baffled and defeated, lay groaning and cursing on the ground.

Followed by the friends, the landlord of the inn darted down a passage, and opening a door, they all passed out into a large garden at the back.

"Have you got the horses all right, Jem?"

"Am awake? Does I ever shut my eyes when the grabs are out?"

With a laugh, Lutterworth led the three companions down a long avenue of chestnut trees, at the end of which was a large orchard. Winding his way through this, their conductor at length halted before a grotto or cave, in front of which grew a beautiful linden tree, the drooping branches curtaining the entrance to the grotto.

A little brook running beside the cave, gave out a pretty rippling noise, whilst its crystal waters, like a mirror of liquid silver, glittered in the sun's rays.

"Here we are, boys, safe at the secret cave! Now whilst you mount your steeds and away, Jem Lutterworth will return to the inn, and show those cursed runners that the Cat and her Kittens has sharp talons to claw with. I'll show them a trick."

"How can we repay you, Jem?"

"Repay, repay! Damn it, had it been any one but Sixteen-String Jack that asked me that in a case like this, I'd pretty soon have shown them another way out of the grounds belonging to the Cat and her Kittens. Understand once for all, that Jem Lutterworth, and all that he has, is ever at the service of the gentlemen of the road. Sixteen-String Jack, Dick Turpin, and dashing Tom King, rather than let you fall into the hands of the Philistines, damme boys, I'd burn the old inn about their ears whilst you made off."

Shaking hands warmly with the companions, the jolly host made his way back to look after the movements of the officers.

"Well, Jem is a first-rate cove. A damned good-hearted fellow, Jack."

"Yes, Dick, he is one of the right sort, and well I know would peril life itself to do me service. I some five years back rendered him assistance in the hour of need, and Lutterworth has never forgotten it; but come, let us get our steeds. Zounds! I long to be astride my bonny nag, and ho! for a canter to London!"

"Aye, Jack; I too am all anxiety to again cast eyes on my dear, bonnie Black Bess."

"And I to mount my beautiful White Wizard," exclaimed King, following his friends into the dark recesses of the huge grotto or cave.

Leading the way, having more knowledge of the place than his comrades, Jack crossed the cave, the roof of which glittered with spars and pendant drops of moisture. Reaching the further end, he groped with his hands against the uneven wall of rock till his fingers searched out an iron ring. Pulling this with all his force, a large piece of the wall rolled aside, leaving a space sufficiently wide to admit of the passage of two men. A short, narrow passage was now before them, lighted by an oil lamp that hung from the roof. Making their way down this, the three companions halted before a large door that faced them, and barred their further progress.

An unmistakeable odour of a stable now greeted their nostrils.

"Here we are, pals, at the old cave stables of the Cat and her Kittens!" exclaimed Jack, as pushing the door before them, which yielded at once to the pressure, he entered a large, roomy underground chamber, in one corner of which was a low door, with a small grating at the top, through which rushed a current of air.

A loud whinnying noise greeted their appearance, whilst their three steeds that had been feeding from a trough, fixed against the left side of the stables, pawed the ground, and gave signs of the utmost pleasure.

The highwaymen, patting their dumb but sagacious animals, breathed words of fond endearment in their ears. The which were apparently well understood by the noble beasts.

"Well, this is a fine snug retreat, Jack. I was never in it before, though I knew that Lutterworth was of the right metal, and to be trusted," ejaculated King.

"Ah! this and the blue room aint the only secrets of the Cat and her Kittens," replied Jack, with a laugh.

"Well, but how the deuce did they come into existence? Were they got up by Jem merely for the accommodation of the knights of the road."

"Oh, no; they were discovered by Jem when he took the house. Originally a high toby man, and in his younger days a dashing highwayman, when he turned landlord he nosed about the old inn, to see if there were any means of serving a pal at any time, and happened on these hiding places."

"But how the devil did they come to be in existence?" exclaimed King.

"Oh! the inn is an old building, and was formerly a manor house, tenanted some years ago by an old Jacobite. Doubtless he constructed them, little imagining that they would one day serve as a hiding-place for knights of the road."

"Well, good luck to his ancestors, Jack say I," ejaculated Turpin, with a laugh.

"And may the secret haunt of the Cat and her Kittens often throw the runners off the trail of the knights of the road."

"I echo that, Tom! But come pals, let us away. Are you ready, Dick?"

"All right, Jack."

"And you, Tom?"

"Yes, lead on!"

Each now took the reins of his steed, and led them through the low door in the corner of the strange stables, that Dick had opened with a key he took from a shelf.

The horses were obliged to sink down upon their haunches, and crawl through the narrow, low-roofed opening.

"Who'll see to the locking-up of the stables, Jack?"

"Oh, Jem and his confidential help—a rough, honest fellow, one Joe Watson—will see to that."

"Rather dark here, Jack."

"Well, yes; but we shall soon get out now."

Jack leading the way slowly, walked his mare down the dark passage, which was just of sufficient height to allow the horse to stand upright.

Followed on by Dick and Tom, he at length emerged through a large opening into another cave. This outer cavern was flooded with light, that poured in from an aperture nearly fronting them.

Making their way through this, to the surprise of Tom King, who had never traversed the underground and secret way before, they all three stood upon the brink of a silvery pool, in the waters of which drooped the pendant branches of a beautiful weeping willow; the leafy shadows of the tree curtaining the entrance to the cavern.

Upon the other side of the pool was a thick copse through which brawled a little streamlet, fed by the waters of the spring.

Mounting their steeds, the highwaymen led them across the pool, the waters reaching to their saddles, and presently were threading their way through the thick copse; the air ringing with their shouts of laughter, as they thought upon how cleverly, by the aid of their friendly host Jem Lutterworth, they had eluded the pursuit of the officers.

"I wonder how Anstey is by this time, Jack?"

"I should imagine that friend Bolt, Dick, begins to think we've all made a clever bolt of it."

"Well, we've certainly done them now."

"Right and tight, Tom."

"No bowling us out this time."

"I say, Dick, that was a close shave in the parlour."

"Yes, Dick, I just came in the nick of time."

"Where were you, Jack, the first few minutes?"

"Oh, I ran upstairs to speak to Jane Lutterworth."

"Or the pretty Dora, which, Jack?" exclaimed Dick, with a laugh.

A crimson flush overspread the handsome features of Jack, who pretended to be busy with his horse's trappings. King, noticing the tell-tale blush, burst into a roar of laughter.

"Hallo, Jack—scornful Jack! The railer against the darling petticoats caught at last, eh?" King leant back in his saddle, whilst the copse rang with his hilarious shouts.

"Ha, ha, ha! Jack in love! See, Dick, by all that's holy, he blushes like a maid! Come, tell us, Jack, who is she? What is this peerless beauty? You must keep her from me; thou knowest my failing, Jack! For lovely woman I would give my life. Ha, ha, ha! Come, Jack, out with it. Is she young, pretty? any money? What is she? a farmer's buxom daughter, or the only child of some rich squire, whom you eased of his purse on the road?"

"Tom! we are now good friends."

"Damm it, yes. Don't talk like that, Jack. If I've said anything wrong, I'm heartily sorry, my dear pal. I did but jest."

With surprise, King noted the serious, thoughtful look upon the flushed features of his friend.

"Tom King, I love—love to madness—the young girl I have left behind me at the inn. Though I met her for the first time but yesternight."

"Indeed, Jack! Then must she have made a wonderful impression upon you, my dear pal. Ah! Jack, such love as that now burns in your bosom once flamed in mine, for one that, curses on her! jilted me for another."

A dark cloud gathered over the features of Tom King, that was the next moment dispelled by a merry smile, as he dismissed the unpleasant remembrance from his mind.

"Tom, you have not seen the young girl, Dora Annersley! Her lovely face bears the impress of every virtue. I would stake my existence upon her truth, did she give her troth-plight to one she professed to love."

"You are quite right, Jack! So too, would I!" exclaimed Turpin, who with his friend had been much struck with the beauty and innocence of the unfortunate and persecuted girl.

Upon King expressing a wish to hear the particulars of Jack's adventure the night before, our hero at once told his story; his handsome countenance flashing with passion, as he related how he had been followed up by the villain dwarf and monster, Silas Vaughan, upon whom he vowed to wreak a fitrible revenge. "I'll hunt the hideous cur to the death, though I risk my own life in the pursuit!" exclaimed Jack, as he finished his relation.

"Well, from your description of him, I should say he is one of Satan's own."

"He bears more the form of devil than of man, Tom."

"Well, if I come across him, Jack, I'll give him something to remember Dick Turpin by."

"Curses on him! 'Twas he that brought a fresh troop of runners at our heels then, Jack, at the inn, an hour back."

"Yes, Tom, so I was told by Jem."

"Well, then, of course, Dick, you and I owe this half-made man one as well as Jack?"

"Right you are, Tom."

"And of course we'll pay him?"

"Religiously! And find him a parson's lodging (a grave) free gratis for nothing."

"Just the very identical, Dick. But, hallo, what's this?"

The little party had during this converse left the copse far behind them, and were now wending their way at a trot down a lane that opened out on the high road. As they neared the end, Tom had discerned a horseman cantering along at a rate that would bring him to a meeting with them as they emerged from the lane into the road. Pointing to the stranger with his whip, Tom cast a significant smile upon his friends.

"I tumble to you, Tom."

"Well, what do you say, Dick?"

"Oh! with all my heart."

"And what's your opinion, Jack?"

"Why, to stop the pigeon by all means, and see if it's worth plucking!" exclaimed Jack, who had understood the intention of his companions, which was to waylay the traveller.

Patting the necks of their steeds, at a word, the noble beasts dashed on out of the lane into the high road.

The approaching horseman, somewhat startled at their sudden appearance, drew in his reins, and glanced at the little party with eyes of suspicion.

Slowly cantering up to where the stranger had reined in his horse, Jack, who took the lead in the affair, with a jaunty, saucy air, lifted his hat slightly from his head, exclaiming—

"Good day to you, sir! I must ask your pardon for the liberty I am about to take, but the fact is I have lost my purse. Will you kindly lend me yours? and your watch, too, for mine being a lever left me three months ago, and has not yet returned."

"A highwayman!" ejaculated the stranger, a tall, dark, handsome man, about whose appearance, however, there was a rather sinister bearing. His countenance, though handsome, having a highly sensuous and villanous expression; whilst coal-black hair and eyebrows gave him a forbidding aspect, and increased his disagreeable and repelling ensemble.

"A highwayman!" he again ejaculated, as tapping the heel of his boot with the whip he held in one hand, Jack coolly held out the other for his purse; whilst Dick and Tom took care to let him see the butts of the pistols from beneath the lappets of their coats.

With his countenance livid with rage, the stranger drew a well-filled purse from his pocket, and gave it to Jack, then making as though he would ride on.

"Stay, my dear sir. I've got an appointment in London; to know how the time goes, as I journey on, is of the utmost consequence to me. You must lend me your watch."

"Anything else!" exclaimed the stranger, in a voice choking with rage.

"Well, really you are very kind!" replied Jack. "I don't want to be intrusive, but, since you ask me, I'll borrow that ring."

"Won't this do instead?" With a touch of his spur he caused his steed to rear back. As he did so, the stranger snatched a pistol from his pocket, and fired it in the face of Jack

There was a loud report, followed by the noise of a desperate conflict; and the next moment the horse of the traveller went dashing riderless along the road, whilst its master lay bruised and helpless at the mercy of his foes.

Dick and Tom, jumping from their steeds, hurried to that part of the road upon which their victim lay. Jack, who had been the one to hurl him from his horse, was coolly riding him of everything he possessed.

"How is it, Jack?"

"All right, pals. My friend here has only made my hat a ventilator." Jack here held up his hat, through which had passed the bullet from the stranger's pistol; a round hole in the centre pointing out the course of the leaden missive.

"A little lower, Jack!"

"And Sixteen-String Jack would have had his dose, Tom. But my time aint come yet. Hallo! what the —— is this?" Jack, who had taken a pocket-book from the vest of the stranger, started, and turned first pale, then red, whilst his brow contracted into a deep frown. "This is your piece of pasteboard, is it not?" He here held before the eyes of the enraged traveller a card he took out of the pocket-book.

"It is, villain; and by all the saints below you shall have cause to remember its owner. I'll follow you, highwayman, thief, robber, till I bring you to the gibbet." The stranger foamed at the mouth with passion as he beheld Jack conning over the different papers he found in the book.

"Look you, Captain Lester, your threats I value at their worth; and were it not that highwayman as I am, I am incapable of deliberate murder, by —— I'd put a bullet in your brain, with as little remorse as you would have planted one in mine. But you are unarmed, helpless, and at liberty to go; but a word of warning ere I depart. Give up the business the letters I have glanced at treat of, or by the fiend Satan himself, I swear I'll follow you like a bloodhound the fugitive slave, and know no rest till I have dismissed you in your travels to the vale of death. Remember the warning of Sixteen-String Jack, who never broke his word, for good or ill, to friend or foe."

"Sixteen-String Jack! I have heard of you ere to-day, and shall not forget you!" replied the bruised and enraged traveller, staggering to his feet. "Were you to seek refuge from my vengeance in the icy regions of the north, or under Afric's burning sun, I'd find you out. You are the man of whom I heard something last night, in connexion with the matter to which you just now alluded. Look to it! you shall be hunted, felon as you are, not alone by me, and those in my pay, but by the emissaries of the law, whom I will fee with gold to hunt and drag you to the scaffold. By all things earthy and unearthly, I swear it! I will prove a serpent in your path where'er you go, and ere forty hours are passed you shall feel the venom of the serpent's sting."

Livid with rage, his lips colourless and covered with flecks of foam, whilst the veins on his brow stood out like knotted cords, the enraged man resembled an incarnate fiend, as he glared with wild fury upon the form of Jack, who, seated in his saddle, calmly listened to his invectives.

"Put a bullet in his brain-pan, Jack," ejaculated Dick.

"Don't hearken to his threats, but send him to ——!" exclaimed King, who glared viciously at the enraged victim they had plundered.

About, notwithstanding a warning look from Jack, to fire Captain Lester, who, choking with fury, clutched madly at the reins of our hero's horse, Tom was deterred from his purpose by beholding the forms of some half-dozen men dashing along the road.

"The runners from the inn, by the devils!" shouted King.

"Hillo! ho, away!" shouted Turpin, giving his bonnie mare the reins.

"Ware hawks, Jack! let us away."

"I'm with you, lads," said Jack, who, failing to compel the enraged captain to release his hold of his horse's reins, gave him a blow with the butt of his pistol that sent him bleeding and senseless to the earth.

In another moment the three highwaymen were at a gallant pace dashing down the road in the direction of London.

Turning their heads as they flew along, they beheld two of the officers dismount, and place the helpless Lester on horseback; the rest keeping on in pursuit.

"Another race for us, Dick."

"Yes, Jack."

"Where shall we go to, Jack?"

"Well, we had best do a gallop to London, Tom, hadn't we?"

"The very thing I wish."

"What house shall we go to, Jack, when we get into the long village (*London*)?"

"I don't know, Dick. I can't show my face at the Red Rose."

"Nor I!"

"Suppose we put up our steeds at old Mac's, in Oxford Street, and then betake ourselves to Rat's Castle."

"Not a bad idea, Tom! Only there's such a crew of the worst of our profession there."

"So there is. Suppose we give a look in at the Devil's Punch Bowl, at old Westminster."

"Aye, that will do! The Devil's Punch Bowl be it. The house is a queer den, but its landlord, Joe Noggins, aint altogether a bad sort."

"Especially if you tip him plenty of palm oil (*money*)."

"Well, you're about right there, Dick. However, we shall be safe from the cursed runners in the Punch Bowl. There arn't many officers that will venture across its threshold after dark."

"Right you are, Jack. But hark! By the devils, the enemy behind are well mounted."

The clatter of horse's hoofs sounded plain to their ears in the distance.

The officers were gaining on them.

About to put their brave steeds to their quickest flight, an accident occurred that caused blank despair to appear in the faces of Turpin and Jack.

Tom King, slightly in advance of his friends, suddenly reeled in his saddle, like a drunken man, and a moment afterwards fell with a low moan from his horse, striking his head with fearful violence on the ground.

To spring from their seats, and raise him in their arms was the work of a moment.

The sun poured its full rays upon the upturned face of King.

It was pale and wan.

A thin stream of blood issuing from his temple increased the horror of his appearance.

Seized with dizziness, barely having recovered from the wound received in the churchyard at Fulham, Tom had fallen from his horse, incapable of giving even a timely alarm to his friends.

For some minutes Jack and Turpin stood irresolute by the side of the road, holding their companion in their arms.

The clatter of horses' hoofs on the road behind sounded each moment plainer to their ears.

Their foes were rapidly nearing them.

"We are in for it now, Jack!"

"Curses! what a mischance, Dick. Poor Tom! he has overtasked his strength."

"What do you advise, Jack?"

"I know not."

"Are we to wait here?"

"If we do we are booked."

"Safe as the bank."

"Got your barking irons all right?"

"Yes."

"Of course you'll show fight?"

"Just what I shall do, Dick."

"It's no use giving in."

"Not a bit."

"It's escape or death."

"Aye, for both of us."

"By —— I won't be nabbed."

"Nor I, if I know it."

"Well, you slipped them out of the jug very neatly lately, Jack."

"Yes; but I had a friend inside."

"The devil you had."

"Yes."

"Who was it?"

"The deputy-governor."

"Whew! Well, you were in luck."

"Ah! I'll repay him some day."

"No, Jack, that's impossible."

"How?"

"He is dead."

"Dead!"

"Yes, poor fellow. I remember him. A kind-hearted man, quite unfit for his office. But by the devils, Jack, our foes are close at hand. Are there no means of escape?—poor Tom is in a dead faint. Curses! a draught of water now would set him right, perhaps."

"There is only one chance, Dick."

"And that?"

"Is to make our way into that old house." Jack here pointed to a large, red brick-built tenement that stood at the end of the lane near which Tom had met with his mishap.

This turning, opening on the high road, was some quarter-of-a-mile in length. At the further end was a large house that was falling rapidly into decay; its casements all shattered and broken in, giving free ingress to the warring elements.

When King first fell from his horse Dick and Jack carried him in their arms to the beginning of the lane leading to the deserted house, their steeds, at a word, following in their steps. Here they were all concealed from the eyes of their enemies the officers.

As the sounds of their rapid approach fell upon their ears the two friends hastened with all speed to the end of the lane.

"They will be safe to follow us, Jack."

"Yes, there is no doubt of that Dick, but we can better offer resistance against such odds within a building than without one."

"Very true. I never thought of that."

"I have, though."

"Well, here we are."

The two friends now drew up their steeds at the entrance of the old, ruined house, and once more alighted. Carrying the still senseless form of their comrade in their arms, they now forced their way through the gate, which, hanging half off its hinges, offered but little resistance to them.

The horses, led through by Dick, now followed them as they wound their way along a path that was surrounded on both sides by thick brambles, that completely hid them from view of any one in the lane. Emerging from this path out upon a wild waste of weeds, that once had been a beautiful lawn, Turpin and Jack had a full view of the old house.

The sun sinking in the horizon, it now being about four or five o'clock in the day, cast a bright, yellow light upon the ruined house.

It was a desolate-looking building, even in the glorious rays of the summer's sun.

And when gilded by the pale, ghostly light of the moon, was, doubtless, a wild, dismal, and dreary pile.

"What a cursed miserable place, Jack!"

"Rather, Dick. Never mind, it will answer our purpose."

"What do you suppose is the cause of the building, originally a fine one, being thus left to decay and ruin, Jack?"

"Ah! its doom is easily guessed at, Dick. Does not all this desolation and ruin of a once splendid house tell a tale of vindictive hate and passion, of bitter foes, of a war between brother and brother, or near relations, who, in their malice one against the other, doomed the property to ruin rather than yield a portion to another, though that other had a legal right?"

"Oh yes, Dick! there is no doubt that this fine old house has fallen a victim to Chancery."

Forgetful of their foes, the two friends gazed upon the old, red-bricked building that reared its height before them, each absorbed by the strange, wild scene of desolation, ruin, and decay. Anon they were startled from their reverie by the sound of voices in the lane. Both at once turned, and catching up the form of Tom, who with half open eyes glared wildly round, hurried across the weed grown lawn, and halted at the large oaken door of the house. This they found it impossible to force. Leaving Dick with the helpless Tom, who was now slowly recovering, Jack made his way up to a casement. Thrusting his lithe figure through the decayed and shattered window, he soon gained an entrance to the house. Casting but one glance of surprise upon the floor of the room into which he made his way, he observed that it was ankle deep in dust, that in thick clouds rose in the air, as he hurried across the chamber.

Thrusting open the door of this room, which yielded to his touch, Jack made his way out into a corridor, at the bottom of which was a wide oaken staircase leading to the hall below. Hastening down these stairs, startled by hearing the voices of the officers in the garden, Jack with feverish haste drew back with some difficulty the rusty bolts of the door, and after some delay forced it open. Glancing with surprise out into the garden, where he had left Turpin with King and the horses, he found that the latter had disappeared. Noting his alarmed look, with a smile, Dick, hurrying into the house, and closing the door behind them, exclaimed,—

"It's all right; leave me alone, I have seen to the cattle, Jack.

"But where the deuce have you put them?"

"Why I found a large opening in the side wall of the garden, on the left hand, big enough to pass a hayrick. Through this I led our bonny steeds, and by a word got them to hurry away through the thicknesses of a copse that surrounds the grounds, I find, on every side, and which, had you not entered the house, might have hid us from our foes."

"Well, no matter, Dick. We are safe enough here, and can with ease beat back our enemies should they find us out."

"They are in the garden."

"So I heard when I was forcing the door. How is it with Tom?"

"All right, Jack," replied King himself, rousing up from the stupor that had held possession of him.

"Well, my dear pal, you can have a little rest here, and when it's dark we will resume our journey to London."

"My dear friend, what dangers you are encountering for my sake; but for me you might have outridden our foes."

"Pshaw, Tom, don't talk like that. Are we not sworn pals?—have we not vowed never to desert each other in the hour of danger?"

"Of course not; it wasn't likely, Tom, that I or Jack were going to leave you to the mercy of the cursed runners; but hark! there they are. By the devils, they are trying to force the door!"

A loud bang sounded upon the strong oaken door of the ruined house that sent a hundred echoes through the old building.

The friends knew not why, but they all felt a cold shudder dart through their frames, as the knock sounded with a hollow noise in the old house.

"Curse me, I don't like this place, Jack!"

"Nor I."

"Nor I," ejaculated Tom, who, now thoroughly recovered, stood by his friends in the hall of that old house, casting a nervous glance at the dark shadows thrown in through the interstices of the door.

Bang! bang! How dismally the echoes rang through the old building.

"It's no use trying that door, Geoffrey; it aint been open for years."

The friends listened intently to the converse of the officers without.

"Look here, Newton. Suppose, as Anstey is so sure our men must be here, we get in through that casement up there. It's all broken in; a climb up that cherry tree and the thing's done."

Jack cast a significant look on Dick, and put his pistols at full cock. The officer proposed to enter the house by the very same means that he had used.

"Well, look here my men!" exclaimed the leader of the runners, his voice sounding hollowly to the ears of the little party in the hall. "I don't see how our slippery customers

could have escaped us. We lost the sound of their horses' hoofs on the road, and it struck me upon reaching the end of this lane, that nothing was more probable than that they, to throw us off the scent, had sought refuge in this old house."

"Nothing more likely," replied a voice, the sound of which caused a dark cloud to gather on the features of Jack. "I think that it is certain the villains are here, officer, and advise you to search the old house before you go further."

"Never fear, Captain Lester; I'm not one, yer honour, easily thrown off a trail by such men as Sixteen-String Jack and his pals. I'll have 'em; I've sworn to nail them; and by the bones of the criminals rotting in Newgate, I'll keep my oath."

"Well, shall we get in at that casement, Anstey?"

"Ay, Newton, by all means; and do you go with him, Geoffrey. We will wait your opening of the door. Yet, stay, you can give a glance through the rooms of the old house, while we search the grounds; a pistol shot can be the warning for assistance."

It was evident from the tone of the speaker's voice, that he had no great faith in the idea of the men of whom he was in pursuit being in the old house.

With beating hearts the three friends stood motionless in the hall.

Anon they heard the two officers scrambling in at the casement above, their heavy footfalls sounding plainly in their ears!

"It's all up, Jack, when they come down here."

"Hush, Dick! we may elude them yet. Hark! by all that's fortunate they are going upstairs first."

The companions, with exultation, heard the officers making their way to the upper part of the house. A few minutes afterwards they lost the sound of their footsteps, as they ascended to the topmost chambers, and all was silence in the old hall.

Five minutes passed away! Ten! breathlessly the companions stood in the hall of the old house listening for the slightest sound.

All was quiet.

Still as death.

The glinting sunbeams cast a thinner, paler light through the crevices of the door, as the glorious orb began to sink to rest.

A semi-darkness began to fall on all around.

With a cold, nervous shudder they could not control, the three companions watched the approach of darkness.

"Well, the sooner we get out of this place the better I shall like it, Jack."

"Better be here, Dick, than in the hands of the Philistines."

"Oh, yes! but it is such a dismal old den, Jack. Curse me, it smells for all the world like——"

"Like what, Dick?" exclaimed Tom, as his companion paused.

"Why like a charnel-house! There, now it's out," replied Turpin, with a shudder, casting his eyes round the hall, and drawing closer to the side of his friends.

Jack, on being questioned by his companions, was fain to admit that he too had noted the strange earthy odour that loaded the air in the old house.

"But that of course is easily accounted for, Dick. The old house is falling to ruin and decay. Everything is rotting, and an unwholesome damp, of course, prevails all through the building."

"Very true, Jack; that's right enough. God of heaven, what's that?"

Such a piercing yell now sounded through the old house, that it curdled the blood of the bold, daring highwaymen, as it rang in their ears.

It was a shriek—a yell of frenzied horror!

Of maddening terror!

Again and again it rang with shrill echoes through the old building.

Then there was a loud report—a crash of glass, and a wild yell of voices in the garden without. There was the sound of hurrying feet in the garden, and cries of horror and alarm. This was succeeded by a low, muttered conversation, carried on, however, so far from the house, that Jack and his friends could not distinguish the voices.

In surprise and with some amount of fear, though of what they knew not, the three friends stood side by side in the hall, glancing uneasily into each other's faces.

"Dick, what the —— was that cry?"

"Cuss me if I know, Tom. Jack, what do you think of all this?"

"I know not what to think."

"I wish, Jack, we were well out of the place."

"We dare not leave it yet, Dick."

"What the deuce was the meaning of that scream; it was like the death shriek of some terrified human being."

"It rings in my ears now, Dick."

"So it does in mine, Tom. Well, I'm for leaving the old house."

"To fall into the hands of our enemies the runners?"

"Well, no, Jack. That won't do, either. I suppose we must remain in here, like rats in a trap, or birds in a cage."

"Never mind, Dick, the officers will soon raise the siege, and then we can make our way out, secure our brave steeds, and laugh over this adventure when we get to London."

"Damn it, I wish we were there now."

"I say, Jack, do you think the grabs have gone? All's quiet in the grounds!" exclaimed Tom, who, with his ear placed against the door, listened intently for any sound from without.

"It won't do to leave the shelter of the old house yet, Tom," replied Jack. "Our foes may be lurking in the grounds without to surprise and capture us when we make our exit."

"Very true, Dick Curses on them, we must bide our time!"

"Tom! Did you hear that?"

"Hear what?" King and Jack both gave a nervous start, as the sound of a footfall on the staircase above fell upon their ears.

"Well, I can't stand this any longer!" exclaimed Turpin, drawing his pistols from his belt, and loading them, at the same time glancing nervously up the dark staircase.

"Dick, listen to me."

"Well, go ahead, Jack."

"You and Tom get your barking irons all in readiness, and follow me up above, I'll get at the bottom of this or I'm mistaken."

"What! do you think it is one of the runners left to watch?"

"I can't say, Dick; but I'll speedily find out the clue to this mystery."

"I say, Jack, do you know I think the best thing to do is to get out of the house."

"Yes, Tom; but I don't want to be sold, and fall victim to the cunning of Jonathan Anstey; and I tell you what, I firmly believe this is some trick of his."

"Well, if that be so, God help him if I get a crack at him," muttered Turpin, following Jack, who, with pistols in hand, cautiously made his way up the wide oaken staircase; reaching the landing at the top the companions paused.

All was pitchy dark.

Not a ray of light shone in that dismal corridor

All was silent.

Still and quiet as the grave.

"Hist! Jack! by heavens, there's some one in the first room on the left!" murmured Turpin, in a low whisper.

"One of Anstey's men! by the fiends, 'tis as I suspected!" muttered Jack.

"I think you are mistaken, Jack. For God's sake let us leave the house!"

Tom King, a bold, daring fellow, urged his companions in such tones of alarm to quit the old house, that he infected them with the terror that possessed himself.

"By the fiends, I'll not go till I have fathomed this mystery!" ejaculated Jack, coolly, making his way to the door of the room, from which plainly sounded the footfalls of a man.

With his hand placed upon the lock, he was about to throw the door wide upon its hinges (for it was the one through which he had passed two hours before, and yielded to his touch,) when he was startled by hearing a noise from the room as of some man whistling.

Loud, shrill, and clear, it rang through the house.

A sad, melancholy melody, that sounded horrible and ghastly in that lone tenement.

The companions knew not why, yet did the sound give them a horrifying terror—a wild feeling of alarm of they knew not what seized upon them.

"Jack, let us quit this accursed house; there is something dreadful in all this."

"All right, Tom; but we must go through this chamber."

"Can't we go down and let ourselves out by the door?"

"No, the bolts are rusty with age and damp. 'Twas with difficulty I opened the door to admit you. Follow me!"

With a muttered curse, Jack pushed open the door before him, and stepped into the chamber, through which he had made his way on entering the house.

Followed by his companions, he approached the shattered casement.

The moon just appearing, threw a flood of silvery light into the room.

With freezing horror, Jack and his friends pause, as they glare with distended eyes at the casement.

Fully revealed to them in the pale blue light of the luminary of the night is a dark form.

The figure of a man, with folded arms, gazing out into the grounds.

Again that mournful melody rings in their ears.

The stranger, unconscious of the presence of others, whistles on.

Bereft of speech, with the cold drops of fear hanging on their brows, those three daring men, who hourly faced death upon the road in their perilous calling, shuddered as they stood behind that figure by the casement of the deserted house.

At length a loud report rang through the chamber, as Jack, with a curse discharged his pistol at the figure, and dashed to the window.

There was a cry of horror and alarm from the lips of the highwaymen.

All glared wildly round and at each other, as they stood by the broken, shattered casement.

Jack, with unerring aim, had fired direct at the motionless form that had barred their exit from the chamber.

But when dashing up to the casement there was no one there.

The figure was gone!

A harrowing feeling of intense horror filled the bosoms of the three companions, as again that strange whistle sounded in the room. But this time just behind them!

With a loud cry of horror, they simultaneously sprang from the casement into the branches of the tree that grew before it, and the next moment were on the ground.

Jack, as he turned his eyes up at the window ere he hurried away, was seized with a cold chill as of death, for standing at the opening, fully revealed in the pale blue rays of the moon, was the figure of a man, but with a face so livid and stern that it chilled the life-blood of the highwayman as he gazed upon it.

With a cry of terror, Jack followed in the flying steps of his companions, whom he reached as they were vaulting into their saddles; the horses dashing from the coppice as they heard the footfalls of their owners.

Half an hour afterwards the friends were on their way to London.

Nor drew rein till they reached Oxford-street. Here they put up their steeds, and by mutual consent made their way to the neighbourhood of Westminster.

As the clock of the old abbey was giving out the hour of twelve, they all three entered the Devil's Punch Bowl, nor noted that they were observed by a dark, muffled form that passed in just before them.

Had Jack and his companions beheld the features of the stranger, who dauntlessly made his way into the house, possibly they would have paused ere they entered.

Scarce had they passed the threshold of the thieves' ken cre the muffled figure darted out, and with all speed hurried from the spot, soon disappearing in the darkness of the night.

CHAPTER XXXVI.

THE PARLOUR OF THE DEVIL'S PUNCH BOWL—THE CONSULTATION UPON THE MYSTERY OF THE RUINED HOUSE—DEPARTURE OF TOM KING—THE YOUNG SAILOR AND THE HIGHWAYMEN — BILL BURKER AND THE KNIGHT OF THE ROAD—THE QUARREL—A SCENE OF HORROR IN THE OLD BOWL HOUSE—FLIGHT OF JACK AND DICK—DANGER WITHIN AND PERIL WITHOUT—THE WARNING WARE HAWKS!—TOO LATE — THE AMBUSCADE — THE STRUGGLE—THE CAPTURE—LODGED IN NEWGATE.

PASSING through the crowd that thronged the bar of the Bowl House, the friends who had the last few hours gone through suchstrange and perilous adventures made their way to a parlour at the back of the bar, kept for special customers, and calling for some refreshment, prepared to enjoy a rest from the fatigues of the day.

"Well, Jack, here we are, then, at last, safe in the old Bowl House."

"Yes, and infernally glad I am that we are here!" exclaimed Tom.

"Ditto!" replied Jack; "and now I say, Dick, what do you think of that affair at the ruined house?"

"Why, I've only one opinion about it, Jack."

"And that is?"

"That it's haunted!"

"Just my opinion, Dick!" exclaimed King, with a shudder.

"Well, Jack, what do you yourself think of the matter?"

"I don't know what to think, Dick; I've always before tonight treated tales of ghosts and apparitions as stuff to frighten children; but the horrors we witnessed in that old, ruined house have, I confess, shaken my ideas on the subject."

"Well, ghost, man, or devil, I don't care to visit the old house again to encounter it!" exclaimed Tom.

"Nor I either, Tom!" ejaculated Turpin.

"Well, a strange, horrid curiosity would take me there," said Jack. "I should like to sift the matter to the bottom; and, after all, remember, we may have been imposed upon."

"No, no! Jack, that was no flesh and blood, that figure in the old house. I that have hitherto scoffed and jeered at such things, with a horror I cannot express, feel convinced that our eyes beheld not a corporeal form in that old, ruined house, but an immaterial being—a shadow from the other world."

"I think with Dick, Jack; though by all that's holy, I never thought to believe in spirits."

"Except those in the bottle; eh, Tom?" exclaimed Jack, with a smile, not convinced in his own mind. But, finding that his friends had but one idea on the subject, Jack turned the conversation, and the companions were anon arranging their plans for the morrow.

Upon counting out the gold secured from Captain Lester in the afternoon, Jack found that there was altogether thirty-five guineas, along with this was a beautiful gold watch—a rich, brilliant ring, and some notes amounting to a hundred pounds.

"A nice little haul, Dick!"

"Rather, Jack."

"And shared out like a prince of high toby men!" ejaculated Tom, placing some of the booty in his pocket.

It had been arranged by the three friends that all the proceeds of their calling were to be equally divided amongst them, so that the bad fortune of the one would be counteracted by the good of another.

A close, firm bond of friendship now existed between the three knights of the road.

A friendship terminated only by death.

An hour had passed away, when King, rising from his seat, first appointing where to meet them on the morrow, left the Bowl House, replying only with a smile to the badinage of his friends as to the cause of his hurried departure.

"Well, Jack, when do you intend to leave the Bowl House?"

"In an hour or so, Dick."

"When do you mean to return to Lutterworth's?" Turpin cast a meaning smile upon his friend, as he put this last query.

"I shall leave town early to-morrow, Dick. I have a little business on hand. The fact is, to be plain, I wish to see Mrs. Malvers, and learn how that poor devil, Grantley, has got on, and whether he has received the will all right. I must also give old Shadrach a look in, and get him to tip me some shiners for the watch and ring of my friend, Captain Lester."

"And after that is settled you are off to Willesden?"

"Yes, Dick, I shall make all speed to the Cat and her Kittens, for though I know that the unfortunate Dora Annersley is safe, and will be well protected from harm whilst under the roof of Jem Lutterworth, yet am I anxious to return and secure her some fitting abode, where she may reside without fear of being discovered by her enemies."

"Do you purpose, then, Jack, taking her under your protection?"

"I do."

"With an idea, of course, of eventually making her yours?"

A dark flush crossed the features of Jack as Turpin spoke, whilst a look of sorrow and pain clouded his brow.

"Dick, I confess to you, dear old pal, that I love this young girl with all the ardour of my impassioned nature. Never till I cast my eyes upon her lovely features, have I experienced aught of the tender sentiment for the other sex that ennobles the soul of man. I would perish to save the life of Dora Annersley, but yet am I well aware that I can never hope to call her mine. What, I, Sixteen-String Jack, the highwayman, the knight of the road, the daring robber, whose name is in every mouth, dare I, the hunted felon, hope to make that innocent girl my wife? No, no, Dick, I must control the passion that consumes me, for with terrible bitterness I feel that the girl for whom I have such love can never, never be mine."

With folded arms, and eyes filled with moisture, Jack sat glaring steadfastly at the face of his friend. Never before had our hero felt any regret or pain for his position; yet as he sat reflecting with bitterness on his wayward fate, he was compelled to acknowledge that it was now to late to retrace his steps, he had embarked in his dangerous calling too far to recede. The die was cast, he must go on.

"Cheer up, Jack! do not despond. You say the young girl has no friends. You have saved her from a fate far worse to her than death: from what I have seen, I am sure you have but to ask to win. You are framed to please the eye of woman, Jack; take my word for it, Dora Annersley will soon love the man who is prepared to protect her as you have made up your mind to do. She is young, guileless, and if she is what I take her to be, will not withdraw her affections from you, though she may learn that you are a knight of the road, and at war with society and its laws; besides, you are looking far ahead: it may be months, years, ere she discovered your calling."

"And think you I would deceive that young innocent girl, win her love, gain the affection of her fond virgin heart, and know that any hour might remove the hideous mask, and tear away the veil that enshrouds me? No, no, Dick, she shall be made aware who it is that shields her from her foes. I am a highwayman; my cruel fate has thrust upon me a profession that, till now, I felt no pain from pursuing; but I will prove, that though an outlaw and at war with my fellow-men and the laws of my country, I still have an honest heart, that shall cease its pulsations ere I act basely to one who might tender up to me her affections, as I think Dora Annersley is prepared to do. Oh! Dick! I could almost wish I had never met this unfortunate girl."

"Nay, Jack, talk not thus; all will yet be well. The clouds that now hover overhead will disperse. I do not wonder at your feelings towards this young girl. She is lovely, innocent and has crossed your path under circumstances that won your pity and your love. You are prepared to shield her from her foes?"

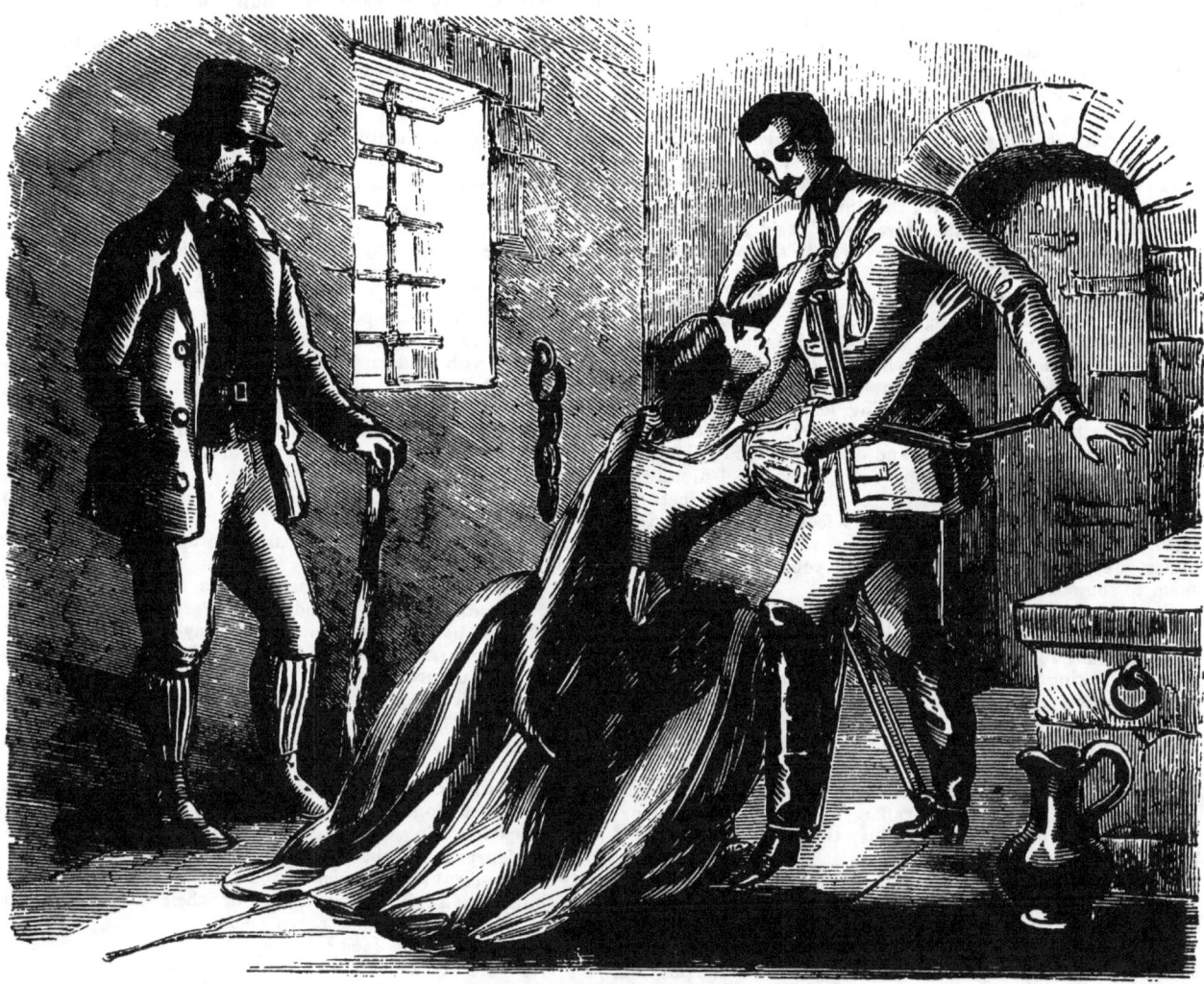

THE SCENE IN NEWGATE.

" Aye, Dick, to the death !"

" She owes you now a debt she can but repay with her affections. Depend upon it, Jack, that though you make her acquainted with your perilous profession it will not deprive you of her love. I am older in the world, my dear pal, than you, and know well the heart of woman. A true, virtuous girl, Jack, is a prize to be treasured by the man upon whom she bestowes her heart, as we would treasure our very existence. The love of woman, Jack, is a precious jewel which we cannot prize enough. Act straightforward with this young girl, tell her all, Jack, and my life upon it, she will not turn from you, though she read your fate, and could be told your doom would be Tyburn tree."

" You think, then, Dick, that, despite my calling, I might secure her love ? "

" I'm sure of it, Jack."

" If I dared imagine it ! "

" You may, and not be deceived, Jack ; there is everything in your favour to win you her love."

A smile of joy wreathed the features of Jack, as Turpin thus raised hopes in his breast. About to make a reply to his companion, he was startled from his purpose by the entrance of a young sailor, who, with a look of surprise, glared, with a half-drunken stare, at the two friends.

" I beg your pardon, gentlemen ! I think I have made a mistake."

The young man, a dark, handsome sailor, of some three or four and twenty years of age, stared, first at the two highway-men and then round the apartment, as if trying to bring to his recollection where he was.

" This is a public parlour, my dear sir, sit down," said Turpin.

Bowing his thanks, the young sailor staggered to a seat, at the same time putting his hand to his head, and complaining of dizziness.

" I—I feel so strange ! that last glass has upset me. Let me see, where am I ?" again the young man glanced round the room, and then at the forms of the two friends.

" Jack ! "

" Dick ! "

" The poor young fellow has been hocussed."

" Yes, and brought here to be skinned."

" Aye, and perhaps——"

A shudder darted through the frame of Jack as Turpin paused in his whispered converse, and drew his hand across his throat.

Both were aware that seldom, if ever, did a stranger, who appeared thus at the Punch Bowl, again leave its doors.

" I say, Dick, it's a mistake—his coming in here."

" Yes, they have lost him at the bar—perhaps gone into the kitchen, and left him to himself for a moment,"

" No doubt,"

" He's quite a young fellow."

" Yes."

" Well, I for one won't let them do him further harm,"

" Nor I, Dick ; but hush ! he speaks."

No. 14.

" Gentlemen, I don't feel very well. I fear I have fallen into bad hands. Ill, sick, and half stupefied as I am, I have just discovered that my watch and purse have been stolen. Though I cannot afford their loss, yet would I sooner they had gone than a locket I wear round my neck that is valuable to me beyond its worth. I will protect this trinket with my life. I know you not, but you appear to my dazzled eyes as those who would lend me a helping hand, rather than assist those from whom I have escaped. A something seemed to whisper danger in my ears as I entered this inn."

" Who brought you hither, stranger ? " said Jack.

" Two men, of whom I asked my way to the neighbourhood of Vauxhall."

" Hem ! they proffered to conduct you there, I suppose ? "

" Yes ; and, as a stranger in London, I accepted their offer. We had some drink on the road ; I found 'twas getting late ; I asked where I could anchor for the night, making up my mind to visit my friends in the morning. I scarce remember coming here, but on being led into the bar I was alarmed at the appearance of the assembly. I made my way into this parlour, to be alone, and discovered you ; thanks to my not, though a sailor, being fond of liquor, I drank but sparingly of the spirits given me by those whom I met, else had I been even worse than I am. I feel still dazed and ill, but have strength left to battle with anyone who attempts to molest me. Now, may I trespass on your kindness, gentlemen, to show me from this house ? "

Staggering up from his chair, the young sailor made for the door ; about to follow him, Jack, with Turpin, started back, as the ruffians Bill, Burker and Churchyard Dick, entered the room. Taking no heed of the highwaymen, the villains, accosting the young sailor, exclaimed,—

" Hullo ! here you are ! What made yer leave the bar ? "

" Because the looks of those congregated there did not please me."

" Oh, there's all sort of visitors, stranger, at the Devil's Punch Bowl ! " exclaimed the ruffian, Burker, but come along, I'll introduce you to Joe Noggins, the landlord, and we'll have some drink."

" No ; I require no more. I thank you for the trouble you have taken in relieving me of my watch and money, and will quit the house."

His brain getting clear of the drug that had before dazed and confused him, the young man began to get aware of his position.

" Oh ! curse me, Churcher, did you hear that ? "

" What ? "

" Why, the lily-livered salt says we've got his goldfinches and his ticker."

" Curses ! he does, does he ? Well, I'll give him summat for that."

The villain here bared his sinewy arm to the elbow, and clenching a formidable looking fist, advanced towards their victim.

The young sailor, his lips compressed, assumed immediately a defensive attitude, and awaited the attack.

" Let him have it, Churcher."

" Leave me alone, Bill, I'll bruise him."

" No you won't."

The ruffian, about to rush upon the young man (who despite his youth, stood dauntless, prepared for the attack) drew back, with a deep breathed curse, glaring wildly upon Jack, who had stepped between them.

" What the —— is the cove to you ? "

" Knock him over, send them both to ——! " exclaimed Burker, with a fearful oath. Then darting forwards to where Jack stood, as if to attack him, he drew back. " Sixteen-String Jack, by the fiends ! "

" Yes, Bill Burker, I think we've an old score to settle, haven't we ? "

" We have, Stringer, and curse me, but I'll give yer summat to-night, though you are backed by Dick Turpin, there, and though I swing for it."

With cool ferocity, the ruffian here drew a knife from his pocket, and, unclasping a formidable blade, grasped the handle firmly in his hand, glaring with wild fury at Jack.

" Oh, that's your game, is it Bully Burker ? Well, you're welcome as the flowers in May."

In a moment, Jack drew his pistols from his belt, and presented them at the head of the murderous villain, who had advanced a step towards him.

" Come on, Burker, don't hang back," ejaculated Turpin, as, following the example of Jack, he pulled out his pistols.

" Never mind the barking-irons, Bill ; at 'em ! "

In another moment, with howls of savage fury, the villains rushed upon the highwaymen.

The Burker, receiving a bullet in his shoulder, uttered a cry of pain accompanied by a fearful imprecation as he closed with Jack, who catching the hand that held the knife, twisted it round, nearly wringing it out of the socket and causing the ruffian to drop the weapon.

A desperate struggle then ensued.

Cursing with wild fury, Burker endeavoured to hurl Jack to the ground, but retaining his hold of the villain's neck, our hero defeated him in his intentions.

The young sailor rushed to the aid of Turpin, who was overmatched by the strong sinewy frame of the ruffian Churchyard Dick.

A wild scene of uproar now took place in the old Bowl House.

Some of those from the bar rushed in upon the scene of the struggle.

A few of those who recognised Turpin and Jack sided with them and attacked the friends of the ruffians Burker and Church, who had sprung upon the highwaymen.

Knives were raised, pistols fired, whilst the inn echoed with the din of murderous conflict.

An end at length was put to the scene of horror by the landlord, who, rushing into the parlour, exclaimed,—

" Ware-hawks ! the grabs are without ! " A loud crash now sounded upon the door of the old Bowl House.

With oaths, curses, and imprecations, the combatants in an instant rushed from the room, the villains Burker and Churchyard Dick following the rest.

Jack, Turpin, and the young sailor were alone.

For a moment the two friends stood in the centre of the room breathing heavily from the effects of their exertions in the desperate struggle that had taken place.

" Any harm done, Jack ? "

" No ! are you hurt, Dick ? "

" Only a scratch. But hark ! by the devils the runners have ventured into the Punch Bowl. We had better clear out, Jack."

" I think so."

" Follow me. We must dash for it through the door."

" Yes, it's our only chance ; we cannot secrete ourselves in this cursed den."

" No, for we have foes within as well as without."

" Well, lead on. I'm ready."

" All right, Jack, got the barking irons loaded ? "

" Yes, Dick."

" Then now for it."

Turpin, pistols in hand, followed by Jack and the young sailor, the latter in wondering surprise, gazing at the actions of the men who had preserved him, now made way out of the parlour.

In the passage were three dark figures.

" That's him ! secure him lads ! "

There was a rush upon Jack, but Dick and the young sailor in an instant beat back the men who attempted to seize our hero, and following Jack dashed through the now deserted bar of the Bowl House out into the open air.

Scarce had they passed the threshold of the door when the landlord looked out, ejaculating, " Ware-hawk ! Dick, the grabs have surrounded the house. Come back ; I'll put you both out of harm's way."

The warning was too late.

A dozen dark figures rushed upon the friends.

Turpin, firing his pistols and then using the butt ends, beat back three or four officers and succeeded in effecting his escape.

Desperately Jack struggled.

But borne down by some half dozen of his foes he was secured.

The young sailor, who had valiantly assisted Jack to escape was at length stretched senseless by a blow upon the head.

Ten minutes from the time he had dashed out of the door of the Bowl House Jack was a prisoner.

A prisoner in the hands of his enemies the Bow-street runners.

"Got yer at last, Jack! Pop the darbies on him, Nabem."

In a moment the manacles were placed upon his wrists.

Jack, his face all bleeding from a cut on the forehead, from which the blood welled out in streams, with a smile exclaimed,—

"Well, Anstey, luck's against me to-night, but I'll be out of your hands in a week."

"Yes, trussed up at Tyburn, Jack."

"No, free, free as air! and mounted on my bonny steed, coursing over Hounslow-heath and stopping travellers with the cry of 'Stand and deliver!'"

"Ha, ha, ha! you think that, Sixteen-String Jack, do you?"

"Yes."

"Well, you'll find yourself mistaken, that's all."

"Yes, we shall see."

"Jack dancing a hornpipe on nothing at Tyburn tree," ejaculated another of the officers with a loud laugh.

"Twenty to one he dies game."

"I won't take yer, Geoffrey, cos I know the Stringer's got pluck."

"Now, then, lads, bring him along." Jonathan Anstey, the leader of the runners, now stepped up, accompanied by a tall muffled stranger with whom he had drawn aside a few moments before.

The officers, raising Jack to his feet, prepared to lead him to a vehicle that approached the spot. Afraid of a rescue, they were anxious to be off.

A loud exultant laugh close beside him caused Jack to raise his head.

With a curse of wild fury he glared upon the face of the stranger, who had let fall the cloak that had before shrouded his features.

It was no other than Captain Lester.

The face of Jack purpled with impotent fury as he gazed into the features of the man he had robbed.

Vainly he tried to struggle from his bonds.

But his wrists were confined by a pair of steel bracelets, whilst his feet even were bound together.

The officers had well secured their captive.

His wild attempts to gain his freedom were useless.

The low chuckling laugh of the man before him drove him into madness.

"Sixteen-String Jack, you see I have kept my oath," then leaning forward as the officers thrust him into the vehicle that now drew up, Captain Lester whispered in the ear of our hero, "Dog, thief, robber! For the robbery on the Willesden road I can send you to Tyburn, but even now I will save you from your fate if you will tell me where you have hidden the girl Dora Annersley."

With eyes that fairly blazed with light, Jack glared into the features of his enemy, exclaiming,—

"Captain Lester, if I were now placed beneath Tyburn tree with the rope about my neck, I'd say, No! She you seek shall never be your prey."

"Curses! Die—perish—then, romantic fool!" ejaculated the enraged captain, as with a muttered oath of furious disappointment he banged to the door of the vehicle, in which were seated two officers in charge of the highwayman. Turning to the leader of the runners, who was about to mount the outside seat of the vehicle along with the driver, he exclaimed,—

"Look you, Jonathan Anstey, you found my watch upon the highwayman, did you not?"

"Yes, captain, it's all right."

"Think you he will hang?"

"Oh yes! safe as beans."

"'Tis well; call upon me at my town residence then, to-morrow, in Park-lane, and I'll give you the promised reward; use all your influence to send him to the gibbet. I'd give anything rather than he should escape."

"All right, Captain Lester, have no fear, there are too many charges against Sixteen-String Jack for a hope of his escape, and as to his getting out of the stone-jug a second time, I'll forgive him if he does it, that's all." With a hurried adieu to his employer, Jonathan Anstey then drove off.

Folding his cloak around him, Captain Lester was about to depart when a hand was laid upon his arm, with a start he drew back, his detainer exclaiming,—

"Can you tell me, sir, where those men have conveyed their prisoner?"

With a grim smile, as he glanced upon the form of the questioner, a young sailor, Captain Lester replied,—

"Yes, Highwayman Sixteen-String Jack, is being driven to Newgate."

"My preserver from a fearful death a prisoner, and taken hence a captive by his foes! By heavens, he shall not want a helping hand while Harry Halyard lives!" With a bound the young sailor darted off, quickly disappearing from sight.

"Hem! This knight of the road gains friends it seems at every turn. He has, it appears, rendered this sailor a service. Ha, ha, ha! Sixteen-String Jack is like a knight-errant of the days of old: always ready to aid the distressed. Well, I think his friends will find it a hard matter to save his neck from the rope that I shall be the means of placing round it. 'Twas a fortunate chance that led me hither to the Devil's Punch Bowl to-night, else for a time the highwayman would have escaped my vengeance. And now for the Ivy Manor House—the pretty Clarisse Howard; and to-morrow I'll take measures to find out the hiding place of the fair Dora Annersley."

With a laugh of triumph Captain Lester hastened from the spot.

An hour after the struggle with the officers outside the Devil's Punch Bowl at old Westminster, Sixteen-String Jack was led a captive into London's grim receptacle for criminals, Newgate.

CHAPTER XXXVII.

THE CAPTIVE OF THE IVY MANOR HOUSE—CAPTAIN LESTER AND HIS VICTIM—THE PRAYER FOR MERCY—THE STRUGGLE—TRIUMPH OF THE ROUE—LEFT ALONE—THE RETURN TO CONSCIOUSNESS—MAD DESPAIR OF THE LOST ONE—THE THOUGHTS OF FLIGHT—THE LUMBER ROOM—THE DISCOVERY OF THE ROPE—THE FALL OF NIGHT—THE ESCAPE FROM THE CASEMENT—THE DARK SHADOW IN THE MOONLIGHT—TERROR OF CLARISSE—THE STRANGE MEETING OF TURPIN WITH LESTER'S VICTIM—THE TALE OF SORROW—THE OATH OF VENGEANCE.

UPON the verge of Wimbledon-common, at the period of our narrative, stood a large white house, called Ivy Manor House.

The whole front of the building was covered with the creeping tendrils from which it derived its name.

In thick masses the luxuriant ivy grew and clustered up the grey stone with which the house was built.

It was a sombre, gloomy looking tenement, was the Ivy Manor House.

Standing on the verge of the common, just off the high road, leading on the one hand to London and on the other to Putney, it stood grim and solitary, surrounded by dark dismal heath and copse.

Wimbledon a century ago was thickly wooded.

Not as now, boasting of lovely villas, but with scarce more than one or two tenements within a mile of each other.

The Ivy Manor House stood alone, without another habitation near it.

In front was Wimbledon-common, with its dark furze, its bushes, and open heaths; at the back of the house was a thick copse, upon the edge of which towered up some fir trees, among the topmost branches of which the rooks had built their nests, revelling in the dreary scene, and adding to its dismal gloom with their incessant caw, caw, caw!

It was certainly a wild, dismal habitation, was the Ivy Manor House.

As dismal and as sombre as the plant that grew in such rich luxuriance in front of the tenement.

The grey stone, eaten away here and there by the destroying plant, gave note that the building was an old one.

The morning after the apprehension of our hero by the runners was a bright and beautiful one.

The sun poured down a golden light upon the old Ivy House.

The rooks circled, with their black wings outspread, round and round the building, and then anon flew to the dark branches of the firs near the copse, their incessant caw, caw, being the only sound that broke the stillness around.

It was a glorious sunny morn.

All nature was gay and joyous.

Even the disagreeable, cheerless looking old Ivy House wore somewhat of a gayer appearance that bright summer's morning.

The breeze sighing gently through the trees shook the loose foliage, and made a pleasant murmuring lullaby in the air.

All without the old Ivy House was peace and joy.

But within was the storm of human passion, and the wretchedness of a heart's despair.

Sitting near a casement that overlooked the wild open country at the back of the house was a young and lovely girl; dark but very beautiful was she. The crystal dew drops were depending from her eyelids, which were red with weeping; tumultuously the richly developed bust of the young creature heaved under the corsage of her boddice, as rising from her seat she wildly wrung her hands and paced up and down the room.

"There is no hope more!" she gasped. "Oh! why am I thus left at the mercy of the base villain who has torn me from my home and all I hold dear on earth?"

In an agony of sorrow she walked up and down the chamber, wildly wringing her hands, and weeping with all the pain of a terrible despair.

A half shriek escapes her lips as the door of the apartment is opened, and a tall dark handsome man enters, with such a satyr-like smile wreathing his features that he resembles some incarnate fiend. He exclaims,—

"How is this, sweet Clarisse? Still in tears? I had hoped ere this to find you reconciled to your fate."

Heeding not the cold sarcastic sneering way that these words were uttered, the young girl staggered forwards, and throwing herself on her knees, with hands upraised, exclaimed, with a voice nigh choked with sobs,—

"Oh! have mercy upon me, Lester! You surely do not mean me harm! you would not, could not, injure the daughter of Colonel Howard, he with whom you have fought side by side in the battle-field! You owe my father, too, some thanks for favours past: you surely cannot mean to harm his child. Say you repent, let me free, and the past shall be locked a secret in my bosom for ever. Say you will spare me, Captain Lester, and let me go."

"Clarisse Howard, you plead in vain. I have sworn to make you mine, and I'll keep my oath."

With a shudder the poor girl turned her eyes from the roué and villain. There was a look upon his features as he gazed into hers that sent the blood with an icy chill rushing to her heart.

"Listen!" he exclaimed, lifting her up and leading her tottering to a couch. "You mentioned but now that I owed your father thanks for favours past: I will tell you now, girl, I owe him a life's revenge. Some ten years' back he put upon me a terrible shame, for which I registered a vow to have revenge if I waited years for its fulfilment; years have elapsed, but at length the time has arrived. I have watched for it, waited for it, and it has come. Well I know the news your parent will receive ere to-morrow's sun sinks to rest will kill him. You scorned, rejected my proffered love, months back; your father, with lowering brow and bitter words, forbade me the house. Had you consented to be mine, though he your father refused his consent to our union, I'd have cared not; but, dismissed with contumely by both, I renewed my vow of vengeance, and I will keep my oath, Clarisse, though the fiend himself stood forth to save ye."

"No, no, no! you mean it not! you will spare me! Say indeed you have a cause, for some reason I know not of, to hate my father: you will not be so base as wreak your vengeance on his child."

"Granted, lovely Clarisse, but I burn for possession of your exquisite charms, and though death were the reward you shall be mine."

Wild screams for mercy issued from the young girl's lips as the roué stepped forwards and clasped her in his arms.

"Help, help, help!"

"Nay, my lovely prize, you shriek in vain, no help can reach you here."

"Mercy, mercy!"

"You plead in vain; those ruby lips, those lustrous orbs swimming in tears, but add fuel to the fire that consumes me."

"Oh! pray release me, Captain Lester! For heaven's love, let me free."

"Ask me ought but that, dear girl, and I'll not refuse thee. For months I've prayed for this hour; I cannot let you go, sweet girl. Though everlasting torture be my award for thy ruin I must make you mine."

"No, no, no! Help, help, help!"

Wildly the beautiful girl struggled in the close embrace of the villain Lester, shriek following shriek in rapid succession.

But no answering cry echoed that of the wretched maid.

The servants of the Ivy Manor House were the tools of their villain employer, and answered not.

Panting, struggling, and wrestling with the roué, the poor girl sent forth her piercing shrieks for aid.

His face flushed with passion, and with his eyes gloating upon the beautifully rounded and heaving bust of his victim, exposed in her fruitless struggles, the villain Lester held her in his close embrace, till, with a last despairing shriek, the lovely girl fell from his arms in a death swoon.

No spark of pity was there in the breast of the villain as his victim fell senseless from his embrace.

'Twas well, perhaps, that her senses were steeped in her trance-like swoon—

That she had not the horror of being sensible of her ruin.

For the villain Lester released her not till he had accomplished his desires.

With a grim smile of triumph he at length, leaving his victim on the couch, slowly recovering her senses, quitted the room, an aged crone being sent to attend upon the hapless victim of his base passions.

The hours flew by; the golden sun, with a crimson hue, was sinking to rest, when the real consciousness of her situation flashed upon the hapless girl, who during the day had been like one in a dream.

"Lost, lost, lost!" she moaned, as glaring wildly round she found she was alone; then as the remembrance of the scene of the morning flashed upon her, the poor victim of the villain Lester, casting her eyes round, sought in her despair for some means of self-destruction. These dismissed from her frenzied brain as impracticable, her thoughts recurred to an escape. The preceding day she remembered finding in an ante-chamber used as a lumber room, adjoining the apartment she was in, a coil of rope; this she had thought would aid her to escape by the casement, from the prison in which her persecutor had confined her, and in the morning that saw her ruin at the hands of her abductor, the poor girl had returned thanks to Providence that had opened to her the means of an escape.

With beating heart the poor victim watched the sun sinking to rest.

With sickening terror she feared a recurrence of the scene of the morning, and determined when the curtain of night had fallen, to effect her escape from the Ivy house, or perish.

At length the sun disappeared, like a ball of burnished copper, in the crimson-tinted skies, and twilight fell on all around.

Twilight, with its dim shadows and ghostly gloom.

Like a statue, Clarisse Howard stood by the casement of her prison watching the approach of night.

The moon anon rose in the heavens, casting a thin blue and spectral light upon the earth.

With an exclamation of despair the poor girl beheld the pale luminary rise up in the clouds. She had hoped that thick darkness would veil her movements, but determined to seek refuge in death rather than remain a prisoner at the mercy of the villain Lester.

She prepared to carry out her project of escape through the casement.

All was still within the Ivy House. Fearing each moment now that the villain captain would pay her a visit, the wretched girl, with feverish haste, prepared to effect her escape, but had scarce directed her footsteps towards the door of the ante-room when she was startled from her purpose by the entrance of the old crone, who mumbled out to the terrified girl that her master had gone to London and would not return that night, and had desired her, ere he left, to ask his victim if there was anything she desired. Hurriedly answering that she wanted nothing, with beating heart, the poor girl beheld the door closed upon her.

She was once more alone.

Alone! with no fear of interruption in her task.

Her villain seducer had left the house.

Would not return that night.

There was no fear of a fresh visit from the villain who had effected her ruin.

Hours might elapse ere the old servant would again enter the room.

Making her way to the ante-chamber, Clarissa now produced the coveted rope.

Returning with trembling eagerness, she fastened it to a heavy piece of furniture close to the casement and threw it out.

She now gently opened the window, and glanced out into the grounds below.

With a thrill of joy she found that the rope reached within two or three feet of the earth beneath.

The moon, shining brightly as it rose in the horizon, cast a flood of silvery light on all around.

With a prayer to Providence, the brave girl, catching fast hold of the rope, lowered herself from the casement.

For a moment she swung to and fro in the air, till the motion of the rope ceasing, she began to glide down.

The friction hurt and wounded her soft hands, but with true heroism the brave girl held on, gliding, slowly but surely, lower and lower down the rope.

She is at length within ten or fifteen feet of the ground.

She has passed in safety a casement, before which her means of escape was swaying to and fro.

With a thrill that sent the life blood bounding through her veins, she at length reaches the ground.

She has loosed her hold of the rope and falls to the earth.

Staggering to her feet she prepares to hasten away.

Every minute is an age.

She is not safe till she has left the precincts of that terrible house.

Wildly she hurries through the moonlit grounds.

In an agony of fear lest she should meet any of the servants belonging to the house, at length she pauses, as she reaches a part of the garden thick with shrubbery.

About to dart on, she stays her steps, whilst with difficulty she prevents herself from giving utterance to a wild shriek of terror.

There, before her in the shrubbery, making his way towards the house, is the figure of a man.

The moon shines full upon him.

Nearer and nearer he approaches the spot upon which the terrified Clarisse stands transfixed, incapable of flight.

She is rooted to the spot in an agony of fright.

The blood, like ice, darts through her veins.

Thoughts of suicide, of death, float through her brain; she is determined not again to become the victim of the villain Lester.

She cannot doubt that the figure, slowly but surely approaching her, is one of the myrmidons of her destroyer.

With an icy coldness, as of death, thrilling through her frame, the unhappy girl stands statue-like, awaiting the fatal moment that shall bring the stranger to her side

An exclamation fall upon her ears.

She is perceived.

She discerns the figure of the man dart towards her. She catches sight of a face she knows not, then all the bushes and trees seemed to blend themselves with the skies, the whole mass whirling round and round with fearful velocity.

All is then a blank.

With a moan of pain the poor girl sinks like a stone to the earth.

Her senses are wrapt in a death swoon.

When again she opens her eyes she glares with surprise around her, like one awaking from a dream.

Recovering slowly from her death swoon, she first observes with a shudder that she is still in the garden of the Old Ivy House.

A stranger stands beside her, gazing with pitying eyes upon her.

She notes the look of distress upon his features, with a prayer to heaven that he may be a friend, then fall at his feet beseeching him not to drag her back to the house from which she had but just before escaped.

"Take you back, my poor girl? No."

"You are no friend to—to—" the poor girl's tongue at first refused the utterance of her destroyer's name, but mastering her emotions she added, "you are not on terms with Captain Lester?"

"A friend?" replied the stranger; "oh, no." A black scowl gathered over the speaker's features as he answered the young girl.

"You will then aid me to fly from his power?"

"Will I, my dear girl, yes ; and put a bullet in the skull of him who would stay me.

"Oh! thanks, thanks, stranger! But come, come, let us at once away; I breathe in terror whilst I remain here."

Nay, fear not, my poor girl, they shall none of them harm you now—not whilst I've an arm to use in your defence. But tell me, why do you stand thus in fear of the villain Lester?"

Such a look of unutterable woe passed over the beautiful face of the poor girl, that her companion instantly regretted the question, put without thought of giving pain.

At length, mastering her emotions, Clarisse, in a voice nearly choked and unintelligible from her sobs, exclaimed,—

"Stranger!" she gasped, "you have called the man, Captain Lester, a villain. Drag from the dark abyss below one of the master fiends, and it shall whiten beside the wretch and villain Lester. The greatest criminal that ever swung upon the gibbet—the veriest wretch that ever crawled the earth—is an angel compared to the owner of yonder accursed house. When I come to think of my wrongs, from a weak, timid girl I become a stern revengeful woman. By the heavens above me—by the mother that gave me birth—by the gray hairs of my poor father, who will be stricken to death by the news of my shame, I swear to exact a fearful reckoning from Captain Lester, for the deed of this morn. Torn from my father's roof at the still hour of night, I was borne thither to the residence of this my destroyer—he who owed much to the parent of the child whose ruin he has wrought. But the hour of reckoning will come ; and he that has robbed me of my honour shall pay the cost of his crime!"

With a wild, hysterical laugh, the young girl staggered towards the stranger, and, but for his protecting arms, would have fallen to the ground.

Overcome by the recollection of her wrongs, the poor girl again relapsed into insensibility.

It was a strange scene that, in the gardens of the Ivy House that summer night.

The lovely victim of the villain Lester, like a beautiful corpse, reclining in the arms of the stranger, whose brow contracted in a deep frown, looked like some spirit of vengeance, as he stood there in the bright moonlight, glaring with eyes that sparkled with fury at the house, the roof of which was plainly discernible through the trees.

" So, then," he muttered, " this lovely girl is another victim of the accursed Lester. 'Tis strange that this young creature should have crossed my path to-night—to-night, when I had come prepared to satiate my rage in the blood of this cursed roué, and fiend. This poor girl's wrongs obliterate those of my friend, on whose account I am here. Well, I have now a double debt to pay Captain Lester, and it shall go hard but this night shall liquidate it."

Glancing at the pallid features of the senseless girl he held in his arms, the stranger was struck by the beauty of the victim of the roué.

" She is very beautiful! How young, too! I could find it in my heart to rail at the powers above that let such a blooming flower fall a prey to the poisonous breath of the accursed Lester."

A tear stood in the eye of the stranger, as he gazed in pitying sorrow upon the pallid features of the hapless Clarisse Howard.

Recovering from the swoon that had seized upon her, she at first started with a shriek from the supporting arms of the stranger ; then, as she cast her eyes upon his, and observed them filled with a moisture that he in vain attempted to check, she rushed to his side, and, falling on her knees, seized his hands in hers exclaiming.—

" Oh, forgive me! I remembered you not ; my brain is nigh turned to madness by the events of the past four hours, but I recollect all now. You are the stranger whom I crossed in escaping from the Ivy House. I think you told me you were no friend to the villain Lester."

" I am his deadliest enemy, my poor girl."

" His enemy! then may I ask what is the reason of your presence here ? "

" His death! " A dark flush of passion darted athwart the features of the stranger as he, in a voice husky with rage, answered his companion.

" His death! Then you have, as well as I, some heavy debt of vengeance against the black-hearted villain, Lester."

" A debt of vengeance, girl, that will only be appeased by his death."

" Indeed! Well, this revenge will not be achieved to-night."

" What mean you ? "

" Why he upon whom you would wreak your vengeance is not here."

" Not here! "

" No, he is in London."

" In London."

" Ay, he is away, else had I not escaped my prison house."

" If that be the case, I will at once retrace my steps, and now tell me, my dear young lady, where can I take you, for I swear I will not leave you till you are safe with your friends."

" I have no where to go to, but my poor father's roof. Oh, how shall I face him, and tell him of this wrong ? " agonising sobs here choked the poor girl's utterance.

With pain and distress the stranger gazed upon the lovely girl before him. Her face bedewed with tears, with her hands clasped, she stood in the pale moonbeams looking like some sorrowing angel weeping over a lost soul.

With a deep breathed curse upon the man who had ruined the lovely girl before him, the stranger, with knitted brow, stood beside the pale shivering form of the poor victim.

" It needed not this," he murmured, " to urge me on in my task of vengeance. By ——," muttered the stranger, with an oath, " if Captain Lester had fifty lives I'd have them all."

Arousing from the stupor that had seized upon her, Clarisse Howard seized the stranger by the arm, exclaiming,—

" Come, come, lead me hence, or I shall go mad ; my brain e'en now turns to madness, as I gaze upon the walls of that fearful house. Oh, for love of Heaven, lead me from this place ! "

With a wild, hysterical sob, the poor girl staggered from the spot, darting through the brushwood in frenzied haste, as she more fully recovered her senses.

Following in her footsteps, the stranger in vain besought her to dismiss her fears.

" Be not alarmed," he cried, " the fiend himself should not do you harm now, unless I were stretched a corpse at your feet."

Paying no heed to the voice of her companion, however, Clairisse Howard hurried on, nor paused until a high wall stopped her further progress.

About to take the young girl's hand in his, and breathe assurance of safety in her ears, the stranger was startled by a dark shadow in the moonlight.

With a shriek the frenzied girl threw herself into his arms, at the same time glaring wildly at the hideous object that stood fully revealed before them in the bright rays of the moonlight.

The stranger, with a curse, drew a pistol from his belt, and in an angry, excited tone, exclaimed,—

" Who the fiends are you ? "

" Eh, eh, eh ! stranger, I return the same query ; who are you that are thus traversing the grounds of Captain Lester at this hour, and during his absence ? "

" I do not choose to answer the question of such a cursed ape as thou art, and if I am not mistaken, though I have not before gazed upon your hideous form, you are no other than the servant of one Mark Annersley, named Silas Vaughan."

" Eh, eh, eh ! right. I am he ! Oh, oh, oh ! I should know you, too, though we have not met before. Doubtless you are the friend of him whom we have safely lodged in Newgate. Sixteen-String Jack. You start, ha, ha, ha ! I am right, you are—— "

" Dick Turpin! you imp of darkness, and take that as a gift from the friend of Sixteen-String Jack," shouted the stranger, who was, indeed, no other than the daring highwayman, who had come to execute a deadly revenge upon the man who had been the principal means of placing his friend in gaol.

Scarce had the last words issued from the lips of Turpin ere a loud report rung upon the air, followed by a howl of pain.

The next moment two dark figures were struggling wildly in the moonlight.

Oaths and curses, mingled with eldritch screams of laughter, echoed through the gardens.

Like a statue of marble the helpless girl stood glaring at the struggling figures before her : one a strange unnatural libel on humanity, in form and appearance, the other, the fine, noble, well-knit frame of a handsome man.

The struggle was desperate, but brief.

Seizing the dwarfish form of his adversary in his iron grip, Turpin, exerting all his strength, lifted him off his feet and threw him with fearful violence to the earth.

There was a dull thud, a hollow groan, then all was still.

The dwarf, Silas Vaughan, was stunned and helpless.

With a curse, Turpin, his eyes gleaming with fury, was about to discharge one of his pistols at the head of the senseless dwarf, when his hand was stayed by the young girl, who, starting forwards, exclaimed,—

" No, no, no ! kill him not thus, whilst helpless at your feet, but let us leave him to his fate. A higher power than thine will punish his and his master's crimes. Come, stranger, aid me to escape from hence, lead me to my father's residence, and he will remain your debtor ever, for my parent loves his daughter as his life. Come, then, come."

Besought thus to quit the spot, Turpin, casting a vicious glance at the motionless form of the dwarf, Silas Vaughan, drew one arm of the beautiful girl in his, and gaining a door in the garden wall, forced it open, and anon led his fair charge from the precincts of the Old Ivy House upon the high road that crossed the common.

It was a lovely night.

The moon in silvery lustre shone upon the purpled heath and wooded copse.

Side by side the two young people walked at that silent hour of night across that bleak, wild, open common.

Dick Turpin, a highwayman, and an outcast, a breaker of the laws, a man upon whom the law had set its ban, in all honour conducted the friendless girl across the lonely heath. No thought of harming his lovely charge entered the brain of that highway robber.

For two hours the strange companions journeyed on, nor paused till they neared the village of Putney. Here, turning off the high road, the young girl led the way down a long lane, lined on either side with hedges of hawthorn and blackberry.

"We are near my father's house," ejaculated the poor girl, her voice choked with sobs. " See the roof o'ertops those trees. Oh, God of heaven, little did I think to enter thus my father's doors, when borne off three nights since by the miscreant tools of the villain Captain Lester!" In a paroxysm of grief, Clarisse Howard hurried on ; Turpin, bewildered by the strangeness of the scene, slowly following in her footsteps.

At length they reached the end of the lane, and paused before a pair of huge iron gates. Placing her hand upon them, they yielded to her touch, and the poor girl, closely followed by her companion, hurried on.

No words now fell from her lips. With loud hysterical sobs, Clarisse Howard tottered on towards the house of her father— the home from which she had been forcibly borne three nights before.

There was a strange kind of desolation upon all around.

The Fir-tree Grange looked dreary and dismal that summer night.

The silvery moon, with her ghastly rays, added to the dismal aspect of the scene.

With a strange feeling, as though something terrible was about to take place, Turpin hurried on after his lovely conductress.

At length they reached the hall door of the Fir-tree Grange. Staggering back, seized with a sudden faintness, the young girl murmured, with trembling voice,—

"Do you demand admittance, I cannot. Oh! would that I were dead." With a moan of heartfelt woe the unhappy girl sunk down upon the marble steps of her parent's residence, whilst Turpin, with a hand that trembled, he knew not why, gave a loud imperative summons at the door.

The knock sounded dull and hollow to the ears of the young girl and her companion.

Waiting impatiently a few moments, Turpin again raised the knocker, this time giving such a bang that it woke up the echo around.

The noise of the angry summons had scarce died away, when a light appeared from one of the upper casements.

There was the noise of a window being opened, and then a voice sounding shrill and clear in the night air, exclaimed, "Who's there?"

" Come down and see, and don't let the daughter of Colonel Howard remain here without her father's residence this chill hour of night," replied Turpin, angered at the delay, whilst his fair charge, shuddering and trembling with cold and terror, clung to his arm.

A few moments elapsed, when above the noise of the wind that rustled the foliage of the trees and surged dismally round the old Grange, Turpin heard the rattling of bolts and the clanking of a chain ; the door then thrown open revealed the wizened, stunted figure of an old man, who with a lamp in his hand peered out into the darkness upon the forms of Turpin and the young girl.

"Who—what are you?" exclaimed the old man in vexed querulous accents.

"I am a stranger to the owner of this house," replied Turpin, "but have with me in my company his only child, torn from his dwelling a few nights back. Can we not see Colonel Howard?"

"No."

The old man gazed with a strange stare of wonder and ill concealed vexation upon the intruders, who had now made their way into the hall. Clarisse, worn down with fatigue, and speechless and shuddering, with a gloomy dread of she knew not what, still clung to the side of her preserver.

"Not see Colonel Howard! Absurd! Why he will only be too glad to see his beloved daughter."

"Oh yes, lead me to my father, old man ; you are a stranger to me, else would you ere this have hurried to acquaint my dear parent of my presence."

Turpin and his fair charge gazed bewildered at the strange conduct of the old man, who, fidgeting about the hall and mumbling some unintelligible sentences, seemed as if undecided what to say or do. Turpin, who had closed the door, with a muttered ejaculation of anger, now snatched the lamp from the hand of the old man and exclaimed,—

"Come sweet Mistress Howard, this old dotard knows you not, and is more fitted for an asylum of the insane than your father's house. Come, allow me to escort you to your parent ; perhaps my half-witted friend here can tell us where he sleeps?"

"If the young lady be Colonel Howard's daughter she should be able to lead you to his chamber," muttered the old man, who with a grim frown added, "but I forgot she left her father's house at the dead of night in company with a libertine some three days back, and is unaware of the events that have since occurred."

"Old man, were it not your grey hairs protect you, by the fiends I'd fell you to the ground and make you rue the words that have just passed your lips."

Turpin, who beheld poor Clarisse turn deadly pale as the stranger adverted to her absence from the Grange, darted such a look of fury upon the old man that he shrank back in alarm.

"My dear Miss Howard, heed not the babbling words of the drivelling dotard before you, but show me at once to your father's chamber. I will explain all your sad story, and it shall go hard, my friend," ejaculated Dick (turning upon the cowering figure of the stranger), "if I do not succeed in having you kicked from the house ere the dawn of another day. Come, dear Miss Howard, let us to your father without further delay."

"Well, he will await your coming ; you will find him in the walnut-wood chamber above. Eh, eh, eh ! you will have me kicked from the house will you? we shall see." With a chuckle and a grim smile wreathing his withered features the old man hurried after Turpin, who, with the trembling and bewildered Clarisse was ascending the wide oaken staircase leading to the corridor above.

"The walnut-wood chamber is the second door on the left," gasped the unhappy girl, who in a whisper of terror murmured, " What does my father there at this dead hour of night? Oh I fear something terrible is about to happen."

"Something terrible has happened, young lady," ejaculated the old man, who, hurrying forwards turned the key of the door before which he had paused, and threw it open. "There, enter the walnut-wood chamber and see your father," he muttered, "but he will give you cold greeting." With a chuckle and a glance of spite and triumph at Turpin, he then slunk aside as Clarisse Howard staggered across the threshold into the chamber.

Upon a sideboard in the chamber (a large and lofty one) was a candelabra, the lights in which cast a yellow lustre throughout the apartment.

Wildly Clarisse Howard gazed at the scene before her.

In the centre of the room was a large table upon which was thrown a huge black velvet cover, the fringe of which trailed down to the floor.

It was not the sombre drapery of the table that chilled the life-blood in the poor girl's frame as she gazed upon it, but the outline of a something beneath the rich velvet.

A something that bore the appearance of a human form.

With a stare of horror and frenzy Clarisse Howard gazed round the apartment.

In vain she sought to discover her parent.

He was nowhere in the room.

"My father, my father!" she gasped, at the same time staggering forward and clutching at the black velvet cover of the table.

Like a block of marble, like some beautiful statue, the wretched girl stood, transfixed with horror.

Bold, daring, as he was, a cold shudder stole through the frame of Turpin as he stood beside the poor girl.

All was silence in the vast apartment.

A minute of time elapsed whilst Clarisse, her hand convulsively clutching the velvet drapery, stood immovable, glaring with distended eyes at the table before her.

What was the object concealed by the sombre covering?

About, as he guessed the fatal truth, to bear the distracted girl from the room, Turpin gave a nervous start, as a wild piercing shriek of dire agony pealed through the chamber from her lips.

Suddenly wrenching the velvet from the table a terrible object was revealed.

An object that near turned the poor girl's brain.

A sight nigh changing her to stone.

A sight that caused the blood like threads of ice to course through her veins.

The object stretched upon the table beneath the velvet was a human form.

A corpse—stark, cold, and grim.

The weazen features looking terrible in the yellow light of the chamber.

Poor Clarisse Howard, the events of the last few days had changed her from a happy girl to a sorrow-stricken broken-hearted woman.

Casting one glance upon the features of the corpse, with another wild shriek of dire woe the wretched girl sank senseless upon the floor.

The corpse her hand had revealed—

Was her father's!

The table in the walnut-wood chamber of the old Grange was the bier of him who a few days before was full of life and strength.

Colonel Howard had gone to "that bourne whence no traveller returns."

His daughter returning to his roof the dishonoured victim of a villain, in time only to gaze on his corpse.

CHAPTER XXXVIII.

TURPIN AND THE FAIR VICTIM OF FATE—THE HEIR AND THE HIGHWAYMAN—AN ANGRY INTERVIEW—THE WARNING—CLARISSE HOWARD THE BLIGHTED ONE AND THE KNIGHT OF THE ROAD—THE OATH OF FRIENDSHIP—THE DEPARTURE OF TURPIN FOR LONDON.

At the same moment that the poor heart-broken girl sank senseless at the side of her father's bier, a young man appeared at the threshold of the room, and gazed inquiringly upon Turpin and the fair corpse-like form he had raised in his arms.

"How now, Grindley? What is this? Whom have we here?"

"So please you, Master Lionel, the young lady is your cousin, Miss Clarisse, so I am told. Who the gentleman in her company may be I can not say," ejaculated the old man, a grim smile wreathing his features as he observed a dark cloud gather upon the brow of the young stranger.

"My cousin, Clarisse, come hither at this unwonted hour, and in company with a stranger? Impossible!"

"Not at all impossible, sir," ejaculated Turpin, "and I think as the nephew of the man now lying a corpse before you you might leave all explanations of your cousin's sudden arrival here till the morning; humanity alone urges the removal of the unfortunate girl to her chamber. Death and the devil young man! don't stand glowering there as though you imagined we were impostors, but arouse some of the females of the house and let them conduct Miss Clarisse Howard to her bed." Turpin, with a hectic flush of passion on either cheek, gazed sternly at the immovable figure that stood within the doorway

"May I ask to whom I have the honour of speaking, sir?" exclaimed the young stranger with a sneering voice and a look of fury at the highwaymen.

"I am Richard Palmer, gentleman, at your service," replied Turpin ironically.

"Well, Mr. Richard Palmer, you will please follow me to the library and explain this strange arrival. Grindley do you arouse the housekeeper, who will convey Miss Clarisse to her chamber," added the young man, as he left the room followed by Turpin, who, bearing Clarisse in his arms, placed her in an apartment adjoining the chamber of death, and then leaving her in the charge of a female who now arrived, hastened after the stranger against whom he at once had conceived a detestation and aversion he could not control.

Reaching the library, a large and handsome apartment, and dismissing the old man, Grindley, who had followed with a lamp, the nephew of the deceased Colonel Howard, pointing haughtily to a chair, exclaimed—

"Be seated, sir, and now kindly oblige me with the particulars of my cousin's sudden and strange reappearance at the Grange four and twenty hours after her parent's death."

"Well, sir, I must at once acquaint you with the fact that till this night I was a total stranger to your unfortunate relative, Miss Clarisse Howard."

"Indeed."

"Ay, but 'twas my good fortune to rescue her from the power of the villain, who, a few nights back, had her forcibly abducted from her father's roof. She told me her tale of wrong; at her solicitation I brought her hither. You were witness of the scene beside her dead parent's bier, nor can I speak my indignation at the cruelty of the hoary-headed scoundrel who left us but now, and who allowed the poor girl to discover the corpse of her parent, whom she expected to meet in life and welcome her return."

"Have you done, sir?"

There was a sneering, biting, irony in the young man's tones as he gazed contemptuously at Turpin, that caused the latter to clench his fist with rage, and inwardly mutter vows of future vengeance for the other's scorn.

"I have told you all it is in my power to acquaint you with."

"Very good, Mr. Richard Palmer; then, at the same time that I, in my cousin's name, beg to thank you for your services, allow me to show you from the house. But perhaps you wish for some more profitable reward." The young man here took a well-filled purse from his pocket, and made as if he was about to tender some loose coin to the man before him.

A dark flush mantled the cheeks of Turpin at the uncalled-for insult, and starting forward, at the same time placing his hand upon the other's arm, he exclaimed,—

"Look you, Mr. ——"

"Lionel Faversham," said the stranger, as Turpin paused.

"Well, Mr. Lionel Faversham, you have chosen this night to offer me the most uncalled-for insolence. Now, I am one that neither forgets an injury nor forgives an enemy. From this night I hold you as a foe. As to my quitting this house, that shall be as it pleasures the poor girl, your cousin—not you, but she, shall order me to leave the Grange."

"Indeed! it is as I will whether my cousin herself stays beneath the roof she quitted unknown to her father a few nights back!"

"What mean you?"

"Why know, Mr. Richard Palmer, I am heir by my uncle's decease to all his property and entailed estates—my cousin is penniless without I will it otherwise."

"The devil!"

"Just so. You now see I have it in my power to order you instantly from the house."

"If your story be true, yes, and I have the power to resist all attempts made to remove me; and curse me, Mr. Lionel Faversham, if I don't exercise that power, should you endeavour to force me hence."

"We will see about that."

"Yes, you will see. Try it on!"

"I shall certainly do so." About to ring the bell. Lionel Faversham started back, as the door opened suddenly and Clarisse Howard, pale and ghostlike, glided into the room.

"Hold! Lionel Faversham! I have heard the latter part of your altercation with my preserver and friend. 'Tis years since you and I have met; as children we could never agree, and from this time forth we meet but as strangers. As my only male relative, and to avoid ill words whilst yet my poor father's corse lies in the house, we must remain as friends, but when my dear parent rests in his grave, Lionel, we part for ever." Terrible sobs choked the unfortunate and bereaved girl's utterance, who now, staggering over to Turpin, besought him to remain with her at all events till the following morning.

THE VISION IN THE HAUNTED HOUSE.

" Look you, my fair cousin, your stranger friend leaves this house within the hour."

" Lionel Faversham, you are mad. My poor father who is dead, and who was wont to be your mediator between us years gone by, would not council me to accede to your wish of compelling the instant departure of one to whom I owe more than life. I hated you from childhood, Lionel, and your conduct this night has increased my loathing and abhorrence."

" Indeed. You will have to conquer your aversion, sweet cousin. and sue to me for the means of livelihood." A grim smile of malicious triumph flitted athwart the features of the young man as he noted the pallor of his cousin's face deepen to a death hue as she gasped,—

" Cousin Lionel, are you mad? What mean you?"

" Your father is dead—my uncle is no more."

" Well."

" He died suddenly. Your flight from his roof-tree was a blow that struck to the old man's heart."

" Wretch! my parent knew I was torn from him by ruffians when I could not resist." The poor girl clung to Turpin, glaring wildly at the purpled features of her cousin, who, in a voice hoarse with passion, exclaimed, —

" Well, no matter—the old man is dead. The estates entailed devolve to me, whilst you, fair cousin, there being no will, are left penniless. Ha! ha! ha! Now who shall say I am not master here?"

" Why I will, and whilst I've an arm to aid the distressed will use it in their defence."

Driven to fury by the taunting villain, Turpin took one stride, and reaching his side, with a fearful blow, sent him reeling to the floor, senseless and bleeding at his feet.

" When a serpent strikes with envenomed fang, we crush it beneath us. Fear not, dear Miss Howard, I will be your friend, will risk my life in your defence. Your villain cousin cannot drive you from your father's house whilst yet his poor, cold, clay rests beneath the roof; and hear me: I swear, dear girl, by that dead parent, to bitterly avenge you upon your accursed relative, should the law indeed wrest your father's wealth from you; fear not, for I, Richard Palmer, will not see you want. I am one scarce fit to be your friend, but though without the pale of society, and a banned being, yet I would not exchange places with that villain cur—to be Lionel Faversham, and he Richard Palmer. Do you now, dear girl, seek your chamber, your deceased parent's servant will not see you harmed. I will away at once, and return hither on the morrow."

" Oh no, no, no! leave me not. My brain already appears as though about to turn to madness. I seem as if haunted by some fearful, hideous dream, or the victim of some dreadful spell, from whom my home—ruined, dishonoured—my dear father no more—I shall go mad! mad! I am mad. Ha, ha, ha!" Glaring wildly, first at Turpin and then at the senseless, bleeding form of her villain cousin, the poor girl gave utterance to a fearful shriek, and a peal of frantic laughter, sinking afterwards in the arms of the highwayman, unconscious and delirious. Ringing for assistance, the servants, who were now all about, hastened to the library, and delivering up his fair charge, Turpin, bidding them fetch a surgeon, hastened from

No. 15.

the Grange, his brain confused and dazed by the strange incidents of the past few hours.

"Poor girl! what a fate is her's!" muttered Turpin, as he hastened through the grounds casting his eyes thoughtfully upon the clouds in the east, that were now tinged with a light golden tint, giving note of the coming day. "Poor girl, so young, so lovely, her fate is even worse than that of Dora Annersley. 'Tis a strange coincidence that these helpless girls should be thrown thus under our protection. Myself and Jack, knights of the road as we are, possess not the black hearts of the villains who thus pursue these helpless girls. Strange, that on the night of my visit to the Ivy Manor House, the residence of the accursed Captain Lester, I should meet with his poor victim, the beautiful Clarisse Howard. Well, I have vowed to pursue him to the death for placing Jack in the hands of his foes, and I will keep my oath. I have now a fresh incentive to urge me on in the pursuit of vengeance, for I entertain a feeling of both love and pity for the wronged Clarisse, and by the blue vault of heaven I'll some day revenge her cruel fate." With gloomy brow and in thoughtful mood, Turpin hurried from the house of death, and with all speed took the road to London.

CHAPTER XXXIX.

NEWGATE—SIXTEEN-STRING JACK IN HIS CELL.—JONATHAN ANSTEY AND HIS PRISONER—EXULTATION OF THE THIEF-TAKER—DARING OF THE HIGHWAYMAN—THE WAGER—THE VISITORS—DORA ANNERSLEY AND HER PRESERVER—THE DAWN OF LOVE IN NEWGATE'S CELL—THE PROJECTED ESCAPE—DEPARTURE OF THE VISITORS—THE MIDNIGHT HOUR—THE FRIENDLY FILE—THE IRON BAR—THE PASSAGE IN THE GAOL—THE MEETING WITH THE OFFICER—THE STRUGGLE—THE FLIGHT—OUT ON THE LEADS—THE CONFLICT—THE LEAP FOR LIFE—THE EMPTY HOUSE—THE MEETING WITH ANSTEY—THE WAGER—THE ESCAPE.

NEWGATE! what horror is brought to the mind at the mere name of that terrible prison-house.

Newgate, dark, drear, and dismal.

Sombre and terrible, even in the rosy hue of sunset.

The dying sunbeams of a glorious summer's day are thrown upon the gloomy old pile, serving but to increase the chilling aspect of the dismal prison.

The wayfarers who have listlessly approached the dreary prison-house quicken their steps as they near the little, black door through which so many criminals have passed out on their way to death without the gaol, or at Tyburn tree.

Some ask themselves with a shudder, may not the shades of those who once were imprisoned in the terrible gaol and suffered death outside its gates yet haunt its precincts?

Had the solid blocks of masonry power to speak, what hideous scenes would be unfolded.

The stranger, gazing for the first time upon Newgate, and recalling to mind the names of the notorious criminals and murderers whose bones lie mouldering in its very passages, passes on his way with a cold, nervous shudder.

Who shall say that the dark, weird, mystic forms of those who have perished for their crimes, haunt not the gloomy pile?

How many, with throbbing hearts and dizzy brains turned almost to madness at a near approach to a terrible death, have passed beneath the dismal portals of Newgate?

Led forth to suffer a dreadful doom.

A fearful, hideous death by strangulation on the gallows.

The gallows, whose black, frowning front and horrible beam, met the last dying gaze of the doomed one.

What hideous scenes have taken place in the dismal, terrible prison.

A murderer, whose doom has been pronounced, and whose sands of life have near run out, gazes with a fascination of horror at the dying sunbeams as they glint through the grating of his cell.

'Tis Sunday evening—the hour near night—the evening a bright and glorious one.

There are two criminals in Newgate at that moment, watching intently the sinking orb of day and rapidly approaching twilight.

But each with far different feelings.

One, with white, livid features and pallid lips, stares wildly around his darkening cell, his fingers convulsively clutching at the edge of the stool upon which he is seated.

The wretched man with a terrible shudder, notes the fall of day.

With a terrible throbbing of the heart, whilst drops of fear pour like rain down his brow, he counts the hours of life that yet remain to him.

There are only a few hours betwixt him and death.

The doom of the wretched man is sealed; the coming day is black Monday at the Old Bailey.

The shivering, horror-stricken criminal, sitting watching the sun in his condemned cell, dies on the morrow without the gaol.

The following morning, beneath the gallows that will be erected in the roadway without, the murderer is doomed to perish on the scaffold.

Ernest Malvers, for 'tis he, at length approaches his last hour.

The meed of his crimes is about to be paid out to him.

For the murder of the old wicket porter he is doomed to suffer death.

His crimes at length have found him out.

With a shudder, the wretched man stares wildly at the dying sunbeams—the last he will ever see.

To increase the horror of the miserable murderer's mind, he has heard that whilst yet he lives the hangman has sold his body to an enthusiastic student for anatomical purposes.

Ernest Malvers was at last suffering for his many crimes.

Far different are the thoughts and feelings of the other prisoner to whom we now introduce the reader of these pages.

Sixteen-String Jack, heavily fettered, glances unconcernedly at the approaching twilight.

Well he knows the meaning of the busy hum of voices without the prison walls, which reach his ear that summer eve.

He is aware that the villain Malvers on the morrow expiates his crimes upon the gibbet; and, notwithstanding his knowledge of the man's murderous intentions towards the innocent Grantley and himself, yet breathes a prayer for his forgiveness, and pities the murderer, as he reflects upon his near approach to death.

Gazing dreamily at the rich, golden rays of the sun that stream through the grating of his cell, Jack hears not the drawing of bolts or clanking of chains, nor is he startled from his reverie until the hand of a visitor is laid upon his shoulder. Starting up, he then recognises the form of a man well known to him, and to whom he owes it that he is at that moment a fettered captive in Newgate.

"Jonathan Anstey!"

"Yes, Jack; 'tis I. Art not glad to see me?"

"Well, I could have dispensed very well with your company."

"You don't say so. That's a poor compliment, Jack; but I disturbed your pleasant thoughts. You were brooding, I suppose, upon the fate of the condemned Malvers, who swings to-morrow, and thinking how many days you have got ere you may expect to follow him."

"Not at all. I was, on the contrary, asking myself where I should be this time to-morrow."

"Why, in this cell, of course."

"Oh dear no! I shall be a few miles from Newgate."

"Ha, ha, ha! Devilish good! Well, you are a deuced clever fellow, Jack, and devilish cool; but clever as you are, you won't a second time escape from the stone jug. We have you hard and fast, and damme, we mean to keep yer."

"Say, if you can!" retorted Jack, echoing the other's laugh. "I'll bet you fifty guineas to five I'm out of this before another eight-and-forty hours."

"I'll take you, Jack!" replied Anstey, with a laugh, seating himself upon the small table in the centre of the cell. Then peering eagerly into the face of the prisoner, he added,

"But come, Jack, seriously, I can aid you to flit, if you are agreeable."

"I can get away without your kind assistance, friend Jonathan."

"Pshaw, man! You are jesting. Now, listen to me," said the thieftaker, sinking his voice, and leaning forwards. "I can put twenty guineas in your pocket, and point out a means of escape, upon certain terms."

"And those terms?"

"Are that you give to me the intelligence of the whereabouts of the young maid, Dora Annersley."

"I thought so, and am prepared with my answer."

"And that is——"

"A decided refusal."

"Nonsense! Reflect 'tis life itself you forfeit by refusal."

"You are mistaken."

"How so? You will be convicted for the robbery of Captain Lester. Curses, the watch found upon you will be the means of signing your death-warrant!"

"I care not! Jonathan Anstey, the rope aint yet spun that will end the career of Sixteen-String Jack."

"This bravado is madness."

"'Tis a madness of which you will not cure me."

"You, then, refuse the means offered you to escape a death at Tyburn? Think again, ere it is too late."

"I have decided."

"Be it so! Fool, perish on the gibbet, beneath which you shall swing a few days hence."

With a deep breathed curse of disappointment, Jonathan Anstey left the cell, followed by the jeering, mocking laughter of the prisoner.

Sixteen-String Jack was again alone. But scarce had the door been made fast behind the officer who had left him ere the clank of a chain and the drawing of bolts again fell upon the ears of the young highwayman, and a gaoler opened the door, ushering in two figures, one the muffled form of a female, the other that of a rough, uncouth looking countryman.

"Visitors, Jack! Don't keep 'em long. I say, Stringer, I could almost find it in my heart to turn knight of the road myself!" exclaimed the gaoler, with a significant wink at the muffled figure of the female as he left the cell.

Jack, starting up from his seat, stared amazed at the two strangers. From the civility and jocose manner of the gaoler (generally a morose and surly fellow) he was sure his visitors had well feed him. But who was this, he asked himself, that thus purchased a way to his presence? A cry of amazement now escaped the lips of our hero, as, stepping forwards, the female, removing her cloak and veil, revealed the face and form of Dora Annersley.

With an exclamation of joy, Jack seized her hands in his, at the same time gazing astounded into the lovely features of the beautiful girl, who, half sinking on one knee, whilst bitter tears started from her eyes, exclaimed.—

"Oh! my friend—my preserver! Is it thus we meet again? And for me! for me! have you fallen captive into the hands of your foes!"

"No, no! dear Miss Annersley, you are mistaken."

"You would hide it from me; but well I know Captain Lester, the villain Vaughan, and my father, will pursue you with their undying hate for your aid to me; for your generous assistance, to one who has escaped their toils, you are now a captive in this fearful prison; for rescuing me from peril you are imprisoned here."

"Nay, indeed, dear Miss Annersley, it is not so!" exclaimed Jack, at the same time leading the weeping girl to a seat. Then glancing at the man, who had stationed himself near the door, he stepped forwards, and in a hoarse whisper, ejaculated, "Mark Tapley, can you tell me if Jem has explained my antecedents to her? Does she know that I am no other than Sixteen-String Jack?" murmured our hero, pointing to the young girl.

"She knows it not, Jack," replied the man. "She heard you were in gaol, and persisted in coming hither."

"'Tis well; leave me for a few moments."

"All right, Jack. Jem expects to see you soon; he sent you this." The man here handed to Jack a small pie, with a grin, telling him to eat the inside for his supper, and leave the crust for the gaoler. Then quitting the cell, left him alone with the weeping girl.

Sinking on his knees, Jack besought her to check her tears.

"Believe me, dear girl, 'tis not my aid to you has placed me captive here, and if 'twere so, indeed I should be overjoyed, knowing that I had saved you from a fate to you worse than death."

"How can I ever repay this generous kindness? And to see you thus, and to know that I, who owe you my more than life, can aid you not, drives me into frenzy. When I heard from the kind innkeeper that you were a prisoner in this dreadful gaol, I on my knees besought him to let me visit you. I thought the least I could do was to testify by my presence the gratitude I felt for you, my preserver, for your kindness in the past. They tell me you can perchance escape. Oh! Heaven grant that it may be so! But tell me what would be your fate if you remained here?"

"Ask me not, dear Miss Annersley; besides I shall get hence. Even this very night as I hope to effect my escape."

"Heaven grant you aid, for yours must be a venial crime, if, indeed, aught else but being my friend led you hither, a captive in one of Newgate's dreary cells."

"Dora Annersley, would you know to whom you are indebted for the slight service of which you think so much?"

The young girl gazed with surprise at the troubled features of her companion.

A dark cloud gathered over the handsome face of the highwayman, as he cast a glance into the liquid depths of the lustrous orbs of the beautiful girl by his side. Impelled by a sudden impulse he could not control, he prepared to acquaint her with his real position. Should he fail to escape, and, indeed, perish on the scaffold, he would never see her more. The present interview might be the last, and he could not bear the idea of parting with the lovely girl, for whom he now entertained a strong passion, without acquainting her with the truth and telling her all.

"Dora Annersley, ere I throw aside the mask, and unveil myself to you in my true colours, tell me, dear girl, if ever you have entertained towards any one whom you have met other than a feeling of mere friendship?"

Jack Rann gazed inquiringly into the face of the young girl, who at first appeared not to comprehend the question put. Then, as the truth dawned upon her, a bright flush crimsoned neck, brow, and cheeks, whilst, casting her eyes down upon the ground, she murmured, "Never! The feeling you hint at, dear friend, was never felt by me. Why do you ask?" faltered the beautiful companion of our hero.

"Because I love you, sweet girl—love you more than life! And in the heartfelt sincerity of my passion, dear one, am about to tell you that that will cause you to fly from me as from a being stricken with the plague."

"Oh! no! no! Say not that. Nought that you can tell me would now deprive you of my friendship." The young girl again crimsoned with a deep flush, as she uttered those words with a vehemence that a moment afterwards she was abashed at.

Then, bending down her head, she ejaculated, "But rise! Kneel not to me, my preserver, for I that owe you life, can deny you not my heart, which is yours, if you deem it worthy of your love," murmuring the last few sentences hurriedly, and in a whisper, the young girl, frightened at her own boldness, sank her head upon the shoulder of Rann, who with a cry of joy started up from the ground upon which he had knelt, and, winding his arms around her form, pressed her in a close embrace.

The sun was now sinking to rest in the horizon; but a dim light was thrown into the cell; the gathering darkness it was that veiled the wild look of despair that suddenly took the place of of the radiant beam of pleasure that had a few seconds before rested on the features of Jack Rann.

"Dora! Dora Annersley! you must not yield your heart to me! for if, indeed, I had saved your very life, I am not worthy of your love."

"Say not so! Oh! you know not the pain I feel at the words you now utter. You are the only one I have met towards whom I could entertain other than a feeling of friendship."

"Then you think you could love me?" The interrogation came in a thick, hoarse tone, whilst, with one hand upon his fair companion's shoulder, the other was raised to his face to hide a tear that started from his eyes.

"Oh, yes! Do I not owe you more than life? have you not perilled yours to safe me from harm?"

"And you love me?"

"Yes!" The answer came in a low whisper that only the quick ear of a lover could have detected.

A moan of anguish burst from the lips of Jack, who then, driven to frenzy by the thought that the lovely girl could never be his, exclaimed,—

"Dora Annersley. I must now tell you all. I am not what I seem! I know not what madness prompted me to draw this avowal from you, for I feel and know, sweet girl, that there is a barrier between us that can never be surmounted. Dora, I am a man upon whom the law has set its ban—an outcast of society—I am a breaker of its laws. Dora Annersley, the man who aided you in your distress is one whom the officers of that law will hunt to the death. Hark to the noisy hum of voices without! It proceeds from the gathering concourse, who have come hither to feast to-morrow upon the dying agony of a miserable criminal. That criminal is a murderer, and well deserves his fate. But, Dora, the sage judges and wise law of our country condemn alike the robber and assassin to death upon the gibbet; and I, who never dipped my hand in the blood of my fellow man, save in defence of life, by the accursed laws stand alike the chance of perishing on the gibbet as he whose hands are crimsoned with the blood of his victim. For know, Dora, that he who has rendered you assistance in the hour of your peril, is none other than Sixteen-Stringed Jack, the highwayman, the well-known and daring knight of the road!"

Staggering back, the young girl, with her features of the livid pallor of a corpse, glared wildly upon the form of the prisoner before her, who, with his hands clasped, stood statue-like in the centre of the cell, despair and woe imprinted on his handsome features.

For a few moments Dora Annersley stood speechless, and like one in a dream gazing upon the figure before her; then rushing forwards, she placed her fair arms around her lover's neck, exclaiming,—

"Hear me, my preserver! Though the hand of your fellow man be against you—though you have outraged your country's laws, you have still the love and friendship of the one for whom you have done so much. Well I am assured that 'tis not your fault, but a cruel fate, that has driven you in the path of crime. The soul of honour must be he who proclaims to one he loves a terrible secret, as that you have revealed to me this night, despite your perilous calling. Though you be he whom I oft have trembled at the mention of, yet do I render up to you my heart. My life, my very life, is yours." Her voice, choked by sobs, the devoted girl, now threw herself into the arms of the young man, whose generous aid and chivalrous sense of honour towards her completely won her heart.

A thrill of exquisite bliss, as in his life he had never felt before, now darted through his frame. Enfolding the fond girl in his embrace again and again, he pressed his mouth to hers, kissing by turns her flushed cheeks, dewy lips, and spotless brow.

Lost to all around him, Jack Rann was only aroused from his transports by a warning from the gaoler that the utmost limit of time was passed.

For the last time pressing his lips to hers, he exclaimed,—

"Dearest Dora, fear not for me, love. We shall soon meet again. To-morrow I'll be with you at the residence of Lutterworth, in the village of Willesden. The consciousness that I have your love, sweet one, will give me strength to combat with the perils I may encounter."

Whispering these words, as weeping hysterically the young girl drew herself from his arms, Jack followed her to the door of the cell, that a moment after was closed and securely fastened up for the night.

Sixteen-String Jack was once more alone.

Alone for the night.

The moon streaming in through the grating cast a silvery light upon the stone flooring of the cell, throwing the dark shadow of its occupant upon the opposite wall.

For some few minutes Sixteen-String Jack remained seated with folded arms, wrapped in a delicious reverie of the scene that had just passed.

Highwayman though he was, he had secured the love of this young, innocent, and lovely girl. Might not there yet be for him a bright and happy future?

A thrill of exquisite joy started through his bosom, as he recalled the words of Dora Annersley.

She loved him truly and sincerely, that he could not doubt.

That there was some mystery connected with her parent and the villains Vaughan and Captain Lester, Jack was also certain; and as he sat there in the darksome cell of Newgate he vowed to know no rest till he had unravelled the secret, be it what it might.

Rousing himself at length from the train of thought that had enwrapped him since the departure of the loved young Dora, he now began to think of making an escape from his prison.

There was a double incentive now to urge him on.

He loved and was beloved.

The lovely young girl, who had rendered him up her virgin heart, was praying for the time that he would be free and by her side.

Recovering all his usual light-heartedness, Jack now began to see about the means of escape.

First placing the small pie given him by the man Mark Tapley upon the table before him, he cut the upper crust right out, and from beneath the layers of fruit within drew out a small but finely-tempered file.

Making his way to the door, he now listened for any sounds from without. But all was quiet in the prison.

Only from without came a low hum of voices.

As he turned from the door of his cell, the dull clangour of the prison bell woke up dismal echoes through the gaol as it tolled out the midnight hour.

With a shudder, Jack counted the chimes, at the same time breathing a prayer for the wretched criminal Ernest Malvers, whose time was now but short.

"He is a villain and a murderer!" murmured Jack, as he sat upon his stool in the centre of the cell; "but his hour of doom is at hand, and may the Lord have mercy on his sinful soul."

Applying himself now to the work before him, Jack proceeded first to file at the fetters that bound his wrists. An hour passed away ere the highwayman's hands were free of the gyves that had secured them.

With the perspiration streaming down his face, from the strenuous efforts he had made to free his wrists of the galling fetters, he now for a few moments paused in his labours.

"Come, Anstey, my hands are free, and I have now small doubts but what I shall win my wager."

Then again applying himself to his task, our hero next proceeded to file at the rivets that confined the fetters to his ankles. This, after some delay and with fearful labour, he effected; but not till his ancles streamed with blood, and his hands likewise were torn and bleeding, did he accomplish his object; and then so stiff and numbed were his limbs that for some few moments he could not rise from his seat.

At length, staggering to his feet, Jack with a smile of triumph dragged the small table in the cell beneath the grating; upon the top of this he placed the chair, and mounting up was just enabled to clutch at the stone-work, in which were embedded the cross bars of iron.

To draw himself up and cast his eyes without was the work of a moment.

With a curse, Jack, after taking a hurried glance through the grating, let go his hold, and presently after stood with folded arms and clouded brow upon the floor of his cell.

"There is no chance that way; the accursed watch in the court yard below would detect at once the noise occasioned by the file, as I removed a bar of the grating; and if, indeed, he heard me not, he would secure me as I fell to the ground; the height from which would in a fall for a moment numb my limbs. Curses on it, what's to be done? To give in now, when I am ric of my galling fetters, is not to be thought of. I will escape this night, or perish! To-morrow! to-morrow shall behold me at liberty! Free, free, as the birds in the air! Ah! little do those who have never been confined in prison walls know the blessed feeling of liberty. Methinks I am once again mounted on the back of my brave steed, and careering o'er hill and dale; the light breeze fanning my fevered brow, and singing plaintive melodies in my ears. But, come, I must to my task, or the morning's sun will find me still a prisoner in this accursed prison-house."

Making his way to a small grate in the corner of his cell, Jack proceeded to draw his lithe and slender frame up the chimney, a narrow and uneven one. Climbing up some six or seven feet, he found his further progress stayed by an iron bar, that ran across. With a curse, Jack drew his friendly file from his vest, and with persevering energy worked laboriously upon the iron, till at length he had sawn one side right through. Seizing that end in his powerful grasp, he then pulled with all his force, tearing the bar from the fastening, at the same time that a cloud of mortar, stone, and soot, descended into the cell beneath.

Panting and struggling, he, still retaining the bar, made his way up the chimney, till again stopped by an impediment he little looked for.

A deep-breathed curse of rage and disappointment escaped his lips.

The part of the chimney he had now reached had been walled in.

There was no exit.

A firm, compact mass of brickwork roofed over his head, opening out, doubtless, originally upon some other flue, the one in Jack's cell had been done away with and bricked up.

Descending again to his cell, bar in hand, Jack stood for some moments lost in alarm and dismay.

All hope of escape seemed gone.

He must remain a prisoner, to be jeered and mocked by the thief-taker, Jonathan Anstey, on the morrow.

Laughed at and derided for his futile efforts to break from his cell.

Jack bit his lips, till they streamed with blood, at the thought of the exultation of his foe, the thieftaker, when visited by him in the morning.

"There is no hope—none!" he muttered between his clenched teeth. "The grating, the door, and the stone, all alike present no means of escape. There is not one chance, unless——"

A bright smile suddenly illumined the face of our hero.

He had cast his eyes upon the stone flooring of the dungeon.

Perchance, if he removed one of the huge, square flags of which it was composed, he might find some avenue of escape open to him.

It was, at all events, worth the chance.

He determined to raise one of the stone flags with the bar of iron he yet held in his grasp, and which would serve as a crowbar.

He could not be worse off if he failed to find any means of escape this way.

To remain inactive in his cell was to give up all hope.

With Jack, to determine on a course was to carry it out.

No sooner did he conceive the project of escaping by means of raising one of the flag-stones of his cell, than he set to work.

By means of the file, that had already stood him in such good stead, Jack picked out the mortar all round a stone in the corner of his cell, and which he fancied gave a hollow reverberation when struck with the iron bar.

Having removed the cement, he then, using his bar as a lever, by an exertion of strength raised the solid mass of stone up on end.

An exclamation of joy escaped him.

Below was a dark cavity.

Peering down into the void, Jack endeavoured to pierce the thick veil of darkness ere he attempted to descend.

But in vain.

All was black as a funereal pall.

Drawing a deep breath of suspense, Jack now dropped the bar through the hole.

It fell with a ringing noise on some masonry beneath.

As near as he could guess by the sound, he was but a few feet from the flooring on which the bar fell with such clangour.

For some few moments, Jack waited silent by the dark cavity, fearing the noise might have caused an alarm.

But all was quiet in the dreary prison-house of Newgate.

'Twas perchance better for our hero that it was the morning fixed for the execution of the miserable Malvers, as the gaolers and warders were all intent upon preparing for the hideous spectacle.

Taking one glance round his cell, Jack now lowered himself through the cavity made by the removal of the stone, and, hanging by the hands, prepared to drop to the ground beneath.

For a moment he hung suspended in the dark abyss.

A cold, nervous shudder darted through his frame, as he asked himself might not the ground be many feet beneath him; but dismissing the idea as soon as it was conceived, with drawn breath and compressed lips, he let go his hold.

With such suddenness reaching the ground beneath, that he could scarce believe he had fallen at all.

Staggering to his feet, Jack, with surprise, now found that when hanging by his hands from above his feet had nearly touched the earth upon which he now stood.

"Hem! so far so good! Jonathan Anstey, I think I shall win my wager," muttered Jack, who now, stooping down, groped about in search of the iron bar. Discovering it at his feet, he next began to inspect the place he was in.

To his surprise, he found it was a narrow, circuitous passage, evidently long disused, as nought but the loathly toad and hideous rat met him in his search.

Arriving at the further end of this subterranean path, Jack came to a stout oaken door, the other side of which, by the sound given back when struck, was walled up.

What was to be done?

Jack, nonplussed, stood for some few minutes undecided how to act.

Should he force the door, he would then have to work his way through a wall of brick or stone, of what thickness he knew not.

To return to his cell was to remain a prisoner till such time as his trial might take place, and then!

A shudder shook his frame as he thought upon the end of the scene in such a case.

Would Dora Annersley survive his execution?

No; he was sure that his death upon Tyburn tree would hurry her also to an early grave.

With a muttered curse of despair, Jack was about to retrace his steps, when the bar he had held in his hand struck against the wall on his left; but it gave out no ringing noise, as it would have done had it fallen against brick or stone.

There was only a dull, hollow sound.

With a cry of joy, Jack paused, and felt over the spot which had been struck by the bar, with a thrill of delight, finding another door.

The hollow reverberation given back, when hammered upon, told him that there was another passage or chamber on the other side.

The door, strongly bolted and locked, offered stout resistance to his efforts at opening it.

But again the bar of iron aided him. With the desperation of despair, Jack, who knew that morning would soon surprise him in his labours, worked vigorously at the obstacle before him, till he succeeded by the help of the bar and his file in forcing the door back on its hinges.

He now stepped out of the dark passage into a small

chamber, from a little window in which streamed a thin white light.

The dawn of day!

With surprise, Jack stood for a moment gazing round the apartment.

From the little window he perceived the leads of some of the outhouses belonging to the gaol.

The door through which he had made his way he found was painted like the walls of the chamber, a dull brown.

It was evident that the passage behind it had long been disused.

With a smile, Jack noted, hanging from nails driven in the opposite wall of the little chamber, gyves, handcuffs, cutlasses, and pistols, together with articles of apparel.

About to snatch a coat and hat from one of the nails, Jack was diverted from his intention by an unexpected occurrence.

A door he had not noticed, in a corner of the room, suddenly opened, and closing it behind him, a man, a big herculean officer, made his way into the chamber, at the moment not recognising the person of our hero. Raising his eyes, however, as Jack gave utterance to an exclamation of annoyance, the officer, with a curse, drew back to the door.

"Hallo! what the —— is this? Sixteen-String Jack, by all the fiends."

"Yes, MacNabem! Right! it is Sixteen-String Jack! Quite at your service."

"The devil!"

"No, not exactly! I'm a knight of the road."

"Curses! how got you here?"

"By aid of this iron bar, which shall assist me to crack your skull, if you raise the least alarm."

"Damnation!"

"Yes, it is vexing, aint it."

"You shall not escape. Curse yer, I'll call for aid."

"No you wont."

"What will prevent me?"

"Why this." Jack here held up the heavy iron bar.

The officer, his face livid with suppressed passion, glared wildly and vindictively at our hero, meditating the advisability of an attack upon him; but the same officer had once before had an encounter with Jack, and was aware of the strength and agility of his agile, youthful form, and, therefore, hesitated over a second conflict.

"What's the use of all this, you can't escape," muttered the man, thrusting his right hand into his bosom, at the same time staring fixedly upon Jack.

"But I shall escape, MacNabem!"

"Oh dear no. I'll prevent you!"

"How?"

"Why, thus."

With a curse the treacherous officer drew forth a pistol and fired at Jack.

There was a loud report, followed by a moan of pain.

Darting aside as the bright barrel of the pistol caught his sight, Jack had avoided the shot, and with a tremendous blow of the iron bar he broke the upraised arm of the officer, the pistol falling from his grasp, and the limb dangling useless at his side.

With horrid curses and moans of pain, the wounded man made for the door, but another blow from the fearful instrument wielded by our hero stretched him groaning and bleeding on the floor.

"Sorry for you, MacNabem, my boy; but you brought it on yourself. I did not want to hurt you, my dear friend, but as the starving man says, when picking of pockets, 'necessity compels.'"

"Curses!"

"Oh, curse away, with all my heart."

"Ten thousand devils! You shall suffer for this."

"Well, you are suffering now, so you can't cry best."

"You shall hang! hang! hang!"

"You don't mean it."

"Upon the gallows!"

"Thank you; I didn't suppose you meant on a clothes line."

Jack here made his way to the little window, and, throwing it open, gazed out upon the leads some three feet beneath.

Perceiving a coil of rope in a corner of the room, Jack picked it up, and throwing it over his arm, prepared to leave the room.

The officer, groaning and cursing on the floor, tried to rise, but fell back, the pain of his crushed arm and the agony from a wound by the side of the head causing him to feel faint, sick, and dizzy.

He was incapable of offering the least resistance, or attempting to stop the flight of the highwayman.

"Well, MacNabem, my boy, I'm off. Luck's against you this time. Give my compliments to Ansteg; tell him he owes me five guineas, and tell him I mean to have it, too. That was a cur's trick of yours, Mac, and you are rightly punished. But, as Johnny Crappeau the Frenchman says, Au revoir! or in the language of an auctioneer, I'm going, going, gone!"

With a loud laugh Jack drew himself through the small casement and dropped upon the leads, but scarce had his loud shout of mocking laughter ceased ringing on the air, ere it was succeeded by the report of pistols, accompanied with oaths and cries of infuriated men.

Standing on the leads, Jack perceived five or six dark forms at the casement he had just before got through.

His foes, the runners, were upon him.

With loud shouts they scrambled after each other out on to the leads.

The early light of morning shone dim and hazy on the scene.

A scene of savage, fierce encounter.

A desperate struggle took place upon the leads.

Like a beast of the wild woods brought to bay, the hunted highwayman turned upon his foes.

Oaths, curses, and loud shouts rang in the air.

"Go, sound the alarm bell."

"He's given poor MacNabem a dose, let him have it."

"Never mind his cursed bar."

"Rush at him."

"Put an ounce of lead in his skull."

"Down with him."

"Get the darbies ready."

"Go, fetch Anstey."

"Drag him back."

"Give him one on his cocoa-nut, Bolt."

"Curses on him, let him not escape!"

These and such like cries rang in the air, whilst the enraged runners, in a confused posse, fought desperately with their determined and dauntless victim.

Wielding his fearful bar of iron, Jack, stretching two of his adversaries senseless beside him, kept the others at bay.

Anon the dull clang of the prison bell rang upon the air.

The alarm had been given.

The officers in the gaol were made aware that a prisoner had escaped.

Those persons without Newgate who had already assembled to witness the execution of Malvers, were startled by the loud clang of the bell of the prison.

"The prisoner has cut his throat."

"The condemned has escaped."

"There'll be no hanging."

"There's a reprieve."

"He'll hang at Tyburn, instead of the Old Bailey."

Such were the reports circulated by the dissolute mob, who were standing without the gaol.

Meanwhile the desperate struggle of Jack and his enemies went on upon the roof.

Miraculously escaping the random pistol shots of his foes, our hero began to despair as he discovered his strength failing him; wielding his terrible weapon less vigorously than before, the officers perceived that he could not much longer keep up the contest.

"He's ours."

"At him, and wrench away the bar!"

"Get ready the darbies."

Paying no heed to the threatening cries that rang in his ears, Jack glared wildly round him for a means of escape.

His quick eye detected one only chance.

One full of danger.

At the back of the gaol, facing the leads, was a half-ruined house, empty and deserted. The back windows of this tenement looked out upon the courtyard of the gaol. The leads upon which our hero stood, lying rather in the corner of the prison, these outbuildings having been only recently built, and being quite a new part of the gaol.

From the leads there were some dozen yards of brick wall, leading to the outer wall of Newgate, along which was a grizzly looking row of spikes. Between this and the house was a narrow turning or alley, some six feet wide. Jack's object was to gain the outer wall, make a spring to one of the dilapidated casements of the old house, and thus elude his foes. Should he succeed, however, in gaining the outer wall unharmed, he was aware that a failure in reaching the casement of the ruined house would be attended with death, the court below being a fifty feet or more.

Summoning up all his energies for this last chance of escape, Jack, first knocking down one of the foremost of the officers, threw the fearful iron bar with all his force at their heads, at the same time bounding along the dizzy height of the wall.

Below, in the courtyard of the prison, Jack now discerned a crowd of dark figures.

The rich light golden hue of early dawn now shone upon the scene.

With bated breath, and thoroughly exhausted by his late exertions, Jack at length arrived at the part of the prison wall facing the back of the ruined house.

Hurrying along the narrow perilous path he had come, were his foes.

Singly they were obliged to tread the dangerous path; the wall, narrow at the top and many feet from the ground.

With a cold chill of despair, Jack observed that the casement towards which he must make his daring leap was some few feet above the height upon which he stood, consequently he would have to spring up when he made the leap—a wide and dangerous one.

"Better a death upon the flags below than be dragged back to Newgate's dismal cell and from thence to Tyburn tree," muttered our hero.

"Ha! ha! ha! we have him—he can't escape."

"Yield, Jack; it's no use; you are ours."

"Come, you are a game fellow, give in. You may escape Tyburn after all, Jack; yield yourself a prisoner," exclaimed the foremost of the runners, approaching the highwayman, who, with pallid face and compressed lips, stood upon the wall, glaring at the casement of the ruined house before him.

"Yield yourself a prisoner."

"Never!" shouted Jack.

There was a cry of horror from his enemies as they beheld his light, agile form whirling through the air.

Bounding from the wall, as the leading runner, handcuffs in hand, approached him, the daring knight of the road had made his dreadful leap.

The leap for life.

Astounded and terrified, the men gazed upon the scene.

Clearing the space between the wall and the casement of the old house, Sixteen-String Jack had succeeded in clutching at the window sill.

For a few moments he clung to the frail support, endeavouring to draw himself up to a level with the casement.

The woodwork of the sill, old and rotting, crumbled and gave way to his grasp.

With a shudder, the officers beheld him struggling in the air, expecting each moment to see him dashed to the ground below.

But hanging on with tenacious grip, Jack at length succeeds in his efforts.

He is presently kneeling without the casement, and two minutes after making his fearful leap gains an entry into the ruined house.

The shouts of the officers and alarm bell of Newgate ringing in his ears.

When scrambling through the battered casement into the room of the old building, Jack, casting a glance at the wall from which he had made his perilous leap, shuddered as he noted the distance that lay between the house and the gaol.

That he had succeeded in leaping the chasm in safety was almost miraculous.

Breathing heavily and panting with exhaustion for some few moments, Jack stood in the room of the old house, gazing dreamily at the prison from which he had just escaped.

At length, rousing himself up from his reverie, and recalling to his mind the fact that every second of delay was a fresh chance of recapture, he hurried from the room and made his way to the lower part of the house.

All was silence in the old building.

Nor could a sound be heard from without.

A proof that the officers had not yet gained the narrow street or court, in which the old house stood.

With beating heart, Jack listened intently at the outer door.

All was still and quiet.

Seeing first to the pistols he had thrust in his pocket ere quitting the prison, he now cautiously drew back the bolts of the door, which, rusty with disuse, at first refused to move; these at length forced back, the lock alone held it fast.

Unfastening this after some little trouble, Jack threw the door back upon its hinges and made a step out into the street, starting back, however, with a curse, as he found himself face to face with a man.

"Damnation, Anstey!"

"Yes, Jack; and you must go back with me to the jug."

"I'll die first."

"That you shall do if you refuse to give yourself up. For curse me if I don't make you a stiff un, or lodge you in your cell from which you have so cleverly escaped."

"Try it."

"I will. Curses! take that."

There was was a loud report, accompanied by the banging to of the door, as Jack, writhing in the grasp of Anstey, drew the officer with him back into the house.

A violent scuffle now took place in the passage of the deserted tenement, the stamping and swearing of the struggling foes waking up echoes in the old building.

Bang! bang! bang!

The door fairly shook on its hinges, as it was hammered on by those without.

The companions of Jonathan Anstey had arrived, and in vain for a time endeavoured to force their way in, to the rescue of their leader, whom they had observed dragged by Jack out of the street into the passage of the house.

Staggering and wrestling wildly in each others fixed grasp of deadly hate, Jack and his enemy at length reached the edge of a flight of steep stairs leading to the lower part of the house.

Neither perceived their dangerous position or vicinity to the staircase.

"Will you yield?" yelled Anstey.

"Never!" replied Jack.

"Curses! you can't escape; even now my men are about to burst the door."

"But they have to catch me when they do; and by —— they shan't find it easy to drag me back to the lumber ken (prison)."

"Indeed! we shall see."

"We shall."

About to reply to Jack, Anstey gave utterance to a yell of rage and pain, as, enfolded in the arms of the highwayman, he fell with a crash down the stairs.

Locked in each others embrace the two foes with fearful violence were precipitated down the steep staircase, and scarce had their bodies reached the bottom ere a crash at the hall door gave note that it had been burst open.

The loud trampling of feet sounded from above, mingled with the shouts and cries of the officers.

Staggering, dazed and confused, to his feet, Jack, for a few seconds, stood irresolute at the bottom of the dark staircase.

Anstey, who had been under Jack when they reached the end of their dangerous descent, was rendered unconscious by a fearful blow upon the back of his head, that stunned him and rendered him helpless.

Jack, now hearing the officers descending the stairs, bethought him of a means of escape.

His position was critical.

His foes were all but upon him.

Escape seemed hopeless.

Registering an oath to heaven that he would not be retaken alive, Jack pulled out his pistols, and prepared for the coming conflict.

The officers, some six or seven in number, now paused, when near the bottom of the staircase they perceived the figure of the highwayman.

" There he is ; on to him."

" Yield, Jack, it's no use, you can't escape us."

" The odds are too many for you, Jack."

" You had better let us shove the darbies on quietly."

" Very kind advice of yours, lads, but I don't see it."

" You won't yield yourself our prisoner ? "

" No."

" Then we must take yer."

" Just so.   Come and do it."

" Don't parley with him, Ned, on to him."

" Ay, friend, Bolt, and do you come first with Ned, and have a bullet in your brain-pan."

Jack, standing defiantly at the bottom of the stairs with his pistols presented at his foes, somewhat awed them.

" Oh, we ain't going to stand this."

" Not by no means."

" Let us all fire, and rush at him."

" Anstey wants him back safe and sound ; he has sworn to see him scragged.   By-the-by, where is Anstey ? "

" There he is," shouted Jack, who, by an amazing exertion of strength, lifted up the senseless form of the leader of the runners in his arms, and, making his way up two or three of the stairs, hurled his body, with all his force, at the men before him.

There were cries of alarm and rage, accompanied by a loud report of pistols.

Taking advantage of the surprise he had occasioned, Jack dashed up the stairs, knocking down two of the men who attempted to capture him, and then firing at another who met him near the door, bounded from the house.

He was now out in the street.

Casting one glance at the old house, Jack, discerning several of the runners in pursuit at a terrific speed, bounded up the street.

Hurrying wildly on, after turning in and out of some narrow streets and courts, he reached Snow-hill.

The offices, like blood-hounds, following in his wake.

Though yet early morning, there were a large assemblage of persons outside Newgate.

It was black Monday at the Old Bailey.

The black and hideous scaffold, upon which the wretch Malvers was doomed to perish, reared its hideous height up in the air.

With a shudder, as his eye caught sight of the grim structure, Jack dashed on, making his way straight for Holborn-hill, his object being to seek refuge for a time in the house of his friend, Peter Pattypan ; but this he soon found was impracticable, for many of the mob, joining the officers, a vast yelling crowd was at his heels as he reached the foot of Holborn-hill.

" Stop him ! stop thief !"

" It's Jack Rann ! stop him ! "

" Seize the highwayman !"

" Twenty guineas to him who makes a prisoner of Sixteen-String Jack."

" Stop him ! stop him ? "

The cries of his pursuers rang loud and clear in the ears of our hero as he hurried on.

Wildly Jack dashed up the hill, panting and gasping for breath.

His pursuers, like hounds on the track of the hunted hare, following close upon him.

Here and there an adventurous pedestrian or workman that crossed his path attempted to seize the young knight of the road, but with agility and cunning, Jack either diverged from his course or with a blow of his clenched fist sent the obnoxious stranger reeling in the road.

Meanwhile the spring of rattles, cries, shouts and pistol shots woke up echoes in the silent morning air.

Bravely Jack dashed on in his wild race.

A race for life !

For liberty !

Sweet freedom, and the arms of his beloved Dora !

The thought of this it was that lent the highwayman powers of endurance he had ne'er imagined he possessed.

The cool morning breeze fanned his heated brow as he darted wildly on, giving him fresh strength to keep up the race.

It was a strange scene, that young man hunted like a beast of prey by his fellow beings,

Hounded to the death, followed by a yelling crowd, eager to behold him dragged back to imprisonment and the gallows.

The pursuers increased in number as he sped on."

The officers at the head of the mob shouting out the promise of reward for the capture of the escaped highwayman, gave an incentive to those who might otherwise have given up the chase.

" Stop him !"

" Seize the highwayman ! "

" It's Sixteen-String Jack ; stop him !"

The officers shouted with hoarse voices of rage and fury as they found themselves distanced by their man.

They foresaw that if he kept up his present terrific speed, he would escape them.

He was now far ahead.

Many of the mob who followed in the pursuit from Newgate fell back.

Others accompanied the officers, but all were far behind the object of their pursuit.

With a thrill of joy, Jack discovered that he was distancing his foes.

Their shouts now subsided, and presently ceased,

Only a dull patter of feet behind told him that he was still pursued.

At lightning speed, Jack dashed up Oxford-street

His project now was to reach the place where he had left his mare, when reaching town, the night of his capture at the Devil's Punch Bowl.

Once astride his bonnie mare he cared not.

He would then escape, and reaching Willesden set his foes at defiance.

A sudden end, however, was put to the race.

It was then, as for one moment he paused to catch his breath, that Jack heard a shout of triumph from behind.

Looking ahead, he perceived the meaning of the exultant cries of his enemies.

Hurrying forwards to meet him, and evidently preparing to make him their prisoner, were some half-dozen mounted patrols.

To hope to escape their intentions was madness.

With a cry of alarm and a curse of rage, Jack gave himself up for lost.

The yelling pack behind, headed by the runners, rapidly approached.

The patrols, dashing forwards, with loud cries called upon him to surrender.

It seemed, indeed, as if all chance of escape was gone.

Hemmed in, both before and behind, nought but capture appeared to await him.

Glancing wildly round, Jack, like a famished wolf at bay, stood motionless in the roadway.

All hope of escape had left him.

How the wild, exultant shouts of his foes rang in his ears, driving him into madness !

When the patrol are within a few yards of where he stands, however, and the officers behind are close behind him, the keen, sharp eyes of Jack light upon a refuge, that he breathes a prayer to heaven may open the means of escape.

At the side of one of the shops, on his left, is a narrow alley.

As the patrol dashed up to where he stood with a bound, Jack dashed away into the little court.

The yelling cries of his enemies ringing loudly in his ears.

SIXTEEN-STRING JACK RELEASES JOE JOBBINS.

CHAPTER XXXIX.

JACK AND HIS PURSUERS—THE ESCAPE OVER THE WALL——THE PERILOUS ASCENT OF THE DRAIN-PIPE — THE GARRET WINDOW—THE CAPTIVE IN THE GARRET—JOE JOBBINS, THE ORPHAN, AND THE KNIGHT OF THE ROAD—VOWS OF FRIENDSHIP — DEPARTURE OF JACK — THE SECOND FLOOR BACK AND THE HIGHWAYMAN — A WIDOW'S PITY -- THE ARRIVAL OE THE OFFICERS — ANSTEY AND THE FAIR ONE — THE RUNNERS OUT-WITTED — DEPARTURE OF THE OFFICERS AND EXULTA-TION OF SIXTEEN-STRING JACK — THE SPY AND THE HIGHWAYMAN—SEIZURE OF JACK.

RUSHING blindly down the court, Jack, arriving at the further end, discovered that there was no thoroughfare.

The court was only a kind of side entrance to the houses on either side.

The wall on his left appearing the easiest of ascent, Jack proceeded to mount it: a brick or two having been removed near the bottom allowed him a foothold. Taking advantage of this, Jack placed his feet in the cavity, and clutching at the top of the wall, drew himself up.

His enemies were now hurrying down the court.

" On you go, Nabem ; he can't escape now."

" Oh, no ! he's booked for the stone jug."

" Yes, we have him, hard and fast."

" Like a rat in a trap."

" Or a fox in a hole."

" Just so."

" There he is, on the wall."

" After him, or, curses, he may yet double on us!"

With a rush, the officers, headed by the revengeful Ans'ey, darted forwards, as they caught sight of Jack, who now, having safely gained the wall, jumped down into the yard behind the house.

One glance sufficed to show him that there was small chance of hiding himself from the lynx eyes of his foes.

There was not an article that would serve to conceal him.

Taking a last hurried look at the place, Jack determined to risk the only opening of escape that was offered to him.

To gain an entrance into the house was impossible. Besides, the officers would, he was sure, search it through and through to find him.

At a glance, Jack perceived the only means of, for a time, at least, eluding his enemies.

At the end of the yard, and close to the wall of the house, was a huge water-butt, placed there to receive the drainage from the roof. Up the pipe that ran up against the wall, till it reached the leads above, Jack made up his mind to make his way.

Darting forwards, Jack clambered up on the butt ; grasping hold of the pipe, he then began with the agility of a monkey or a squirrel to ascend in his dangerous course.

The shouts of the officers sounding in the yard below, apprising him that he had only quitted the yard in time.

Look below he dared not, as the utmost care was required in his perilous task; one false step, or should his fingers lose their hold, he would be dashed to the ground below.

In nervous terror Jack ascended higher and higher towards the roof of the house, fearing every moment that the frail support would give way.

To his surprise he heard no exclamations from the officers below giving token that they beheld him; he distinguished the murmuring of their voices as they tramped about the yard, but there was no exultant shout of his discovery.

Wondering that he was not perceived, Jack scrambled on up the dizzy height, till at length he gained the stone coping above. Leaving go of the friendly drain-pipe with his right hand, he now clutched at the abutment over his head; then drawing himself up, reached in safety the parapet. To conceal his body behind this and sink upon his knees in the gutter was Jack's first course. He then cast his eyes into the yard below, shuddering as he gazed from the height. Had he lost his hold a few moments before, or had the pipe given way, he must have been dashed a shapeless mass upon the stone paving of the yard, many feet below.

Upon glancing down, Jack now perceived the cause of his not being discovered in his ascent. Running by the side of the pipe was some two feet of brickwork belonging to the next house. This abutment it was had overshadowed his figure. After the first few yards, the danger of being seen was small. Intent, too, upon discovering their man in the yard, not one of the runners had cast his eyes above. Thus Jack reached the roof in safety.

Smiling as he observed the officers congregated in a perplexed group in the yard below, Jack now made his way along the gutter till he reached a garret-window. Here he paused, startled by a noise from the garret, as though proceeding from some one in rage and pain.

The intentions of Jack had been to pass on to the next house, but despite his perilous position, he halted by the little casement of the garret, determined to take a glance at its interior. Upon looking through the window, to his surprise he beheld a young lad of perhaps fifteen years of age, fastened by a rope to the wall of the chamber; a ring let into the woodwork to which the rope was looped effectually forebade all hope of escape. And at the moment that Jack was taking his survey, the lad, with tears streaming down his face, was making frantic efforts to free himself; but in vain, the cord held him securely a captive.

With his usual impetuosity, Jack, forgetting his own danger, made up his mind to free the lad, and without hesitation, forced open the little casement and stepped into the garret.

There was a look of surprise upon the countenance of the young captive upon the appearance of our hero, who, standing by the window, exclaimed,—

"Well, young cocky, who the devil are you?"

"I'm Joe Jobbins."

"Who put you there?"

"Old Grunter."

"What for?"

"Cos I found sixpence."

"Found it before it was lost, I suppose."

"Oh, ain't you artful! but I say, cut this ere rope—pity Joe Jobbins, a poor horphan."

The lad here cast a half serious, half jocose look at Jack, that caused the latter to burst out into a fit of laughter.

"Damn it, you're a rum un."

"Pity Joe Jobbins, a poor horphan."

Jack made a dart to the casement—he fancied he heard footsteps on the landing without. Pausing a moment, and finding all was still, he then hurried back, and taking a clasp-knife from his pocket opened it, and cutting the rope that held the lad a prisoner, set him free, exclaiming,—

"There, you young whelp! Now hark ye: one good turn deserves another. Just answer my questions, and if I need it aid me to elude some foes of mine who have followed me to this house."

"Oh, won't I! crikey Sarah, rather, or my name aint Joe Jobbins."

"Well, look here, Joe Jobbins, the Bow-street runners are after me."

"Oh, crikey Sarah!"

"I've sworn to escape or perish."

"Criminy! You're a flash cove, then, I suppose?"

"I'm Sixteen-String Jack."

There was a something in the countenance of the lad that won the confidence of Jack, who was rather surprised, however, at the effect his name had upon the youthful Joe Jobbins.

"What? you Sixteen-String Jack, the knight of the road. Oh, here's a lark. I say, pity Joe Jobbins, a poor horphan. Let me be your servant. Crikey, Sarah. I'll die for yer, so help my tater. I'll tell yer where old Grunter puts all his cash—I will. Do you know, you saved my life once, you did?"

The lad, seizing hold of Jack's hands, wrung them heartily, at the same time dancing and testifying the utmost delight at his presence.

Jack began to have misgivings as to his sanity.

"Saved your life, my lad. Nonsense."

"Oh, is it though? Dont you remember, six months ago, horsewhipping an old cove as was licking into a young kid on Blackfriars-bridge."

"I do! What of that?"

"Why I'm, the kiddy—the old man was Grunter, who was agoing to chuck me, like a dead kitten or blind puppy, into old Father Thames, but you saved me; and crikey Sarah, you have saved me again from a licking and the penance of swallowing a half-pint of Grunter's sky blue. I say, let me go with yer—pity poor Joe Jobbins, a poor horphan."

Amused at the eccentricity of the lad, whose twinkling grey eyes and merry features, bespoke a good deal of cunning, despite his apparent simplicity, Jack had almost forgotten the peril of his position. At length, starting, as he heard a loud angry summons at the door of the house, he exclaimed,—

"Look you, my lad, I'll do what I can for you if I escape, in the meantime, should I do so, do you make your way to the Green Dragon, in Field-lane, ask for the landlord, tell him you came from me, and he will make you comfortable. Now tell me how I had best make my way from here. You know this house well, I suppose."

"Don't I? Rather."

"Hark, the runners have even now entered its doors."

The trampling of feet and sound of voices reached the quick ears of Jack from the lower part of the house.

"Yes, they're arter yer, that's certain, but we'el do em, or my name arn't Joe Jobbins. Look here, old Grunter will be up here soon, he's a nervous old beggar, and will send me down to the officer coves. Do you make your way to the second floor front room, it belongs to a young chap that is now out of town. You can hide stunning in there. I'll keep the coves in blue down stairs, and tell 'em I seed you cut along the roof to Still's, at the Magpie and Stump, four doors off. They'll rush there, I'll come up, show yer out, and you can hook it like a bird; and you'll take pity on poor Joe Jobbins, a horphan, and let him be yer sarvant."

"All right, Joe, aid me to escape, and reckon Sixteen-String Jack your friend."

"Won't I, rather. But get down stairs, I hears old Grunter coming up. Don't forget, second floor front."

Catching the sound of footsteps ascending the stairs, Jack hurried from the garret, scarce hearing the last instructions of Jobbins as to the place he was to seek a refuge in. Hastily descending the staircase, the voices of the officers below came plainly to his ears; reaching the second floor, he had but just time to open a door on his left and dart into a room, ere the person of an old man, a cripple, appeared just below.

"A close shave," muttered our hero, "another moment and old Grunter, or the officers following him, would have been upon me; but where the devil have I got to now?"

Jack cast a glance round the room, at once making two discoveries: one that he was at the back of the house and not the front, and another that he was in a female's bedroom—the loud and regular breathing of some one in a deep sleep sounding from a curtained bedstead in the corner of the chamber.

Loud and angry voices overhead now told Jack that the officers were in converse with the lad Jobbins.

"If the boy can persuade them I have bolted over the roofs, and the blessed feminine slumberer does not awake, I'm safe," muttered Jack, coolly locking the door he had found merely on the latch. With deep drawn breath and cautious footsteps, he then made his way to the casement, intending to take a survey of the yard below, but in his progress overturning a chair, it caused such a clatter among some articles it shook from a dressing table near, that it awoke the fair sleeper in the bed, who, in a voice sounding strange and smothered behind the curtains of the bedstead, exclaimed—

"Gracious heavens, what's that?"

Jack, who did not vouchsafe to return an answer to this query, sank down by a table in the centre of the room, endeavouring to shield himself from the sight of the occupant of the bed. With a nervous thrill he heard the curtains pulled back, whilst again the voice of the female sounded in his ears—

"Dear me whatever is the matter? Can it be that that old villain who keeps the house is flogging that poor lad again? If so, I'll leave the place without warning, and have the old villain locked up, that I will. Dear, dear! what a noise! Why, there must be a whole parish in the house! Murder!" A shrill scream burst from the lips of the female, who had suddenly caught sight of the stooping form of our hero. "Murder! fire! thieves! robbery! help! a man in my bed-chamber! I shall die! Oh you monster, go away." The occupant of the bed, a fat buxom dame of some forty years of age, thrust her head out through the curtains, gazing in astonishment at Jack, who, with a bound, rushed forwards.

Her shrieks of alarm must be stayed, or all would be lost. Seizing the hands of the astounded female in his, Jack sank upon his knees, at the same time casting a beseeching glance into the not unhandsome features of the lady.

"Dont, I pray you, be alarmed, dearest madam; lovely specimen of your dear sex, deign to cast upon your humble and devoted servant a glance of pity. That charming face, those resplendent eyes, bid me hope you will hear the prayer of one in imminent danger. You will not give me up to my foes. Hear me, dear madam: a cruel fate pursues me; I am, through unfortunate circumstances, hunted by the officers of the law, for a crime, dear madam, by your bright eyes I swear, I never did commit. The emissaries of the law are even now in this house, and I am sure, nay, I would stake my life, that now stands in such peril, that the lovely woman whose privacy I have unwittingly intruded on, will not be one to give up an innocent man to the myrmidons of the law."

Jack, who saw the face of his companion cease to bear the impress of alarm, urged upon her in the strongest terms not to betray him to his foes. The occupant of the bed, as we have said, was a fat, jolly, good-looking woman of forty, who now cast an admiring eye upon the handsome figure of our hero, who, kneeling at the side of the couch, gazed with bold but beseeching glance into her eyes.

Blushing scarlet under the glance of her strange visitor, the female exclaimed,—

"Dear me! what shall I do? I feel I ought to scream an alarm and give you to your foes; but yet I do not wish to do you harm; but to think that I should be seen like this, a man beside my bed, oh dear! I wish you would go away! the idea, me in bed!"

"Nay, my dear lady, think not of it, but I will at once depart, nor longer cause alarm in that lovely bosom. Ah!"

Jack, who had approached the door to catch any sounds from without, uttered the last exclamation, and started back as he heard a loud noise above.

From whom it proceeded he easily guessed.

'Twas from his accursed foes the runners; they had now left rooms above.

He could hear their voices as they descended the stairs.

What was to be done?

What could save him?

How could he escape?

It seemed as though capture was certain.

Should he leave the room he would meet his enemies on the stairs.

In his departure he would fall into their very arms.

But should he stay, he asked himself, was not capture equally certain?

Whilst standing irresolutely by the door, the fair occupant of the bed was taking a minute survey of Jack.

This survey was favourable to our hero.

Jack was young and good looking, with a merry, rogueish twinkle in his eye that won upon the other sex. Fortunately for Jack the female whose rest he had disturbed, and upon whose privacy he had broken, was rather partial to the male gender, and accordingly Sixteen-String Jack unknowingly made a conquest.

"Hem! Mister! my good young man! I wish you would go, I do indeed! Lor, to think now that I should have a he thing in my bed-chamber—an event that has not occurred since I lost my dear good husband. Dear me! what shall I do?"

"Why, save me from my cruel foes! my enemies are hunting me to the death. Is there no place, lovely pattern of excelling nature, where I can hide till my foes have left the house?"

Jack, perceiving that the widow was inclined to aid him, and was evidently prepossessed in his favour, like an astute general immediately laid siege to the fortress. Sinking on his knees beside the bed, he caught the plump soft hands of the fair widow in his, and praising her hair and eyes, hurriedly told her he was sure such beauty would not be the means of handing him over to his foes, and then, snatching a kiss from her full, rosy, and pouting lips, besought her to acquaint him how he could hide from his enemies.

"Dear me! what am I to do? Good heavens, my dear young man, if you were discovered here in my bed-chamber, my character, hitherto spotless, would be tarnished for ever!"

"But to save a life!"

"Good gracious! I don't know what to do."

"Why, conceal me, sweet angel, till my accursed enemies, the myrmidons of the law, have left the house."

"Well, for my character's sake you must not now be discovered! You must not be seen here—I think I should die. I have kept my virtue, praise to the Lord, intact ever since the loss of my dear departed husband, Timothy Toodles, and would not for worlds have it supposed that in an unguarded moment I had given way to the temptations of the flesh and lost my honour, or in any way departed from the paths of righteousness. The worthy Zekiel Graball bids us aid our fellow beings, and therefore will I, for pity and my own honour's sake, hide you from these wicked men, that, like beasts of prey, hunt you to your ruin."

"Thanks, my dear madam. I am yours for ever."

A loud shout was now heard on the stairs without, and a voice expostulating with the officers.

Bang, bang, bang! There was a rude and angry summons at the door of the room in which Jack was concealed.

"Indeed, it arn't no use knocking there, my covies, on the honour of a poor horphan; that there is the bedroom of a female woman; and crikey, Sarah, I expects she'll tear yer eyes out if yer goes in. I do so, sure as my name's Jobbins."

"Oh go to the devil."

"Arter you, mulberry nose."

"No impudence."

"Got lots on hand and sells it for nofin. I say, arn't yer going to take the word of a poor horphan?"

"Damnation! stand aside."

"Don't swear, it's a bad habit; take the advice of the poor horphan, don't swear. Remember the fate of Annias."

"Oh, go to blazes."

"Thank you, I'm warm enough."

"Take no notice of that idiot, McNab, but force the door. Our gentleman must be in the house, and, curse me if I don't search every hole and corner but what I'll find him."

"All right, Anstey."

There was now a loud crash as the officers dashed with all their force against the door.

Loud piercing screams burst from the lips of the buxom

widow, who, with Jack, had been listening to the converse of the youth Joe Jobbins and the runners.

Bang, bang, bang!

The door shook on its hinges.

" Remember, my life is in your hands, dear madam."

" And by the blessing of the Lord I'll save it; and may that kind good Lord forgive me for the sin I now commit."

The rosy-cheeked dame here placed her mouth to Jack's ear, blushing crimson as she told him of the only hiding place she could think of.

There was no time for consideration on either side, for with a loud crash the door was nearly kicked off its hinges.

Without a moment's hesitation, then, Jack scrambled into the bed of the fair relict of Timothy Toddles.

In another moment the officers, headed by Jonathan Anstey, and followed by the lad Joe Jobbins, burst into the chamber.

" Murder! fire! thieves!"

At the appearance of the officers the widow gave utterance to shrill shrieks of alarm, whilst Jack, notwithstanding the peril he was in, was nigh choking with suppressed laughter, as he lay by the side of the plump body of the widow.

" Sorry to a'arm yer, madam, but we're looking for a highwayman—"

" Thieves!"

" And as we know he is in this house—"

" Murder!"

" We means to find him."

" Just so."

" The very identical hammer."

" Murder! help! fire! thieves!"

" Don't go to be a fool, marm; we arn't going to ruinate yer."

" Monster!" Mrs. Toodles looked from behind the bed curtains at the officers, who now began to search the room. " I'll have you locked up for this, you horrid hairy-faced wretches."

With a grin, the lad, Joe Jobbins, turned to one of the runners, ejaculating—

" And I'll be witness of the outrage; the oath of a poor horphan will go for summat."

" Kick them out, Joe," screamed the excited widow.

" Don't I wish I could! Rather. They should soon taste he leather of the poor horphan."

" Now then, McNabem, and you, Bolt, just haul those curtains back," exclaimed Anstey, stepping forwards. " Now, marm, get up, let's see what you're made of."

" See what I'm made of? you beastly indecent ruffian! Oh you shall be punished for this if there's justice in the land. See what I'm made of, indeed!"

The enraged Mrs. Toodles, leaning forwards, caught up a candlestick that stood upon a chair beside the bed and hurled it with all her force at the head of Jonathan Anstey, who, though much enraged at the escape of Jack, could scarce forbear laughing at the fury of the widow. Ducking his head as he observed the missile coming, it struck the shoulder of the officer Bolt, who was told facetiously by Jobbins that he had better now make a bolt of it.

" Curses on the vixen," exclaimed the runner, rubbing his arm.

" I say, pudding face, she's well up in brass, ain't she? Well, yer would come in; yer wouldn't take the word of a poor horphan."

" McNabem."

" Yes, Mr. Anstey."

" Kick that precocious youth down stairs."

" Don't, you'll hurt yerself, mulberry nose." With a grin Joe dashed between the officer's legs as he darted forwards and sent him staggering to the floor, at the same time that the poor horphan darted out of the room laughing loudly at the enraged officers.

Anstey, calling his men together, now quitted the chamber, uttering a volley of fearful oaths at the escape of his victim.

Shortly afterwards the loud banging to of the outer door gave note that the officers had gone; then and then only did Jack venture to draw his head up from beneath the clothes.

" How can I ever repay this kindness, my dear madam?" ejaculated Jack, as he pressed the soft plump hand of the widow to his lips.

" The lord will repay me, my dear young man; and as your safety and getting away from here are as of deadly import to me as to yourself, seeing that my character is lost for ever if you are discovered, you must use every precaution in effecting your escape. What evil there may be in having allowed you to hide from your enemies in this room cannot now be recalled, therefore your longer stay does not signify. We must beware of being premature. Should you be discovered my honour is lost to me for ever."

The fair widow here heaved a deep sigh.

Jack, who found his position novel and interesting—

Alone with a buxom handsome woman who had saved his life.

The rich luxuriant outlines of the fat widow's form were fully exposed to the eyes of the young highwayman.

Her firm fully developed bust heaved tumultuously beneath the thin texture that covered it.

Jack began to think he had best make off.

His position began to get disagreeable; he observed the eyes of the fair widow cast upon him with glances of admiration.

Jack had unwittingly made a conquest.

The widow, the relict of Timothy Toodles, was in love.

Our hero was in a fix; he had escaped the clutches of the officers, and now had aroused the fires of love in the widowed breast of his protectress.

What was to be done? If he departed too suddenly the buxom dame might be angry at his apparent ingratitude, and perchance give him over to his enemies.

Jack remembered the old line, " That the infernal regions know no fury like a woman scorned."

Mrs. Toodles, struck by his handsome figure, had fallen in love.

To rudely repel her advances after her late assistance he felt was both unwise and unjust.

Besides that, he himself was young and impassioned, the fair widow plump and handsome.

Jack, therefore, determined upon his course, and dismissing the idea of at once making his escape from the house, remained with his preserver till the bell of a neighbouring church gave out the hour of eight.

Conducted then by his fair protectress unseen to the side door of the house, Jack bade her farewell, promising to see her again at a future time.

Scarce had he emerged from the court out into Oxford-street ere a hand was laid upon his arm, a voice exclaiming in his ear,—

" This way, Stringer. Ha, ha, ha! you're done this time."

There was a short sharp scuffle, and then with a pair of handcuffs on his wrists, Jack was thrust into a vehicle, followed by McNabem, who, left behind by the wily thief-taker Jonathan Anstey, had been ordered to watch the house.

The runner, as he gave his orders to the driver, noticed not the figure of a lad dart from the court and conceal himself behind the vehicle, that was presently rattling down Oxford-street in the direction of town.

CHAPTER XL.

A RIDE TO HOLBORN—THE OFFICER AND HIS PRISONER—EXULTATION OF THE RUNNER — FURY AND DESPAIR OF SIXTEEN-STRING JACK—A STRUGGLE FOR LIBERTY—THE CRY FOR HELP — STRANGE CONDUCT OF THE DRIVER— THE HALT BY THE HAY-CART — THE CUNNING DEVICE OF JOE JOBBINS, AND ESCAPE OF THE HIGHWAYMAN WITH THE POOR ORPHAN—DEPARTURE OF JOE — THE NON-RETURN — A BRIEF REPOSE — THE STRUGGLE BY THE HAY-CART — SUDDEN APPEARANCE OF A FRIEND—THE JOURNEY TO WILLESDEN.

" WELL, Jack! yer have given us a sharp chase! But, damme, we earthed you at last, cunning as you are. Ha, ha, ha! I swore I'd nail you. I told Anstey I was sure you were burrowing fox-like in a hole, and I said 'Leave me to the job, Jonathan, and I'll have him.'"

"Did you indeed, McNabem? hark you. I owe you one, then, and will pay the debt when I have a chance."

"Ha, ha, ha! You'll never have that chance, Jack."

"Why?"

"Because you will be topped (*hanged*) at Tyburn before you are a fortnight older."

Jack glared savagely at the officer, who, with a malicious chuckle, sat opposite to him, seeming to enjoy the misery he was inflicting.

Jack was well aware that once again in Newgate escape was impossible.

Jonathan Anstey evidently pursued him with a determined hate that would only be satiated by beholding his victim swinging on the gallows.

The villain thief-taker was urged on in the prosecution of his task by the accursed Captain Lester.

Jack grated his teeth with savage fury, as he thought upon how he had been trapped.

After successfully eluding his pursuers to be again made prisoner, when all thought of danger had left his mind, nigh drove him into madness.

MacNabem, with folded arms, sat with his ferret-like eyes gazing with malicious glee upon the gloomy countenance of his captive.

"You don't seem to like returning to old quarters, Jack."

The prisoner returned no answer, but gazed moodily out into the roadway.

"What, sulky, are yer! Damn yer, now will yer speak?"

The ruffian here with all his force kicked the shins of his victim till a moan of pain escaped his lips.

"Still dumb. Saucy, eh?"

Jack's eyes blazed like live coals of fire, as again the brutal officer gave him a severe kick.

"So you thought to do us all, did you? But it was no go, you see; you're booked for Tyburn, and damme if I wont see yer dancing the polka of small back before I've done with yer. Do yer like it?"

Again a dreadful kick; the pain from which brought the water to the eyes of the helpless prisoner.

"Well, if yer won't talk, I must cackle for both, I suppose. I say, do yer know that swell cove that you eased of his turnip and trimmings (*watch and seals*), Captain Lester, I mean, has found the blowen (*girl*) you so cleverly concealed from his sight."

"Liar!"

Jack half started up from his seat.

"Oh! You have found yer tongue, have yer?"

"Yes, Mr. McNabem, Bow-street runner and jackall to the hound Jonathan Anstey. And hear me: though I am again a prisoner, though you hold me, clever McNabem, now a fettered captive in your power, I will yet escape your toils."

"Ha, ha, ha! devilish good. Why in an hour I'll have yer safe in quod, with enough clinkers (*fetters*) on yer to prevent yer doing aught but dorse (*go to sleep*) in your chair, and next week you shall be scragged at Tyburn, my clever high tobyman."

"No, McNabem, I shall escape."

"When?"

"To-night."

"Why not do the trick at once?"

The runner here, a sarcastic grin wreathing his features, pointed to the handcuffs that confined the wrists of Jack, "Yer bracelets won't interfere with yer, my flash cull," added the officer, noting with malicious satisfaction the rage that was consuming his helpless prisoner.

"You are right, you hound!" yelled Jack, who, suddenly starting up, dashed his manacled hands full in the face of his tormentor.

Astounded at the ferocity and suddenness of the attack, the officer fell from his seat, offering scarce any resistance to his ferocious captive.

His face streaming with blood, McNabem, doubled up and half-blinded from the fearful blow, received full between the eyes, fell at the feet of Jack, shouting loudly for help: but a sudden commotion in the roadway, arising from the overturning of a wagon, drowned his feeble cries.

A desperate struggle now took place.

Whilst battling with the officer, Jack perceived the driver dismount, and hasten forward to aid the wagoner. A moment afterwards the vehicle drove on, much to the surprise of our hero, who observed the owner hurrying after them.

Being yet early, there was not a great number of people about, so that the incident did not attract much attention.

Meanwhile a terrific struggle took place between Jack and his enemy.

Driven to desperation by the critical nature of his position, Jack fought madly for a means of escape.

Kneeling upon the broad, heaving chest of his foe, he beat mercilessly his upturned face with his fettered hands, the cries of pain and rage of the officer being drowned in the rattle of the vehicle, as it dashed along the road.

Fortune favoured our hero, for those that had the horse in charge drove along at lightning speed.

The rattle of the wheels and clatter of the horses' hoofs effectually drowning the noise of the conflict in the vehicle.

Once down in the confined limits of the vehicle, with his antagonist kneeling upon his chest, the wretched officer found it impossible to regain his feet.

Madly he struggled with the prisoner! but rendered furious by his situation, and merciless when recalling to mind the savage ferocity of his enemy, Jack beat his upturned face with his fetters till the wretched man's countenance was a mass of blood and bruised flesh.

"Help! help! help!"

"You cry in vain, you hound! The noise of the vehicle overwhelms your shouts for aid."

"Help! help!"

Furiously the two men struggled. At length the officer McNabem, rising by a fearful exertion of strength from beneath the kneeling body of the highwayman, hurled him from him.

There was a crash and a cry of exultation from the lips of the wounded runner.

A moment afterwards, Jack, falling through the door, burst open by the force with which he was hurled against it, with a shout rolled out into the roadway.

The vehicle, drawn up by the driver, stood beside a cart that, laden with hay, was stationed at one corner of a street.

On rising, half-stunned and bewildered, to his feet, the first sight Jack discerned was a young lad battling with the exhausted and already fearfully punished runner.

Giving the wretched man a blow on the head with a life-preserver he snatched from his pocket, he thrust him back into the vehicle, slamming to the door, and shouting,—

"Take that, old cove, and don't forget the poor horphan!"

With the quickness of thought, Joe Jobbins, for it was he, then gave the horse such a slashing cut with a whip that the animal at once rushed off like mad.

"Now's our time, Mr. Jack. Here's a lark! here they come."

Jobbins pointed with a grin to a crowd that, shouting and hallooing, came rushing towards them.

"What the devil are they after?"

"Why, the vehicle, in course, the driver of which won't in a hurry forget the poor horphan! But we mustn't be seen, or we may drop into queer street. What shall we do?"

"Hide at once, boy, or else shall I again become a prisoner."

"Hide, I think you said. Blowed if I knows where we can hide."

"I do, Joe."

"The devil you does. Where?"

"Why, there."

"What, in the hay-cart?"

"Yes."

"Well, I'm blessed if it ain't a stunning idea; but you get up fust; don't mind me, I'm only a poor horphan."

With a grin, Joe Jobbins aided Jack to mount the side of the cart, their actions hidden from the advancing crowd, as the vehicle was drawn up at the corner of a by-street. Clambering

In, Jack buried himself in the hay that was heaped up loose in the cart, and was presently afterwards joined by the youth Joe Jebbins, who had shown himself a useful and serviceable follower to the highwayman.

Jack and his companion, buried up in the hay, heard the loud snouts of the crowd, as they dashed along the high road, as the voices died away in the distance, succeeded by the sound of a voice by the side of the cart.

"Dang moy buttons. What be all that, I wonder. These Lunnunners be queer folk. Well, I must go. Now, then, Dobbin; thee hast had a good feed, and must come along a little further wi' I."

There was the sound of a cracking whip, a muttered "Gee-up!" from the countryman, and anon the cart with its extra load moved slowly on.

For some few minutes, Jack and his companion lay upon their soft, sweet bed, silently gazing at each other, as the cart rumbled on. At length, breaking the silence, Jobbins, in a whisper, and with a look of dismay pointing to Jack's wrists, exclaimed,—

"How the devil will you get rid of those, Mr. Jack?"

"I don't know; that's a puzzle. Which way are we going?"

"On the back track," replied Joe, peeping over the side. "We's going straight for Oxford-road again."

"'Tis well—better my chances of escape. Curse these darbies, they are the only hindrance to my flight!"

"Yes, and blow me if I know how you'll get rid of them."

"Nor I, Joe."

"We've worked the trick very well up to this time; old mulberry nose won't soon forget the poor horphan."

"No, you gave him a stinger on the tater-trap; but tell me, Joe, how the devil did you come so mysteriously to the rescue?"

"Why, you see, when fat Mrs. Toodles, at old Grunters," Joe gave a mischievous wink at Jack as he mentioned the name of the fair widow, "let you out by the side door, I hurried from the other end of the court where I had been hiding till you left the house. In course I knowed where you was when the officer coves was sold in the second-floor back. Well, when I hurries up to remind you there was such a person as Joe Jobbins the poor horphan, I beheld a big cove bounce out of a doorway on to yer, like a parched pea from a frying-pan. Says I, 'Hallo! Jack's collared.' Well, I sees the officer clap the cuffs on and shove you in the blessed vehicle, jumping in arter—off they goes; says I 'This will never do,' so I scrambles up behind, waiting a chance of doing a good turn for the man as rescued me from the cruelty of old Grunter. Well, when the blessed trap reached the place where the wagon had come to grief with the fore wheel off, and the driver of our concern jumped down to assist, says I, 'Now's your time, Joe. Show 'em what the poor horphan can do;' so I scrambles on to the box, gives the blessed hoss a taste of the whip, and rattlin off stunning, says I 'Driver's got rid of and I'll next circumvent Mr. Mulberrynose inside, and give him summat as a keepsake from the poor horphan.' Once I peeps through the glass from behind the seat. Says I 'Here's a lark. They're hard at it, playing at strike up and lie down.' Well, a minute arter bang goes the door—out tumbles you—down jumps I, the rest you knows, and I hopes arter to-day you will allow the poor horphan to become your sarvant."

"I'm afraid you'll find the situation a hard one, Joe."

"I doesn't care—I wants to be yer sarvant—I doesn't want not no wages."

"That won't pay you very well, Joe; however, we'll settle that some other time. Now look here, do you think you can slip down behind the cart without being seen by the yokel?"

"Can a duck swim?"

"And do you think, Joe, you can keep the vehicle in sight and rejoin me again, after you have done what I am going to propose?"

"In course I can, I ain't a fool though I'se a poor horphan."

"Very well, Joe, now put your hand in the pocket of my coat."

Doing the bidding of Jack, Joe Jobbins dived his hand into the pocket and drew it out, with the purse clutched in it Jack [illegible]

"Now take some silver out of that purse, Joe, get down out of this, and walk along till you come to a locksmiths, then get a file or a picklock and return to me."

"Oh, isn't you a downy one!"

Joe cast an admiring eye upon our hero, whom he seemed literally to reverence, then with a sly grin he slid at out the back of the cart and disappeared.

Jack was now alone.

Alone, a fettered prisoner in the hay cart, incapable of flight or resistance should he be discovered before the return of Joe.

The cart rumbling on, and the sun rising in the heavens and pouring down its burning rays full upon the face of our hero, caused a drowsiness to steal over him.

Time passed. But Joe returned not.

Jack each moment grew more uneasy.

What kept the lad?

Why did he not return?

Over and over again Jack asked these questions of himself as the cart rumbled on.

The sun now rising higher and higher in the horizon cast a burning ray of light into the vehicle, the motion of which increased the sensation of drowsiness that some short time before Jack had succeeded in shaking off.

At length, despite his perilous position, worn out with fatigue and want of rest, Jack fairly dropped off into a sound sleep.

How long he had lain thus he knew not, but when he again opened his eyes the cart was no longer rumbling along the road; it was stationary, evidently drawn up by the way side.

Where was he?

Jack, shaking off the dreamy effect of his slumber gradually awakened to his position.

Where was Joe?

The boy was Jack's first thought.

He had not returned.

Surely the lad had not played him false for the sake of the paltry pittance he had taken from the purse. No that was not so after what he had seen of the lad, Jack would have staked his life upon his truth.

But why did he not return?

This was a mystery.

The lad had given proof of a cunning beyond his years, he was also strangely devoted to Jack, and remembered with gratitude the other's services rendered on two occasions.

Some misfortune—some accident must have happened.

What to do Jack knew not.

He was unaware where he was.

He dared not rise up for fear of being discovered.

His manacled hands, should he be seen, would betray him.

He would be seized upon as an escaped felon.

Jack ground his teeth and bit his lips with fury as he thought of his helpless position.

He savagely cursed the runners who had placed him in his strait.

The minutes flew by, but the cart moved no further nor did the boy return.

The sun was now at that height in the sky that Jack calculated it must be mid-day.

If so, the stoppage of the vehicle was explained.

The driver had doubtless halted on his road to eat his dinner, Jack now asked himself were he was most likely to be.

First, not in town, for there was no noise of passing vehicles.

Then he must be in the country.

But how was it the hay was still in the cart?

The rustling of foliage sounded in his ears as the summer breeze fanned his heated brow.

This was proof that he was right in his conjecture as to being in the country.

Determined to solve the mystery, Jack at length boldly rose his head up to a level with the hay and cast his eyes around him.

He to his surprise now found that he was on the Tyburn road, some half a mile beyond the spot where at the fatal tree, to which he doubted not he would be sent were he again recaptured.

The cart was drawn up outside an inn luxuriating in the sign of the Bald-faced Stag.

Jack had often passed this inn, and had been told that its landlord was one not unfriendly to men of his calling, but never having occasion to test the landlord's feelings on this point, Jack was wary and cautious as to exposing himself.

But remain as he was, prison bound in the hay cart, he could not.

He would risk all.

At once boldly descend.

He might be able to effect his escape from the cart unseen.

Once fairly away he could find a means of ridding himself of the galling manacles that fastened his wrists.

Yes, he would at once away.

'Twas torture he could no longer endure to remain thus inactive.

With deep drawn breath, Jack now prepared to quit the cart in which he had lain secure for so long.

Drawing himself to that side of the vehicle that opened upon the highway, first taking a glance both ways, and discerning no one in sight, our hero let himself fall into the road.

For a few seconds he lay helpless where he had fallen.

Bruised and shaken by his sudden descent.

The height was greater than he had supposed.

All was still and quite, however.

There was no sound of an alarm.

Loud shouts of laughter proceeded from the inn.

But no cries indicative of his having been seen fell upon his ears.

For the present he was safe.

Hope once more began to revive in the bosom of Jack.

He would yet be enabled to escape.

Would once more be free and at liberty to rejoin the young the young girl to whom he had sworn his troth.

About to start hurriedly away from the spot, Jack paused, as two figures appeared emerging from the inn door.

With a curse, he recognised them at a glance.

Both were his implacable foes.

Should he be discovered by them he was lost.

For the strangers making their way out of the inn were men who would hunt him to the death.

No others than Captain Lester, and the dwarf, Silas Vaughan.

Jack bitterly cursed his impatience in leaving the secure hiding place of the hay cart.

Concealed in the load of hay he was safe.

But now the next moment might give him to his foes.

His doom was then sealed.

Captain Lester would stay not in his course till he had given up to the gibbet the victim of his hate.

Slowly they approached the spot near which stood the cart with its load of hay, the dwarf listening intently to some muttered converse of his companion, the villain Lester.

With compressed lips and close set teeth, Jack, with his fettered hands upraised, awaited the moment of his discovery.

It came, and with it aid from a quarter little expected.

Endeavouring to make his way unseen from his hiding place, Jack was discovered by the lynx eye of the deformed Silas Vaughan, who, with an unearthly eldritch screech, rushed upon him, followed immediately by the villain Lester.

" Eh, eh, eh! so the doomed would fly his fate ! "

" Ah ! the accursed highwayman, the escaped prisoner from Newgate cell here ! What ho ! help ! within there ! " shouted Lester, rushing upon Jack.

In a moment the two were upon him.

Well prepared, however, Jack offered brave resistance.

Lifting up his right foot, with a fearful kick that caught the wretch, Silas Vaughan, full in the face, our hero sent him howling in the roadway, and as Captain Lester, with eyes flashing fury, came up, Jack struck him with his clenched and manacled hands in his face. Not expecting such resistance, the villain Lester staggered back, failing to avoid the blow that broke two of his teeth from his mouth, at the same time filling it with blood.

With wild fury, both again rushed upon him, at the same time shouting loudly for help from within.

It came, not for the wretches Lester and the dwarf, but for their victim.

" Zounds, and the devil! two on to one! not if I know it."

A young man who now rushed out seized the dwarf, who had savagely caught Jack's arms with his teeth, and giving him a stunning blow on the head with the butt of a pistol, stretched him senseless in the road, then, catching Lester by the neck, hurled him off his feet, throwing him heavily to the ground, his skull striking with fearful violence against the wheel of the cart.

The two aggressors of our hero were now rendered *hors de combat*, and, for a moment, unable to make further attempts at his capture.

The young stranger who had so opportunely rendered him aid, now turned to Jack, bidding him hasten away, as a crowd of persons began to pour out of the inn.

" Off with you, lad, while you have a chance."

" That voice!" cried Jack, " Damn it, is it you, old pal ? "

The stranger, who had begun to hurry Jack away, now, for the first time, raised his eyes to his face, and recognised the friend he had saved.

" What ! Jack ? "

" Yes, Tom ! and but for you I'd have been secured just now by that accursed dwarf and the villain Lester."

Tom King, for it was he who had rushed from the inn, with a shout of joy hurried on beside his friend, and reaching the Edgware-road, darted behind a fence that surrounded a large house standing some way back from the roadside. Here, by means of a file he drew from his pocket, Tom quickly released Jack of his manacles, and presently, after making their way from behind the fence, the two friends betook themselves to the neighbourhood of the Oxford-road, halting at the place where Jack had left his mare on the night of his capture at the Bowl House, and where King had unharnessed his steed only two hours before.

Securing their brave steeds, the two friends were presently afterwards cantering along the road, in high spirits at having met again together.

" Well, now that there's no fear of being run down by our cursed foes, tell us, Jack, all your adventures since the time I left you and Dick at the Bowl House in old Westminster. I was afraid that you were both in the stone-jug, for I have seen nothing of Turpin since that night."

" Doubtless we shall hear of him at Willesden, Tom," replied Jack, who now recounted to his companion events already known to the reader. " Thanks to your timely aid, Tom," said Jack, in conclusion, " I am once more free, and again breathe with heavenly rapture the air of blessed liberty. When seized upon by the hideous dwarf and the miscreant Lester I feared a cell in Newgate would again receive me. However, 'twas not to be. I am free, and a little time hence trust to be seated at rest in the snug blue parlour of the Cat and her Kittens."

" Ay, Jack, and the devil's in it if we don't make a night of it."

Conversing as they journeyed on, the companions, without misadventure, at length reached the pretty little village of Willesden, and meeting their friend, Dick Turpin, at the very door of the Cat and her Kittens, accompanied by Jem Lutterworth, the landlord, all adjourned to the chamber contiguous to the secret parlour, and seated to a welcome repast each laughed at the dangers he had passed, the only alloy to Jack's pleasure being that his beloved Dora, disguised, accompanied by Jane Lutterworth, had made her way to London, to carry tidings of her lover, only the persuasions of his companions preventing Jack from at once making his way from the inn the road he had come.

CHAPTER XLI.

THE ALARM OF JACK AT DORA'S ABSENCE—A CONFERENCE
—A LOVER'S DETERMINATION—DEPARTURE OF THE
HIGHWAYMEN—THE UNEXPECTED MEETING NEAR THE
HAUNTED HOUSE—THE SHRIEK FOR AID—THE CON-
FLICT—ARRIVAL OF THE RUNNERS—THE MELEE—
ESCAPE OF CAPTAIN LESTER WITH HIS VICTIM—FURY
AND DESPAIR OF JACK—THE RETREAT OF THE FRIENDS
TO THE HAUNTED HOUSE—BLOCKADED IN—THE DARK
SHADOW ON THE STAIRCASE—TERROR OF THE COM-
PANIONS—THE STRANGE DISCOVERY OF THE SECRET
PANEL—A DARK PASSAGE AND ITS TERMINATION OUT
IN THE AIR—THE ESCAPE FROM THE DRY WELL—
EXULTATION OF THE THREE FRIENDS—RETURN TO
WILLESDEN.

As time passed and the young girls returned not, Jack grew
more and more uneasy.

Again and again he made his way to the door of the inn,
hoping to catch a sight of them on the road.

But they appeared not.

And with a sigh of disappointment Jack would return to
his friends.

At length, as the sun began to sink to rest, his friends, and
the father of the pretty Jane, the companion of Dora, began
to share Jack's fears that ill had befallen the wanderers.

" Well, Tom, what do you think of this ? " exclaimed
Jack, as for about the hundredth time he turned away from the
door of the inn, whence he had gone, hoping to catch a glimpse
of the figures of those for whose return he was so anxious.

" I don't know what to think, Jack."

" Nor I, Tom," ejaculated Turpin.

" It is certain something has happened."

" Possibly, Jack, my dear boy," exclaimed Lutterworth,
joining the group by the inn door. " But that something may
have nothing to do with what you are thinking of."

" What do you mean, Jem ? "

" Why, that though my Jane and the pretty Dora may
have met with an accident, we must not jump to the conclusion
that that accident has given them to the hands of your foes."

" That may be, Jem, but you have divined my thoughts,"
replied Jack, dejectedly. " Would I could hope that only
some trifling mischance has befallen them ; but, remembering
that only this very morning I encountered the accursed Silas
Vaughan and the fiend Lester on my road hither, I cannot
rid myself of the horrid thought that 'tis into their hands my
beloved Dora has fallen."

" Well, Jack, should that be so, I am one with you to hunt
this Lester to his lair, nor know no rest until we have his
heart's blood ! I owe him a debt of vengeance. The tale of
sorrow related to me by the unfortunate Clarisse Howard, and
with which I made you acquainted a little time back, has raised
within my bosom a feeling of vengeance against this roué and
scoundrel, that nought but his death can assuage, I will hunt
him to the grave."

" And so will I, my dear pals," ejaculated King.

" Let us, then, start at once upon our errand, my friends,"
exclaimed Jack, excitedly, " an inward conviction forces itself
upon me that my dear Dora has again fallen into the powers of
the wretches from whom I saved her when first we met. Should
I be right in my conjecture, Dora will either be conveyed by
her captors to the manor of her father, the Blue Bells, or to
the residence of the villain Lester, Ivy Manor House, at Wimbledon. Into both of these places will I force my way, and
tear her whom I have sworn to protect from those who now
hold her in their power."

" Well said, Jack ! I'm with you," cried Turpin.

" And I, pals ! " echoed King.

" Luck go with you, brave boys," exclaimed Lutterworth,
who, now as much alarmed as the three friends, brought out
their steeds, and with anxious brow saw them depart.

" Farewell, lads ! hasten your return."

" All right, Jem. Mind, I shall expect the hand of the pretty
Jane if we succeed," shouted King, with a laugh, as with his
companions he dashed away from the inn.

Soon afterwards the highwaymen were cantering leisurely
along the road leading to London.

" Do you think I am right in my suspicions about the
girls, Dick ? "

" I do, Jack."

" And so do I ; and curse me if I don't give the varmints
a remembrancer if we meet them. I own to a sneaking kindness for rosy-cheeked Jane, and, damme, our foes shall account
to Tom King for any harm they may have done her. If, indeed,
you are right, Jack, it won't be the first time Messrs. Humpy
and the gay captain have received the marks of my respects."
With a laugh the knight of the road here reminded Jack of the
scene in the morning.

With gloomy brow, Jack, taking the lead, rode on, ceasing at
last to join in the converse of his friends.

It was a lovely summer evening, and had his thoughts not
been so engrossed and his mind so harassed, Jack would have
noted with joy the beauties of the scenery around him.

Arriving at an avenue of trees the tall branches of which
near joined above their heads, the rich golden rays of the
dying sun glinted in bright threads across their path.

The gentle summer breeze stirring the foliage, cast a delicious
coolness around, whilst the feathered songsters, twittering their
evening notes as they basked and whirled in the roseate hues of
the sunset, gave a cheerfulness to the otherwise dull quiet of
the scene.

Anon the golden orb sank deeper yet deeper in the horizon,
till at length, like a huge globe of fire, it disappeared from
sight, tinging the clouds about its bed with a crimson liquid
lustre.

The friends, riding on, relapsed into silence, the sound of their
horses hoofs the only noise that rang upon the air.

Twilight, with its dusky mantle, now descended on all around,
casting dark shadows on the scene.

Slowly the three friends journeyed on.

Save a humble pedestrian, not a living creature had passed
them on the road.

It was as Jack, drawing in the reins of his bonnie mare,
pointed out to his companions a narrow lane turning off the
road, that final darkness enwrapped them.

" Do you know that place, Dick ? "

" I should do so."

" And I, Jack."

" It's the lane leading to the ruined house."

" Yes, Dick. I should like to fathom the mystery of that
night some time or other."

Jack, who in his remembrance of the strange occurrences
when last himself and friends had been in the neighbourhood
of the old lone house, paused, and leaning forward in his saddle,
bent his ear to the ground.

" What do you hear, Jack ? "

" The sound of horses' hoofs."

" I, too, can hear them," ejaculated King ; " and I'm much
mistaken if they are not at full gallop."

" You are right, Tom."

" What shall we do, Jack ? "

" Draw our steeds out of the highway."

" I see your move, Jack. Into the lane, eh ? "

" Yes."

" A fine dodge ; come on, Tom."

Turpin, followed by Tom King, now turned his bonnie
Black Bess into the dark lane.

The sound of horses' hoofs now fell plainly on their ears.

" I suppose if it ain't those we're after, you'll make these
strangers pay toll, Jack ? "

" Well, yes ; but something tells me it is our foes who
approach."

" Got your barking irons all right, Tom ? "

" Yes, Dick, leave me alone. Catch a weasel asleep, not
Tom King."

" Hush, pals. Hark ! By heavens, that is a female shrieking for aid."

A muffled shriek now sounded on the air, heard by the
friends above the noise of the horses hoofs, that each moment
neared them.

JACK'S FLIGHT FROM THE BLUE BELLS.

"Dick Turpin, my pal, get ready for some warm work; I hear other horses on the road, besides those now close upon us."

"All right, Jack. I'm good for three enemies any day."

"And I, Dick. I'll show them a trick."

"Yes, Tom, I think you can bite as well as bark."

Reins in hand, the three highwaymen awaited impatiently the moment that those who approached would reach the road near the lane.

The moment came.

With loud shouts the three friends dashed out upon the strangers.

Jack, the first to appear, with a scream of wild fury, dashed forward at the foremost horseman. In his arms he held a young female.

Though he saw only a muffled form, yet did Jack feel assured that he gazed upon the figure of his beloved Dora. Even as he dashed upon the stranger, with pistol raised, a piercing shriek echoed on the night air, and the muffled female struggling in in the arms of her captor, tore away the scarf that enwrapped her features, uttering loud cries for help.

Well Jack knew that voice.

It was, indeed, the unfortunate girl, Dora Annersley, whom he beheld a prisoner in the arms of the horseman.

And the horseman no other than the villain Lester.

With a curse of mad fury, Jack seized the reins of the roué's horse, a fierce struggle ensuing.

Shots, oaths, and curses sounded in the air, accompanied by piercing shrieks.

No. 17

Beaten back by three strangers who now galloped up, with maddened brain, Jack beheld the villain Lester, still retaining his prize, dash away from the spot. About to follow him, Jack found himself surrounded by some half-dozen Bow-street runners, the warning shouts of his friends, who had backed their horses into the lane, ringing in his ears, above the sounds of the conflict.

"Back, back, Jack. They are too many for us."

"Away, away, Jack!"

But Jack, surrounded by the officers, found it impossible to join his friends.

"Upon him, Bolt."

"Down with him."

"There's twenty guineas hanging to his capture."

"Don't let him escape."

"Knock him off his horse."

"Revenge poor Nabem."

"Bullet him."

The shouts of the runners and thup thup of the bullets, as shot after shot was fired at Jack, rang loudly in the air.

Fighting furiously with his enemies, our hero still remained firmly seated in his saddle, effectually keeping the officers at bay. Having fired his pistols, he only now had his riding whip to beat his foes back; but this weapon served him in good stead, as the handle was loaded with lead. Wielding this with fearful blows, he kept off his foes.

Turpin and Tom King, for some few minutes engaged with a couple of officers, who had followed them into the lane when they made their retreat, having got rid of their assailants, now galloped back to the assistance of their comrade.

A fierce conflict now took place in the roadway.

The second that had occurred between the highwaymen and the officers in the same spot.

The officers, in numbers four to one, bade fair to gain the victory over the three friends.

" Curses! ride over them, Dick."

" Chine (stab) them."

" Beat them back."

The highwaymen, now close together, more easily effected their purpose of beating a retreat. Perceiving how much they were outnumbered, their object was to back their horses into the lane and thence seek a refuge in the ruined house.

" Circle round them, lads! Don't let them escape."

" Clap the darbies on the Stringer. There's some sweetmeats (rewards) to be had for his capture."

" Down with him."

" Send him to grass."

" That's right, Bolt : hold on to him."

" Let him try!" yelled Jack, furious with rage as he thought of the escape of Captain Lester with his unfortunate captive, the helpless Dora.

The officer Bolt, who had seized hold of Jack, clung tenaciously to him, despite the shower of blows rained upon his head by the enraged highwayman. Having succeeded in backing his brave mare from amid the runners, Jack now followed after Turpin and King, who had made their way successfully into the lane. The officer Bolt, still clinging to Jack, had been torn off his saddle, and now, stunned and bleeding from a fearful blow given by Turpin as Jack dashed up, sank with a groan to the ground.

No sooner were the three friends in the lane, than they bounded off, followed by the shouting crowd of runners, the foremost of whom, however, less well acquainted with the darksome lane, remained somewhat in the rear.

" What are we to do now, Jack?"

" Make our way into the ruined house, Dick."

" But, damn it, the hole is haunted!" muttered Tom King, with a nervous shudder, as he galloped on beside his friends.

" No matter; better a night with the spirits, than be collared by the grabs (officers), and dragged back to the stone jug, Tom."

" Very true, Jack."

" Here we are."

The friends, now dismounting, led their horses through the broken gateway into the grounds of the old house, that loomed dimly and indistinct before them.

The moon was not yet up—all was thick, heavy gloom in the gardens of the ruined house.

Dark, dreary, and dismal.

Scarce had the companions made their way into the deserted garden ere the officers arrived at the gateway, their loud shouts ringing in their ears.

" After them! they can't escape."

" Curses! they are going into the haunted house!" shouted another, one of the very officers that had followed the friends to the lone building along with Anstey a few days before.

Unheeding the cries of their enemies or their close proximity, Jack, followed by his companions, now reached that part of the wall that, broken and decayed, opened upon the little copse. Here the steeds of the highwaymen were let loose, the sagacious animals cautiously making their way into the little wood. Well the friends knew they would not allow the runners to approach them, but at sound of their masters voices would, with lightning speed, bound to where they stood.

Aware that a watch would be placed round the grounds, the friends thought the safest refuge for a time would be the haunted house, as a more effectual resistance could be offered in the building than in the garden or the little copse.

Arriving at the tree by the shattered casement, the friends hastily by its branches made their way into the house, not without a shudder as they thought of the strange occurrence that had taken place it when last they were in the ruined chamber.

The officers made their way up to the hall-door as the friends disappeared in the old house.

" Well, Jack, here we are—what next?"

" Oh, a game at hide and seek with our friends outside, from room to room of this pleasant, old building, enlivened every now and then by a chance shot from behind a door."

" That's about it, Tom."

" Well, Jack, you're captain, lead on."

" All right, pals! Let us stay here first and reconoitre the proceedings of the enemy."

Standing some few steps from the broken casement, Jack peered out into the grounds below.

The moon now rising, threw a pale, sickly light through the gardens of the old house. Grouped about by the tree and round the door of the ruined building, the friends beheld the runners in earnest converse, ever and again casting their eyes up at the shattered casement. As they expect, two or three of their foes at length mounted the tree, whilst others prepared to burst the door.

" They mean it, Jack."

" Yes, curse them!"

" What's to be done?"

" Why, we must fight them from room to room."

" That's our only plan."

" Yes."

" Got your barkers all right?"

" Yes, Dick; come on. Where's Tom?"

" Just gone out of the room."

" I did'nt see him go, Dick."

" No Jack, you were looking out on the grabs (officers)."

" How cursed dark it is, again."

" Yes, Oliver (the moon) has just disappeared under a cloud."

" Hark! what's that?"

" Bang—bang!"

A dismal, horrible echo rang through the lone house.

" 'Tis our friends at the hall-door."

" We had better make for the upper part of the house."

" Yes."

" Bang—bang!"

" They'll hurt themselves at that."

" They shall have an ounce of lead from my barking irons, Jack, if they give me a chance."

" Ditto. Hist, Dick—see there!"

Jack turned as they reached the door of the chamber, and pointed to the forms of three of the runners who appeared at the casement.

" Shall I fire, Jack?"

" Curses, yes! They hunt us like dogs, let them pay the penalty."

There were two loud reports, and cries of pain.

" There's two rubbed out—come on, Dick."

Followed by his companion, Jack now made from the room, as a fearful crash at the hall-door below gave note that it had been burst from its hinges.

" They are in the house, Jack."

" Never mind, we can tackle the odds against us better here than without. Flying from room to room, we can reload our barking irons," muttered Jack, ready to give them a fresh dose ; " but where the deuce is Tom?"

" I don't know—perhaps gone up stairs."

" How foolish to separate from us. Come on; they are hurrying up from below."

The loud tramp of the officers' footsteps fell plainly on their ears as they burst into the hall.

Loud oaths and curses were uttered by the runners.

Two of their comrades had perished,

A fierce feeling of revenge now urged them on in pursuit of the highwaymen.

Leaving the chamber as two more of their foes cautiously entered by the casement, the two friends hurried along the wide corridor that opened out from the suite of rooms on that floor, and made their way up a large, oaken staircase, the balustrades of which were two feet broad, so firm and solid was the old house built.

"Hist! is that you, Tom?"

A dark figure appeared coming down as the two companions hurriedly ascended the stairs.

There was no reply to the question of Jack, who, leading the way, had discerned the figure before Turpin. who was two or three stairs behind his companion.

What did it mean?

Surely Tom was not practising a joke!

Jack could not help a shudder stealing over him as the dark form continued to descend, just discernible in the thick gloom.

Tap, tap, tap!

The sound of the person's feet upon the stairs fell upon the ears of Jack, who staggered back with a cry of horror as his hand, outstretched before him, fell upon a death-cold face.

"God of heaven, Dick, this is awful!" gasped Jack, who, but for the arms of his friend, would have fallen in his fright headlong down the stairs.

"What do you both mean?" exclaimed the voice of their friend, King, who now appeared hurrying up the stairs. "Damn it, Jack, what was the reason of your leading me almost into the hands of the grabs, and then eluding me in the dark—confound it, this is no time for joking!"

Tom, in vexed, angry tones, uttered these words as he rejoined his friends, but neither of them returned an answer; both were intent glaring upon a dark shadowy form that stood before them on the stairs.

"Who's that up there, Jack?"

"Gracious Heaven! what is that?"

"The accursed house is haunted by fiends!" exclaimed King.

Such a piercing scream now echoed from the stairs above them, that the blood of the daring highwaymen curdled in their veins. Scarce had the scream died away in dreadful echoes through the old house, ere it was followed by the report of fire-arms in the rooms below, whilst the sounds as of men hurrying from the lone dwelling sounded in their ears.

"The grabs are clearing out, Dick."

"Yes, Tom, and by Heaven, I think we had best follow them!"

"Nay, pals—and fall into their hands! Look you," said Jack, "why should we who fear not man, fly from before a shadow? By the Supreme Power above, I swear I'll not quit this old house till I have fathomed the mystery that attaches to it. Do you as you like; I am bold and determined. Though an army of spirits crossed my path, I'll search this business out."

A wild peal of mocking laughter now sounded in their ears, accompanied by the noise of a fierce struggle in one of the upper rooms.

Transfixed, the friends remained upon the stairs, listening to the dreadful noises from above. All below was still and quiet.

The officers had left the house, doubtless terror-stricken by some horrible sight.

"This is dreadful, Jack."

"Horrible! Curses! let us go."

"The house is the resort of fiends. Let us away, Jack."

"No, by Heavens! I'll not be frightened like a child from my purpose. Though the fiend himself crossed my path, I'd not turn back."

"Forward then, Jack! Turpin is not one to leave a pal, though surrounded by the devil and all his imps."

"Where is that figure gone that was on the stairs but now, Jack?" gasped King, glaring affrightedly around him.

"To rejoin his fellow fiends below I suppose, Tom," replied Jack, who dauntlessly began to ascend the stairs.

A terrible curiosity impelled Jack on to institute a search through the old ruined tenement.

Not naturally superstitious, Jack Rann was struck with awe and wonder by the scenes of horror in that old house.

And with a kind of morbid feeling prosecuted his search, determined to unravel the terrible mystery, if in the power of man to do so.

Arriving at the summit of the stairs, and taking the first door to his left, Jack unhesitatingly, but not without a chill darting through his frame, pushed it open.

A flood of silvery light from the bright moon streamed upon them.

Entering the chamber, a front one, large and lofty, the three friends made their way with one accord to the open space at the further end of the room, through which poured the moon's rays. This, originally a large casement, was now all broken and decayed away, the winters storms penetrating with devastating effect into the chamber of the ruined house.

"This has been a fine old building, Dick."

"Yes, Jack," replied Turpin, who, conquering his fears, stood with Jack camly gazing out into the grounds below.

"Do you see anything in the gardens, Jack?"

"Yes, Tom. our enemies. Curs that they are, they fear to hunt us in the old house, and have, it seems, determined to blockade us in. Well, no matter, we'll defeat them yet."

It was a glorious scene that from the broken casement of the old ruin.

The moon, round and silvery bright, shone with her pale bluish rays upon all around, tinting the old tenement, the copse, trees, and everything alike, in her ghastly light.

Tu whit! tu whoo! Tu whit! tu whoo!

The old owl that had built its nest in the decayed belfry tower of the ruined house, kept giving utterance to its dismal note, increasing the wild and dreary horror that hung about the place.

Anon a huge bat with leathern wings outspread like a large web, circled in the air, rushing blindly against the walls of the old house.

Ever and again the friends heard the voices of their enemies below, as they called one to another in the gardens.

"This is pleasant, Tom."

"Very."

"How do you feel, Jack?"

"Not very lively, Dick."

"Nor I."

"Curses on it, can't we get out of this?"

"I see no chance, Tom, until our foes leave."

"Then we're booked,"

"Safe as a rat in a trap."

"Well, better this than Newgate."

"Oh, certainly."

"Of course if we are nailed now its all over with us."

"Right you are, Dick."

"A ride to Tyburn and a short shrift."

"Just so."

"You are both of my opinion as to the advisability of remaining here?"

"Oh yes, Jack."

"'Tis well, Dick. How strange those noises have ceased."

"Yes, and curse me if I don't feel as queer now they're stopped, Jack, as I did when they were in my ears."

"So do I, Dick. What do you think of it all, Jack?"

"I know not what to think, Tom."

"Nor I. I can guess now how it was about you when first we entered the house, Jack."

"What do you mean, Tom?"

"Why, when we were in the chamber below I fancied I saw you go out; of course I followed down stairs. You, as I supposed it was, went and then disappeared from my sight. As the door was burst open by the cursed grabs, I rushed upstairs, and to my astonishment discovered you and Dick together."

"It's all very strange."

"Yes, Jack, so strange that curse me if I like it! I don't mind the beaks (magistrates), nor do I care about the grabs (officers), but I'm damned if I like figures that are bullet proof, and damme if ever I get out of this haunted house if I'll trouble it again in a hurry."

"Pshaw, Tom, they can harm us not."

"Very true, but the company of beings of the other world is not very agreeable or pleasant."

"Granted, Tom, but the company of warders and gaolers I take it is worse."

"Well, yes."

Jack now, turning from the casement, was about to make his way to the door of the chamber, when he as well as his com panions were startled by a loud whistling without, as though from the mouth of a man, whilst with a shudder each heard the tap, tap, tap, of a man's foot on the stairs.

"Jack, I have heard that air before."

"And so have I, Dick."

"It's the same whistled by the strange being we saw down stairs."

"It is."

"This is all very awful, Jack."

"Ay, Dick, and by the God that made me I'll find it out."

"Jack!"

"Yes, Tom."

"You cannot doubt this cursed house is haunted?"

"Well, no."

"Then let us leave it."

"No."

"Why stay?"

"For two reasons."

"What are they?"

"First, if we attempt to quit the house we fall into the hands of our enemies."

"Well."

"Secondly, I am determined to find out this mystery."

"To what purpose? How will it advantage you or us?"

"I cannot tell. At all events it will gratify my curiosity as to what has passed. I can but think that some fearful crime has been committed in this building."

"Like enough, Jack, but I do not see, if you become acquainted with the particulars to morrow, what advantage it would be to you."

"Well, never mind, Tom, it is my whim, besides I am glad to-night to think upon anything but the one subject nearest my heart, the fate of the unfortunate girl, Dora Annersley, who has fallen once more into the hands of her accursed parent and the wretch Captain Lester; but I'll follow in the track of the villain, and wrest his victim from his arms in the hour of his triumph; like a bloodhound I'll follow in his path, till I rescue the young girl whom I have vowed to protect from the machinations of her foes. I'll save her. I will tear her from them, though I peril a dozen lives to effect my purpose."

"And I will aid you in your task, Jack," ejaculated Turpin.

"And I," exclaimed King.

The two friends now followed Jack from the room out into the dark corridor without.

All was still and silent.

The strange horrible sounds ceased to echo through the old house. A silence as of the grave rested now upon the place.

A silence even more distressing and fearful to the companions than the mysterious noises that had before so startled and terrified them.

"Dick."

"What is it, Jack?"

"Did not those screams appear to you to issue from one of the rooms on this floor?"

"Yes. I could have sworn they proceeded from a chamber close to the one in which we stood but now."

"I think so too, Jack," exclaimed Tom.

Jack, with his friends, now paused at a door situate on the left hand, and at the further end of the passage.

About to place his hand upon the lock, Jack started back in wild terror as again that piercing shriek sounded in his ears.

Such a shriek as had before terrified himself and his companions.

Such a shriek as sent the blood like ice darting through the veins to hear.

A shriek as of one in a last dying agony.

A shriek that might have escaped a victim perishing beneath the assassin's knife.

Again it rings upon the air, sounding horrible and clear in the lone house.

"For heaven's sake let us quit this accursed house!"

"I'm of Tom's opinion, Jack. Let us away."

"Hold! God of heaven! Look there!"

Jack, impelled by a horrible curiosity he could not control, had turned the handle of the door.

The three friends, with a wild stare of affright, now gazed spellbound upon the scene before them.

The room into which they glared with horrified amazement was a large and lofty bed chamber, and it was at the back of the old house; but what struck the friends with awe and terror was the fact of the room being not only well furnished but tenanted. By the glare of the bright silvery moon that cast its rays full into the chamber, Jack and his companions beheld a richly draperied bedstead standing against the wall at the further end of the room. By the casement was a table with books and an open casket, and papers strewn upon it; near the table was an ottoman; beside the bedstead, on the floor, apparently lifeless, and lying in a pool of blood, was a young man; upraised in the bed was a lovely young woman, and by her side, fast locked in sleep, was a boy of perhaps eleven years of age.

Transfixed with wonder, Jack glared into the chamber upon the strange and terrible scene.

Turpin and King, with exclamations of horror, staggered back from the door; but Jack, fascinated by the sight as by the fiery charmed glare of the rattlesnake, remained rooted to the spot, his eyes fixed upon the chamber.

The female, at first with eyes staring at the casement, now turned her head and leaning forward in the bed cast a glance at the door of the room.

Jack's blood fairly stagnated in his veins as the strange form turned its gaze upon him.

The face of the lovely woman was of a livid hue.

Whilst the eyes shone with a dull stare like pieces of polished tin.

Drawing his breath short and thick, with his blood cold and freezing with terror in his veins, Jack pushed the door wide back upon its hinges and strode into the chamber.

Despite his terror, a strange coolness and indifference of danger was in his breast.

An invisible power seemed to urge him forwards.

He seemed drawn to the spot irrespective of his will.

A morbid curiosity, a determination to fathom the mysteries of the ruined house, enabled him to master his fears.

Stepping boldly into the chamber, Jack, turning his eyes from those of the woman, that were fixed upon him with a stony icy glare, made his way to the table.

The moon shone bright and clear in the skies, bathing the grounds of the old house in a flood of silvery lustre.

Jack cast his eyes in vain without to catch sight of any-one near.

Not a living creature was to be seen.

Fancying from the fixed gaze of the female at the window that some one was about to enter by that way, Jack had first, on entering the room, made his way to the casement.

With a feeling as though his whole frame were plunged in ice, Jack now became aware that there was another person in the room.

Turning away from the casement he beheld, standing by the bedside, he beheld the form of the grim shadow he had seen the first time he had entered the ruined house

There were the same features, the same tall well-made figure Jack had gazed on the night that in terrified alarm he and his friends had rushed from the house.

The stranger whose whistling had so startled them was again before him.

With feet that seemed chained by an invisible power to the floor, Jack remained standing by the casement witness of a strange and horrible scene.

His heart almost ceased its pulsations, his whole frame becoming icy cold, appeared as though turning to marble, so rigid, so resistless to his will were his limbs.

He could not move from the spot.

The cold beads of terror trickled down his brow.

Bold, daring as he was, Jack Rann shuddered, as spellbound he gazed upon the scene before him.

A strange and terrible one.

Of crime and bloodshed.

Whilst standing by the casement, Jack fancied he heard the sound of a child's voice, but this was drowned in one of those piercing shrieks that had before rung in his ears. The figure of the man then started from the bed, but now holding in his arms the form of the boy. With horror, and incapable of staying the monster in his bloody purpose, Jack now beheld the man strangle the hapless child.

Loud harrowing screams burst from the mouth of the female, who bounded from the bed, hurling from him the lifeless child; the murderer with a yell of laughter seized the woman by her long hair, and with merciless ferocity sheathed a keen and glittering knife in her bosom. Her shrieks died away into gurgling sobs, her blood spurting up in the face of her assassin. Jack, driven to madness by the horror of the scene, darted forward to avenge the murdered ones, but even as he rushed across the room a young man dashed in, presenting a pistol at the head of the assassin. There was a ringing report, followed by a wild shout of demoniac laughter, and with a feeling as of approaching death Jack staggered back and falling against the wall, that seemed to give way before him, with a cry of terror he sank into space.

From that time he remembered no more.

When again he opened his eyes the bright rosy hue of early dawn shone around him.

"Come to at last."

"Thank heaven, yes."

"Well Jack, old fellow how do you feel?"

"Had enough of the haunted house?" .

"Damn it, old fellow, don't stare at us like that."

"What! Dick? Tom?"

"Yes! Dick and Tom, of course. Why, did you suppose we had made a bolt of it without you? But come, tell us, Jack, how the devil did you come to tumble down those cursed stairs?"

"What stairs?" Now thoroughly aroused and in possession of his senses, Jack staggered to his feet.

"What stairs? why those there behind that secret panel, and which you tumbled down, I suppose, in the dark, in your pursuit of a ghost."

In the broad bright light of the sunny dawn Turpin felt not the fear that had possessed him over night.

"Where are we?" Jack gazed like one awakening from a dream around him.

"Why in the haunted house, to be sure."

"But this chamber?"

"Is the one we looked into last night and fancied was furnished; for the matter of that so it is, only the furniture, what there is of it, is rather antiquated."

Jack, as Turpin ceased speaking, gazed at the room in which they stood with a feeling of nervous terror.

It was the same in which he had beheld the murders of the preceding night.

But how changed.

The bedstead was there but all dropping to decay.

The casket and papers on the table, the floor of the chamber were all alike inches thick with dust.

All about the room was ruin. Time's corroding hand was upon all about the place.

With amazement Jack glanced around the chamber, in vain searching for evidences of the terrible scene that had been enacted the night before.

"'Tis very strange," he murmured, then turning to his friends he added, "where and how did you discover me, Dick?"

"Why, finding that you did'nt follow us, after a time we made back to the room here, and just as we reached the door we heard those cursed noises again; though startled we determined not to leave you by yourself with the fiend, ghost, or devil, and so at once burst into the chamber. All was dark and silent, however; we searched the room in vain; you were not to be seen. Now thoroughly alarmed for your safety, not knowing but what you might have been secured by one of the grabs, we hunted through the old house, and despite our fears of supernatural beings, leaving no room or closet without scrutiny. At length the light of morning shone upon us, but found you not. It was at Tom's suggestion that we returned hither to search the ghost room, as we called it, by daylight, having in the dark given it but a cursory survey. On entering it a little while back we were startled by hearing a low moan; to our surprise, on glancing round we beheld that secret panel open in the wall, and upon looking through, at the bottom of a short flight of steps, beheld the party of whom we were in search. Yes, Mr. Jack, in a blissful state of unconciousness, you were stretched at your length upon the floor of the passage at the bottom of the stairs behind that panel."

"All this is very strange, Dick."

"Yes, you are right, Jack, and I have another strange fact to tell you."

"What is it?"

"Why our cursed foes are still without."

"The devil!"

"Yes, they have determined to blockade us in."

"It would seem so."

"What are we to do, Jack?"

"Escape."

"But how?"

"May not this strange discovery aid us?"

Jack with a smile pointed down the dark cavity behind the panel, to which he had now made his way.

"I never thought of that, Jack."

"Nor I, Dick," exclaimed Tom.

"I say, Jack."

"Well, Dick."

"This haunted house may, after all, be useful, if we can only get used to the phantoms."

"How do you mean?"

"Why the grabs are downright afraid of the haunted house."

"Of course they are."

"Well, they will never attack us wi thin its walls again."

"Granted; what then?"

"Why, damn it, don't you see, we can make it a capital retreat."

"Yes, Dick, that is what I think of; but do you think you will be as valorous and careless of the shadows, that I am fain to believe haunt the old house, to-night, as you are now?"

"Damn the ghosts!"

Turpin, somewhat vexed at having shown fear to his friend the preceding night, turned away and conversed with Tom.

"Oh! with all my heart; but, come, let us find out where this passage will take us."

"Lead on, Jack."

Followed by his friends, our hero, passing through the secret panel, closed by Turpin, who was last, descended along a passage so narrow that only one person could make his way at a time.

So thick was the accumulation of dust upon the floor of this secret way, that it rose up in clouds, as the friends proceeded on, quite drowning the noise of their footsteps.

"This is a lively place, Jack."

"Damn it, I am choking."

"Curses! what's that?"

Jack, who was first, halted, as King, uttering an exclamation of alarm, placed his ear against the wall, listening to the sound of voices.

A low chuckle of triumph fell from the lips of Jack, as he, too, placed his ear to the wall.

"What is it, pals?" ejaculated Turpin, too far behind to hear the voices.

"Hist! Dick! on your life be silent. Our foes are in the old house!" ejaculated Jack, in a whisper.

"The devil!"

"We've doubled on them fine by means of this passage."

"Yes, Tom, this old house will, from now, be a first-rate refuge for us when we are coming from or journeying to London."

"Rather! We'll make it habitable."

"Yes, Dick; but how about the ghosts?"

About to return an answer to the query of his friend, Dick was silent as the noise of the officers sounded louder and louder in the old house.

They were now evidently in a room adjoining the passage in which stood the three companions, and were engaged in a dispute as to the mysterious disappearance of the highwaymen.

" It's no use, Gregson ; they have cleared out somehow."

" But, curses on them, they couldn't have got from the house without being seen."

" They must have done so."

" How ? "

" That I can't tell."

" What do you think of it, Bolt ? "

" Curse me if I know."

" Well, they aint in the house,"

" Right you are, Gregson. What do you propose to do ? "

" Why, we must return to London."

" What will Anstey say ? "

" I don't know or care a damn ! Let him come and hunt 'em up himself."

" It's a strange affair ; here have we been watching the cursed place all night."

" Yes, and now the birds have flown."

" And poor Tony and Smith lie stiff uns in the garden."

" Well, I don't think we shall have any luck while we are here."

" Why so, Smithson ? "

" Because the cursed house is haunted. I have heard of this place before."

" What about it ? It's only in Chancery."

" Yes, and likely to remain so. Mark my words, this crib will never be inhabited again. I've heard talk of the haunted house near Willesden, but never thought to be in it."

" Well, I don't like this place."

" Nor I, and I think, mates, the best thing we can do is to get out of it."

" Smithson's right. Let us cut it."

" All right ; come on, lads."

" Back to London, Gregson ? "

" Oh, yes, our men are off, therefore its no good waiting here. Curse them ! "

With rude oaths and curses the officers now made from the room, the sound of their retreating footsteps falling on the ears of the highwayman.

" What do you think of that, Jack ? "

" Why, they are sold again, and we've got the dibbs (money)."

" Hurrah ! for the haunted house say I."

" Yes, Tom ; we won't mind the shadows, if we can elude the substance."

" Kious (be quiet), they may hear us."

" No fear, Dick, they are fairly off."

" That was a fine trick, doing the door nobbling (listening), Jack."

" Yes, Tom, it gave us a first-rate insight into the movements of the enemy."

" Well, come on, pals, let us get out in the open air."

" All right, Dick. I'm as anxious as you to be off. We have much to do—work of vengeance is before us."

" What mean you, Jack ? "

" Why, to-night I intend to crack the crib called the Blue Bells."

" Right you are, Jack, I'm with you."

" And I, Jack."

" All right, pals. While I secure my Dora again to my arms, you two can collar the wedge (plate) belonging to the worthy Mark Annersley."

" The very identical thing we shall do, Jack.

" And if any of us happens to cross Captain Lester——"

" We slits his weasand" (cut his throat).

" Just so, Tom. I for one have sworn to pursue that man to the death, and I'll keep my oath."

" And so will I," muttered Turpin.

Groping along the dark secret passage, the friends now arrived at the edge of a flight of stairs.

Descending these, which they found of interminable length, and like the passage thickly laid with dust, they again stepped into a narrow passage, but this time it was earth that they were treading, not decayed and rotting boards.

" This is an improvement, Jack."

" Yes, Dick, rather."

" Don't you think there is more air."

" I do. But we must be under the old house now."

" I fancy it's getting lighter."

" So do I."

" Tom."

" All right, Jack, here you are."

" Hurry after us. I'm anxious to find out where this will lead us."

" Right you are, Jack. Go ahead,

As they proceeded onwards in their path, the friends each noted the underground passage, growing lighter and lighter.

A thin white glare of light appeared at length before them, which, as they drew nearer and nearer, grew stronger and more discernible.

Loud shouts of exultation and surprise escaped the lips of the companions as they reached the end of the passage.

A large opening was before them, through which making their way, they found themselves at the bottom of an old dry well, the bed of which was choked up with bricks, grass and wild creeping plants that trailed up its sides to the summit above.

The sky, bright, blue and beautiful, shone overhead, whilst a thin ray of the golden orb of day darted across the mouth of the old well.

The three highwaymen, for some few minutes, stood lost in wonder and joy at the novel scene.

Here was a means of escape from the ruined house invaluable to them.

The officers, whilst searching the old ruin, would give the friends ample time to escape, and make their way far from the spot.

" Jack."

" Dick."

" This is just the place for us."

" Yes."

" We'll take the house on lease."

" Yes, Dick ; but how about the ghosts ? "

" Damn the ghosts ! "

" Oh, of course ; but take care they don't fly away with you, Dick, out of spite for your disrespect."

" Pshaw ! But I say, Jack, how are we to get out of this well ? "

" Easily, Dick."

" How so ? "

" You see those spaces in the side of the old well."

" What, where the bricks have fallen out and rotted away, Jack ? "

" Yes, Tom."

" Well, how will that help us, my dear pal ? "

" Can't you imagine, Dick ? "

" No, I'm damned if I can."

" Nor you, Tom ? "

" No, Jack ; I really cant see a way of escape any more than Dick."

" Well I do."

" Glad to hear it."

" Let us have it—time flies."

" You are right, Dick ; and we have yet much to do. Now the only way of getting out of this old dried up well we have happened on so strangely is this: the nearest opening in the rotting brickwork is some four feet above our heads. Now I must mount upon your shoulders, Dick, you are the tallest, and then, placing my foot in the cavities by aid of the strong plants and rough sides of the well, gain the summit, and once I am in the grounds all is over."

" I don't see it, Jack."

" Nor I either. How about your pals ? "

" Why, Tom, I shall hurry back to the house, procure some pieces of old rope, return, and haul you both up."

" Capital."

" Excellent."

" Jack, you are a trump."

" A first-rate general."

"But away with you; stand beside me, and steady me while he mounts, Tom."

"Right you are, Dick. Now Jack, up with you."

"Here goes, pals."

"Steady, Dick."

"Easy does it."

"All right, Jack?"

"Yes."

"Luck go with you; make haste back. It's confounded dull down here."

Jack, who with little difficulty, had clambered up, by means of the numerous apertures in the sides of the old well, now reached the grounds above, and, casting a glance back at his friends, exclaimed,—

"Dick! Tom!"

"Well, what is it?"

"Why, we are close to the broken part of the wall through which we leave the horses to find their way into the copse. I will now away and return on the instant."

The sounds of their companion's feet hurrying along the gravelly walk presently told the two companions in the dried well that he had left the spot.

"Well, Jack's off, Tom."

"Yes; and curse me if I care how soon he returns."

"There was no other way for us to get out."

"None."

"I don't think it would have been advisable to go back to the old house by the way we came."

"Oh, no, Tom. If the grabs (officers) are still foxing about we shall be able to double on them now."

"Right you are, Dick."

"And I didn't much care about going back down that cursed musty passage."

"No! It's a pity, Dick, the old house is haunted; it is a fine slum (hiding place) from the enemy."

"Yes; but I must be hard pushed to reek refuge here, Tom."

"But Jack seemed to think of making it a regular hiding crib."

"Well, as regards its fitness for such a purpose, it is not to be equalled by even the Cat and her Kittens; that we know has a few slums. But the confounded strange noises and the sights we have seen in the old house, near cause me to vow I'll never enter its doors again."

"Well, Dick, after all, as Jack said, the strange beings that haunt the old house are not to be feared by us; they can do us no harm."

"True."

"Our foes can drag us to the gallows; but these shadows can harm us not."

"Right, Tom."

"Therefore I am with Jack inclined to make the old building a regular rendezvous."

"Well, Tom, we can certainly effectually bid defiance to our enemies here; and damme if I'll hang back where you and Jack go forward. And despite the dark shadows and mystic forms that evidently haunt the ruined house we'll make it our regular hiding place."

"It's our best plan, Dick, and we must not forget that this retreat is on the road to another equally secure."

"You mean Lutterworths?"

"Yes, the Cat and her Kittens will afford us shelter when we may want to leave the ruined house. 'Tis but a short canter from here to Willesden."

"Very true, Tom; but hush! I hear footsteps. 'Tis Jack."

The sound of feet in the grounds above now sounded plainly in the ears of the companions.

Tom, about to shout out, was restrained by Dick, who, observing his friend's intent, motioned him to silence.

"Safe bind, safe find, Tom; it may not be Jack," whispered Turpin.

The noise in the garden above approached nearer and nearer to the vicinity of the well.

"Dick, by heavens, I think it's one of the runners."

"So do I, Tom."

"Curses! if it is so, Jack is nabbed."

"He may have escaped."

"Should this be an enemy, we must return by the passage to the old house."

"Yes; but hush! they are here."

"Anstey, the officer, by ——, Dick!" exclaimed King, with an oath, as a dark shadow was thrown over the mouth of the well.

The companions crouched down by the opening in the old well leading to the secret passage, as the sound of footsteps ceased above, and two dark forms leant over, peering into the darksome cavity.

"You don't think you'll find our men down there, Nabem, do you?" ejaculated a voice.

"There's no saying, Bolt. We've sharp customers to deal with."

"Well, the Stringer tricked you fine in the drag."

"Yes, Bolt, and left his mark upon me, for which I'll yet have a reckoning."

"Do you mean to persist in it, McNabem, that you saw Sixteen-String Jack come out of this old well-hole, as you made your way into the grounds?"

"I do, Mr. Anstey."

"It's incredible," replied the thief-taker, peering down into the well hole.

"It may be incredible, but it's true, as I'm a living man."

"You are sure you were not mistaken?"

"Sure of it, Anstey."

"Curses on the slippery hound, how came he to elude you in the ruined house?"

"I know not; I'm mystified in that respect, Mr. Jonathan Anstey. I was close upon his heels, and panted to revenge the punishment I received at his hands when he so cleverly escaped, aided by a comrade, when I was conveying him to Newgate. He was no sooner in at the window of the old house than I was after him. I dismissed from my mind the stories of my brother officers, respecting the place being haunted, and notwithstanding I fancied I beheld a dark shadow standing in the corridor without the chamber, dashed up the wide oaken staircase after our man. He disappeared in the room which was searched an hour or so back by Bolt here and the rest of them. I was in the chamber a minute after he had banged the door to, but when I entered I saw no trace of him."

"There was no other room opening from this?"

"None, Anstey."

"And here you lost him?"

"Just so. I searched the chamber minutely, but found him not—he was gone."

"'Tis a strange business; and by the fiends I'll fathom the mystery, though a legion of devils stood in my path to shield this accursed Jack Rann and friends from my power."

"So, too, will I, or my name ain't McNabem; but howsomever, suppose we fire down into this old well? who knows? His pals may be hiding there now."

"You are certain you saw Sixteen-String Jack emerge from this hole?"

"As sure as I stand here now, Anstey."

"Then fire into the well by all means; the idea is not a bad one."

Anstey, who, with MacNabem, had arrived at the old house, having met the other officers on the road to London, now leant over the well-hole, and discharged their pistols into the bramble pit, for it resembled nought else, when standing in the garden above.

"Bang! bang! bang!"

There was a low chuckle from the two friends, who, at the opening of the secret passage, had heard all the foregoing converse of their foes.

Jack, it appeared, had been seen, but had effected his escape. Anxious to hear what was said by the officers, Tom, with Dick, remained by the end of the underground passage, opening into the dried up bed of the old well, laughing as the report of the pistols fell on their ears, the leaden bullets from which buried themselves in the earth.

"There's no one there now, McNabem."

" Let us have another fire, Anstey."

" As you will, but 'tis wasting powder and shot."

Bang ! bang ! bang !

Another chuckle escaped the lips of Tom and Dick, whilst oaths and curses of disappointment issued from the mouths of the runners.

" Curses, it aint no go."

" What shall we do, Anstey ?"

" Why, there is only one course, Bolt."

" And that ?"

" Is to keep a watch upon the house and grounds."

" Very good ; we must keep watch and watch."

" Exactly ! remember there is fifty guineas for the capture of Sixteen-String Jack."

" All right, Anstey, we'll earn the shiners."

" Come now to the house, 'tis useless staying here, and by all the devils, clever as he is, by —— I'll lay Mr. Sixteen-String Jack by the heels before the rising of to-morrow's sun."

The sound of the officers leaving the spot had scarce died away upon their ears ere the two friends, Turpin and King, were startled by a voice close beside them.

" Well Dick ! well Tom ! my Trojans, are you dull down here ?"

" Curse me if it's very lively, Jack !" exclaimed Turpin, as he turned in the passage and faced his comrade, who had returned to them, as they expected, by the underground way.

" How the devil did you manage to slip that cursed fellow, Bolt, Jack ?" exclaimed Tom.

" And how the deuce, may I ask, came you to be aware that I had to double when I got out into the grounds ?"

" Why, we nobbled (listened) to the patter (conversation) of some runners who congregated around the old well, fancying that because they saw one old fox tumble out of it, others were in the hole."

" Ha ! ha ! ha ! and so they fired their barking irons into the hiding place of my pals, and 'twas that I heard as I hurried onward hither," ejaculated our hero, laughing and chuckling over the triumph they had achieved over their foes the runners.

" Yes, Jack, they popped away quite regardless of the loss of powder and lead," exclaimed Tom.

" I say Jack !"

" What is it, Dick ?"

" Anstey, as he left the well-hole, swore he'd have you before the rising of to-morrow's sun."

" Curses on the hound ! did he so ? Well, we shall see ; but come, let us back to the old house ; night will soon enwrap all in her black dark mantle ; under its cover we must escape hence. I tremble as the hours fly on for the fate of my dear Dora, and have sworn to rescue her this night from the hands of the accursed Lester, or perish in the attempt."

" I am with you, old pal !"

" And I, Jack, with you to the death !"

" I know it, dear friends ; but come, let us at once by the secret passage to the house. The fact of my having been seen by the accursed McNabem emerging from the well, precludes the hope of a safe retreat from it on this occasion ; come, then, come."

Followed by his friends, Jack now led the way through the subterranean path, till at length, mounting without adventure the old staircase, they came upon the winding passage behind the walls of the house.

All was quiet. Still as death.

Save the throbbing noise of their own beating hearts, not a sound fell upon the ears of the three friends.

Anon they paused.

They had arrived at the panel opening upon the haunted chamber.

In the secret passage all was thick darkness.

Black and ghastly.

Notwithstanding they were bold dauntless men, the companions shuddered as, recalling to mind what they had witnessed in the ruined house, they stood with cold nervous feelings behind the secret panel of the haunted chamber.

" Curses, how dark it is, Jack !"

" Black as ink."

" Or a funeral pall."

" Damn it, Dick, don't be so grave in your similes !" ejaculated Tom, trying to force a low laugh at the attempted pun.

" Hush, pals ! remember our voices may be heard by our wily foes should they be in the adjoining room."

" Never fear, Jack, the runners won't seek us in the house ; they'll watch the building without for our departure ; they stand in awe both of our barking irons and the shadows that undoubtedly haunt the old house, and which they have seen as well as we."

" Very likely, Dick, may be you are right ; but still, we were best act with all caution ; we must escape somehow to-night, if I rescue not Dora Annersley within a few hours I may be too late, and, by the fiends, I'll pay Jonathan Anstey a heavy debt of vengeance for this bloodhound-like following on on my track."

Waiting in silence in the dark secret way, intently watching for any sound of alarm, Jack at length slowly and cautiously opened the panel.

Breathlessly Tom and Dick stood beside their companion, whilst they, with an involuntary shudder, cast their eyes into the haunted chamber. All was quiet.

Save the rustling of the ivy that grew about the casement of the chamber without, or the "tu whit tu whoo" of a solitary owl, not a sound could be heard.

All was as silent as the grave.

The chamber in which Jack had beheld such visionary horrors was as he had last left it, quiet and deserted.

Stepping through the panel, followed by his friends, Jack, with a shudder he could not repress, stood again in the deserted room.

Tom and Turpin, nervously glancing round, drew their pistols out of their pockets and put them on half cock.

Night now falling, the lone chamber in the ruined house was wrapped in darkness.

A thin murky light stealing through the casement increased the dim aspect of the room.

Large dark shadows appeared to hang upon the walls.

There was no bright moon in the horizon to pour its silvery rays in the haunted chamber.

All was thick darkness within and without.

Black heavy clouds shut out the silvery light of the moon.

All was dark, drear, and dismal.

A strange odour of damp and mildew hung about the room, causing a shiver to pervade the frames of those who detected it.

" Hist ! I say, Jack, are we in a charnel house ?"

" No, Dick, we are in the old ruined house, from which I speedily intend to escape."

" The sooner the better ; go ahead, Jack, let us get out of this cursed room ; it contains the odours of a vault."

" By heavens, you are right, Dick !" exclaimed Tom, who, more heedless of danger and less cautious than Jack, hurried to the door and threw it open.

The tall figure of a man stood upon the threshold.

With a curse Tom started back.

About to fire, he was restrained by a hand being laid upon his arm.

With a horrible shudder Tom glared round, as though expecting to behold some hideous sight.

He encountered the steadfast gaze of his friend Jack, who, pointing to the figure by the door, in a whisper exclaimed,—

" Hold ! fire not ! By heavens, 'tis but a shadow ! The report of your pistol will only rouse our foes."

" Jack, this is horrible !"

" Better fall into the hands of our enemies than remain here," muttered Turpin.

A low chuckle and sharp click of a pistol now fell upon the ears of the companions ; at the same moment the figure that had remained so erect and motionless by the door, darted forwards, presenting a brace of pistols at the heads of the highwaymen.

THE SCENE IN THE COURT--DEATH OF FARMER ASHFORD.

"Ha, ha, ha! good evening, lads. You are tricked at last! I owe you one, Stringer, and curse me if I don't soon pay the debt, if you don't surrender; damme, I'll lodge an ounce of lead in your brains if you don't give in. It's no use, you're trapped at last; give in, you know you're wanted. What ho! Anstey, Bolt! up with you! I have found the birds."

McNabem shouted loudly as he stepped backwards to the door of the room.

The three friends at first discovery that the wily officer had tricked them, stood undecided and irresolute as to their course.

"Up with you, below, our men are here! Help, help, help!"

The voice of the runner rang loud and shrill through the old house.

Echoing cries answered from below.

The noise of trampling feet and exultant shouts sounded through the house.

Bang, bang, bang!

McNabem and the highwaymen fired their pistols, but without injury to each other, the darkness in the chamber being now so great that one could scarce discern the other.

With a cry of rage, Dick Turpin had rushed, when recovering from his surprise, upon the exulting McNabem, and endeavoured to hurl him to the ground.

But the officer was a strong, herculean, active man.

Turpin found that he was unable singly to conquer his enemy.

Oaths, and curses of fury, escaped his lips.

"Jack! Tom! curses, help! or damme, I shall be nabbed."

There was no reply to his cry for aid.

There was a loud crash that shook the flooring of the chamber.

Deep curses escaped the lips of Turpin.

He was hurled to the ground by the officer, who, with a shout of triumph, pulled a pair of handcuffs from his pocket, and prepared to manacle his prisoner.

Turpin shouted loudly for King and Jack.

But his friends had disappeared.

He was alone with the officer.

Alone and overpowered.

In vain he tried to wriggle himself from beneath his foe.

McNabem, kneeling on the chest of the highwayman, coolly prepared to slip on the handcuffs he had drawn from his pocket.

The runners, who had rushed up from the lower part of the house upon hearing the cries of their comrade, were now in the corridor without.

Another moment, and they would be in the room.

Turpin gave himself up for lost.

In wonder and alarm he kept asking himself where were his friends, who had so strangely and suddenly disappeared.

With rage and fury he listened to the ejaculations of triumph that fell from the lips of the officer McNabem.

His comrades were now at the door of the chamber.

They dashed it open with a loud crash.

No. 18.

Headed by Jonathan Anstey they crowded into the room.

"I've got one of them, Anstey."

"Who have you there?"

"Dick Turpin."

"Shove on the darbies and carry him below."

"Just what I am going to do, governor; now then, my tulip, easy does it, you're booked for the stone jug this time, my clever high toby man."

"Liar!" Turpin, taking advantage of the officer turning round to his leader, with a sudden exertion of strength hurled him from his position and staggered to his feet.

"Ha, ha, ha! McNabem, you see I'm not nabbed yet."

"Upon him."

"No, don't."

There was the sharp ominous click of the lock of a pistol.

Through the murky darkness of the chamber Jonathan Anstey and his men discerned Turpin, with a pistol in each hand, stepping backwards to the wall of the chamber on his left.

Dick, who suspected his companions had started upon the first surprise through the panel, prepared to dash through it himself, but, anxious that his enemies should not see the means by which he escaped, made up his mind to reserve the fire of his pistols till he was close to the secret means of egress from the chamber, and in the tumult of the discharge and inevitable rush upon him by the officers, make his way through the panel unseen.

He was foiled in his intentions, however.

The enraged McNabem, whose pistols were unloaded, hurled one with terrific force at the form of the highwayman.

It struck with fearful violence upon the temple of Turpin.

With a curse, Dick, sick and faint, staggered back.

The officers, with a yell, rushed upon him.

"Seize him!"

"Curse him, let him not escape."

"Drop him one on his nut."

"Let him have it, Mac."

"I've got him."

"Then mind you keep him."

McNabem, who had gripped Turpin by the throat and was about to hurl him to the ground, was struck down by a fearful blow in the face.

To the surprise of the officers, two dark figures appeared before them.

Standing by the side of Turpin.

Coming from they knew not where.

With rage and fury Jonathan Anstey glared through the darkness at the figures before him.

He guessed whom it was.

The companions of the highwayman Turpin.

Tom King and Sixteen-String Jack.

For the apprehension of the latter a good reward had been offered by Captain Lester.

Grinding his teeth, and biting his lips with rage, the officer determined to make a desperate effort to capture the highwayman.

He had with him six of his men.

Strong herculean officers.

There were but three of the highwaymen.

Surely his victim could not escape.

Wary and cautious, being aware that the three friends were better acquainted with the old house than his runners, and fearing Jack might elude them and escape in the souffle, Anstey began a parley with the three friends; signing to his men to stand back, he exclaimed,—

"Come, Rann, 'tis useless to attempt an escape, you are wanted, and had better go quietly."

"Really, you don't mean it;" replied Jack, in a bantering tone.

"If you will go quietly I will say a good word for you on the trial."

"You are very kind."

"Allow Bolt to shove the darbies on, yield yourself my prisoner, and I'll be your friend."

"Are you in earnest, Jonathan Anstey."

"On my honour, yes."

"No, don't, pray don't talk of that."

"Of what?"

"Your honour! you well know you never had any."

"On my soul."

"It's a bad one, Anstey, don't swear by it."

"Will you yield, before I order my men to fire!"

"Are all your hands here, Anstey?"

"Yes; you see we are seven to your three!" With a chuckle, Anstey drew near, he fancied that Rann was daunted by their numbers.

"Hold a minute! don't come nearer, Jonathan."

"What would you say, Jack?"

"You promise to use your influence on my behalf when I'm placed before the beaks (magistrates)?"

"I swear it."

"Will you do this also for my pals, Tom King and Dick Turpin?"

"Yes; I'll get them off."

"You swear it."

"On my honour."

"Well, never mind about your honour! You hear what Newgate Jonathan says, dear pals; will you, with me, give in?"

"Like flies!"

"No mistake, we'll yield like lambs!"

"Get ready the darbies!"

"We are your humble and obedient!"

"How are you off for soap?"

"Who's your barber?"

"Do you want to shave us for the simples?"

"Have you got a humble (cart) to convey us to the long village (London)?"

"We have all got bad feet."

"We can't pad the hoof (walk)."

"Come in, Anstey, don't eat your lips for supper!"

"He looks cross!"

"Poor fellow, he's vexed!"

"Give him one of your blue pills, Dick."

"I'm afraid his inside won't digest it."

"Well, let him try."

"All right; ready, Jack?"

"Yes, pals."

"Then let them have it."

Bang! bang! bang! followed by oaths, shouts, and curses.

Whilst parleying with Anstey, the highwaymen had edged towards the door of the room.

Tom King and Dick, whose pistols had been unloaded, managed to reload them in the darkness unobserved.

Giving a cough, to intimate to Jack that all was ready, the friends, ceasing to banter the officer, who knew not whether to take their jests as earnest, fired their weapons and dashed to the door of the room.

Two of the runners, with loud groans, fell upon the floor.

The other four, with the enraged and infuriate Anstey, rushed upon them.

The sounds of desperate conflict sounded through the old house.

Beating back their foes, Jack and his friends passed out of the room into the corridor.

Behind them was the flight of stairs leading to the suite of rooms below.

Down this staircase Jack, King, and Turpin made their way.

Step by step retreating downwards, their foes facing them, yelling and uttering cries of fury, as they descended.

"Rush at them! Curses, let them not escape!" shouted Anstey, in a voice hoarse with rage.

Bang! bang! accompanied with a moan or shriek of pain.

It was a strange scene, that fight upon the staircase of the ruined house: Jack and Tom King retreating only step by step, beat back their foes with two of the thick oaken rails of the banisters of the stairs, that had fallen out from decay.

Snatching the heavy pieces of wood up when dashing from the haunted chamber, the friends found them invaluable weapons of defence against their enemies.

Heavy sticks of oak, they were dangerous weapons.

Wielding them over their heads like clubs, the highwaymen were successful in keeping off their foes.

Turpin, ever and again firing at the officers, aided his friends in effecting their retreat.

All was pitchy darkness in the old house.

The flash of the pistols, looking ghastly as they were fired, illuming for a second the inky, murky air.

When about half-way down the staircase, a strange interruption took place, causing each of the combatants to cease hostilities,

In the midst of the clamour of the combat, a sound came upon the ears of all from below.

A sound recognised both by the officers and the highwaymen.

A loud, strange whistle.

Sad, melancholy, and sharp.

Followed by the noise of a door being banged to, and footsteps ascending the stairs.

"The accursed phantom of the haunted house!" yelled one of the officers, who, stepping backwards in his fright, endeavouring to retreat up the staircase, lost his footing, and with a shriek of horror fell headlong down the stairs.

There was one yell of pain and terror, then all was still.

The officers, with Anstey, the thief-taker, collected in a horrified group upon the staircase, peered down into the darkness.

But all was a black, impenetrable veil

Nought could be seen.

For a moment all was silence.

Then again came upon their ears the strange, shrill whistle.

Tap, tap, tap!

The footsteps were now close behind the highwaymen.

With a chill of horror, Jack and his companions drew on one side.

Afterwards, when conversing together upon the matter, Turpin averred upon his oath that he saw the figure of a tall man pass them, whilst a sensation as of the air being laden with frost was felt by him.

This feeling was also experienced by his friends Jack and Tom.

Tap tap, tap!

The steps passed them.

Whilst a cold breath as of ice fanned their cheeks.

The runners, as the sound of the ascending steps approached nearer, rushed back with cries of horror up the staircase.

"Now's our time," gasped Jack, hurriedly descending the stairs, followed by Turpin and King, when at the bottom a cry of terror escaped the lips of Tom, who stumbled and fell upon the floor of the corridor.

"What's that, Tom?" ejaculated Turpin, in a voice of alarm.

"Curses, it's only the body of the officer who fell down the stairs. I thought it was some fresh horror of this cursed house; but away with you, go ahead, Jack, for here they come, and it's devil take the hindmost."

As the friends dashed into the room through the casement of which they were in the habit of making their way out into the garden in the front, a loud, piercing shriek echoed through the ruined house, whilst the yells of the officers and rush of their frantic descent down the stairs sounded in their ears.

"They have seen some horrible sight, Jack!" exclaimed Turpin, at a bound following Jack through the casement into the garden below.

Not waiting to descend by the branches of the tree that flapped against the casement, as they had done when leaving the house on a former occasion, the three friends jumped down into the grounds below, risking any mischance from leaping such a height, some fifteen feet or more. Not only were they anxious to leave the horrors of the haunted house, but they were aware that the runners were close behind, rushing from the place with the wings of fear. When the panic was over, the friends knew enough of Jonathan Anstey to be sure that his first thought would be their capture.

Escaping without any mishap into the garden, Jack and his companions bounded on, the noise of the flying officers sounding close behind them

With no moonlight to guide them, the highwaymen rushed on through the dark grounds.

Jack, who led the way, at length uttered a cry of joy.

He had discovered that part of the garden wall that, broken away and fallen to ruin, left a huge gap, opening out upon the thick copse.

Darting from the gardens of the ill omened house, Jack and his friends wound their way through the belt of wood without the grounds of the ruined building, till at length they reached its outskirts, and stood by the side of a long country lane, lined on either side with the thick copse.

A few hundred yards away, to their joy, the highwaymen discerned three tall forms looming through the darkness.

Giving a low whistle they were answered by a neighing sound, and the trampling of hoofs.

In another moment their brave and sagacious steeds were standing beside them.

Mounting them with all speed, the companions dashed along the lane, the clatter of their horse's hoofs sounding like music in their ears.

A quarter of an hour after this they drew rein in the high road leading to Willesden.

"Well, Jack, we're safe out of that!"

"Thank heaven, yes," ejaculated King.

"What's our next move, Jack?"

"My destination is the Blue Bells."

"The residence of Squire Annersley, some three miles beyond the Cat and her Kittens?"

"Yes, Dick, I shall, without pause for refreshment, at once make my way to the Blue Bells. I will rescue my Dora from the clutches of her foes this night, or perish."

"Well, Jack, I'm with you, heart and hand."

"And so am I! Damme, we may as well crack a crib as cry, Stand and deliver!"

"Right, Tom! And oh for the Blue Bells! Away with you, Jack! Forward."

There was the sharp clatter of horse's hoofs, and, with the speed of the wind, the companions were dashing along the road, soon leaving the scene where they had gone through such perils and encountered such horrors far behind them.

Half an hour afterwards six horsemen galloped by the same spot, hurrying on in the direction of Willesden.

Loud oaths and curses rung upon the air, sounding high above the clatter of the horse's hoofs.

The bloodhounds were on the track.

The fiendish thief-taker, urged by the prospect of gain and insatiable malice, hunted, with the fierceness of a beast of prey, his victim, that had so cunningly and effectually escaped him, and on so many occasions eluded his vigilance and revenge.

CHAPTER XL

A DARK NIGHT—THE STORM—THE BURGLARY AT THE BLUE BELLS—THE SEARCH FOR THE LOST ONE—THE MEETING WITH THE HUNCHBACK—THE THREAT—THE LONE CHAMBER IN THE EAST WING—THE MEETING OF THE LOVERS—THE ALARM WITHOUT—FURY OF THE HIGHWAYMAN—THE PRAYER OF THE HAPLESS DORA—THE FLIGHT OF SIXTEEN-STRING JACK—THE ENCOUNTER IN THE LIBRARY—MARK ANNERSLEY AND THE KNIGHT OF THE ROAD—THE OATH OF VENGEANCE—THE SECRET PAPERS AND THE JEWEL BOX—THE LEAP FROM THE CASEMENT — THE MEETING WITH THE DWARF — SCUFFLE AND A RESCUE—ARRIVAL OF THE RUNNERS AND CAPTURE OF SIXTEEN-STRING JACK.

IT was a wild, dark, stormy night.

The wind in hollow, fitful gusts raged through the branches of the trees.

Black, inky darkness was on all around.

The black, heavy clouds hung low down over head.

Not a star was visible in the horizon.

All was dark drear, gloomy, and dismal.

A large pile of buildings, standing not far back from the

high road, some three miles from Willesden, looked sombre and ghostly that tempestuous night.

The trees surrounding the house creaked and groaned in the blast.

The tenement stood alone, without other habitation near.

The mansion and its owner were well known.

The Blue Bells, as it was called, and its tenant Mark Annersley, were, however, avoided by all

There were some strange reports about the resident of the Blue Bells.

No one visited Mark Annersley.

A morose, reserved man, with a wild, story of past wrongs, circulated about him. He was not sought after by the neighbouring gentry.

He was avoided by the rich.

And feared by the poor.

Heartless and cruel, a worshipper of mammon, he pursued without pity or remorse those who were in his debt.

A deed of bitter wrong, enacted some two months before, increased the hatred and dislike of those who knew the man.

Squire Mark Annersley was the landlord of a large building, called the White Farm, situate about two miles from the Blue Bells.

This farm, rented for years by one Matthew Ashford, at length became tenantless.

Bad crops and other misfortunes caused Matthew Ashford a fall in arrears.

He sued for time when pressed by the agent of Mark Annersley.

He was refused.

The vile agent of the landlord, however, offered a means of release from the embarrassment.

Matthew Ashford eagerly clutched at any chance that might give him time, and save him from being thrust a beggar from the farm he had rented so many years.

He asked the agent what he could do to save the farm.

With a grin the hideous-looking tool of Mark Annersley, a being scarce human in his deformity and ugliness, demanded for himself the hand of the farmer's pretty daughter, Rose.

Rose Ashford, young and beautiful, was motherless and was her parent's only joy.

For her, the old man was prepared to give up life.

Not crediting that he had heard aright, the old man requested the agent to speak again.

With a hideous leer the proposal was repeated. " Better my wife than the mistress of another ; for, eh! eh! eh! that will be her fate! Should you be turned out of the farm, I know one has sworn to possess her, and——"

The remainder of the wretch's speech was lost in a howl of fury.

With a curse of fury, the old farmer, seizing a huge billet of wood, hurled it at the head of the monster before him.

Hideous and bleeding, the agent of Mark Annersley staggered from the farm.

In an hour he returned, and at his heels the officers of the law.

The next day the bailiff took possession of the farm.

Matthew Ashford was carried to gaol for the assault upon the agent.

Three days after his committal to prison the poor old man learnt that his only and beloved child had disappeared from the cottage of those with whom she had taken refuge.

A week—ten days—elapsed !

Rose Ashford was nowhere to be found.

The old man on the morning of his trial had to be carried in the court.

Upon asking if he was guilty of the assault upon the agent of his landlord, the judge received no reply.

Upon his entrance in the dock, Matthew Ashford, sinking into a seat placed for him, drooped his head upon the railings before him, and never moved, apparently lost in agony at his situation.

Again the judge put his query, with the same result.

Matthew Ashford stirred not.

Surprised and alarmed at the silence of the prisoner, an

officer of the court stepped forward and raised the old man's head, letting it fall with a cry of horror.

Matthew Ashford was dead !

His heart had broken.

All knew the sad story of the farmer.

Curses loud and deep were raised against the villain squire and his agent, the latter barely escaping with his life from the enraged populace.

The story of the poor farmer increased the detestation of those who had before hated and scorned Mark Annersley.

The Blue Bells was passed by all with glances of dislike.

Its owner anathematised by every one, far and near.

On the night that Sixteen-String Jack and his friends determined upon breaking into the house of Mark Annersley, the weather was stormy and boisterous.

It was a night well suited to the purpose of the highwaymen.

The wind soughed and moaned in dismal cadences round the gables and outhouses of the old manor house.

Anon the rain, that had first descended from the inky clouds but slowly, now poured down in torrents, dashing and pattering against the casements, and upon the leafy branches of the trees.

In the height of the tempest three dark figures stole cautiously through the grounds in front of the Blue Bells.

Like weird forms or spirits of the storm, the figures glided phantom-like towards the house.

Reaching the large lawn that stretches before the hall door, the wanderers of the night pause. A low, muttered converse takes place.

The three friends, for it was Jack, with Turpin and King, who now halted in front of the residence of Squire Annersley, began to arrange how best to carry out their project.

" It's a nice night, Jack, to crack a crib."

" Yes, Dick. even the weather favours me."

" They're not all gone to dorse (sleep)."

" What makes you think that, Tom ? "

" Why look there." King here drew the attention of his friends to a small casement at the east end of the manor house, through which shone a glimmering light.

" King is right, Jack. Some one's up in the crib."

" No matter. The devil himself should not deter me from making my way into that house to night."

' Right you are Jack, I'm with you."

" Crack the crib is the word."

" The very ticket, Tom."

" Just the identical."

" And no flies."

" Go ahead, Jack."

" All right, but kious (softly), or we may be piped (discovered)."

Jack now crossed the lawn, and reaching the hall-door the three friends paused again, and at once made preparations to enter the house.

" Hold the glim, Tom ! " exclaimed Jack, handing a lantern he lighted to his companions.

" All right. Got the jemmy ? "

" Yes ! but I suspect the door is sheeted with iron."

" If it is, we are balked, Jack."

For a few moments there was silence between the friends.

A drill-grinding noise alone sounding in the air.

At length an exclamation escaped the lips of Jack.

An ejaculation of disappointment and vexation.

" Its no use trying to force the trap (door); as I suspected it's sheeted with iron."

" Damnation ! Jack, what are we to do ? "

" Try an entrance at the back."

" All right, Jack—lead the way."

Leaving the door in the front of the house, the companions were about to make their way to the back, when Tom called the attention of Jack to the short stinted figure of a man that appeared crossing the lawn. The friends, who were close beside a thicket of holly, started behind it, and watched the stranger approaching the house unseen.

" Hist ! Jack—by —— I know that bloak ! "

" And I, Dick."

" Once seen, he aint forgotten."

"He's one of Satan's own."

"Who is it, Jack?"

"One Silas Vaughan, Tom, an unscrupulous tool of the villain Mark Annersley."

"The devil!"

"Right, Tom. The devil he certainly is, or one of his imps!" exclaimed Turpin.

"'Kious, Jack; he nears our hiding-place. Now whilst I and Tom follow the humpbacked whelp, who, of course is about to enter the crib, do you stop here on the touting-lay (*looking out*). If you see anything likely to interrupt us give warning; a shrill whistle will summon us from the crib. Yet, stay; follow us; you can sleek the trap (*fasten the door*) after we are in the house, and do the touting from the room above, the casement of which overlooks the lawn."

"Right you are, Jack! I can't say I much cared to do the piping business out here, and you and Tom perhaps, require a helping hand inside."

Cautiously the three figures of the highwaymen followed after that of the dwarf, Silas Vaughan.

The wind howling through the branches of the trees, and the pattering of the rain that again began to descend from the inky canopy above, drowned the footsteps of the determined men who were bent upon forcing their way into the manor house.

Passing the hall-door, the dwarf turned off down a narrow path lined on either side with elder trees, the thick foliage of which made all as dark as pitch.

Guided alone by the sound of the dwarf's footsteps on the soft, gravelly walk, Jack and his companions hurried on.

Anon they emerged upon a more open path, at the end of which was a high wall.

Halting in front of a door, the dwarf, pulling a key from his vest, thrust it in the lock, and pushing back the door was about to pass through, when he felt a heavy hand laid upon his shoulder and a cold substance pressing on his brow.

With a horrible curse, he struggled to free himself from his detainer.

But he was held in an iron grip.

With an exclamation of fury, he beheld two dark figures standing by the side of the man, who firmly grasped him by the collar.

"One cry for help—the least alarm, you son of the demon below! and by —— I'll send the bullet from my pistol crashing into your skull."

Jack, who, with his pals, had darted upon the dwarf as he opened the side-door, pressed the barrel of his pistol hard upon the temple of the terrified and enraged dwarf.

With eyes that blazed like live coals beneath his black, pent brows, the hideous servant of Mark Annersley glared upon the figures of the men who held him in their power.

He ground his horrible tusk-like teeth with suppressed fury, foaming with impotent rage.

"Silas Vaughan, your efforts to escape, with your fury, are alike of no service. You know me, and by the Heavens above and your companion fiends below, I'll put an ounce bullet in your thick skull if you answer not my queries, and act as I desire. Do you hear?"

A low guttural cry of rage was the only reply.

"Now, in the first place, Silas Vaughan, you must conduct myself and friends into your master's house."

"Where we'll behave like gentlemen."

"No error; we are high, toby men, Humpy! Come, speak up."

King, who was possessed of less patience than Jack, here gave the dwarf a tap on the side of the head with the barrel of his pistol, that caused the wretch to utter a cry of pain.

"Now, speak up, Satan." Turpin here administered a by no means gentle kick.

"I say, Jack, he don't seem to like it." Another blow from the fist of King.

The dwarf fairly foamed at the mouth with fury.

"Eh, eh, eh! You shall all swing—swing upon the gallows, yet," he gasped, "and I, I! Silas Vaughan, will help you to the tree of death!"

About to strike the hideous creature to the earth at his feet, King was restrained by a warning look from Jack.

"Hold your hand, Tom! leave him to me. Now, Silas Vaughan, do you choose to show us into the manor house, or shall I send my leaden messenger into your villanous skull and let you sup to night with your fellow fiends below?"

Jack, putting the pistol on full cock, pressed the muzzle hard upon the brow of the infuriate dwarf.

"I will lead you into the house," gasped the wretch, glaring at Jack with eyes that sparkled like those of an enraged serpent or wild animal.

"Very good. And now tell me, no prevarication, is not Dora Annersley held now a prisoner in this, her father's house?"

For a moment the dwarf hesitated; then, as Jack with a curse pressed his fingers on the trigger of the pistol as if about to fire, the terrified wretch exclaimed,—

"She is! Eh, eh! your purpose is to carry her off!"

"Just so; and I require you to show me the chamber in which she is confined."

"I dare not."

"What mean you, wretch?"

"My life would pay the forfeit."

"How?"

Captain Lester would strangle me should he find I had aid you to bear off his future bride."

There was a savage gleam of joy upon the hideous countenance of Silas Vaughan, as he noted that the features of Jack clouded upon hearing this speech.

"Dora Annersley become the bride of Captain Lester! You lie, you imp of hell!"

Losing his self-command, Jack struck the dwarf a fearful blow with his clenched fist, that caused the dwarf to sink upon his knees and shriek with pain.

The howling wind and storm of rain, however, drowned the cry.

No answering cry echoed that of the dwarf.

All was silent in the Blue Bells.

The tempest roared on, the wind howling, bleak, and shrill, round the manor house, whilst the rain plashed upon the thick foliage of the trees and upon the gravel walk.

It was a fearful night.

A fit one for the scene that was about to occur.

"Jack, finish the cursed whelp, and let us crack the crib."

King, with a curse, drew a large knife from his pocket, an stepped up to the dwarf. The latter, starting to his fee exclaimed,—

"No, no! I will lead you into the house! I will conduct you to the chamber in the east wing, there, where Dora is prisoner. But you will spare my life?"

In abject terror Silas Vaughan now clung to the side of Jack.

He saw that Turpin and King were disposed to summarily settle matters, and terror of approaching death dispersed all feelings of rage and fury that had before alone possessed his fiendish breast.

Jack, whose only thought was the rescuing of his beloved Dora, swore to the shuddering dwarf that he should not die by the hands of himself or friends, if he did but as they desired.

"Come, then—come! and I will lead you to the chamber of the captive."

"Stay one moment. Dick, fasten his arms behind his back, so he shall not slip us in the house."

Biting his lips till they streamed with blood, Silas Vaughan submitted to be pinioned; he saw there was no chance of escape.

His enemies were bold and determined.

Well he knew that attempt at deceit or escape would be his death.

Seizing the dwarf in his iron grip, Jack now told him to lead on.

Passing through the door in the garden-wall, they now walked on, till Silas Vaughan reached a passage at the end of a gravel walk. This passage was covered over with a verandah about which clustered thickly the woodbine, clematis, and sweet-scented honeysuckle, that even in the night air, smelt delicious and refreshing.

At the end of this covered-in pathway was a door.

This entrance, it appeared, led into the servants' offices.

Unlocking this obstacle with a key he drew, by desire of the dwarf, from his vest, Jack with his friends, was presently standing in the house.

"Now look, Silas Vaughan, ere we proceed further, understand, if we are interrupted in our project and alarm takes place, my first business will be to stretch you a corpse at my feet. By —— I swear it, so look to it, we are not disturbed."

"Or you'll be made a stiff un."

"Sent to —— with a blue pill in your nut."

Turpin and King, each pulling out a pair of pistols, now put them on full cock, the sharp click causing a nervous shudder to pass over the frame of the wretch, Silas Vaughan, as it fell upon his ears.

"Jack."

"Well."

"A word before we go further."

"What is it, Dick?"

"I suppose you won't mind I and Tom collaring some wedge (*plate*) while you're up stairs. Humpy dare not play any tricks, and while you search out Mistress Dora, damme, me and Tom can pay ourselves for the trip."

"As you will, Dick. Where shall we meet?"

"Out in the passage of the garden."

"'Tis well."

"Of course if we hear an alarm, we shall join you in a trice."

"All right, Dick. I will now away. An hour hence we will be far away from here, and she, my Dora, once again at liberty! Come, Silas Vaughan, and beware you play me not false. Better had you tamper with the savage tiger or the deadly serpent, than with me this night."

Following in the footsteps of the helpless and enraged dwarf, Jack, now leaving Tom and Turpin below, ascended a flight of stairs, and anon stood in the hall of the manor house.

Passing along this, they ascended another wide staircase that led to the upper part of the building.

All was silent in the old house.

Save the howling of the tempest without, nought was to be heard.

Treading softly along a short corridor, the dwarf turned off into a little passage, and then began to ascend another flight of stairs.

Reaching the summit of these, Silas Vaughan, pointing to a door on the right of a long corridor, from beneath which streamed a ray of light, exclaimed in a whisper,—

"In that chamber sits Squire Annersley. Eh, eh, eh! one word of alarm would bring him from the chamber with a brace of pistols in his hands."

"And that moment would be your last, Silas Vaughan," hissed Jack in the other's ears. But come, I grow impatient—lead on."

Again they moved onwards, silent and cautious.

Like two phantoms gliding noiselessly along the corridor.

The other end is reached.

A whole suite of rooms is passed.

For a moment the dwarf pauses by the threshold of a door that stands half open.

A night-light burns upon a table.

The flame from the oil-lamp giving a dull flicker through the chamber.

By its light, Jack has a full view of his companion's hideous features.

They are ghastly livid.

The horrible pallor of a corpse rests upon the features of Silas Vaughan.

A thin stream of blood trickling down his chin from his mouth, bruised and cut by the blow Jack had administered in the garden, increasing the hideous aspect of the wretch's countenance.

A low, muttered exclamation from the lips of the dwarf was answered by a noise in the chamber.

With a start, Jack renewed his former grip of his foe that for a moment he had somewhat loosened, and placing his pistol in his pocket, drew out a knife similar to the one King had displayed to the eyes of the dwarf in the grounds.

"No treachery, or by —— I'l cut your cursed throat from ear to ear!" Jack, furious at the thought that the fiendly dwarf might yet thwart him in his purpose of rescuing the hapless Dora, flashing the keen, glittering blade of the deadly weapon he held in his hand before the wretch, placed its sharp edge to his bare throat.

Even the slight touch caused a stream of blood to start from the neck of the terrified Silas Vaughan.

"Remove your knife," gasped the alarmed wretch. "Back back, Dido! Down down, boy!" ejaculated the dwarf in an agony of terror.

A huge black dog, that had issued from the chamber at the first sound of the voice of Silas Vaughan, now slunk back, giving utterance to a low growl, and glaring with fiery red eyes upon the figure of Jack.

"Silas Vaughan, imp of Satan, beware! play me not false, or by —— your life shall pay the forfeit." Jack enraged at the appearance of the dog, gripped the dwarf so tightly by the throat that only a strange gurgling noise escaped him as he strove to reply to the highwayman.

"Mercy, kill me not," gasped the struggling dwarf, who now feared that Jack indeed meant to sacrifice him in his fury.

"Vile imp of —— I want not your black blood upon my soul: lead me to the chamber in which is concealed she whom I seek, the hapless Dora Annersley, and I will spare your worthless life; but if you attempt to play me false, ere aid can reach you I'll sheathe my knife in your black heart and send you howling to your fellow fiends below. Come then, lead on, lest you wish your soul sent to instant perdition, thou fiend of the devil!"

Releasing, to some extent, his desperate grip, Jack now followed by the side of the trembling dwarf.

Thoroughly cowed by the fury and evident determination of our hero, Silas Vaughan now led him on along the corridor unhesitatingly, and with silence but haste.

Well the wretch knew that an interruption now would be his death.

Should anyone cross their path the knife grasped by his enemy would be thrust into his body.

Cold drops of fear and agony trickled down the face of Silas Vaughan as he hurried on.

Any moment might be his last.

Any alarm would be his death warrant.

At length with a sigh of relief the dwarf paused.

They had now arrived at a door at the end of a narrow passage running off the corridor.

"That is the room, eh, eh! you will now let me free."

"Softly, Silas Vaugham. Is Dora Annersley in that chamber?"

"Yes."

"Good. Is the door locked?"

"It is. But, eh, eh, eh! that is nothing to you, you know."

"Perhaps not. And now, I suppose, as you have led me hither you are anxious to leave me?"

"Eh, eh, eh! I would be gone."

"Just so."

"You will let me depart?"

"Of course."

"Then loose your hold."

"Are you in a hurry?"

"Eh, eh, eh! . . ."

"Silas Vaughan."

"Ye-s."

"Listen to me."

Jack spoke in a hoarse whisper of suppressed rage as he tightened his grasp of the dwarf.

"Silas Vaughan, what act of mine could lead you to suppose I would be so gross and madbrained a fool as to let you go, now that I have you in my power? No, no, my friend of the devil; by the hump upon your back I swear to hold on to you till I am free of this accursed house. Woe betide you if I am crossed in my purpose, for by —— I vow to send your dog, to ——, if I am interrupted in my business of this night; and now to show you, you imp of Satan, that I am not to be trifled with, safe bind safe find, you know. It's an inscrutable fact, dear Silas. that if we draw the fang of a serpent it cannot sting."

"Curses! Eh, eh, eh! I'll yet have revenge. I'll, I'll drink your heart's blood. Oh, I will have such revenge."

"Silas, sweet, amiable, handsome, Silas Vaughan, don't, or I may hurt you."

Jack, who had thrown the dwarf down, had strongly bound him with a scarf he had drawn from his neck, and now, kneeling upon the heaving chest of the frantic wretch flashed his knife so close to his eyes that a horrible shudder shook the frame of the terrified dwarf, who feared an instant death.

In silence he now lay at the feet of his foe.

No word issued from his lips.

Grinding his teeth with savage fury, Silas Vaughan moved not, stirred not.

White foam gathered around his mouth, but no cry escaped him.

He guessed that the least alarm would ensure his doom.

Wildly he glared at Jack, who now proceeded to force the door.

A moment of time elapsed.

All was quiet in the chamber.

Not a sound could be heard in the old house.

Anon a strange click struck upon the ears of the dwarf.

Followed by the opening of a door.

Jack had effected his purpose.

Seizing the form of the terrified Vaughan, he now dragged him into the chamber.

Jack then closed the door.

He glanced round the room, a large and handsome one.

A taper burning upon a table near a casement revealed the form of her he sought.

A pale spectral figure stood by a draped couch.

The figure of a young and lovely girl.

Very lovely.

Beautiful.

But so pale and wan!

Like a spectre from the other world.

No cry escaped the young girl's lips at the appearance of the intruders.

Wildly she gazed upon them.

Erect and motionless.

Like a piece of statuary she stood by the couch, her lips moving, but no sound escaping her.

Hurling the dwarf to the floor of the chamber, Jack stepped hastily towards the young girl.

The light of the taper now flashes full upon his face.

"Dora! Dora! sweet, dearest love! look not thus upon me."

"Who—what are you?"

The voice of the poor girl was strange and hollow—nervously she clutched at the curtains of the bed as Jack approached her.

"Great heavens, Dora! don't you know me? I'm your own betrothed, Jack Rann."

"'Tis false you are not he! They told me he was dead."

"Dead!"

"Aye, dead! he, the villain Lester, boasted that his bullet it was had slain the man I loved. The one who was prepared to give his life for me has perished."

"No, no, no! Dora, 'tis not so. Look up dear girl, 'tis I, Jack, in health and strength, come to save you from your cruel persecutors."

A low stifled shriek escaped the lips of the young girl as Jack rushed forwards and caught her in his arms.

Winding his arms around her, he again and again besought her to look up, to dismiss her fears; that it was, indeed, her own true, fond lover, who had hastened to her rescue.

"Dear Dora, my own, my beautiful, I will bear you from your foes or perish in the attempt."

Choking sobs now escaped the bosom of the young girl.

Wildly Dora Annersley clung to the form of her lover.

Scarcely crediting that he stood in life before her.

"They told me you had perished! Methought 'twas an apparition from the grave when you first appeared before me," sobbed the unfortunate, persecuted girl.

"Nay, my Dora, I am well in life, and will make those rue who have caused you to suffer thus; but come, dearest, we will at once hasten hence. I come to bear you off this night from the power of the villain Lester, and your unnatural parent. Come, dear girl, we will away at once. I have friends below who will give their lives in your defence; tremble not, dearest, they shall not again tear you from me."

"Whither would you go?"

"I know not yet, dearest, but anywhere were preferable to this place."

"Oh yes, bear me away from this my father's detested roof, and pray heaven I may ne'er return."

"They shall never part us again, dear love! But come, we will from this hated roof at once."

Throwing a cloak over the head of his trembling charge, Jack prepared to quit the room.

About to quit the chamber, he bethought himself of the dwarf.

Casting a glance around, Jack started, and gave utterance to a curse of rage and alarm,

The dwarf, where was he?

A hurried search was instituted through the room.

But to no effect.

Silas Vaughan was nowhere to be seen.

He had gone.

But how?

He must have released himself of his bonds and silently and stealthily effected his escape.

Yes, it was so!

The scarf that had confined the limbs of the dwarf was discovered lying by the door.

The door, too, was now ajar.

Jack, with knitted brow, and a muttered curse, drew a pistol from his belt, and his long keen-edged knife from his vest.

He must be prepared for the worst.

The impish dwarf would, he was sure, raise an alarm.

Measures would at once be adopted for the safe capture of himself and friends.

Jack cursed the folly and pity that had spared the life of the wretch.

He might now be foiled in his purpose.

And she for whom he had risked all be again torn from his arms.

The thought was torture.

In terrified alarm, Dora now followed Jack from the room.

All was quiet in the Blue Bells.

Not a sound could be heard in the old manor house.

Threading the passages and corridor by which he had come, Jack, with Dora clinging to his side, made his way silently on.

Hope began to enter his breast.

They might yet escape.

And yet the dwarf.

Why did he not appear?

There was as yet no alarm.

Would Silas Vaughan allow the man whom he hated with all the ferocity of a black, evil mind, to depart unmolested.

'Twas not likely.

Jack hurried on, endeavouring to elucidate the mystery, but in vain.

No alarm, or indication of interruption, sounded in his ears.

But, knife and pistol in hand, Jack crept on, prepared for danger.

'Twas well he did so!

Danger was at hand.

Unexpected and terrible.

A hideous and fearful one.

A danger that, when it faced him, caused the stout heart of Jack to throb with fear.

Reaching the door of the room he remembered as being the one tenanted by the wretch Silas Vaughan, Jack was startled by observing a dark mass stationed beside it.

A stifled shriek escaped the lips of the terrified Dora.

"The brute, Dido! Lost! lost!" she moaned, and fell senseless at her lover's feet.

The noise of her fall startled the watcher by the door.

The silence was broken by a low, fierce growl.

The growl of a dog in furious rage.

Jack, motionless, and with beating heart, stands over the senseless form of her he loves.

The dark black mass by the door bounds towards him.

There is the sound of a heavy fall.

Fierce, angry growls resound through the corridor.

Mingled with a heavy laboured breathing.

As of a man in distress.

Borne down to the ground by the savage brute, ere he could fire his pistol, Jack engages in a terrible struggle with the huge, fierce dog; his only means of defence his knife.

Wildly he tussels with the ferocious animal.

A strange incident saving his life.

His right arm seized by the vicious brute, Jack is unable to use the weapon he holds in his hand.

Involuntarily, as he struggles with the brute, Jack strikes at his muzzle with the butt of the pistol he grasps in his left hand.

With a fierce, angry growl, the dog, leaving hold of Jack, grasps at the pistol.

Seizing it in his jaws, he crunches the butt to pieces between his teeth; then again turns upon his prey.

But the few seconds of time intervening saved Jack.

Though torn and bleeding, there was yet strength left in the right arm of our hero.

As the brute again turned upon him, Jack, with a curse, drove his knife deep into his neck.

There was a wild howl and a gush of blood.

The dog and his antagonist now rolled over the floor in the deadly struggle.

"Eh, eh, eh! hold on, Dido! Good dog! hold on! Ha, ha, ha! Sixteen-String Jack, you are doomed. Oh, oh, oh! The dog will feast upon your life blood. I shall return anon and find you—eh, eh, eh!—a stiffened corse. Hold on, Dido! Shake him! Kill, kill, kill, him! Ho, ho, ho! what ho! help! The pretty prisoner, the fair Dora, would escape. Hold on, Dido! lap his life blood! Shake him! tear him! Eh, eh, eh! Sixteen-String Jack, said I not I'd be revenged? Oh, oh, oh! you are doomed! doomed! doomed! Ha, ha! sound the alarm-bell. Help, help, help!"

Shrieking wildly in exultant fury, the dwarf, lifting up the still senseless form of Dora Annersley, dashed along the corridor, his shouts echoing with horrid din through the old house.

Scarce had Silas Vaughan disappeared, ere, panting and gasping for breath, Jack rose to his feet.

Exhausted by his wild struggle with the dog, and drenched with blood, Jack Rann leaned against the balusters of the staircase to recover his breath.

His late enemy, the dog, lay dead at his feet.

A home thrust of the knife, wielded by the frenzied highwayman, had pierced the heart of the fierce brute.

The wild, exultant shouts of Silas Vaughan had driven Jack to madness.

Had endued him with fresh strength to grapple with his terrible antagonist.

As he beheld the unhappy Dora borne off in the arms of the hideous dwarf, Jack had given a last terrific thrust at the already dangerously wounded animal, that caused it to relax its gripe, and fall dead upon the floor of the corridor, leaving its conqueror to stagger to his feet drenched with its blood, that in copious streams had welled out of its broad and ample breast.

Only for a moment did Jack pause at the scene of the terrible encounter.

Then, with a fierce shout of rage, he dashed along the corridor.

The loud report of pistols below urging him on in his flight.

Bang! bang! bang!

Accompanied with loud shouts.

The noise of a fierce struggle sounded from below.

The incessant clang clang of the alarm bell of the old manor house now added to the horror of the scene.

The whole house was aroused.

Anon a female shriek rings upon the air.

With his blood like lava coming through his veins, Jack hurries on.

He pauses by a door of a room that is situated at the end of the corridor.

At the bottom of the stairs below he observes the figures of several men.

They, with loud shouts, point to the form of Jack.

He starts back with a curse of fury.

The strangers, with shouts and cries of exultation, hurry up the stairs.

At a glance Jack recognises these men.

They are his implacable foes, the officers of justice.

Jonathan Anstey and and his runners have tracked him to the Blue Bells.

Guessing, doubtless, that he would endeavour to rescue the girl from the hands of his rival, the villain Lester, they have made their way to the residence of Mark Annersley.

"There he is—after him, lads, he can't escape!"

"Get ready the bracelets."

"We'll have him in the jug by sunrise."

"With fifty weight of clinkers (*fetters*) on him."

"That'll astonish his weak nerves."

"Rather."

"Nabem owes him one."

"And don't forget there's sweetmeats (*money*) offered for his capture, lads," exclaimed the officer, Anstey, as he hurried up the stairs after his myrmidons.

In a wild throng the officers dashed up the stairs.

Jack at the top, coolly presenting his pistols, awaited their approach.

"On to him!"

"Seize him!"

"Never mind his barking irons."

"Jack Rann, you are booked for the jug—give in."

"Never! Stand back, or curse you, I'll lodge a bullet in your brains!"

"Pshaw, we're six to one; you can't escape! Will you yield?" exclaimed Anstey, pushing his way up the stairs.

"Yield! curses, no!"

"Then perish, rash fool!"

Bang—bang.

The officers, firing their pistols, with loud yells rushed up the stairs.

The report of the pistols of Jack echoed with those of his foes. Then, as the runners gained the summit of the staircase, our hero, bursting open the door of the chamber, banged it to in the faces of his enemies, at the same time turning the key in the lock.

For a few moments he was safe.

The chamber in which he now stood, was situate at the back of the old house.

It was a large and lofty one.

Only when turning from the door did Jack discover that it was not tenantless.

Seated at a large table in the centre of the room was an old man.

With his hand upon a pile of papers, apparently lost in perusing the documents before him, the occupant of the chamber stirred not in his seat.

A lamp upon the table threw a bright light on every article upon it.

With a start, Jack cast his eyes upon a casket that rested near the right hand of the stranger.

The lid raised, exposed its contents to the bright rays of the lamp.

A thousand prismatic hues darted from the box.

Coruscating in the light was a heap of valuable jewels.

The box was filled with trinkets.

Bracelets, necklaces, miniatures studded with rich gems, were all mingled together in the open box.

Even in that moment of peril, Jack thought what wealth the jewels would bring him were they his.

DEATH OF CAPTAIN LESTER.

What happiness might they not be the means of giving him with the lovely Dora.

With a bound Jack dashed to the table, seizing the jewel-box in his hand.

There was a loud crash at the door, which threatened to give way on its hinges.

Jack, as he seized the box in his hand, also snatched up a pile of papers.

He knew not why, but an irresistible impulse led him to gather up the papers along with the precious jewel-box.

The documents might place the parent of his loved Dora in his power.

The papers might be of immense value to the proprietor of the Blue Bells.

At all events, Jack determined to secure them.

Thrusting the documents in his vest, with the jewel box in his hand, he now turned to fly; a bullet crashing through the door warning him that it was time to depart.

The strong oaken door having hitherto refused to give way to the attacks of the officers, must, he knew, at length be burst open.

Astonished that the noise had not awakened the old man, whom he had first taken to be Mark Annersley himself, Jack cast a glance of surprise at the sleeper as he turned from the table.

With a cry of horror, he now became aware of the truth.

The old man, so still and silent, sitting at the table, was in his last sleep.

The sleep of death!

With horror, Jack gazed upon the livid face of the miserable man.

Fascinated and rooted to the spot by the strange sight, he stood gazing at the corpse before him forgetful of his peril.

But Jack is aroused by a loud crash.

The door is giving way.

But even as it gives to the attack of his foes, Jack is startled by the sudden appearance of a tall, middle-aged man, who enters the chamber through a side door he had not before observed.

The stranger, in violent alarm, casting a look upon the old man at the table, turns away with a shudder, and hurries to the door of the room, opening on the passage without.

" Mark Annersley, I would stake my life!" muttered Jack. " There is some terrible mystery here which I will fathom; he has perceived me not. Now to double on my foes. Pray heaven, that Dick and Tom have escaped."

Darting noiselessly across the room, Jack glides through the door, by which the stranger had but just before entered.

He had barely disappeared, ere he heard the officers in colloquy with the master of the Blue Bells, for Jack was, he found, right in his conjectures, as to whom it was that had so suddenly appeared before him.

Casting his eyes round the little chamber he was now in, to his surprise and delight, Jack beheld a secret panel, that in the wall opposite to him stood open, disclosing a winding flight of spiral stairs.

" By all that's holy I'm in luck, and will not yet despair of rescuing my pretty Dora, with an unexpected treasure in my hands. A means of escape opened before me, I yet may triumph over the accursed Lester, and his demon dwarf, Silas Vaughan."

Standing by the open panel, Jack now listened to the converse of Mark Annersley and his enemies, the officers.

" What means this ? "

By the sound of his voice, Jack became aware that Mark Annersley was keeping the officers on the threshold of the chamber.

No. 19.

"Beg your pardon, squire, but Sixteen-String Jack the highwayman, for whose capture you have offered a reward, escaped into this chamber.

"Impossible."

'Nay, Mr. Annersley, he burst into the room and locked himself in."

"Again I say impossible; it could not be; you are mistaken."

"No, your Honor; I seed him."

"And I."

"And I."

"I piped (saw) him dash through, as I reached the top of the stairs."

"So did I, just before he let off his barkers."

"He is somewhere in the room."

"Of course he is."

"Let us nose (find) him out."

"That's the card."

"Come on."

"We'll have him."

"Like beans."

"In yer go."

"Hold!"

The voice of Mark Annersley rung loud and clear through the room, startling the runners, who all, as Jack could hear, drew back.

"What do you mean, squire?" exclaimed Anstey, in a voice of surprise.

"I mean that none of your men can enter here."

"But the robber and scoundrel, Sixteen-String Jack, is in the room."

"No."

"But, curses!—I beg your pardon, Mr. Annersley, we all saw him enter."

"I say, impossible."

"Well, if you will have it so, squire, so be it; only, if you meet our man by and by in the house, and he presents a barking iron at your head, don't blame us."

"He must have escaped."

"Only by the casement in this chamber, Mr. Annersley, or that door there; he went in by this, but curse me if he came out again."

"Not a haporth of it."

"Not the ghost of him came out."

"Though he went in."

"Safe as houses."

"He's a downy bird."

"Up to every move."

"And no flies."

"Mr. Annersley."

"Well."

"Perhaps that old gentleman at the table can tell us something about this strange business."

"No, no, he is asleep—has been so the last hour. You are all mistaken. But I would be alone—go; search through the grounds; the villain cannot be far off; and remember, I will give one hundred guineas for his capture. Let me see you by and by, Mr. Anstey; for the present I would be alone.

There was the sound of departing footsteps, the muttering of voices, the banging of a door, then all was still.

The officers had gone.

Mark Annersley was alone.

Stimulated by curiosity, and with an earnest desire to fathom the mystery that was connected with the strange scene of the old man's death in the other chamber, Jack remained by the door of the inner room, nor attempted to avail himself of the secret panel, by means of which he doubted not he could effect an escape.

Glancing through the interstices of the door, Jack kept his gaze fixed upon the form of Mark Annersley.

Standing in the centre of the room, the owner of the rich rich estate of the Blue Bells, glared first at the table by which sat the grim rigid form of death! and then at the door of the inner room.

The face of Mark Annersley was of a livid hue.

A pallor, equalling that of the grim corpse by the table was on his countenance.

A wild, maddened look was in his dark eyes.

Motionless he stood glaring at the figure of the dead.

"Gone! gone!" he gasped, in a hoarse, low tone, a little above a whisper! Dead! So! He can no more threaten or demand! The potion of this morn has done its fell work: the old man has perished. I must to Lester, and tell him that all is over. Curses! how I shake and tremble at sight of that livid silent form! and yet it can harm me not: he is dead! gone!—removed for ever, and now awaits the dark, dank, and horrible grave. But I must not dally here. I must begone. How still is all now in the house! Could it be that the accursed highwayman indeed made his way into this chamber? if so, he must have seen the—the—dead! Yet, perhaps not, in his hurried flight, but perhaps made one dash through the room, out by yon casement, and by means of the vinery effected his final escape. The daring robber must be stayed in his knight errantry. By the fiends, had it not been for Silas Vaughan, that invaluable and unscrupulous instrument of crime, Mistress Dora would by this have been far from hence. But now for the papers and the jewels brought hither by the old man. I must secure them, though I have to unclasp them from the fingers of the dead."

Staggering to the table, Mark Annersley glared round for the articles secured shortly before by Jack.

Upon finding they were gone he started, as though stung by a venomous serpent. His face, before of a livid pallor, now assumed the purple tint of passion.

Wildly he glared at the door separating the two rooms.

"By the fiends, the thief-taker was right. He, the highwayman, has been here! Yet I dared not let the hounds of the law enter this room, to behold that hideous form. It would have ruined all! But the papers—the jewels—gone! May sulphurous flames devour the hand that seized upon them! But he may yet be here, and if so—the inner room—yes, yes, 'tis so! Ha, ha, ha! Better, Sixteen-String Jack, had you entered the haunt of a famished wolf, than have lingered in the house of Mark Annersley; for if you are still here, instant death shall be your meed. Jack Rann! Robber! Highwayman! Come forth! for by ——, nought can save you from a hideous doom, unless I will it otherwise."

In a loud voice, and nearly choking with suppressed passion, Mark Annersley uttered this threat, at the same time dashing to the door of the inner room.

As he reached it it flew open.

A tall, handsome figure stood before the enraged squire.

The gleaming barrel of a pistol shone in the rays of the lamp that yet flickered on the table.

A low, hoarse laugh fell upon the ears of Mark Annersley.

"Sixteen-String Jack!"

"Yes, Mark Annersley; at your service."

"Thief! dog! idiot! you shall never quit this house alive."

"Ha! ha! ha!"

"You shall die within the hour."

"You don't mean it?"

"You may have your life on conditions."

"You're very kind."

"That jewel box."

"Yes."

"And its contents."

"Yes."

"Together with private papers stolen by you. Give them up."

"Of course I will."

"And you can go."

"Thank you."

"Attempt to keep them, and death shall be your reward."

"Really."

"This bravado avails not with me! By the fiends you shall die within the hour if you give not up that box and papers."

"Mark Annersley, what prevents me putting a bullet in your skull?"

"Fears for your own safety; the noise of the discharge would be your own death warrant."

" Indeed ! Now listen to me, Mark Annersley. I am not only going to carry off the property I now hold, but I am also going to tear from your clutches the lovely innocent girl whom you call your daughter."

" Call my daughter ? "

" Ay, call your daughter; for a blacker lie never issued from human lips, Mark Annersley, than for you to declare that innocent lovely girl to be child of yours."

" Curses ! "

" You don't like the truth : villains never do."

" Fool ! idiot ! what mean you ? " a deadly pallor now stole over the face of the enraged squire.

" Why this : that Dora, that good and innocent girl, came from no such devil's son as thou. There, Mark Annersley, digest that bit of truth if you can."

" By the foul fiend, he has perused the papers and knows all ! "

Jack's quick ears caught the muttered sentences of Mark Annersley, who glaring wildly round, suddenly, with a howl, as of a wild beast, in mad fury rushed upon the highwayman.

At that moment, knowing that Dora owed all her wrongs to the man before him, convinced now that the fair girl was not his child, Jack without compunction fired his pistol at the advancing form.

There was one wild shriek ! a gasping sob ! and the sound of a heavy fall.

Then all was still.

Doubled up in a heap, a stiffened and bleeding corpse, Mark Annersley lay at the feet of his late victim, the old man, who, so still and rigid in death, retained his seat at the table.

With a curse, Jack rushed from the chamber of the dead.

He made for the casement.

Disappearing through it as a crowd of servants and officers poured into the room.

Loud cries of horror escaped the lips of all as they burst into the chamber of death.

But the burglar, whom they sought, had gone.

Jack had effected his escape to the garden below.

Glaring wildly round, he sought to gain a sight of his friends.

But they where nowhere to be seen.

About to hurry from the spot, a strange and hideous object started up before him.

A wild figure.

With long matted hair clinging about its brows.

Its hideousness increased by large smears of blood.

" Silas Vaughan, by ——" exclaimed Jack.

" Eh, eh, eh ! Yes, Silas Vaughan; come to intercept your flight. Ha, ha, ha ! you can't escape. I will cling to ye with the firm grip of undying hate, ho, ho, ho ! You have murdered Mark Annersley, but I will avenge his death ; for you, you shall hang, hang, hang ! at Tyburn. What ho ! Help, help ! The murderer of Mark Annersley is here. Help, help, help ! "

In wild frantic rage, the hideous dwarf shrieked for aid.

The loud tramping of feet sounded upon the soft wet gravel.

With a curse, Jack fired at the impish Silas Vaughan.

His weapon flashed in the pan.

Eldritch shrieks of laughter escaped the lips of the dwarf.

" It's no use, Sixteen-String Jack, you are doomed, doomed ! "

With fierce fury he rushed upon the highwayman.

A terrible struggle ensued.

The noise of hurrying feet sounded nearer.

In frantic rage Silas Vaughan clung to Jack.

The highwayman found it impossible to release himself from the iron grip of his foe.

" Ha, ha, ha ! said I not I'd have revenge ! They come to drag ye to prison—to the scaffold. Eh, eh, eh ! Silas Vaughan will stand beneath the fatal tree and gloat upon your dying agonies."

" No, thou liest ! Curse me if you do."

There was the sound of a crashing blow.

A sickening noise of broken bone.

No cry escaped the dwarf.

Without a groan or sigh he fell upon the wet ground at the feet of the man he had pursued with such remorseless hate.

" Done for, Tom ! "

" Yes, Dick, I let him have it home; he's as dead as a door nail."

" Well, he ought to have fallen by the hand of me or Jack ; but no matter, you have sent him to sup with his father, the devil below, so it matters not. But how now, Jack ? arouse thee, man, the grabs will be upon us if we escape not hence. Lively is the word ; a clean pair of heels and devil take the hindermost."

About to hurry away Turpin was restrained by Jack.

" Dick."

" Well, old pal ? "

" I leave not this house without her I came to rescue. I will carry off Dora Annersley in my flight, or perish in the attempt."

" But damn it, Jack, there is no chance. If I and Tom had not found you here that hound of a dwarf would have quickly summoned aid ; each moment here is at peril to our lives. Let us away."

" No, Dick, by heaven, I go not without Dora."

" Well, then, I stay with you."

" And I."

" Tom."

" Yes, Dick."

" Shove that carrion aside. The runners are here; let us have fighting room."

As Tom King, with a curse, thrust from their path the hideous blood-bedabbled corse of the dwarf, five or six officers, led by Jonathan Anstey, dashed up to the spot.

There were no words on either side.

With one accord the officers and highwaymen engaged in deadly conflict.

Oaths, curses, and groans of pain sounded in the air.

The report of fire-arms added to the din.

It was a fearful night of horrors, that at the Blue Bells.

A night of crime, of bloodshed.

Wildly the highwaymen struggled with their foes.

Anon a piercing female shriek rang upon the night air.

Sounding high above the din of conflict.

A harrowing shriek of dire woe.

" Dick ! Dick ! " gasped Jack, as darting back from one of his adversaries he flew to the side of his companion. " Take these papers and jewels ! value them as your life. Fly ! We cannot all escape ; away, with these precious gems and papers. Leave the rest to me ! If I am made captive, not Newgate itself shall hold me fast. Away with you, or my bitterest curse upon your head."

Thrusting a box and a bundle of papers in the hands of Turpin, Jack now flew to the aid of Tom King, who, with the fair form of the shrieking Dora Annersley (who had suddenly appeared upon the scene), clinging to his arm, was fighting wildly and courageously to beat back his foes.

A crowd of servants now hurried to the spot.

Tom King, burying a knife he wielded in his hand in the breast of the foremost of the fresh arrivals, turned, and with Dora in his arms, bounded from the scene, followed by Turpin.

Jack, on the point of joining his companions in their flight, was borne to the ground by three of the officers, who, staggering to their feet, had dashed like ravening wolves upon him.

A short brief struggle took place.

Then bound and helpless, Sixteen-String Jack, lay upon the torn and blood-stained gravel, at the mercy of his foes.

But a fierce gleam of joy shone upon his face.

A smile of exultation and delight.

Beside him, looking ghastly horrible in the sickly rays of the pale moon, that now burst from a bank of heavy clouds, was the form of one of his merciless foes.

The wretch Silas Vaughan.

With his skull beaten in, by the blow from the bludgeon wielded by Tom King, the hideous dwarf had expired without a groan.

An exclamation of joy and surprise escaped the highwayman as another bleeding figure met his gaze.

Assisted to his feet by a couple of servants, the man stricken down by Tom King glared round with a dazed and confused stare.

In the pallid features of this fresh victim to the horrors of the night, Jack recognised his rival and enemy, Captain Lester.

Pointing to the form of the bound and helpless highwayman, he essayed to speak.

But an unintelligible gurgle alone escaped his lips.

A gush of blood at every attempt a articulation issuing from his mouth.

Captain Lester was doomed.

The wound from the knife of Tom King had struck a vital part.

The wretched man, bleeding internally, had but a few hours to live.

Senseless and gasping for breath, he was conveyed into the house of death.

Sixteen-String Jack, a prisoner, was, under the charge of some officers, sent to London.

The strange incidents that occurred in connection with the capture, must be detailed in another chapter.

CHAPTER XLI.

THE STRUGGLE ON THE BRIDGE—THE BOAT UPON THE RIVER—THE OFFICERS AND THEIR PREY—THE PURSUIT—A DARK NIGHT FOR A BOAT RACE—THE FIGHT UPON THE COAL BARGE—THE ESCAPE OF SIXTEEN-STRING JACK—THE MEETING WITH DICK TURPIN—A RACE FOR LIFE.

Two o'clock boomed out from the dome of St. Paul's.

The streets of London are solitary and deserted.

A strange quiet rests upon the city.

How different to the scene of bustle a few hours before.

The plodding citizens, the merchants, the clerks and the labourers at the warehouses and wharves, are all gone.

The hive of busy London is silent.

Save the tread of the city watch or shout of some intoxicated reprobate, not a sound disturbs the stillness of the night.

Anon the rattle of a vehicle sounds upon the bridge.

An obstruction, not seen by the driver, causes the coach to fall over with a crash.

There are the loud shouts of men.

Oaths and curses ring upon the night air.

" Stop him ! stop him ! "

How the wild cries echo on the bridge at that silent hour.

A dark form bounds along at mad speed.

The steps on the City side of the bridge are gained.

Down these the figure disappears.

A party of five or six men dash up as the dark form vanishes down the steps.

A few wanderers of the night gather about the steps, some hurrying down to the water's edge.

" What is the matter ? "

" Any one drowned ? "

" Have they found a dead body ? "

" What's it all about ? "

" Where are the watchmen ? "

These and such like cries are uttered by the little crowd as they gather on the steps and gaze eagerly across the dark waters of the river.

There is no moon.

The Thames, like a sea of ink, surges on, its waters looking black and hideous in the dark night.

Anon there is the sound of oars plashing in the waters.

A boat pushes from the steps.

In it are seated four officers of police.

" Bow-street runners arter a cove," muttered a ragged creature, that stood upon the lowest step, gazing eagerly after the rapidly receding boat.

With strenuous exertions, the men seated in the boat pulled out into the centre of the dark stream.

Anon the silence of those in the boat is broken by a man seated at the rudder, who exclaimed,—

" Steady, steady, lads ! by heavens we shall have him yet ! Curses on the mischance that overturned the coach ! Had it not been for that, we should have had Mr. Sixteen-Stringer in old old Newgate by this."

" Can you sight him, Bolt ? "

" Yes, Mr. Anstey, he is pulling like a devil. I can just discern him in the thick gloom."

" Give way, lads, by —— he must not escape ! where away, or we shall fall foul of something in this thick darkness."

A dark object now loomed right before them.

" Hold on to your oars ! By the devils, Anstey, the slippery whelp has left his boat and scrambled up on to a coal barge."

" Ha, ha, ha ! hoping by the trick to elude us ; but the clever dodge has failed. Sixteen-string Jack has run his last race ; next week he shall hang on Tyburn tree or my name is not Jonathan Anstey."

The officers, now arresting their boat, cautiously climbed up on to the deck of the coal barge.

The dark object that had loomed upon them in their course.

Like grim spectres they appeared as though emerging from the dark waters of the Thames.

As the runners gain the sides of the barge a dark figure starts up at the further end, and utters a deep breathed curse.

" So, so ! I've failed to double on them ; but by the fiends, Jonathan Anstey, I'm not yet booked for the stone jug."

Sixteen-String Jack, for it was he, now raised an iron bar that lay at his feet, and gripped it with a fierce oath, swearing to give up to his enemies only with death.

Near our hero lay the body of a man bound and helpless.

It was the bargekeeper, whom he had surprised only a few moments before.

A low groan escaped the half strangled bargekeeper, as he beheld the officers mount the sides of the barge.

He feared instant death.

But the runners heeding not his extended form, bounded to where stood the figure of their victim.

With an oath, Jack started back.

With vengeful grip he held on to the iron bar.

A fearful instrument in the hands of a determined man.

The foremost of his foes now called upon him to surrender.

" It's no use, Jack, you're trapped this time ; you played the double upon us exceedingly well, but you must give in now."

" Give in now, Jonathan Anstey—give in now ? and why ? " Jack gave utterance to a jeering laugh.

" Because we've got you hard and fast."

" No ; excuse me, Jonathan Anstey, not yet. Ah, Bolt, how d'ye do ? Dark night, aint it ? What ! MacNabem, are you there, too ? and Smithson, and old Cherry-nose ? Damme, I ought to be proud ! Four such expert officers after me. Do you know, I think I'll place my blessed autograph in Newgate stone, when you get me there."

" Come, come, Jack, enough of this ; come on, and quietly. You know we've wanted you some time."

" Lor, now, Anstey, have you really ? how funny ! Well, now the want is supplied. Here I am : come and take me."

Jack raised threateningly his iron bar.

" Sixteen-String Jack, am I to understand you intend to resist your capture ? "

" That's just what I do intend to do. You see this iron bar ; attempt to fire upon me with those barking irons of yours, and I'll smash your skull in like a piece of card-board. The noise of your finger upon the trigger shall be your death warrant. I'll dash out your brains, though I swing for it."

There was a fierce savage glitter in the eyes of Jack, that bespoke a determination to resist his foes to the last.

" But it's no use your showing fight, Jack, we must have you in the end."

" Come and take me, then."

" Do you persist in your intention to resist us ? "

" The exact card I'm bent on playing. You've hit it."

" Curses ! "

" Don't go on like that ; you'll hurt yourself."

Jonathan Anstey turned away, and in an undertone con

versed with his myrmidons as to their best course, as regarded making a prisoner of the bold, daring highwayman.

He was known by all of them to be a man of his word.

Well they knew his courage and daring defiance of danger.

The officers, with a shudder, cast nervous glances upon the iron bar, held in the grasp of their victim.

It was more than probable that two of them in a scuffle might fall.

It behoved them to attack their man with caution.

Anstey turned round and began again to parley with Jack, whilst the barge, drifting on without guidance, floated with the tide.

"What object do you expect to obtain by resisting our authority, Jack?"

"Why, your defeat."

"Hem! You match yourself, one, against us that are four."

"No. It's two. I'm a match for two, any day."

"Two; how?"

"Why thus: when you fire at me, I shall dash at you, send you over the side, and Bolt, there, after you. Thus you will be two instead of four. Poor Cherrynose I reckon as nobody. The struggle with MacNabem and Smithson I will soon finish. A bath in the waters of Old Father Thames will wind up the scene of the attempted capture of Sixteen-String Jack, the burglar and highwayman, who sets the law and its myrmidons at defiance. I have settled two foes of mine to-night. Are you ready, Jonathan Anstey? If so, come on. Ha, ha, ha! why don't you take me?"

"Very clever! And so you think by this bravado to frighten us. But you are deluding yourself; nought can save you; you can't escape. If you think to elude us and escape the bracelets and a lodging in the stone mansion in Newgate street to-night, you are mistaken. As to so easily settling myself and Bolt, I think you will find yourself in error. Now then, lads, curses! on to him! At him! Ah! Cherry, good! seize him!"

Anstey here glanced behind Jack, as though speaking to one of his men.

The trick succeeded. Jack turned his head.

The officers, with loud yells, now dashed upon him.

A fierce and desperate struggle now took place upon the coal barge.

In another moment one of the runners was shivering with cold and terror, and clinging to the boat that had been made fast by a rope to the barge.

Hurled over in the scuffle, he fell with a loud plash into the inky waters, with some difficulty escaping immediate death in the rolling tide.

Meanwhile the fearful struggle between Jack and his enemies went on.

The thought that his friends were in safety, that his beloved Dora was free, and awaiting the moment when he would be able to rejoin her, endued him with fictitious strength.

Wildly he combatted with the runners.

Aware that if conveyed to Newgate he might only leave it for Tyburn tree, Jack fought with maddening desperation.

"Cherrynose!" shouted the highwayman, heated and flushed with triumph as he found his terrific strength overpowering that of his assailants. "Cherrynose, go and join Smithson in the cooling waters of Old Father Thames, and cool your inflamed proboscis."

There was a curse and a yell of fright, as one of the runners, struggling with Jack, a short stout fellow, with rubicund visage and purple nose, was lifted off his feet and hurled into the stream.

"Help! help! help!" shouted the half-drowned officer, battling with the stream, and struggling to the boat in which stood the shivering figure of his comrade, thrown into the waters a few minutes before.

"Poor Cherrynose couldn't swim, and was in danger of meeting with a watery grave.

But at length he reached in safety the boat in which stood his companion.

Meanwhile the fierce struggle with Jack and his remaining assailants still went on.

"Slip the darbies on him, Bolt," exclaimed Anstey, who had succeeded in throwing Jack off his feet, and was kneeling on his chest.

"How are you going to do it, my rum culls?" ejaculated Jack, struggling and writhing serpent-like in the hands of his foes.

"Curses! on with the bracelets, MacNabem, or he'll have me off."

"All right, Anstey, I'll do the trick."

MacNabem now drew from his pocket a pair of handcuffs, and endeavoured to thrust them upon the wrists of the panting victim.

Jack, who had been for a few seconds waiting to gather fresh strength, now drew up his knees, and with a quick sharp jerk and expert movement, sent the unfortunate MacNabem over the side with a loud plash into the river.

Throwing off the astounded Anstey, Jack then bounded to his feet, and. with a well-directed blow in the jaw, sent Bolt, who rushed upon him, reeling among the coals.

Now master of the field, Jack darted to the opposite side of the unwieldy barge.

About to follow him, Anstey, with a curse, fell over the body of the bound and helpless keeper.

A thin, grey light now appeared in the eastern skies.

The darkness upon the waters began to disperse.

Night was on the wane.

Morning would soon light up the scene.

With a cry of surprise, Jack now discovered that the barge had drifted close to the river side.

Some logs rode upon the tide, within two yards of the barge.

Springing upon them, Jack darted over them, and presently stood upon the shore.

Gaining a wharf, he, bounding on, made his way on till he reached an archway.

At the end of this archway was a pair of iron gates.

They were locked.

An old porter darted before Jack, as the shout of the officers, who followed in his track, sounded in the air.

With a well-aimed blow of his doubled fist, Jack sent the old watchman of the wharf reeling among some timber.

To scale the gates was but a moment's work.

Presently after, at frantic speed, Jack was dashing down a by-street that led him out in the neighbourhood of Blackfriars.

Jack, who was on the Surrey side of the river, at once made for those streets that would lead him to the Old Mint.

Once there he was safe.

Several habitations would hide him from his foes.

Wildly Jack bounded on.

How would it all end? he asked himself.

Upon how many occasions had he not thus been compelled to race for his life?

His life, that by his acts he had made forfeit to the laws.

During his race that morn, when pursued by his implacable enemy, Jonathan Anstey, Jack Rann vowed, if he escaped, to hasten from England, and for ever give up the calling that had so often perilled his existence.

He kept his resolution.

Dashing on, followed by the yelling officers, Jack, as he turned out of the street down which he had been, fell right into the arms of a tall stranger, who, with a curse, exclaimed,—

"Hallo, lad! whither away? Flying from the traps? If so, come with me, and damme——"

The remainder of the sentence was lost in an exclamation of surprise and joy.

"Jack, by ——!"

"Dick! dear old pal! By heavens this meeting bodes well. I do not believe, whatever haps, that I shall again become a prisoner. But, come; hark! my cursed foes are behind. Ah! that shout! they sight you, Dick! Away—away! or, curses, we both shall become the prey of the villain Anstey."

At a mad pace, Jack, now accompanied by the friend whom he had so strangely met, flew from before his foes.

Panting for breath, the friends could hold no converse during their race.

The race for life.

" Jack."

" Well, Dick."

" There's a crib close at hand will hide us from the grabs."

" Whose is it ?"

" Joe Nobber's crib, the Cat and Fiddle."

" I know it."

" Three minutes will bring us to it."

" Less than that."

" Down that court."

" All right."

" Here we are."

" Thank Heaven ! "   Panting and sinking from exhaustion, Jack leaned against the door of a beer-house, outside of which they had halted.

Giving three loud knocks upon the door, Turpin awaited the result.

Scarce a moment elapsed ere a head was thrust out of a window just above the sign that swung above.

A head, large, and covered with a shock of fiery red hair.

A round purpled visage appeared to the eyes of the friends, whilst a deep gruff voice exclaimed—

" Who's there ? "

" Hawks in distress."

" The grabs at hand ? "

" Yes; Joe; and if you aint quick we shall be collared."

The head was at this drawn in, and a few seconds after the door of the Cat and Fiddle was cautiously opened. Jack and Turpin slipped in, and it was again closed.

" Damn ! I didn't know it was you, Turpin ; why didn't you speak out? I'd have bolted down to you like a shot," exclaimed the red-headed landlord, as he hurried the friends down a dark passage.

" It's all right, Joe ! any of the family here ? "

" No.   Some on 'em will curse the ill luck that kept them from a sight of the high toby Richard Turpin ; it aint often the Cat and Fiddle are honoured by such famed coves as yerself. Hallo, are the Philistines so near at hand, lads ? "

There was a loud bang at the door.

Whilst the shouts of the officers who had arrived at the house sounded plain to the ears of the friends.

Bang ! bang ! bang !

" Go it, my hearties, we are all gone to dorse (sleep) in the Cat and Fiddle and we cant hear."

" Where are you going to shove us, Joe ? "

" In the old place."

" All right, old boy, lead on ; it aint the first time you've helped Dick Palmer out of a fix."

Crash !

" They are arter forcing the door."

" Yes; and curse me, Joe, if they wont succeed presently."

" Oh don't fear, it'll hold on a bit, till I've stowed yer both away.   This way, boys, follow me, we'll fog the grabs yet, double on 'em, and leave no] trace behind; come on, this way."

Joe Nobbers, followed by the two friends, now hurried down a passage, opened a door at its further end, and passed out into a yard at the back of the house.

" Here yer are, lads ! The finest hiding-place from the grabs out."

" The devil ! what, in this yard ? " exclaimed Jack.

" Yes, my boy, in this yard, and nowhere else."

Joe Nobbers, the landlord of the Cat and Fiddle, here gave a knowing wink at Turpin.

" Why, damn, there's only the dusthole and water-butt."

" In course not, that's just it.   That's the blessed snuggery where I'll defy the grabs to find yer, once yer inside."

" What ! the dusthole—I'd rather not."

" No, not the dusthole, but the water-butt, my flower."

" Confound it, Dick, a joke now with us is out of place. Why, the butt is full."

The water was in truth running over the top of the butt, trickling down its sides, and falling, with a plash, on the stones beneath.

" It's all right, Jack, you needn't fear a cold bath."

Nobbers now, pulling out a plug, some three feet from the

top, the water gushed out with a loud gurgle for a few moments, then ceased.

" Now, then, in with yer, we arn't got no time to lose."

Jack, now, guessing there was a trick in the affair, rushed forward, and upon examining the butt, found, three feet from the top, a false bottom.

Lifting this up with some difficulty, for it was close and even with the sides of the butt, Jack discovered that all beneath was dry and hollow.

Unhesitatingly scrambling in, he was quickly followed by Turpin.

" All right, Dick ? " exclaimed the landlord.

" As a trivet, Joe."

" Very good, stay you there, and kious (be quiet) till I return.   Cuss 'em, they'll batter the blessed door down."

The loud banging at the door by the officers was heard even by the friends in their curious hiding place.

Having replaced the false bottom ere he left, the landlord had turned on fresh water, and the two companions in their dark abiding place could hear the trickling splashing noise of the stream as it ran over the butt to the stones beneath.

For a few moments all was quiet.

Anon the silence was broken.

Rude voices sounded in the yard, accompanied by oaths and curses.

Joe Nobbers with the officers were in the yard.

" He ain't, genelmen, nor his pal either.   I arn't seen em, on my davy."

" You lie, you thief," exclaimed one of the men, whom by his voice Jack recognised to be Jonathan Anstey.   " We know you before to-day, Joe Nobbers.   Your assertion that you have seen nothing of the two men I am in quest of, don't wash with me.   By —— I'll watch your premises for a month but what I'll lay hands on slippery Sixteen-String Jack, and his mate, Dick Turpin, whom I am certain you've got stowed away in some corner of your cursed house."

" Have I though ? lor you are a funny man.   Perhaps the coveys are in this ere yard."

" As likely as not," exclaimed Anstey, with a curse of rage. " Look into that dustbin, Bolt."

The two companions heard the lid of the dustbin raised, and then let fall.

Then followed a loud jeering laugh from their friend the landlord, who, with a sneer, invited the officers to take a survey of the water-butt.

With loud curses the highwaymen heard the officers make their way out of the yard.

Then all was silent.

Nought fell upon the ears of the companions in captivity save the trickling of the waters, and the dull plash as they fell upon the stones beneath the butt.

A quarter of an hour passed away.

An age to Jack and Turpin, who, cramped and unable to move, were enduring torture in their prison house.

At length there was the sound of cautious footsteps in the yard.

Presently the friends heard a loud rush of water.

A few moments afterwards the covering above their heads was removed.

A broad stream of daylight now dazzled their eyes.

The next moment they made out the rubicund features of Joe Nobbers staring down upon them.

" Well, arn't this a fine place for doubling on em ? "

" Yes, landlord," replied Jack, " but it's confounded close quarters in there."

Scrambling out after Turpin, Jack, with his companion, stamped up and down the yard to relieve his stiffened limbs.

" Well, I suppose you are a little stiff-like lads, but better a cramp in your limbs than a crick in your neck at Tyburn, or outside Newgate ; but come on into the house ; the grabs have cleared out, there's nothing to fear, and ere you go, why, damme, we'll drink confusion to all Bow-street runners."

Readjusting the mysterious apparatus, that had so effectually hidden the companions from their enemies, Joe Nobbers hastened into the house.

Half an hour afterwards Dick Turpin and his friend left the Cat and Fiddle.

Their destination the haunted house near Willesden, where Tom King with Dora Annersley awaited the return of Turpin, who had left them to glean tidings of Jack.

CHAPTER XLII.

THE VOW FULFILLED—THE SECRET OF THE PAPERS—JOY OF JACK AND DORA—THE PARTING FROM OLD FRIENDS —PREPARATIONS FOR A DEPARTURE TO THE NEW WORLD—THE OATH CARRIED OUT—FAREWELL TO ENGLAND—ALL ON FOR THE LAST SCENE—CONCLUSION OF THE ROMANCE OF A LIFE—DENOUEMENT.

UPON the friends reaching the haunted house, a shriek of delight escaped the lips of Dora Annersley, who, observing the approach of her lover with Turpin, rushed forth to meet him.

A few brief sentences explained all.

In wild joy Dora clung to her lover, whom she so little expected to behold return with the one whom she had dispatched to London on his account.

For at the solicitations of Dora was it, that Turpin had so immediately made his way to town.

We have seen how strangely and unexpectedly they met.

Tom King was incredulous at the account of Jack's last wondrous escape.

But when relating his fearful race for life ere he met Dick, and upon informing his companions of the vow he had registered to give up his calling if he escaped, looks of astonishment and annoyance passed over the features of Turpin and King.

"Leave us, Dick!"

"Give up the road!"

"Ay, I have sworn it."

"You surely jest."

No; my resolution is irrevocable. I am fixed in my resolve."

"What, then, is your purpose, Jack?"

"To leave England. By those papers I secured last night at the Blue Bells I find that the villain, Mark Annersley, now no more, was not Dora's father, but her uncle."

"Her uncle?"

"Yes. A villain who had determined to give up his brother's child to the wretch, Captain Lester, because, it appears, the latter held over his head some threats of a disclosure of former crime."

"Both are now dead."

"Yes, and, thank Heaven! by my hand. And now, look you, dear pals, the contents of that jewel box I secured at the Manor are worth some thousands of pounds; ere we part I shall share the riches equally amongst us."

"No, Jack, we want them not; they are the dowry of your lovely Dora; keep them, think not of us."

"And do you think I will leave you thus without sharing to the last coin what we have gained by the last adventure we shall ever have together? No Dick! no Tom! to the uttermost farthing will I equally divide the booty we have secured upon our last journey together as knights of the road."

Half an hour afterwards the companions, seated in the haunted room of the old house, shared the rich jewels found in the box carried off by Jack from the Blue Bells the night before.

On the afternoon of the same day the friends and the beautiful Dora, all dined at the Cat and her Kittens.

It was a happy, yet a sad party.

Jack and Dora, in blissful thoughts of the future, were at times saddened at the downcast looks of the companions, Tom King and Dick Turpin.

Ever and again Jack strove to cheer his friends.

Then as Dora quitted the room, in company with the pretty daughter of the innkeeper, Jane Lutterworth, the wine was passed more freely, and in its intoxicating draughts the friends forgot the parting on the morrow.

For, on the next day, Jack meant to arrange for his journey from London to Liverpool, at which port he purposed embarking in a vessel to America.

How a few short hours had changed the scene!

Little did Jack Rann the day before imagine that the next few hours' incidents would occur that would cause him to give up his dangerous calling.

Inscrutable are the decrees of fate.

Rigidly adhering to his resolution, Jack the next day, in company with Dora and Jane Lutterworth, who, much to the chagrin of Tom King, had gained her father's consent to leave England with Jack and his bride, left Willesden for London.

Here he, in various places, beheld huge placards, offering a goodly reward for his capture.

Effectively disguised, however, Jack escaped the vigilance of his foes.

Making his way to a well-known fence (*receiver of stolen goods*), Jack sold a portion of her rich jewels he had procured at the Manor House.

He next went to a solicitor, accompanied by Dora.

To this gentleman the poor girl told her story of her wrongs, and placing the matter in the attorney's hands, they then left.

The next day they received intimation that Dora could at any time enter into possession of her estates, kept from her by her now deceased uncle.

Jack Rann, by order of his future bride, gave notice to the solicitor that Miss Annersley purposed disposing of the property, and agreeing to sell it for half its value, it was immediately purchased.

Exactly three weeks from the night of horror and bloodshed at the Manor House, near Willesden, Jack, with his now wedded bride, left the shores of England for a far off land.

Little more remains to be told.

With the departure of Sixteen-String Jack from his native shores our history ends.

Turpin and King together pursued their calling as knights of the road.

King in after years falling by the hand of his friend, in a skirmish with some officers.

Richard Palmer, alias Dick Turpin, in time perished on the scaffold.

One more character in our life romance remains to be mentioned.

Clarisse Howard, the victim of the villain Lester, by an interposition of Providence, was revenged upon her villain cousin, who would have wrested from her her heritage.

Attending the very funeral of her parent, the wretch, Lionel Faversham, met his death.

The horses in the carriage taking fright, the vehicle was overturned; falling out and rolling beneath the horses hoofs, he was killed upon the spot.

Clarisse Howard escaped with but a few bruises and an alarm.

The unhappy and orphan girl left England a few weeks afterwards and never returned.

In after years, a man taking to the road who had remembered Rann when a boy, called himself Sixteen-String Jack, like the hero of this life romance wearing a bunch of ribands upon his boots.

This highwayman perished on the gibbet.

But the hero of this drama of life, upon a large estate in the backwoods of America, lived for many years in happiness and enjoyment, blessed with a lovely wife and smiling children.

None knew in that far off land that John Rann, so well-known and respected by all in former years was in England known as SIXTEEN-STRING JACK, THE DARING HIGHWAYMAN!

FINIS.